a death
in custody

a
death
in
custody

T. S. Clayton

Matador
9 Priory Business Park,
Wistow Road, Kibworth Beauchamp,
Leicestershire. LE8 0RX
Tel: 0116 279 2299
Email: books@troubador.co.uk
Web: www.troubador.co.uk/matador
Twitter: @matadorbooks

ISBN 978 1800465 640

British Library Cataloguing in Publication Data.
A catalogue record for this book is available from the British Library.

Printed and bound in Great Britain by 4edge Limited
Typeset in 11pt Adobe Garamond Pro by Troubador Publishing Ltd, Leicester, UK

Matador is an imprint of Troubador Publishing Ltd

To Silvana

The Deal

For Delroy, it began as just another deal – business as usual on Brixton's Railton Road on a July afternoon in the late 1990s.

For his customer, by contrast, their encounter was a completely new experience.

Until a few days previously, PC Andrew Thomas had been a uniformed officer patrolling the centre of Nottingham, a black officer with a high visibility role, a personal message from the chief constable to the city's black community. But now, using the name 'Wes', he was working undercover, trying uneasily, in the grey shadow of his cover, to come to terms with his new role. For, while in Nottingham it had been important for him not only to be a police officer but also to be seen to be a police officer, here it was different. Here, it was essential that his profession should go undetected, and, as he tried to adjust, his sense of himself as black and his sense of himself as a police officer seemed to lose some of their uneasy cohesion, and he felt disorientated.

He walked slowly down the road, loitering with intent.

"Don't do anything," DS Fletcher had told him. "Let them come to you."

It was a warm day and he felt himself sweating.

His progress was watched critically from both sides of the front line.

DC Matthews, operating the video camera from the empty flat over the electrical goods shop, muttered, "He's just too fucking clean!" at which DS Fletcher and DC Jones, to whom this comment seemed not only apposite, but also, although they could not have said why, somehow incongruous, gave snorts of amused appreciation.

The group of black men standing around the entrance to the alleyway on the opposite side of the road watched as Andrew approached them. The more experienced among them regarded him with suspicion, but Delroy, who, though a relative newcomer to this business, was an enthusiastic entrepreneur, sauntered forward to meet him.

They sized each other up. Both in their late twenties and both the sons of parents who had come to England from Jamaica in the early 1960s, they experienced a brief intimation of mutual recognition, lost almost immediately, as they took stock of each other. Delroy, a little lighter skinned, small and jaunty, was wearing a loose-fitting black tracksuit jacket with a hood hanging down at the back, baggy black trousers and trainers, while Andrew, tall and serious, had on a white T-shirt, faded blue denim jeans and open brown leather sandals. ("Sandals!" DC Matthews had sneered contemptuously after Andrew had parted company with them at the police station earlier that day. "What does he think he is? A fucking hippy?")

Delroy was a good salesman. He gave Andrew a friendly smile. "Lookin' for business?" he asked.

Andrew took a deep breath. "Got a rock?" he countered.

Delroy noted the unfamiliar Midlands accent. He looked around. "I can sort you out," he said conspiratorially.

"How much?" asked Andrew, feeling uneasily that he was doing this all wrong.

"Thirty," replied Delroy.

Andrew tried not to appear too willing a buyer. "But is it good stuff? I don't want no rubbish."

"Yeah, man, it's good stuff. Do I look like I'd sell you rubbish? But, if you ain't interested…" With a slightly theatrical gesture, Delroy, always the showman, began to turn away.

"No, no, man, I'm interested," Andrew reassured him urgently. "Look, I've got the money," he said and began quickly to pull several banknotes from the left-hand pocket of his jeans.

DC Matthews, watching through the viewfinder of his video camera, muttered, "Jesus!" and shook his head in disgust.

"Wait here!" ordered Delroy and walked back to the group of men waiting at the entrance to the alleyway.

"Gimme a rock," he said. "He's buyin'."

The rest of the group continued to regard Andrew with suspicion. "Me no like it," cautioned Lewis, a big Jamaican with long dreadlocks. "Him look like Babylon to me."

Delroy glanced back at Andrew, who was waiting with his eyes intent on the ground, fearing that, if he looked up, his gaze might be drawn up to the window from which DC

Matthews was filming, or fix, in too curious a stare, on the group of men in the entrance to the alleyway.

Delroy turned back to Lewis, gave a slight shake of his head and declared confidently, "He ain't the filth. He's too scared. Come on. Gimme one."

He stretched out his right hand towards Lewis.

Lewis looked around. "OK, man," he said, shrugging. "Your funeral." He brought his right hand folded into a fist out of his trouser pocket, reached forward and opened it palm downwards into Delroy's outstretched hand, passing him a small creamy wax-like lump wrapped in clingfilm. As the exchange took place, the two men briefly shook hands. Then Delroy quickly passed his right hand in front of his face and transferred the rock of crack cocaine into his mouth.

This done, he strode purposefully back to Andrew, who asked anxiously, "Have you got it?"

By way of an answer, Delroy briefly opened his mouth, revealing the wrap of crack resting on his tongue.

Andrew glanced round nervously at the passers-by, wondering if they had seen what Delroy had in his mouth. A police siren sounded in a nearby street, making him flinch. He fumbled with the banknotes which he still had in his left hand. "Thirty, you said, yeah?" he asked rhetorically and held out in his right hand one twenty-pound note and one ten-pound note.

Delroy took the money with his left hand and then, with a swift movement of his right hand, removed the rock of crack from his mouth and placed it in Andrew's still outstretched right hand.

Andrew knew that he was supposed to put the rock of crack into his mouth, but he was a fastidious man, and he just couldn't bring himself to do it. The clingfilm wrapping felt slimy to his touch, and he thought of Delroy's saliva on it. He hesitated for a moment and then pushed the wrap into the right-hand pocket of his jeans. "Respect," he said, self-consciously and without much conviction.

Delroy eyed him curiously. The man seemed out of his depth. "'Nough respect," he replied.

Andrew began to walk down the street, trying to look casual, trying not to hurry. As he passed the group of men at the entrance to the alleyway, he avoided looking at them. They continued to regard him with suspicion and, when Delroy, following a few steps behind him, rejoined them, most of them shook their heads in disapproval.

Andrew turned off into a side street.

"Well done!" commented DC Matthews ironically, removing the cassette from his video camera. He turned to the others. "Hardly what I'd call an Oscar-winning performance," he said, "but he's scored. He's pulled that little joker, Delroy Brown. Not my nomination for pusher of the week, but I suppose it's a result."

DS Fletcher was in charge of this operation and determined that it should be a success. "Yeah," he growled, "it's a result. Don't knock it. Now off you go."

DC Matthews caught the note of irritation in his voice. "On my way, Skipper," he said. He put the video cassette he was holding into the pocket of his anorak and clattered down the uncarpeted wooden stairs which led to the door at the rear of the shop downstairs. He let himself out, crossed the overgrown yard behind the shop, opened the back gate and slipped out through it.

In a quiet street not far away, Andrew got into the front passenger seat of the old red Ford Escort which was waiting for him. Donald Arthurs, a black officer from Sheffield, also in plain clothes, was sitting in the driver's seat.

"How did it go?" he asked.

"OK," replied Andrew, trying to appear offhand. He was suddenly aware that his heart seemed to be beating too fast and that he was sweating profusely.

Arthurs, who was more than a little jealous that he had not been chosen for the role of 'test purchaser', was irritated by Andrew's reticence. "But did you score?" he asked impatiently.

"Yeah, I scored," replied Andrew, gingerly pulling the small clingfilm packet from the pocket of his jeans to show Arthurs. He suddenly felt very tired. He was conscious that his performance had not been the heroic success that he had hoped it would be, and he had a vague feeling that he had betrayed someone or something – though he could not say whom or what. "We'd better get this back to the nick," he said.

They drove back to Brixton Police Station in silence, separated by Andrew's experience, a loss of virginity from which Arthurs was excluded.

Back at the police station, Andrew made his way to the room being used as the control room for Operation Fleece. Here, earlier in the day, DS Fletcher had instructed him in his duties as an 'agent provocateur' – what he could, and could not, do as a 'test purchaser' – and had issued him with sixty pounds in notes: two twenty-pound notes and two ten-pound notes, each of which had had its serial number recorded before it was handed over to him.

Now Andrew reported to DC Jarvis, the exhibits officer.

"Hi, Wes," said Jarvis. "Got something for me?"

"Yeah," replied Andrew, holding out the wrap he had bought from Delroy and experiencing, suddenly and unexpectedly, a small thrill of pride.

Jarvis examined it. "Yeah," he pronounced. "That looks like the real McCoy."

He placed the wrap in a thick transparent cellophane bag, which he then closed with a seal bearing the unique number C8707325. Meanwhile, Andrew wrote the exhibit number W/1 on a label, which he and Jarvis signed and Andrew then attached to the cellophane bag.

They then repeated this procedure with the twenty-pound note and ten-pound note which Andrew had brought back from his shopping expedition and which now became exhibit W/2 and were sealed into a cellophane bag bearing the seal number C8707326.

DC Matthews arrived. "Good work, Wes," he said.

Andrew's previous dealings with Matthews had given him some inkling of the other officer's attitude to him, and he examined his face closely, but Matthews was being careful, and neither his expression nor his voice betrayed any trace of irony.

"I'll just run off a couple of copies of this tape," he said, "and then I'll give you one to watch while you're doing your statement."

He disappeared into a neighbouring room and, when he returned a few minutes later, he handed Andrew a video cassette labelled BM/1B, saying, "Here you are, star."

Andrew looked at him intently, but failed to detect any indication of ironic intent in his face. He wondered if he was being over suspicious. "Thanks," he murmured.

He tried to adopt the confident tone of one police officer speaking to another, colleagues working together on the same case. "Is the dealer known to you?"

"Yeah, his name's Delroy Brown. We suspected he was dealing, but, up to now, we'd never caught him at it."

7

Matthews nodded at the video cassette in Andrew's hand and asked solicitously, "Would you like me to help you operate the machine?"

Andrew thought back to his encounter with Delroy. Watching the recording of it on his own would be embarrassing, but doing so in the company of DC Matthews would be mortifying. He suspected that Matthews knew this, but, again, when he examined the other's face, it told him nothing.

"No, I'll be all right, thanks," he replied, and waited for Matthews to leave.

But Matthews did not seem in a hurry to go, and Andrew wondered if, sensing his discomfort, the other officer was deliberately delaying his departure.

At the end of the room were a television set and a video recorder. Andrew went over to them and turned them on. He put the tape which Matthews had given him into the video recorder and picked up the remote control unit which operated the machine. From a table at the side of the room he picked up a blank MG11 Witness Statement form and a biro. He sat down at a desk facing the television set, put the remote control unit down on the desk and began to complete the form.

After the words *Statement of,* he wrote, *Wes,* after the word *Age,* he inserted, *Over 21,* and after the word *Occupation,* he put, *Police Officer.* But, as he wrote the familiar last two words, they suddenly looked somehow different, even alien. Next came the printed declaration: *This Statement (consisting of   pages) is true to the best of my knowledge and belief and I make it knowing that, if it is tendered in evidence, I shall be liable to prosecution, if I have willfully stated in it anything which I know to be false or do not believe to be true.*

Suddenly, Andrew found himself contemplating these words in a new light. What was true and what was false? At the top of the form he had given his name as *Wes* but that wasn't his real name. Was it a false name? He'd given his occupation as *Police Officer*, but, in the events he was about to describe in his statement, he'd been pretending not to be a police officer. Was it true then to describe his occupation, in the context of those events, as that of a police officer? He could give an accurate account of what had occurred between him and Delroy, but would that account be true? Had what he had done that afternoon been dishonest and, if it had, could what he said about it be true? He shifted uncomfortably in his chair.

DC Matthews, tired of waiting for Andrew to start playing his tape, had left the room.

With a conscious effort, Andrew set about writing his statement. When he came to describe his encounter with Delroy, he began playing the video tape. It took him a few minutes to find the place in the film at which he first appeared. He had never seen himself on film before and was, at first, mesmerized by what he saw. The film was in black and white – or, more accurately, and perhaps appropriately, in shades of grey. It did not last long and Andrew played it several times. The faces of those appearing in it were recognizable but not very distinct. The movement in which Delroy passed his hand across his mouth and then placed it in Andrew's hand was a little blurred, but clear enough, and Andrew began to convince himself that he had not done so badly after all. He just wished he could see his face – and Delroy's – a little more clearly. He wondered what Delroy was doing now – and how he would react to the film when he saw it.

Andrew realized that DC Jarvis was watching him. He quickly returned to writing his statement. He wound the

9

video tape back to the beginning of his encounter with Delroy, and played it again, this time stopping it every few seconds, to write a few more lines of his statement, recording, as he did so, the timings shown on the film of the events he was describing.

When Andrew had finished his statement, he handed it and the video tape to Jarvis. He wished he could take a copy of the video back to Nottingham to show his wife and son, but, of course, that was impossible.

He returned to Nottingham that evening by train. Before he left, he was advised by DS Fletcher not to tell anyone what he had been doing in London. "Not even your wife," the DS told him. "Some of these dealers are very dangerous bastards, and, if you're all that stands between them and a stretch inside, they won't have the slightest hesitation in topping you."

For Andrew, this advice was doubly troubling. He had been told when he volunteered for Operation Fleece that the work could be dangerous, but it had not occurred to him that any danger it involved might follow him back to Nottingham where his wife and son were. The admonition not to tell his wife what he had been doing in London also distressed him, for, not only did he not like keeping secrets from her, but also, for him, discussing with her his work and the moral dilemmas and ethical uncertainties with which it presented him was one of the necessities of life. These were not discussions in which his wife, Ella, played a very active part, and, indeed, sometimes he wondered if she was listening to his anxious monologues at all, but, even so, telling her what was on his mind was essential to his attempts to make sense of his life and his work.

As he neared Nottingham, however, Andrew's anxieties began to fade. He thought of Delroy and found it impossible to imagine him capable of violence. The idea of him as a dangerous killer seemed absurd. He thought of Ella and remembered her quiet discretion. He was sure that nothing he told her in confidence would go any further. By the time his train pulled into Nottingham station he felt more relaxed. He was happy to be home.

Operation Fleece continued. Dr Mudd, an analyst at the Forensic Sciences Laboratory, carried out an analysis of the contents of the exhibits bag labelled W/1 and bearing the seal number C8707325, and confirmed them to be '2.95 grams of a white substance containing cocaine in the form commonly referred to as 'crack'.' More undercover police officers made more 'test purchases' from unsuspecting drug dealers on Railton Road. Andrew made two more visits to Brixton, but his forays into Railton Road were not successful. There was no sign of Delroy, and Lewis and the others at the entrance to the alleyway opposite the electrical goods shop pointedly ignored him. Andrew felt, at the same time, disappointed and relieved. He wondered what had happened to Delroy.

Delroy had gone to ground.

The cause of his disappearance was not any inkling on his part that he had sold drugs to an undercover police officer, but an unhappy development in his domestic life. Althea, with whom he had lived, on and off, for about five years and with whom he had two children, and Bernice, with whom he had lived, on and off, for about a year and a half and with whom he had a baby son, had finally become aware of each other's existence. There had been a nasty scene outside Althea's house. At first, the two women had directed their anger against each other, but, when Delroy had intervened to try and separate them, both had turned on him. Althea

11

had long, strong fingernails, and Bernice was wearing boots with hard leather toecaps.

Delroy retreated to nurse his wounds and, for a few weeks, stayed away from his usual haunts.

As a result, he remained blissfully unaware of the arrests made as, in the middle of August, Operation Fleece moved into its second phase.

DC Matthews finally caught up with Delroy late one fine afternoon early in September.

Delroy was making his first cautious visit back to Railton Road and wondering where everyone was, when he became aware of a car pulling up beside him. He jumped back nervously and then, as he recognized Matthews (with whom he had had a number of previous encounters), he breathed a sigh of relief. "Oh, it's you, Mr Matthews," he exclaimed. "You gave me quite a start."

Matthews grinned. "Delroy Brown," he said, "I'm arresting you for supplying a Class A drug, namely crack cocaine. You do not have to say anything, but it may harm your defence, if you fail to mention, when questioned, something which you later rely on in court. Anything you do say may be given in evidence."

"Come off it, Mr Matthews, I'm clean," Delroy protested. "Go on, search me."

"No need for that," said Matthews. "Get in the car."

"This is all a terrible mistake," complained Delroy, but he did as he was told. He knew better than to make a fuss.

In Custody

"This interview is being tape-recorded," recited DC Matthews. "We are in the interview room at Brixton Police Station. I am DC Matthews and the other officer present is…"

"DC Jones," contributed his colleague.

Matthews continued, "We are interviewing… Please state your name for the tape."

"Delroy Brown," volunteered their interviewee obligingly. He had been here before – both metaphorically and literally.

Reading carefully from a laminated card, Matthews advised Delroy of his right to have a solicitor present during the interview.

Delroy was not really listening. He had noticed the television set and video recorder standing on a trolley to the side of the table across which the two officers were interviewing him. He did not remember seeing these the last time he was in this room, and wondered what they were there for.

"Is it right that you've agreed to be interviewed without a solicitor?" enquired Matthews.

"Yeah, that's right," replied Delroy confidently.

"Would you like to say why? You don't have to give a reason."

"Don't need no solicitor, Mr Matthews. I ain't done nothin' wrong," said Delroy, with an air of bravado.

Matthews gave a faint smile. He was enjoying this. "OK," he said. "Well, first of all, I have to caution you." He recited the words of the caution and asked, "Do you understand?"

"Yeah."

"OK, then, do you know why you're here?"

"You said somethin' about arrestin' me for supplyin' crack, but, like I told you, I'm clean. You searched me when we got back here and you didn't find nothin', did you?"

Patiently Matthews explained. "Delroy, I'm investigating an allegation that, at Railton Road, on the 23rd July of this year, you supplied crack cocaine to a man called Wes."

"I don't know no Wes," protested Delroy. "What kind of a name is that, anyway?"

"You may not know his name," conceded Matthews, "but you must remember him." He gave another faint smile. "A black guy in a whiter than white T-shirt."

Something stirred uneasily in Delroy's memory, but he could not quite place what it was.

"No. Sorry. Can't help you," he maintained defiantly. But a note of uncertainty had crept into his voice.

"OK," said Matthews soothingly. "Do you remember being in Railton Road on the 23rd July?"

A look of relief came into Delroy's face. "Don't think I

was," he said, regaining his confidence. "I've been away for a bit. Women trouble. You know how it is."

In the course of his efforts to find Delroy, DC Matthews had met both Althea and Bernice, and had learnt all about Delroy's domestic problems. He felt some sympathy for him, tinged with more than a little envy. ("Keeping two women on the go like that!" he had commented to DC Jones. "I wish I had the fucking time.")

"Yeah, so I've heard," he said, "but I think you may have got your dates a bit mixed up here. I'd like you to have a look at this video."

He stopped addressing Delroy and pronounced, "For the tape, I'm showing the suspect exhibit BM/1B."

He turned on the television and the video recorder and began to play the video tape.

"Look," he said, pointing to the television screen. "There's the date, the 23rd July, and the time, 15.13. That's just before quarter past three in the afternoon."

But Delroy wasn't listening. He was totally absorbed in the picture on the screen. Like Andrew, he had never seen himself on film before.

"Hey, that's me," he exclaimed.

Matthews nodded with satisfaction. That was what he had wanted to hear. There was now no risk that an over-scrupulous jury might acquit Delroy because they felt he was not sufficiently recognizable on the film.

The screen showed the group of men standing in Railton Road at the mouth of the alleyway. Delroy was at the front of the group, facing towards the camera.

A few moments later Andrew entered the picture.

"That's Wes," said Matthews quietly.

Delroy sat very still in his seat. He watched as the film

showed him going to meet Andrew and the two of them standing together – obviously in conversation.

Matthews pressed the pause button on the remote control unit.

"What's going on there, then?" he asked mildly.

Delroy's self-confidence had left him. The interview room felt very hot. His mind was racing.

"The geezer's stopped to ask me the way," he improvised.

"Where to?"

"I can't remember. Maybe it was the Tube. Yeah, that's right. It was the Tube station."

"I see," said Matthews quietly. He restarted the tape.

The film showed Delroy leaving Andrew, rejoining the group at the entrance to the alleyway, and then returning to Andrew. To Delroy's relief, his back had shielded what had gone on between him and Lewis from the camera.

Matthews stopped the film again. "What's that all about?" he asked.

"I was just checkin' out the best way to the Tube station for the geezer." A note of desperation had crept into Delroy's voice.

Matthews looked at him. "You don't know the way to the Tube station?" he asked with exaggerated incredulity.

Delroy said nothing.

Matthews restarted the tape. They watched the exchange take place between Delroy and Andrew.

"And how do you explain that?" enquired Matthews gently.

Delroy was silent for a few moments. Then he said, "The geezer was grateful for my help, so I thought I'd ask him for a fag. He gave me a fag. We shook hands, and then he left. That's all there was to it."

This seemed to him like a good explanation for what they had just seen on the screen, and he sat back, feeling pleased with himself.

"I see," said Matthews. "And why, just before you shook hands with him, did you put your hand to your mouth?"

"Cold sores," replied Delroy. "I get these terrible cold sores round my mouth. I put this cream on them, but they still itch. I would think that's why I was rubbin' my mouth."

Matthews looked at him thoughtfully. "Thing is," he said, "Wes says you sold him a rock of crack which you took out of your mouth to give to him."

Delroy experienced a sinking feeling in his stomach. "The geezer's having you over, Mr Matthews," he said desperately. "I never sold him no crack." He decided that perhaps the best form of defence was attack. "To tell the truth, I don't think he was all there." He tapped the right side of his forehead with his right forefinger. "Know what I mean?"

Matthews decided that this game, though entertaining, had gone on long enough. "Delroy," he explained wearily, as if speaking to a small child, "Wes is a police officer." From under the desk he produced a cellophane exhibits bag. "And this is the crack you sold him," he said, adding, "For the tape, I'm showing the suspect exhibit W/1."

Delroy knew he was beaten. "How long will I get for this?" he asked, his voice scarcely audible.

"Three years, perhaps four," replied Matthews cheerfully.

Delroy looked at him in horror. He had been in prison before and had not enjoyed the experience. He was a free spirit, a man used to coming and going as he pleased. The longest that he had spent in prison until now had been six weeks and that had nearly destroyed him. He knew that a four-year sentence would mean two years inside. The thought was unbearable.

"What if I helped you?" he suggested. "Gave you some information?"

DC Matthews was interested, but at pains not to show it. He was only too aware that Delroy and the others netted by exercises like Operation Fleece were almost invariably small fry – small-time dealers right at the bottom of the supply chain selling small quantities of drugs to customers on the street on behalf of their suppliers in exchange for a few pounds or a free fix. The major dealers kept off the streets, using others to do their selling for them. So, to bring these bigger players in, the police relied largely on informants. An informant would give the police details of an address used by a major dealer and the police, having obtained a search warrant from a magistrate, would raid the address, finding, if they were lucky, a significant cache of drugs, together, increasingly often, with alarming numbers of firearms, usually automatic or semi-automatic weapons. The informants who gave this information to the police risked their lives by doing so and the police went to great lengths to protect their identities. Normally, an informant's identity was known to only two police officers – his 'handler', the officer to whom he supplied his information and his 'controller', the senior officer, usually a detective chief inspector, who oversaw the relationship between the informant and his handler. Even so, despite these precautions, some informants would be identified by those they had exposed, or by these men's associates, and, as a result, would be badly beaten up or killed.

Matthews wondered if Delroy, who must know the risks involved, was seriously offering to become a police informant, as he really seemed unlikely to have the stomach for it. The officer also very much doubted whether Delroy would have access to any information which would be of any real use to the police. He calculated that Delroy's supplier was likely to be another small-time dealer, one link, at most, above Delroy in the supply chain. He decided to test him out.

"OK then, Delroy, who's your supplier?"

Delroy shuddered slightly. "I ain't got no supplier," he replied quickly.

"What, make it yourself, do you?" enquired Matthews with heavy sarcasm.

Delroy ignored this. "I got information 'bout a bad, bad bastard," he persisted. "Yeah, he's a dealer, a supplier, but he's into so much more than that." He paused for effect, before pronouncing dramatically, "Goes by the name of 'Ice'."

These theatrics were missed by DC Jones who had bent down to pick up a pen which he had been fiddling with and had dropped under the table, while Matthews, partly distracted by his colleague's movements, misheard.

"So, what kind of information can you give us about this character 'Eyes'?" he asked sceptically, as DC Jones's head reappeared above the table.

But Delroy was not listening. "No disrespect, Mr Matthews," he said, "but I ain't tellin' you no more. Fact, I've said too much already. I'm only talkin' to your top man – chief superintendent, chief constable or whatever." He looked at the tape recorder which was still running. "An' it's got to be off the record."

Matthews pictured Delroy in conference with the Commissioner of the Metropolitan Police, in effect London's chief constable, and struggled to keep a straight face. "Detective chief inspector do you?" he asked sarcastically.

Delroy looked dubious, as if being offered goods of an inferior quality. "Yeah, OK," he agreed hesitantly.

"Right, then, I'll see what we can do, but, for the moment, we'll be charging you in the normal way."

The officers brought the interview to an end, and took Delroy, by this time thoroughly chastened, back to the custody suite, where he was charged and placed in a cell to be taken to Camberwell Green Magistrates' Court the following morning.

DC Matthews and DC Jones went to the canteen. The only other officer there was DC McKinnon.

Michael McKinnon was a relative newcomer to Brixton Police Station and was not liked by his fellow officers there. He was a big man with an arrogant air and a surly manner. He avoided the company of his colleagues, and rarely spoke to them, unless they spoke to him first. He was rumoured to have a violent temper if crossed. As Matthews and Jones came into the canteen, he was sitting at a table staring morosely into a cup of tea which he was stirring with a teaspoon. Matthews greeted him, but received only an incomprehensible grunt by way of reply.

Matthews and Jones each collected a cup of tea and a packet of biscuits. They did not feel like sitting at the same table as McKinnon, but, equally, they did not feel that they could sit too far away from him. They sat down at the next table.

They spoke in low voices about the interview which they had just conducted with Delroy.

"What do you make of it?" asked Jones. "This stuff about having information about this man 'Eyes' that he'll only disclose to a senior officer?"

Unnoticed by either Matthews or Jones, McKinnon stopped stirring his tea.

"I don't know," said Matthews. "I've never heard of anyone going by the name of 'Eyes', and I don't see any major villain letting a mouthy little runt like Delroy Brown in on his activities."

McKinnon began stirring his tea again.

"And you know what the DCI is like," continued Matthews. "Doesn't like to have his time wasted. If Delroy just gives him a load of shit, we're the ones who are going to get it in the neck. I think I'll leave it for now. Maybe come in early in the morning and have another word with Delroy before he goes off to court. See if he's sticking to his story."

"Makes sense to me," agreed Jones. He looked at his watch. "Well, I'm off home now," he said. "How about you?"

"Yeah, me too," said Matthews. "Mustn't keep the wife waiting."

They got up and made for the door, leaving McKinnon stirring his by now cold cup of tea. This time neither of them said anything to him.

About four hours later, just after eleven o'clock in the evening, DC McKinnon turned up in the custody suite.

The custody officer, Sergeant Leach, was surprised to see him. He had had few dealings with McKinnon, but knew of his reputation and eyed him warily. "What brings you down here?" he asked.

McKinnon attempted a friendly smile. "I believe you've got a man by the name of Delroy Brown here," he began.

"Yes," agreed Leach slowly.

"Well, thing is, Skipper," continued McKinnon, "I think he may have some information on a case I'm working on and I was wondering if I could have a quick word with him."

Leach looked unhappy. Visits by officers to prisoners in the cells were heavily frowned upon.

"It'll only take a couple of minutes, Skip," urged McKinnon insistently.

"Oh, all right, then," agreed Leach grudgingly. "But you can only stay in there for five minutes, the door stays open, and your visit's going in the custody record."

"Yeah, that's fine. Thanks, Skipper."

Leach led McKinnon down the corridor to Delroy's cell, unlocked the door, pulled it open and walked back to his desk.

When McKinnon entered the cell, he found Delroy curled up asleep on the bed running along the far wall, with his back to the door. Although tired out by the events of the day, Delroy had not been sleeping well. He was growing increasingly distressed at the prospect of spending two years in prison and increasingly alarmed as he began to contemplate the possible consequences of his offer to give information to the police about Ice. He decided to say no more, but he was terrified that he had said too much already. He had heard of people who had been killed because they were rumoured to be police informants when they were not.

He became vaguely aware that there was someone else in the cell and turned over to see who it was. The lighting was very dim and, at first, all he could make out was the silhouette of a large man standing in the open doorway facing him. As his eyes adjusted to the light, however, a look of recognition and apprehension spread across his face. "What do you want?" he demanded nervously.

McKinnon took a step towards him. "I think you and me need to have a little chat, Delroy," he said.

Delroy got up from the bed. "I ain't got nothin' to say to you," he said, raising the palms of his hands in front of him, as if to protect himself from the officer. "Get out. If you don't get out, I'm callin' the custody officer."

McKinnon took another step towards him.

As soon as the alarm went off, Sergeant Leach jumped up from his seat, and ran towards Delroy's cell.

As he got to the door of the cell, the first thing he saw, or thought he saw, in the dim light was McKinnon standing with his back to the left-hand wall of the cell, apparently banging the back of his head hard against the wall behind him. Later, however, when he tried to recollect the events of that evening, the bizarre nature of this spectacle, and the confusion created in his mind by the events which followed, led him to have doubts about what he thought he had seen McKinnon doing when he entered the cell, and he decided to say nothing about this to anyone. He reckoned he had enough problems as it was.

Delroy was lying motionless on the floor against the right-hand wall of the cell, his head bent over at an unnatural angle.

Leach dropped to his knees beside him and tried to find his pulse, but without success.

"You stupid prick," he yelled at McKinnon. A regular churchgoer, he was not a man usually given to obscenities, but he knew they were in trouble.

Other officers had appeared at the door of the cell.

"It wasn't my fault," protested McKinnon sullenly. "He came at me like a madman. I just pushed him away, and he fell hitting his head on the wall. I didn't even push him hard."

Leach ignored him. "Get the FME in here right away," he instructed one of the officers standing in the doorway. "She's in her room taking blood from a drunk driver."

He turned to another officer. "And you, go to the duty inspector and get him to call the chief superintendent."

"I'll need to see the FME, too," said McKinnon.

Leach looked up at him briefly. "Yes, you'd better do that," he agreed, "but you'll have to wait until I can get another doctor here. I don't think you should be seen by the same one as him."

He gestured towards Delroy's crumpled body on the floor.

In the Press

At about ten o'clock the next morning, Alison French was sitting at her desk in the newsroom on the first floor of the offices of the *Brixton Chronicle*, a small local newspaper which came out every Thursday and whose offices occupied a former ground-floor shop and the two storeys above it in Coldharbour Lane.

Alison had joined the *Chronicle* as a trainee journalist just four months earlier. She was twenty-two years old, of medium height, with a pale complexion, short, wavy fair hair with just a hint of red in it and pale green eyes. She had a friendly, easy-going manner, but also something about her which suggested a stubborn streak to her character.

She was drinking a cup of coffee, and trying to put together a story about a number of cats which had disappeared from homes in the area in mysterious circumstances.

Her telephone rang. It was Tracey, the newspaper's receptionist.

"Alison," she said, "I've got a gentleman here who wants to speak to a reporter. Do you think you could come down and have a word with him?"

"Yes, sure," said Alison, sorry to leave her coffee, but glad for a break from the disappearing cats. She picked up her notebook and a pen.

When she got downstairs, Tracey, who was sitting at her desk just to the left of the door at the bottom of the stairs, beckoned her over. "That's him over there," she whispered, pointing towards a small, thin man, in a crumpled grey suit, sitting on one of a small circle of chairs arranged around a low coffee table at the other end of the room next to the large shop-front window which looked out onto the street. "I think he's been drinking," she added, wrinkling up her nose. "He says the people have a right to know." She suppressed a giggle. "His name's O'Connor."

As Alison approached O'Connor, she felt a mounting sense of dismay. His thin face was red and blotchy, his thinning grey hair was greasy and unkempt, his suit was ragged and stained, and his shoes were coming apart at the seams. He gave off a strong smell of drink, sweat and urine. She realized why she had been given this assignment. She steeled herself, held out her hand, and said, with a friendly smile, "Hello, Mr O'Connor, I'm Alison French."

He looked back into her face with pale blue, rheumy eyes. To her surprise, she noticed that they had an unexpected gentleness in them. "Very pleased to meet you, I'm sure," he said, taking her hand. He had a soft Irish accent. "Please call me Bertie. It should be Robert, but I prefer Bertie."

"And what can I do for you, Bertie?" asked Alison.

"I don't want to be wastin' your time, but I think the people have the right to know," he said.

She smiled back at him encouragingly. "To know what, Bertie?"

"'Bout that man that died in the police station."

Suddenly, Alison found herself taking him seriously. "Let's go into one of our interview rooms," she suggested, leading him to a door next to Tracey's desk. As they passed her, Tracey raised her eyebrows, but Alison, determinedly businesslike, pretended not to notice.

Inside the small, windowless room the smell coming from Bertie O'Connor was overpowering, but Alison was determined to ignore it. She ushered Bertie into one of the small armchairs in the room and settled herself into another. She rested her notebook on the arm of her chair.

"So, who's this man who died in the police station?" she asked.

"It was a coloured fellah. I saw him lookin' outta his cell when they brought me in."

"When was this?"

"Last night. Haven't I just been after tellin' you that?"

"No," said Alison, gently. "I don't think you have."

"I'm sorry. I get a bit confused at times."

"That's all right. Let's just take this a step at a time. Now, which was the police station you were at last night? Was it Brixton?"

"Yeah, that's right."

"And why were you there?" Alison hoped the question would not offend him.

"Drunk 'n' disorderly, they said, but that's a lie. Drunk, I may've been, but I wasn't disorderly – or I wouldn'ta been if they'd left me alone. No harm in a bit of singin', is there?"

"So, what happened after you got to the police station?"

27

Bertie looked pained. "They put me in a cell. To sleep it off, they said."

"And where was this black man?"

"He was in the cell next to mine. I saw him lookin' outta the little window in his cell door just before they pushed me into my cell," said Bertie, adding querulously, "No need for all that pushin' and shovin'."

"So, what happened next?"

"Well, I was tryin' to get mysel' some kip – which isn't easy on the beds they got in there – when suddenly the alarm goes off, makin' a terrible racket: enough to wake the dead. Then I hears this thuddin' noise. Or was that before the alarm went off? I can't be sure. An' then I hears this police officer – leastways I think it was a police officer – though by rights it shouldn'ta been – usin' this terrible language – sayin' a thing I'd not like to be repeatin' in front of a nice young lady like yoursel'."

Alison was busily writing in her notebook. She glanced up. "Oh, don't worry about that," she said reassuringly. "I'm sure I've heard worse."

But Bertie shook his head. "Then," he said, "I hears this other voice sayin' 'He fell hittin' his head on the wall. I didn't even push him hard'." His voice became indignant. "But he didn't ought to've been pushin' him at all, did he? An' him a police officer 'n' all." He shook his head again, this time in disgust.

"And how do you know it was a police officer you heard saying that?" asked Alison.

"Well, I can't be sure. But it stands to reason, don't it? Who else is it goin' to be?"

Alison considered this. "OK, what happened next?"

"Well, I hears someone callin' for a doctor. An' then there

was all these voices outside my door an' I hears one of them sayin' 'He's dead'. An' then there was another one sayin' how it would mean trouble – him bein' coloured an' all. Then, for quite a while, there's all this comin' an' goin'. An' then, after a bit, it all went quiet, an' I went back to sleep."

"And what happened when you woke up?"

"Well, they got me up really early, gave me my breakfast an' kicked me outta the station. Didn't charge me nor nothin'. Couldn't get rid of me fast enough. I tried askin' 'bout what happened to the coloured fellah, but they weren't sayin' nothin'."

"Did you get this black man's name?"

Bertie shook his head.

"But you're sure they said he was dead?" asked Alison.

"Yeah, I get confused 'bout a lot o' things, but I'm sure 'bout that."

"Right. Well, thank you very much, Bertie. We're very grateful to you for coming in to tell us about this. Now, is there somewhere we can contact you, if there's anything else we need to ask you?"

Once again, Bertie shook his head. "I don't really have what you'd call a fixed address, but most days you'll find me up by Brixton Station."

Alison felt pity at the thought of this frail old man sleeping rough, but all she said was, "OK, that'll do."

They got up and she showed him out of the interview room and towards the front door.

At the door, Bertie turned to her and asked, "Will it be in the paper?"

"Well, it's not up to me, but I should think it will."

"An', if it's in the paper, will my name be in it?"

"Yes, I should think so."

"Well, if my name's in it, perhaps it should be Robert O'Connor, Mr Robert O'Connor, not Bertie," suggested the old man shyly.

"OK," agreed Alison. "Mr Robert O'Connor it is then."

Bertie gave her a grateful smile. "Thanks," he said and shuffled out of the door.

As Alison went back upstairs to the newsroom, she experienced a mounting sense of excitement. She felt this had the makings of a front-page story. What was more, today was Wednesday, which meant that, if she could put the story together that day and get it into the edition of the paper due out the next day, she might even beat the national dailies to it. 'My first 'scoop',' she teased herself.

When she got back to her desk she telephoned the Metropolitan Police Press Office and asked to speak to Muriel Smith, to whom she had spoken on two previous occasions.

"Hello, Muriel," she said. "This is Alison French at the *Brixton Chronicle*. I'm ringing to enquire if it's true that a man died while in custody at Brixton Police Station last night."

For a moment there was silence at the other end of the line. Then Muriel asked, "Who told you that?"

"Come on, Muriel. You know better than that."

"Fair enough. Look, I'm going to have to call you back on this one."

"Can you make it before two o'clock, please?" asked Alison, trying not to appear over-eager. "Otherwise we'll have to go with what we've got," she bluffed, knowing that, without something from the Metropolitan Police Press Office, there was very little chance of the *Brixton Chronicle* running the story.

At almost exactly two o'clock, Muriel Smith rang back. "I'm afraid I don't have much information for you at this stage," she said, "but what I can tell you is this." Then, obviously reading from a prepared statement, she continued, "Last night, a twenty-nine-year-old man named Delroy Brown died while in custody at Brixton Police Station. Mr Brown had been charged with supplying cocaine and was due to appear at Camberwell Green Magistrates' Court on this charge this morning. In accordance with standard procedure, Mr Brown's death is being investigated by the Police Complaints Authority, and the Metropolitan Police is therefore unable to comment on the circumstances of his death at this stage."

"Is it true," asked Alison, "that Mr Brown died after being pushed by a police officer and hitting his head on the wall of his cell?"

Once again there was a silence at the other end of the line, until, after a moment or two, Muriel replied, with more than a little exasperation in her voice, "I've told you all I can. I can't answer any more questions." She rang off.

Alison wrote up her story and took it to her editor. He asked her a few questions, made a few alterations and then, with some hesitation, agreed to run it as the following day's front-page story. It read:

PRISONER DIES IN POLICE CELL
by Alison French

Alleged Drugs Dealer in Suspected Fatal Fall

A suspected drugs dealer died while in custody in a cell at Brixton Police Station on Tuesday night.

At the time of his death, the man, twenty-nine-year-old Delroy Brown, was being held on a charge of supplying cocaine, say the Metropolitan Police.

Little is known at present about how Mr Brown died. But well-known local character, Mr Robert O'Connor, who was being held in the cell next to Mr Brown's at the time, says he heard someone in Mr Brown's cell admitting that he had pushed Mr Brown and saying that Mr Brown had fallen, hitting his head on the cell wall.

Mr O'Connor says he was woken from his sleep by an alarm bell ringing. He told the Chronicle he heard someone calling for a doctor and a lot of voices outside his door. He heard one of them say 'He's dead', and another say that it would mean trouble, especially as the man was black.

The Metropolitan Police have refused to comment on the circumstances of Mr Brown's death, saying that the matter is being investigated by the Police Complaints Authority.

Riot

The next evening there was rioting in Brixton.

Following the rioting, the newspapers reported that it had been caused by anger in the local community at Delroy's death.

The truth was more complicated.

During the day there had been a demonstration outside Brixton Police Station to protest at Delroy's death, but this had passed off peacefully. The demonstrators were few in number, consisting mainly of Delroy's friends and relations. There were also a few protestors from the Socialist Workers' Party and black activist groups, but these were largely ignored by Delroy's friends and family, and were not there in large enough numbers to cause any trouble on their own.

The Brixton Police had learned lessons from similar incidents in the recent past and handled the protest well. Officers known for their tact and good humour were hand-picked by the chief superintendent to police the demonstration. These officers showed a willingness to talk to the protestors and to listen to their concerns, and ignored minor incidents of rowdiness and abuse, which might, in other circumstances, have led to arrests for public order offences.

A small delegation of demonstrators, including Althea and Bernice, was invited into the police station to meet the chief superintendent, who assured them that Delroy's death would be fully investigated and that any officer found to have been guilty of any wrongdoing would be punished.

These measures by no means completely placated the demonstrators, but they took the heat out of the situation, and the small crowd outside the police station remained for the most part calm and even-tempered.

Althea and Bernice renewed each other's acquaintance and, after showing some initial hostility towards each other, found that they had much in common – for Delroy had been a man whose notion of variety as the spice of life had been a limited one.

Alison attended the demonstration with a photographer from the *Brixton Chronicle*.

At first they were treated with suspicion by the crowd outside the police station. The photographer's initial attempts to take pictures were met with hostile looks and threats from the demonstrators, who feared that these pictures would be passed to the police for future use against those taking part in the demonstration. When, however, the protestors realized that Alison was the author of the front-page story in that morning's *Brixton Chronicle*, their attitude softened. Members of the crowd urged her to find out how Delroy had been killed, and to make sure that this information was made public. Althea and Bernice were at pains to tell her that Delroy had not been a drug dealer, and Althea promised to let her have a copy of his criminal record to prove this.

Alison, having initially had some difficulty in understanding the nature of the relationships between Delroy, Althea and Bernice, scented a 'human interest' story to follow on from her front-page story that morning, and arranged to visit and interview the two women.

The photographer was allowed to take a picture of Althea and Bernice and their children outside the police station.

The resulting photograph had an almost surreal quality about it – portraying what looked, for all the world, like a family group on a sightseeing trip to a building of local interest.

Towards the late afternoon, the protestors outside the police station slowly dispersed of their own accord.

Away from the demonstration, in other parts of Brixton, on street corners, in pubs, clubs, betting shops, offices, homes, schools and colleges, Delroy's death was the subject of heated discussions. There was talk of taking action against the police, and, although the form that such action should take remained nebulous and nothing was done to organize it, the level of tension in the community stayed high.

The weather did not help. It had been a long, hot summer and it was a warm, humid day.

The Brixton police were well aware of the dangers which this situation posed, and adopted a low profile, staying away from areas where their presence had led to confrontations with local residents in the past.

As a precaution, however, they drafted into the area, as reinforcements to help them deal with any trouble which might arise, officers from the Territorial Support Group or TSG.

This was a mistake.

TSG officers were not posted to a particular police division, but were called into an area when their help was expected to be needed to deal with anticipated public disorder there. As a result, these officers had little opportunity to learn about the concerns and sensibilities of the residents of the areas they were called upon to help police, and remained unversed in the subtleties of community policing. Nicknamed 'the heavy mob', when they were called into an area, they arrived expecting trouble and, partly as a result, they usually found it.

At about half past eleven that evening a marked police carrier containing eight TSG officers was driving slowly south along Brixton Road.

Walking along the pavement in the opposite direction were three young men. All three were college students and none of them had ever been in trouble with the police. They had been drinking, but were not drunk. They were walking three abreast. In the middle was Mark Wright, a small white nineteen-year-old with red hair. On his left was his friend Peter Lloyd, who was also nineteen, and on his right was Peter's brother, Thomas, who was seventeen. Peter and Thomas were both big for their age and were black.

For Mark, it had been a difficult day. His mother was a traffic warden, which he felt sometimes led his friends to associate him with the police, and today, when all his friends at college had talked of Delroy's death as the killing of a black man by a white racist police force, he had feared that some of their anger and hostility towards the police might come to be directed against him. He wanted to prove to them that he shared their feelings about the police.

So, as the TSG carrier drove past, he lifted his right

36

arm, made a 'V' sign at the carrier with his right hand and shouted, "Wankers!"

The police carrier stopped a few yards down the road.

Mark wanted to run away, but found himself unable to do so. He stopped and stood as if rooted to the spot, his heart beating violently. Peter and Thomas, scarcely aware of what was happening, stopped with him.

The front passenger door of the carrier swung open and one of the TSG officers, PC Harris, jumped out of it, and walked purposefully towards the three young men. He was wearing body armour and, from his belt, dangled a long police baton.

As he approached Mark and his friends, he shouted, "Oi, you, what was that for?"

Mark, inwardly quaking, essayed an air of bravado. "Fuck off," he said. "I haven't done anything."

Harris approached Mark menacingly, his hand resting ominously on the handle of his baton. "Watch your mouth, you little toerag," he said aggressively, "or I'm going to nick you."

"But I haven't fucking done anything," protested Mark.

"OK, that's it," said the officer. "I'm arresting you for disorderly behaviour." He put his right hand on Mark's left forearm. "You don't have to say…"

But, before he could say any more, Mark yelled out, "Piss off. Let go of me," and tried to pull his arm free from the officer's grasp.

PC Harris immediately spun Mark around and, from behind him, forced the young man's right arm up behind his back and pushed him forwards hard, so that his face was squashed up against a shop window. He began reaching for the pair of handcuffs hanging from his belt.

Peter and Thomas, who had been standing helplessly by, hardly able to take in what was going on, appeared suddenly to wake up to what was happening. Almost in unison, they moved forward, took hold of the officer's shoulders and attempted to pull him away from their friend.

At this, as if in response to a signal, the back doors of the police carrier burst open and several officers, some in full riot gear, jumped down and ran towards the four men struggling on the pavement. One officer came up behind Thomas, put his right arm round the young man's neck, and tried to pull him backwards away from PC Harris. Thomas, who felt he was being choked, struggled violently, kicking out backwards with his feet and letting out a strangled cry of pain. Peter, seeing what was happening, put up his right hand to try and pull the officer's arm away from his brother's throat, at which another officer struck him sharply on the right forearm with his police baton. More officers attempted to take hold of the two brothers, causing them to lash out with their arms and legs in panic. As some of these blows landed, the officers retaliated, one kneeing Peter in the groin and another punching Thomas hard in the face.

In the confusion, Mark broke free and ran off down the street, sobbing with shame and terror.

A crowd had begun to gather. It included a small group of young black men who had watched the incident from across the road from the beginning. To them it appeared as if the white boy who had started it all was being allowed to escape, while the two black boys who had had the misfortune to be with him were being brutally beaten up by the police. Some, though by no means all, of these young men had been in trouble with the police in the past, and one or two of those involved in these encounters had received rough treatment at the hands of the officers who had dealt with them. They all wanted to take the TSG officers on, but knew they would be no match for them in their riot gear.

The crowd quickly grew as the noise and the yellow flashing light on the police carrier attracted people from neighbouring streets.

Soon the whole crowd, already fired up by what they had read and heard about Delroy's death, became increasingly incensed as they saw the treatment being meted out to Peter and Thomas becoming more violent. They began to chant, "Pigs, pigs, pigs". One of them picked up a stone and threw it at the police carrier, denting the side of the vehicle. Another ran up behind one of the officers and kicked him on the back of the leg, before running back into the crowd. Others began taking up the chant, "Pigs, pigs, pigs". Someone shouted out "Fucking murderers", someone else, "Racist bastards".

The crowd was getting bigger all the time. Some of its members had sticks in their hands which they were waving threateningly towards the TSG officers. Stones, bottles and other missiles were thrown at the officers. One of the stones broke a shop window.

The driver of the carrier, who had remained in the vehicle, radioed for urgent assistance, while the other officers not involved in the struggle with Peter and Thomas, formed up, wielding shields and batons, to face the crowd.

The crowd moved back a little way from the line of police officers facing them, but continued to throw stones and bottles at them.

A number of other police vehicles arrived and officers spilled out of them to assist the embattled TSG officers.

The crowd quickly retreated, its members dispersing into neighbouring streets, but, as they went, they broke shop windows, overturned and set light to parked cars and erected makeshift barriers to hinder the police officers from following them. Behind the barricades fires were started and shops broken into.

As news of the rioting spread, the rioters were joined by those in the area who were always on the lookout for an opportunity to do battle with the police and by more whose passions had been inflamed by the day's angry discussions about Delroy's death.

The police, attempting to break through the barricades thrown up to block their way, were pelted with stones and homemade Molotov cocktail petrol bombs. Some officers were injured by missiles which hit them, while others had their clothes set on fire by the petrol bombs, and had to be assisted by their colleagues to put out the flames.

In an effort to calm down the situation, senior officers decided not to order their men to try and break down the barricades blocking their way, but to move back so as to put themselves out of range of the missiles being thrown at them. Only where there was a fire on the other side of a barricade which needed to be dealt with by the fire brigade, were officers to force their way through it.

Behind the barricades, the rioting lasted for over four hours, causing extensive damage to shops, businesses and motor vehicles, but it could have been worse. The policies adopted by the Brixton police in recent years had improved the relations between the police and local residents and, as a result, many who, a few years earlier, would have joined in the rioting did not do so now.

Moreover, Brixton's many illegally held firearms played no part in the rioting – mainly because they were held by professional criminals who, although not unhappy to see the police losing control of the streets, were unwilling to do anything which would unnecessarily attract the attention of the police to them and their activities. It would be bad for business.

Shortly before daybreak the police began to clear away the by now abandoned barricades. They found the streets almost completely deserted. In a few shops they discovered and arrested looters – mainly teenagers drawn by a mixture of curiosity and opportunism into premises already broken into earlier.

A few others were arrested for offences connected with the rioting, and, of those who were, almost all were arrested for minor public order offences, when caught during the night on the fringes of the rioting shouting ineffective threats and abuse at the police.

For Peter and Thomas Lloyd it was different.

Once overpowered, they were arrested for violent disorder and assault occasioning actual bodily harm, and hustled, roughly and unceremoniously, into the back of the TSG carrier. The carrier took them to Brixton Police Station, where they arrived shortly before one o'clock in the morning.

The custody officer, who was secretly shocked by their appearance, immediately arranged for them to be examined by Dr Johnson, the forensic medical examiner or FME.

Dr Johnson was also shocked by what she saw when she examined the two brothers. Both were covered in extensive and severe bruising. She directed that they be taken to hospital immediately to establish whether they had any internal injuries or broken bones. In her own mind, she was fairly sure that they had neither, but she wanted a second opinion on this, and was determined that their injuries should be seen and recorded by a doctor who had no connection with the police.

Peter and Thomas were therefore bailed by the custody officer to return to the police station four weeks later, and were taken to hospital in a police car.

The casualty doctor at the hospital did not find either of them to have any broken bones or internal injuries, but was sufficiently concerned at the state they were in to keep them in hospital for twenty-four hours for observation.

When their parents, informed of where their sons were by a telephone call from Peter, came to see them in hospital, their mother burst into tears at the sight of their badly battered appearance.

Dr Johnson was also asked to examine the TSG officers who had been involved in the arrest of Peter and Thomas. She found three of them to have some minor bruising to their arms and legs. The officers later ascribed their lack of more serious injuries to the fact that they had been wearing body armour when arresting Peter and Thomas.

When Mark Wright got home that night, he was violently sick, and spent much of the night sobbing on his bed, but he refused to tell his anxious parents what had upset him.

Four weeks later, when Peter and Thomas returned to Brixton Police Station to answer their bail, they were charged with violent disorder, assisting an offender to resist arrest and assaulting three police officers occasioning them actual bodily harm, and were then further bailed for six weeks to appear at Camberwell Green Magistrates' Court to answer these charges.

The Investigation

For Chief Inspector Anthony Elliott, who had been appointed to investigate Delroy's death on behalf of the Police Complaints Authority, the press and television coverage of the rioting which followed it brought unwelcome attention to his investigation.

Chief Inspector Elliott was thirty-eight years old and had been with the Area Complaints Unit at Surrey Police Headquarters for just under six months. He was a graduate officer who had gained rapid promotion within the police service. He had accepted his current posting in the hope that it would further advance his career, but he was not enjoying the work which the post entailed.

Most of the complaints which he was asked to investigate were brought by complainants with whom he had little sympathy. The majority had criminal records and were hostile to the police. Many of their complaints arose from confrontations between the complainants and police officers which the complainants appeared to have done much to provoke. At the same time, many of the police officers whom he was asked to investigate filled him with distaste. He found them uncooperative, arrogant and shifty. Frequently they had a history of complaints against them.

He also found himself confronted in these cases with a paucity of reliable independent evidence. Where there were civilian witnesses to the events on which the complaint was based, these witnesses were often friends of the complainants, or had some other axe to grind against the police. Those who were genuinely independent witnesses were often unwilling to make statements to the police out of fear of reprisals – either by the police or by the complainant and his or her friends. Police officers who had witnessed the events out of which the complaint arose generally either made statements fully supporting the account of those events given by the officer against whom the complaint had been made or claimed not to have seen what had happened.

In this context, it was even more difficult than in most other police investigations to establish where the truth lay, and, even where Elliott suspected the complainant's version of events to be true (or nearest to the truth), he was usually forced to recognize that it was impossible to prove this.

To add to his discomfort, he usually found himself reaching this conclusion with mixed emotions, for, while he wanted to see police officers who had done wrong identified and punished (preferably by being dismissed from the service), he recoiled from the prospect of the bad publicity for the police which was likely to result from this process.

The investigation into Delroy's death was Elliott's first into a death in custody and, like all such investigations, presented particular difficulties.

In the first place, he and his team were not being asked, as they usually were, to investigate the actions of officers of their own force, the Surrey Police, but, as was usual in cases involving a death in police custody, they had been brought in to investigate the actions of another force, the Metropolitan Police. This inevitably meant conducting their enquiries in an environment which was even more hostile than usual, among officers who treated them with even more resentment and suspicion than usual – a problem heightened by the general contempt felt by officers of the Metropolitan Police for officers from county forces, often dismissed by them with such epithets as 'turnip heads'.

Moreover, the investigation was treated as a murder enquiry and, as such, involved taking statements from a large number of witnesses. As well as statements from DC Matthews, DC Jones, DS Fletcher and PS Leach, Elliott and his team obtained statements from all the officers who had seen Delroy lying on the floor of his cell, the FME who had examined him in the cell, the ambulancemen who had taken him to hospital, the police officer who had accompanied him to hospital, the hospital doctor who had declared him to be dead, his father who had formally identified his body, the pathologist who had carried out the post-mortem examination on his body, the scenes of crime officer or SOCO who had carried out a forensic examination of his cell, the police photographers who had photographed his body and his cell and the FME who had examined DC McKinnon.

The medical and forensic evidence was inconclusive. The pathologist's report and the statements by the two doctors who had examined Delroy established that he had died when his neck was broken as the result of a blow to the back of his head. Bloodstains found on his cell wall provided evidence that he had struck his head on the wall. The hospital doctor and the pathologist had also noted that he had some faint red marks to the tops of his shoulders. Dr Howard, the FME who had examined DC McKinnon, stated that he had found the officer to have two bruises to the back of his head and a small bruise on his left shin. He reported that DC McKinnon had told him that he had received these injuries when a prisoner had made a violent and unprovoked assault on him, pushing him against a cell wall, so that he struck the back of his head on the wall, and kicking him in the left shin. Dr Howard stated that, in his opinion, DC McKinnon's injuries were 'consistent with, but not diagnostic of' their having been caused in the way described by the officer.

Elliott decided that he would interview DC Matthews, DC Jones and PS Leach himself, both to explore further some of the matters covered by their fairly brief original statements and to ask them about other matters not dealt with in these statements. To save time, he tape-recorded these interviews, on the basis that what the officers said in them would later be put in additional statements to be signed by them. At the same time he took notes of what the officers said for his own use and ease of reference.

He found Matthews a confident young officer, more at ease than most at being interviewed by a senior officer from a complaints unit.

At Elliott's request, Matthews began by describing Operation Fleece and the events leading up to Delroy's arrest.

"Did he resist arrest?" asked Elliott.

"No, sir, not at all. He protested that it was all a terrible mistake and that he'd done nothing wrong, but he came quietly enough."

"And, at the station, I assume he was interviewed."

"Yes, sir, that's right."

"And who conducted the interview? Did you do it yourself?"

"Yes, sir, with DC Jones."

"Did Brown admit the offence?"

"Eventually, sir, yes. To start with he tried to deny it but when we showed him the video and told him the buyer was an undercover officer, he threw in his hand."

"And what was his demeanour like during the interview?"

"Well, to begin with, he was fairly cocky, sir. But, when he realized the strength of the case against him, he became much more subdued. He asked me what he was likely to get for the offence and, when I told him he was likely to go down for three or four years for it, he seemed pretty shocked."

"Desperate, would you say?"

Matthews could see where this was leading. He shifted slightly in his chair and hesitated before answering.

"Well, sir, no, not desperate. No, I wouldn't say that. But definitely shaken. He even began trying to do some sort of deal, offering us information."

"Information? What sort of information?"

"Well, sir, he claimed to have some information about a major villain called 'Eyes', and my understanding was that he was hoping to trade in this information in exchange for a reduction in his sentence."

Elliott looked at Matthews closely. "And what did you say to that?"

"Nothing really, sir, because then he clammed up and

said he wasn't going to say any more except to a senior officer."

"So, what did you do? Did you take it to your DCI?"

Matthews looked slightly uncomfortable. "No, sir, I didn't. To tell you the truth, sir, I wasn't sure what to do for the best. I wasn't convinced that Brown wasn't having us on. I've been at Brixton for over five years and I've never heard of anyone known by the street name 'Eyes'. I'd also had a fair number of dealings with Brown over the years and, to be honest, he was small fry. I couldn't see him having access to information about a major villain."

"But isn't it your experience that small-time criminals are sometimes our best informants?"

"Yes, sir, that's true, but not Brown. He talked too much. I couldn't see any major villain in his right mind letting Delroy in on what he was doing."

"So, you didn't tell your DCI about Brown's offer to turn informant?"

"No, sir, I didn't." Matthews hesitated. "The DCI is a very busy man, and I didn't want to waste his time. I was planning to have another word with Brown the next day to try and find out a bit more about this information he claimed to have, and, depending on what he'd said, I would perhaps have taken it to the DCI after that."

"Did you discuss what Brown had said to you in interview with anyone else?"

"No, sir, only with DC Jones."

Elliott changed tack. "How well do you know DC McKinnon?"

Matthews immediately became more guarded. "Not well at all, really, sir. He hasn't been at Brixton all that long and he keeps himself pretty much to himself."

"But, from what you know of him, would you say he is a good officer?"

Matthews once again looked uncomfortable. "Not really for me to say, is it, sir? But I know he's had some really good results since he's been with us."

"Good results? What sort of good results?"

"Well, sir, he's had some major drugs busts. You know, set up raids on dealers' addresses and caught them there with fair quantities of drugs and firearms."

Elliott considered. He knew, and he knew that Matthews knew, that what Matthews had just told him indicated that McKinnon had access to at least one first-class informant, but this was a very sensitive area.

He asked, as if changing the subject, "Did you mention Brown's offer to become an informant to DC McKinnon?"

Matthews shifted uneasily in his chair. He remembered sitting in the canteen with DC Jones after they had interviewed Delroy, and having a discussion with Jones about the interview, with DC McKinnon sitting at the next table. Since Delroy's death, Jones and he had together tried to recall exactly what they had said about the interview in the course of their discussion, and how much of that McKinnon was likely to have overheard, but both officers remained unsure both of what they had said and how much of this might have been heard by McKinnon. They had contemplated taking the issue up with McKinnon himself, but had decided against it. They had agreed that, when questioned by officers from Complaints, they would, while being careful not to lie in answer to any of the questions put to them, avoid any mention of this incident, if at all possible.

When Matthews did not immediately answer his question, Elliott wondered if perhaps the officer had not heard it, and asked again, "Did you say anything to DC McKinnon about Brown's offer to turn informant?"

Matthews answered the question directly. "No, sir."

"Do you know of any reason why Brown or his offer to become an informant might have been of particular interest to DC McKinnon? Could this man 'Eyes', for example, have been the target of an operation being conducted, or planned, by McKinnon?"

"I don't know, sir. I know very little about DC McKinnon's work."

Elliott changed the subject again. "You say you'd had a fair number of dealings with Brown?"

"Yes, sir, I'd dealt with him several times, mostly for minor stuff. You know, shoplifting, possession of cannabis, that sort of thing."

"And, in your experience, was he a violent man?"

Matthews knew of McKinnon's claim that Delroy had attacked him, and could see where this line of questioning was leading. He answered, cautiously, "I've never seen him being violent myself, sir."

"Does he have any previous for violence?"

"Not so far as I'm aware, sir."

Elliott decided that he had got as much as he could from DC Matthews – at least for the time being – and let him go.

DC Jones was quieter and less self-assured than DC Matthews, but told Elliott much the same as his colleague. He said that he had not discussed Delroy's offer to become an informant with anyone other than DC Matthews and had not mentioned it to DC McKinnon. Like Matthews he said that he had had very little to do with McKinnon and knew of no reason why Brown or his offer to become an informant should have been of any particular interest to McKinnon.

Elliott's interview of Sergeant Leach was more difficult.

Leach had been a police officer for almost thirty-five years, and resented having to answer for his actions to an unknown officer who, while his senior in rank, was nearly twenty years his junior in age. His resentment was fuelled by his knowledge that his decision to allow DC McKinnon to visit Delroy Brown in his cell was one which was legitimately open to question. He was an officer who, throughout his career, had tried to do things strictly by the book, and he felt bitter that a rare departure from this manner of conducting himself had laid him open to rebuke. He greeted Elliott with stiff formality, and Elliott, sensing his resentment and guessing its source, realized that he needed to tread carefully in questioning him.

He decided to start with what he hoped was an uncontroversial subject.

"You were the custody officer on duty when DC Matthews first brought Brown into the station, is that right?"

"Yes, sir, that's right. I'd just come on duty," replied Leach stiffly.

"And how did Brown appear to you at that time?"

"How do you mean, sir, how did he appear?"

Elliott gave an inward sigh. He could see this was going to be hard work. "I mean," he explained, "what was his demeanour like? Was he aggressive or subdued, calm or worked up?"

"Fairly average, I'd say," replied Leach stolidly.

Elliott decided to try a new approach. "Can't you help me any more than that? After all, you're an experienced custody officer. You know the different ways people react to being brought into custody."

Leach's manner softened a little. "Well, sir, to the best of my recollection, when he was first brought in, he was fairly cocky."

"Aggressive, would you say?"

"No, sir, not aggressive. Just full of himself, as if he was sure we didn't have anything on him."

"I see. That's very helpful. And when DC Matthews and DC Jones came to take him to be interviewed, how was he then?"

"The same, sir. Full of himself. Saying he had nothing to worry about. Some of it was show, of course, but I think he really believed it."

"And he agreed to be interviewed without a solicitor?"

"Yes, sir, that's right. Said he didn't need one and signed the custody record to say he didn't want one."

"And you've got his custody record there, have you? Perhaps if you could just let me have a look at that."

Leach, who had been the officer responsible for completing the custody record, stiffened visibly, as if this request suggested that the way in which he had performed his duties was being called into question. Sullenly, he handed the document over.

Elliott sensed the change in the other officer's attitude. Carefully he put the custody record down on the desk in front of him without looking at it. He could look at it later. He resumed his questions.

"And, after interviewing Brown, DC Matthews and DC Jones brought him back before you to be charged, is that right?"

Leach relaxed a little. "Yes, sir, that's right."

"And how did Brown appear then? Was he still full of himself?"

"No, sir, not at all. When he came back from interview,

he was very subdued. Seemed to have had the stuffing knocked out of him."

Elliott looked up sharply from the notes he was making. "Are you suggesting that he had been ill-treated during the interview?"

Leach looked shocked. "Oh, no, sir, there was no suggestion of anything like that. I just meant that he looked very depressed, very down in the mouth. I gathered it was because he'd found out how strong the case against him was, and he realized he was facing a long stretch inside."

"But he wasn't aggressive about it?"

"No, sir, not at all. Quite the opposite. In fact he was so subdued when I took him to his cell that I was concerned about him, and I decided to leave the wicket in his cell door open to make being locked up a bit easier on him, and so as I could keep an eye on him when I went past."

"And how often did you check on him after that?"

"About once every half hour," said Leach, adding defensively, "It's all in the custody record."

"I'm sure it is," said Elliott, reassuringly. "And how did he seem when you checked up on him?"

"The first couple of times he was just standing at the cell door, staring out of the wicket, but not really looking at anything, if you know what I mean."

"And then?"

"He just went and laid down on the bed at the back of the cell, but I don't know if he ever got to sleep, because every time I looked in on him he seemed to be tossing and turning on the bed."

"And then," said Elliott carefully, "DC McKinnon came and asked you if he could visit Brown in his cell, is that right?"

Leach stiffened. "Yes, sir, that's right."

"Difficult situation for you," suggested Elliott sympathetically.

Leach looked at him gratefully. "Yes, sir, it was."

He had thought a lot about what to say about his response to McKinnon's request, and without waiting for Elliott to ask him about it, he said, "It's not something I normally allow, and the officers who have been here some time, they know that, but DC McKinnon is fairly new here and was very insistent. Said he understood that Brown had some information about a case he was working on, and that he just needed a quick word with him. In the end, I told him he could have five minutes in the cell with Brown and no more. And I made it clear to him that the cell door would have to stay open during the time he was in there, and that his visit to see Brown in his cell would be fully recorded in the prisoner's custody record. And that's what I did. As soon as I'd taken him to the cell, I went back to my desk and recorded what I'd done in the custody record."

"Did McKinnon raise any objection to your recording his visit to Brown's cell in the prisoner's custody record?"

"No, sir, he didn't." Leach's answer was firm. "And I wouldn't have agreed to its not going in, whatever he'd said."

"No, of course not," acknowledged Elliott quickly, and asked, "Tell me, what was Brown doing when you took McKinnon to his cell?"

Leach hesitated. "I'm not sure, sir. I seem to remember that he was lying on the bed with his back to the door, but I didn't really stay long enough to get a good look at him. I wanted to get back to my desk as soon as I could."

The question of whether, as custody officer, Leach should have taken steps to ascertain what state Delroy was in before leaving DC McKinnon in his cell with him, hovered in the minds of both officers, but neither referred to it.

"Very understandable," said Elliott. His main concern was to get Leach to tell him all he knew about the events leading up to Delroy's death, and he was anxious not to say anything likely to cause the other officer to clam up. He moved on. "What happened next?"

Leach had become noticeably more tense. "After a couple of minutes – I don't think it can have been more – the alarm went off and I immediately ran to Brown's cell."

"Do you know who pressed the alarm? Was it Brown or McKinnon?"

"I don't know, sir. There's no way I can say. It could have been either of them."

"And what did you see, when you got to the cell?"

"Brown was lying on the floor, slumped against the wall to my right, with his head bent over at an angle, sir."

"And McKinnon, where was he?"

"He was standing with his back to the wall on my left, sir."

Leach opened his mouth, as if to say something else, but closed it again.

Elliott asked, "Not down on the floor tending to Brown?"

"No, sir."

"Did he say what had happened?"

Leach hesitated. He knew his answer to this question was important and, despite the anger that he felt at McKinnon for having landed him in this situation, he wanted to get his facts right, to be absolutely fair to his fellow officer.

"Yes, sir, he did, but I'm not sure now of what exactly it was that he said."

"I understand that, but, to the best of your recollection, what did he say?"

"Well, sir, it was to the effect that Brown had made a violent and unprovoked attack on him, and that he, that is McKinnon, had tried to push Brown away, but not hard, and that Brown had fallen and hit his head on the wall."

"So, McKinnon admitted pushing Brown?"

"Yes, sir. But the way he put it was definitely that Brown came at him first, and that, when he pushed Brown, he was only trying to defend himself, and didn't push him hard."

"I see. And, when you got to the cell, what did you do?"

"I got down on the floor beside Brown and tried to find his pulse, sir, but there was nothing there. I didn't like to try and move him, because, from the way his head was lying, I had a feeling he'd broken his neck, and I thought if I tried to move him, I might end up doing him more damage. So, I called for the FME, Dr Johnson, who was already in the station on another matter, and, as soon as she arrived, I left him to her."

Elliott decided that there was probably no more Leach could tell him about Delroy's death, but, before releasing the sergeant, he turned to another subject.

"This man, O'Connor, who I understand was in the cell next to Brown's, what can you tell me about him?"

Leach winced slightly. "Oh, Bertie, sir. He's one of our regulars. Drunk most of the time."

"And where can we find him? Do you have an address for him?"

"Well, there's a hostel he gives as his address, sir, but, more often than not, he's banned from there for coming home drunk."

"OK, well, I'd better get a note of that anyway. Could you write down the address for me, please?"

Grudgingly Leach did as he was asked. He felt offended at the idea that Bertie O'Connor might be accorded the status of a witness in this investigation. He remembered the state Bertie had been in on the night Delroy had died, and he did not believe that the old drunk was capable of giving an accurate or reliable account of what had happened that night. He jibbed at the prospect that Bertie's confused recollections of the events of that night might be accorded the same weight as, or even more weight than, his own painstaking efforts to give a full and truthful account of those events. Moreover, he was irked by the possibility that what Bertie told Elliott might, depending on what the old drunk thought, or imagined, he remembered happening on the night Delroy died, lead to a police officer being charged with murder or manslaughter. That couldn't be right.

Elliott took the note with the address of the hostel on it and asked, "And, if he's not there, where do you suggest we might find him?"

"I really couldn't say, sir," replied Leach stolidly, adding with a touch of malice, "I can only suggest you make enquiries on the streets."

The picture of Chief Inspector Elliott out on the streets of Brixton searching for Bertie O'Connor among the local down-and-outs was one which appealed to his sense of humour.

Elliott realized that Leach was not going to give him any more help in finding Bertie, and let the sergeant go.

Before leaving Brixton Police Station, Elliott went to see the station's detective chief inspector, DCI Greaves. The two men knew each other slightly, and had had a short formal meeting when Elliott had first arrived at the station to begin his investigation into Delroy's death.

Greaves was about fifteen years older than Elliott and, as an officer who had slowly worked his way up through the ranks, felt some antagonism towards his visitor, whom he identified as one of a new class of graduate officers who were, in his view, being unfairly promoted over the heads of more experienced officers. The fact that Elliott was conducting an investigation into the actions of one of Greaves's officers also inevitably created some awkwardness between the two men. Nonetheless, Greaves was determined to show Elliott every courtesy.

"Come in, Tony," he said. "Take a seat. Can I offer you a cup of tea?"

Elliott rarely drank tea, but, in an effort to foster the atmosphere of goodwill which his host was clearly trying to generate, he accepted the offer.

The two men sat facing each other across Greaves's desk.

"How's it going then, Tony?" asked the DCI. "I trust my lads are giving you their full cooperation."

"No complaints," replied Elliott. "It's a difficult situation for all concerned, of course, but no one's given me any problems so far."

"I'm pleased to hear it. And, if there's any way I can help, just let me know."

"Well, there is just one thing you might be able to help me with."

"Fire away."

"Have you ever come across a man known by the street name 'Eyes'?"

Greaves stared down at the top of his desk for a few moments as if in thought, then looked up.

"'Eyes'," he said, carefully. "No, I don't think I've heard of anyone who's known by that name."

"Well, if you do, perhaps you could let me know."

"Yes, of course."

After Elliott had left, Greaves sat at his desk for a while absorbed in thought. On a piece of paper in front of him, he absentmindedly wrote down 'Eyes, Ice, McKinnon'. Slowly he drew a circle around the word 'Ice' and a circle round the name 'McKinnon' and then a line connecting the two circles together. He contemplated the piece of paper. These cases were very difficult, he thought. Lives were at risk. These young graduate officers from outside London could not be expected to understand the realities of these situations. He put the piece of paper into the shredder.

When Bertie O'Connor was finally traced by two officers from Elliott's team, they found him in an uncooperative mood.

Bertie's itinerant lifestyle brought him into daily contact with officers from Brixton Police Station, and, since featuring in Alison French's front-page story about Delroy's death, he had found these encounters taking on a distinctly harsher character. It was not that he was being arrested more often than before, but now he found himself constantly being moved on by police and, in the process, being spoken to more rudely and handled more roughly than he was used to. Officers who had previously shown him kindness treated him as a stranger.

Bertie was left in no doubt as to the reason for this change in the way he was being treated by the police. Some of the more outspoken of the officers with whom he came into contact asked him outright who he thought he was to be running off to the papers and stirring up trouble for the police. One asked him if he realized that he and his big mouth were to blame for the rioting which had followed Delroy's death.

The two officers from Elliott's team who finally located Bertie unfortunately knew nothing of the way in which he was being treated by local officers. They found him late one afternoon, sitting on his own on the pavement outside Brixton Station drinking out of a can of Special Brew. When they approached him, producing their warrant cards and introducing themselves as police officers, he cowered away from them, saying he had done nothing wrong and was just on his way.

The officers tried to explain that they were not accusing him of anything and just wanted to talk to him about Delroy's death, but this only made things worse.

"OK. It's all right. I've got the message," he babbled frantically. "You don't want me sayin' no more 'bout it. Well, that's fine, I won't say no more 'bout it. But there's no need for all this pushin' an' shovin'. See, that's what's wrong with you lot today – too much pushin' an' shovin'." He took a swig from his can, and muttered under his breath, "That's why the fellah died in the first place – too much pushin' an' shovin'."

The two officers found it difficult to make much sense of what Bertie was saying, and they put this down to the fact that he had obviously been drinking heavily. They tried to explain to him that, far from wanting him not to say any more about Delroy's death, they wanted him to tell them all he knew about it, and to make a statement about it. But it was no good. Bertie suspected a trick.

"Oh, no!" he protested. "You're not gettin' me like that. Just to give you an' your mates another excuse to start pushin' an' shovin' me 'bout again. No, I'm not makin' no statement an' that's me final word. Now, if you don't mind, I'll just be after movin' along, gettin' outta your way."

With that, Bertie shuffled off down the road, casting anxious looks behind him to make sure that he was not being followed.

The two officers were not sorry to see him go. They had done their best, they told themselves, but there was no way they were going to get any sense out of that drunk old dosser.

Elliott was disappointed to hear that his officers had not managed to get a statement out of Bertie and initially suggested that they should make another attempt to do so, but both officers were adamant that there was no point in doing this, as Bertie had made it clear that he was unwilling to cooperate with them and, in their view, he was too much of an alcoholic to carry any credibility anyway, and, in the end, Elliott accepted this.

With most of his enquiries complete, Elliott arranged to interview DC McKinnon.

McKinnon attended for the interview with his solicitor, Mr Jessop.

Roger Jessop was a tall, thin man with a slight stoop. He was in his early fifties and had practised criminal law for most of his career. A clever and hardworking lawyer with an extensive knowledge of the criminal law and of the rules of evidence and procedure which apply in criminal cases, he had, during his career, become adept at performing the delicate balancing act involved in exploiting every opportunity to further the interests of his clients, while, at the same time, taking care to avoid doing anything dishonest or unethical by the standards of his profession. Over the years, his skill at advising and representing his clients and the frequency with which he secured acquittals against the odds had gained him the grudging respect of many police officers, and, as a result, the Police Federation had begun to instruct him to act for those of its members who found themselves facing criminal or disciplinary investigation. It was the Police Federation which had arranged for him to represent Michael McKinnon.

Once Mr Jessop and DC McKinnon had taken their seats facing Elliott and one of his colleagues across the table in the interview room, the solicitor handed Elliott a statement by his client.

The statement had been drafted by Jessop after long and careful consultations with McKinnon. It read

STATEMENT
Statement of Michael McKinnon
Age: Over 21

I make this statement of my own free will. I understand that I do not have to say anything, but that it may harm my defence, if I do not mention, when questioned, something which I later rely on in court. This statement may be given in evidence.

Dated: 29ᵗʰ October   Signed: Michael McKinnon

I understand that I am to be questioned about an incident in which Mr Delroy Brown died while in custody at Brixton Police Station on 6ᵗʰ September of this year.

The incident in which Mr Brown died and the events which followed his death have caused me great

distress, and have left me in a very emotional state. I therefore believe that it is in the best interests of all concerned that I give my account of what happened in a written statement.

I deny that I committed any criminal or disciplinary offence in my dealings with Mr Brown.

I consent to this statement being used in the investigation into Mr Brown's death and in any criminal or disciplinary proceedings which may follow that investigation.

Dated: 29*th* October   Signed: Michael McKinnon

At 11.30 p.m. on 6*th* September of this year I was on duty at Brixton Police Station.

Earlier that evening I had received information that a man by the name of Delroy Brown was being held in the cells at the station, and that this man had information about a case which I was working on.

Having heard this, I went to the custody suite and obtained permission from the custody officer, PS Leach, to visit Mr Brown in his cell. I agreed with PS Leach that my visit to see Mr Brown in his cell should be fully documented in Mr Brown's custody record.

PS Leach took me to Mr Brown's cell, unlocked the door to the cell, and then left to continue with his duties.

Mr Brown was lying on the bed at the far end of the cell. As I entered the cell, he sat up and looked at me with wild, staring eyes. Then, before I had a chance to say anything, he suddenly jumped off the bed and came at me in a frenzy. He took hold of me by the throat, and started banging the back of my head hard against the cell wall behind me. At the same time he was kicking out at me with both feet. I put my hands on his chest to try and push him away from me. I only used reasonable force, and did not push him hard. He lost his grip on my throat, and stumbled backwards. As he did so, he seemed to lose his balance, and, apparently as a result of losing his balance, fell back heavily, striking his head hard on the cell wall behind him. He then collapsed on the floor.

For a few moments I was too shocked by what had happened to do anything. Then I rang the alarm.

PS Leach arrived almost immediately, and I reported to him what had happened. He attempted to render first aid to Mr Brown, and called for the FME, Dr Johnson. I then left the cell.

Following this incident, I was examined by the FME, Dr Howard.

As a result of this assault on me by Mr Brown, I received bruises to the back of my head and a bruise to my left shin.

The assault on me by Mr Brown in his cell was totally unprovoked. The violence used by Mr Brown in this assault caused me to fear that I was about to suffer serious injury at his hands. In defending myself against this assault, I used no more force than was reasonable in the circumstances.

Dated: 29th October   Signed: Michael McKinnon

As he was reading this statement, Elliott glanced up from time to time to look at the officer opposite him. DC

McKinnon did not look to the chief inspector like a man 'in a very emotional state'. Indeed, the only emotion which Elliott could discern in McKinnon's face was one of arrogant defiance.

He wondered what McKinnon's reaction would be if confronted by a suspect who, as he was about to be interviewed, claimed that, given the emotional state he was in, he believed that it was in the best interests of all concerned that he provide the police with a written statement about the events in question, and then handed over a carefully worded statement setting out his defence and clearly drafted with the assistance of a lawyer. Elliott suspected that McKinnon would be among the first to condemn and deride such a manoeuvre, but then, as Elliott was aware, it was a situation which DC McKinnon was unlikely to encounter very often, as it was rare for a suspect to have the time or the opportunity, before being interviewed by police, to set out his or her defence in a statement prepared with the assistance of a good lawyer.

Elliott turned on the tape recorder. He formally reminded McKinnon that he wished to question him about the death of Delroy Brown at Brixton Police Station on 6th September and cautioned him. He referred to the fact that, before the start of the interview, Mr Jessop had given him a statement by DC McKinnon, and he read out the account of events given by the officer in his statement.

He then asked McKinnon, "When did you first learn that Delroy Brown was in the cells at Brixton Police Station?"

McKinnon sat up in his chair, looked Elliott straight in the eye and recited stiffly, "Having taken legal advice from my solicitor, I do not wish to add anything to what I have said in the statement which I have already submitted to you, sir."

Elliott was not surprised. He had expected something like this. Nonetheless he persevered.

"Had you had any previous dealings with Mr Brown?"

"I have nothing to add to my statement, sir."

Was there, Elliott wondered, a ring of insolence about the way in which McKinnon stressed the word 'sir'? He pressed on.

"What were you told that led you to believe that Mr Brown had information about a case you were working on?"

"I have nothing to add, sir."

"Who led you to believe that Mr Brown had this information?"

"As I've said, sir, I have nothing to add."

"What was the case you were working on, about which you believed Mr Brown had information?"

"Again, sir, I have nothing to add."

"Do you know a man who is known by the street name 'Eyes'?"

"I have never heard of anyone who is known by the street name 'Eyes'."

Elliott was surprised to get an answer to one of his questions. He looked closely at McKinnon. Mr Jessop put out his hand, and touched his client's left forearm, and, as McKinnon turned to look at him, silently shook his head.

McKinnon answered the remainder of Elliott's questions by saying he had nothing to add to his statement and Elliott eventually gave up and brought the interview to a close.

Having interviewed McKinnon, Elliott began preparing his report for the Police Complaints Authority. He was good at writing reports and did not find this a difficult one to write, but it was not one that he enjoyed writing.

The central issue was a simple one: was there sufficient evidence against DC McKinnon to charge him with the murder or manslaughter of Delroy Brown?

Elliott had taken an instinctive dislike to McKinnon, but he put this out of his mind. There remained, however, the issue of McKinnon's credibility. Elliott's extensive experience of interviewing witnesses and suspects (including police officers) led him to distrust McKinnon, but he had no hard evidence that McKinnon had lied to him.

Elliott also remained acutely aware that there were important questions in this case which remained unanswered, things he had not been told. What exactly had McKinnon been told which had led him to visit Brown in his cell? Who had given McKinnon this information? Why had McKinnon refused to say more about his reason for visiting Brown in his cell? Was it just that he'd been told by Jessop not to add anything to the statement which the solicitor had drafted for him? Why had McKinnon been so keen to say that he had never heard of anyone known by the street name 'Eyes'? Did McKinnon's visit to Brown's cell have anything to do with Brown's offer to provide the police with information about 'Eyes'? If so, how did McKinnon find out about this offer? Did 'Eyes' exist and, if so, why did no one at Brixton Police Station appear to have heard of him?

Elliott's instinct was that there were things in this case which were being deliberately withheld from him – not only by McKinnon, but also by others. Was this, he asked himself, just a product of one of those walls of silence he came up against so often in investigating complaints against police officers, the result of a closing of the ranks and a generalised unwillingness by the officers serving at the station at which the investigation was being carried out to allow officers from outside to pry too deeply into the station's affairs? He half wished one of his team could be posted to Brixton Police Station to work on this case under cover. Would this, he wondered, provide him with answers to his unanswered questions?

As it was, Elliott had to acknowledge that he had no evidence to disprove McKinnon's claim that, in pushing Brown, he had only been defending himself against an assault on him by Brown.

He was also forced to admit that he had difficulty in seeing how anything more he might find out about McKinnon's motive for visiting Brown in his cell could provide sufficient evidence to undermine McKinnon's claim that he had only acted in self-defence.

He did not like the feeling that he had not discovered the whole truth about Delroy's death, but the sensation was one he was used to. He prepared his report, detailing the evidence which he and his team had gathered. He made little reference in the report to the questions to which he had been unable to obtain answers, on the basis that, as unanswered questions, they were of no evidential value. He gave his assessment of the evidence which he and his team had collected, and concluded by saying that, in his view, there was insufficient evidence against McKinnon to charge him with any criminal offence relating to the death of Delroy Brown.

When he had finished his report, Elliott took some comfort in a confident belief that it was a well-written report, and that no one could fault the conclusions he had reached in it. He felt, too, relief at not having to recommend that a police officer be prosecuted for murder or manslaughter.

Elliott submitted his report to the Police Complaints

Authority and a copy of it, together with a copy of his file of evidence to the Crown Prosecution Service, which would now have to advise on the case.

Peter Rotherhithe, the branch crown prosecutor in charge of the branch of the CPS to which Elliott submitted his file, was not a man who was good at making decisions. A forty-seven-year-old barrister, he had joined the CPS soon after its inception at a time when it was very short of lawyers and, largely as a result, he had risen to a position where he was earning far more than he had ever earned during a relatively unsuccessful career at the bar, in which he had discovered that, although he had a good knowledge of the law, he was not an effective advocate. Now, never a decisive man, he had become rendered incapable of making almost any decision at all by a fear that one day he might make a wrong decision which would cost him his job. This fear he assuaged by delegating almost every decision he had to make to one of his subordinates. In doing this, he told the lawyers working for him that he would support them in any decision they might take and accept responsibility with them for any errors they might make.

His staff had learnt not to take these assurances at their face value.

Elliott's file remained on Rotherhithe's desk for nearly six weeks. During this period, it was moved to several different positions on the desk, as, from time to time, Rotherhithe nervously dipped into it and then quickly put it down again, telling himself he would consider it later. He quickly realized that this was a sensitive case which could have political repercussions and, as such, was a case he ought to review himself, but he could not face the responsibility of doing so.

Eventually, he called Linda Fawcett, one of his principal crown prosecutors, into his office.

"Linda," he said, "I've got this little advice file here I'd like you to have a look at, if you wouldn't mind. It's a case involving a death in police custody. I've had a quick look at it, and it looks fairly straightforward. There seems to be a good report on the case by the investigating officer, a chief inspector, who's basically come to the conclusion that there's insufficient evidence to charge the officer involved with anything, so it's probably just a matter of rubber-stamping his recommendation. I'd do it myself, but I'm afraid I'm rather snowed under at the moment."

Linda Fawcett looked at Peter Rotherhithe's almost bare desk, and thought of her own almost collapsing under the weight of the files on it awaiting her attention. Inwardly sighing, she replied brightly, "Yes, of course, Peter."

"Oh, and there's just one other thing," added Rotherhithe, as she was about to leave the room with the file in her hand. "This is one we ought to let the police have our advice on as soon as possible. As you know, these death in custody cases have a high priority, and I'm afraid that it's some time since the police submitted this file to us. So, perhaps, if you could get something off by the end of the week…"

"Well, I'll do what I can, Peter," she said, "but I do have rather a lot on at the moment."

"Yes, of course, Linda, I understand," said Rotherhithe, filled with benevolent relief at having shed responsibility for reviewing a potentially controversial case. "All I ask is that you do your best. And remember, I'll back you up on any decision you take."

His PCP, who had already turned to leave, grimaced and left his office.

Linda Fawcett was a brisk, businesslike woman in her mid-thirties. She was a solicitor who knew that her skills as an advocate were limited and her knowledge of the criminal law adequate rather than exceptional, but she prided herself on the common sense which she brought to her job, on her capacity to manage a heavy workload and on her ability to make decisions.

Late the following day, she spent twenty minutes reviewing the file submitted to the CPS by Elliott, quickly decided that she agreed with the conclusions reached by the chief inspector in the report by him which accompanied the file, and drafted her advice accordingly.

It read:

Dear Chief Inspector Elliott,

Death in Custody of Mr Delroy Brown
DC Michael McKinnon

ADVICE

Thank you for the file submitted to me for advice in relation to the incident in which Mr Delroy Brown died while in custody at Brixton Police Station on 6th September.

I have now carefully considered this file and, by reference to the criteria laid down in the Code for Crown Prosecutors 1994 issued pursuant to section 10 of the Prosecution of Offences Act 1985, advise as follows:

At the time of his death, Mr Brown was clearly in lawful custody at Brixton Police Station, having been charged with supplying cocaine to an undercover police officer. The evidence to support this charge was substantial.

It is undisputed that Mr Brown met his death when he broke his neck as a result of striking the back of his head against the wall of the cell in which he was being held.

DC Michael McKinnon, an officer at Brixton Police Station, who was in Mr Brown's cell with him at the time he met his death, has admitted pushing Mr Brown backwards just before he struck his head on his cell wall, but DC McKinnon says that, in pushing Mr Brown backwards, he was only using reasonable force to defend himself, after Mr Brown had made a violent and unprovoked assault on him.

There is no evidence to contradict DC McKinnon's assertion that, when he pushed Mr Brown, he was acting in self-defence. Indeed the injuries to DC McKinnon found by the FME, Dr Howard, tend to support DC McKinnon's account of events. Moreover the evidence of DC Mathews, DC Jones and PS Leach that Mr Brown was in a disturbed state on the evening of his death lends weight to DC McKinnon's assertion that Mr Brown made an irrational assault on him.

Accordingly, I advise that there is insufficient evidence against DC McKinnon for there to be a realistic prospect of his being convicted of any criminal offence in relation to Mr Brown's death, and I recommend that no further action be taken against DC McKinnon in this matter.

Yours sincerely,
Peter Rotherhithe
Branch Crown Prosecutor

When Linda Fawcett had had her advice typed up, she took it to Rotherhithe for his signature.

He affected to be too busy to look at it.

"Just p.p. it for me, Linda. It's all right. You know I trust you."

She did as she was told, thinking to herself that the problem was not that he did not trust her but that she did not trust him.

When Elliott read the advice from the CPS, he gave a wry grimace, as he noted that it said, more briefly and in slightly different language, much the same as he had said in the conclusion to his report. He guessed that the advice was Ms Fawcett's own work and he wondered critically how old she was, how much experience she had as a criminal lawyer and how long she had spent on this case. Had anything been achieved, he asked himself, by submitting his file to the CPS?

He informed the coroner's office that an inquest could now be held into Delroy Brown's death.

Inquest

The inquest into Delroy Brown's death was held at Southwark Coroner's Court.

A hearing formally opening the inquest had been held shortly after Delroy's death, but, at that hearing, the coroner, sitting alone without a jury, had immediately adjourned the proceedings to await the outcome of the police investigation into the case.

Once Chief Inspector Elliott had informed the coroner's office that the police investigation was complete and that Delroy's death was not to be the subject of a prosecution for murder or manslaughter, the inquest hearing was resumed to hear evidence.

The witnesses attending the resumed hearing included Delroy's father, Malcolm Brown, and DC McKinnon, while also there were other members of Delroy's family, including Althea and Bernice, some of the family's friends and supporters, Alison French, who was there to report on the case for the *Brixton Chronicle*, and Chief Inspector Elliott, who was there as an observer.

Roger Jessop was there to represent DC McKinnon, and Neeta Patel, a young local solicitor, was there to represent Delroy's family.

Neeta Patel was twenty-nine years old, small and slim, with jet black shoulder-length hair. She had gained a first class degree in law from Cambridge University and had passed the Law Society's Final Examination with flying colours, but had encountered difficulty in securing the two-year training contract with a firm of solicitors which she needed to complete her qualification as a solicitor. Despite her outstanding academic record and glowing references, none of the large firms to which she had applied for a training contract had offered her an interview, and most had not even acknowledged her application. She had therefore been very grateful to accept the training contract offered to her by a small two-partner firm in Brixton, though she was at first dismayed by the firm's cramped, dingy and none too clean offices. It was not the sort of place she had imagined herself working in as a lawyer. Most of the firm's work was legal aid work, and it specialised in criminal, matrimonial and immigration cases. This was also not the kind of work which she had imagined herself doing, but she soon came to enjoy it, and built up a strong relationship with her clients, many of whom recommended her to their friends. The steady stream of clients which she brought into the firm led the partners to ask her to stay on with them when she qualified, though they told her that, regrettably, they were not able to pay her as much as they would have liked to nor, at least for the time being, to offer her a partnership. She had now been qualified as a solicitor for five years, and had enjoyed some modest increases in her salary, but had still not been made partner in the firm.

At the resumed hearing, the coroner sat with a jury, because, although some inquests were conducted by a coroner sitting alone, section 8 of the 1988 Coroners Act provided that a coroner conducting an inquest into a death must summon a jury when he had 'reason to suspect that the death occurred while the deceased was in police custody, or resulted from an injury caused by a police officer in the purported execution of his duty'.

The coroner, Sir Montague Thirske, was a small, bald man in his late fifties, sporting somewhat incongruously, a brightly coloured bow tie. Before being appointed a coroner he had had a successful career as a barrister specialising in medical negligence cases, but his present role was one he relished.

He began by agreeing to an application by Neeta Patel to represent Delroy's family and an application by Mr Jessop to represent DC McKinnon. He then addressed the jury.

"Ladies and gentlemen, we are here today to conduct an inquest into someone's death. The coroner's court, as some of you may be aware, is one of the oldest courts in this country, and, as you will find out, is rather different from other courts which you may have been to or have seen on television or in films. In the first place our procedure is, as we lawyers say, inquisitorial rather than accusatorial. What that means is that the purpose of these proceedings is not to determine a dispute between two sides. It is not for us to determine whether anyone is guilty of a criminal offence or whether one party has committed a civil wrong against another. Indeed, it is generally prohibited for us to return a verdict framed in such a way as to appear to determine the criminal liability of any person or any question of civil liability. No, ladies and gentlemen, what we are here for is simply to determine the identity of a person who has died and how and why he died."

Sir Montague paused to take a sip from a glass of water, and then continued, "One of the consequences of the fact that there are no opposing sides in these proceedings is that all the witnesses who are called to give evidence in this case, will be called by me, rather than by the lawyers present, and most of the questions which these witnesses will be asked will also be asked by me. Having said that, it is possible for interested parties to be represented by lawyers at an inquest, and, ladies and gentlemen, as you have heard, I have agreed that Ms Patel may represent the deceased's family in this hearing, and that Mr Jessop may represent one of the witnesses, Detective Constable McKinnon, in the proceedings. These lawyers will be allowed to ask questions of the witnesses who appear before you, but it is not the job of either of them to try and persuade you to find in favour of his or her client or clients or against anyone else. This is not the kind of case in which witnesses are called by the lawyer for one party and then cross-examined by the lawyer for the other. So, there'll be no Perry Mason stuff here!"

As he delivered the last words of this address, Sir Montague gave a benevolent smile to the jury and then turned a meaningful look on the two lawyers.

Roger Jessop smiled to himself. He remembered with affectionate nostalgia the television series of the 1960s featuring the famous fictional American lawyer referred to by the coroner, but he wondered if his colleague, Ms Patel, or indeed the younger members of the jury, would ever have heard of Perry Mason. In any event, he mused, he could not imagine that there was the remotest possibility that this inquest would take on the characteristics of the fictional American trials depicted in the television series.

The first witness called by Sir Montague to give evidence was Delroy's father.

Malcolm Brown was a small man of about the same age as Sir Montague, with slightly greying closely cropped curly black hair. He was wearing a shiny black suit, a white shirt and black tie and clutched in his right hand a black and grey checked cloth cap. He looked ill at ease in the crowded courtroom, but gave his evidence with quiet dignity, speaking in a soft Jamaican accent.

In answer to questions from Sir Montague, he gave his name and address and described how in the early hours of 7th September, he and his wife had been visited by two police officers, and how he had been taken by the officers to see a body which he had identified as that of his son Delroy. He gave his son's full name and date of birth. When asked for Delroy's address at the date of his death, he hesitated, and then replied, "He moved around a lot, but I suppose that our address was what you could call his official address."

"What sort of man was your son?" enquired Sir Montague gently.

Malcolm Brown, a law-abiding man, who had worked hard all his life and had held down his present job as a bus driver for over thirty years, struggled with conflicting emotions, as he tried to find the right words to describe his son.

"Basically, Delroy was a good boy," he said at last. "He just never seemed to manage to settle to anyt'ing, never seemed to take life serious, just seem to drift. But there was no real harm in him." He paused, then added with unexpected feeling, "He never deserve to die."

Mr Brown's wife, a large woman, who was sitting towards

the front of the courtroom wearing a brightly coloured dress and a large navy blue hat, let out a loud, dramatic sob, setting off a tremor of emotion around the courtroom.

Sir Montague looked slightly embarrassed, and gave a short cough. "Quite so," he said. "Thank you, Mr Brown." He turned to the family's solicitor. "Any questions, Ms Patel?"

Neeta Patel rose to her feet. "Sir, yes, thank you, sir," she said, and, turning to Malcolm Brown asked, "Mr Brown, was your son, Delroy, a violent man?"

"No, not at all. Quite the opposite. First sign of trouble, he'd be off. Even when he was a boy, he was like that. Never one to get into a fight, if he could help it."

"Thank you, Mr Brown," said Neeta and sat down.

"Mr Jessop?" enquired Sir Montague.

DC McKinnon's solicitor got to his feet. "Thank you, sir," he said, and turned to Mr Brown. "But your son did take drugs, didn't he?" he asked quietly.

Malcolm Brown was aware that Delroy had smoked cannabis, but he resented the question, which seemed to him an attempt to cast an unnecessary slur on his dead son's name. "I don't know not'ing 'bout that," he said.

Jessop persisted. "But you know that he had been charged with supplying crack cocaine to an undercover police officer?"

Malcolm Brown found it hard to accept that Delroy had been a drug dealer, but was acutely aware of how little he knew of his dead son's activities. In recent years he had seen little of Delroy, and most of the time he had had little idea of what his son was doing or even of where he was. "That's what the police say, but I don't know not'ing 'bout it," he replied defensively.

"Thank you," said Jessop and sat down.

"Thank you, Mr Brown," echoed Sir Montague. "You

may step down now. Thank you for coming, and my sincere condolences to you and your family."

As Delroy's father left the witness box, he experienced a sudden unexpected sense of loss. He had never felt close to his son, but now, suddenly, he missed him. He had a vague sense that he had let Delroy down, but did not see what else he could have said or done.

DC Matthews, who gave evidence next, first confirmed, in answer to questions from the coroner, that he had known Delroy, and that he had seen him on 6th September. He then explained that, on an afternoon in July, while engaged in a surveillance operation, he had witnessed Delroy selling cocaine to an undercover police officer, and that, as a result, when he had seen him on 6th September, he had arrested him for that offence. He then went on to describe how he had taken Delroy to Brixton Police Station, interviewed him, charged him with the offence, and left him with the custody officer, PS Leach.

"What sort of state did Mr Brown appear to be in when you interviewed him?" asked Sir Montague.

"To begin with, sir, he was quite cheerful, but when he became aware of the strength of the evidence against him and realized that he was facing a fairly long prison sentence, he seemed to take it quite badly."

"Would you say he was upset?"

"Yes, sir, I think I would."

"Thank you, Detective Constable. Ms Patel, do you have any questions for this witness?"

"Yes, sir, thank you, sir," replied the solicitor, getting to her feet.

She turned to DC Matthews. "Officer, you'd had a number of previous dealings with Mr Brown, hadn't you?"

"Yes, that's correct."

"Are you familiar with his record of convictions?"

"Yes, I am."

"Do you have a copy of that with you, today?"

"Yes, I do."

"Looking at that record, Officer, did Mr Brown have any convictions for offences of violence?"

"No, he didn't."

"Did he have any convictions for offences of supplying drugs or possessing drugs with intent to supply them?"

"No, he didn't."

"Did he have any convictions for the possession of any Class A drugs?"

"No."

"Before you interviewed Mr Brown, did you arrange for him to be examined by the police doctor?"

"No, I didn't. There was no reason to."

"From that I take it that you were satisfied that he was not under the influence of drugs."

"That's correct. If I had believed him to be under the influence of drugs I would not have interviewed him and, if I had had any suspicion that he was under the influence of drugs, I would have asked for him to be examined by the FME, and would only have interviewed him if the FME had certified that he was fit to be interviewed."

"Thank you, Officer, I have no further questions."

Neeta Patel sat down and Sir Montague turned to DC McKinnon's solicitor.

"Mr Jessop?"

"Thank you, sir," said Jessop getting to his feet to question DC Matthews.

"Officer, you don't have any medical qualifications, do you?"

"No, I don't."

"So you are not really qualified to say whether Mr Brown was under the influence of drugs or not when you interviewed him, are you?"

"Well, in the course of my duties as a police officer, I have had to deal with a large number of people who have been under the influence of drugs, and I'd say that I can usually tell when someone is in that state."

"Usually, but not always, Officer? So, it is possible that Mr Brown was under the influence of drugs when you interviewed him, but that you didn't realise that, isn't it?"

"It's possible, but I wouldn't say it's very likely."

"Thank you, Officer. Now, if you could turn again to Mr Brown's criminal record," said Jessop, stressing the last two words. "It is correct, is it not, that he had convictions for possession of cannabis?"

"Yes, that's correct."

"How many?"

"Three."

"And had he ever been cautioned for possession of cannabis?"

"Yes, once."

"So, that's four offences of possession of cannabis altogether, isn't it, Officer?"

"Yes, that's right."

"As for cocaine, the mere fact that Mr Brown had no convictions for possession of cocaine does not mean that he never used cocaine, does it?"

"No, it doesn't."

"It's over eleven years since Mr Brown was first cautioned for the possession of cannabis, isn't it?"

"Yes, that's correct."

"And isn't it your experience that those who start off by using cannabis often move onto using hard drugs, like cocaine?"

"Often, but not always, by any means."

"Very well. You arrested Mr Brown for supplying crack cocaine to an undercover police officer, didn't you?"

"Yes, as I've said."

"And isn't it your experience that those who deal in crack cocaine on the streets are usually also crack users?"

"Again, that is often the case, but not always."

"You've said that, in the course of your duties, you have had to deal with a large number of people who have been under the influence of drugs, is that correct?"

"Yes, it is."

"And is it your experience that people under the influence of crack cocaine are often violent?"

"Yes, that's correct."

"And you said that, when you returned Mr Brown to the cells after you had interviewed him, he was upset?"

Sir Montague intervened. "I think," he said, "'upset' was my word. I think you, Officer, said…" He looked through his notes. "Ah, yes, here it is. You said, 'he seemed to take it quite badly'. Perhaps we should clarify what you meant by that. How did his reaction to what he had learned in the interview manifest itself in his behaviour? Was he worked up? Aggressive?"

"No, sir," replied Matthews. "Quite the opposite. He was very subdued, very quiet. Seemed quite shaken."

"Thank you," said Sir Montague. "Any more questions, Mr Jessop?"

"Just one, sir." Jessop turned to Matthews. "So, Officer, would it be fair to say that, when you left Mr Brown with the custody officer, PS Leach, Mr Brown was in an emotional state?"

"Yes, I suppose that would be fair."

Matthews was allowed to leave the witness box. He had not been asked any questions which required him to tell the court about Delroy's offer to become a police informant, and he had not felt the need to raise the subject himself.

PS Leach, who was called upon to give evidence next, looked nervous as he entered the witness box and took the oath. He was worried about what he might be asked about his decision to allow DC McKinnon to visit Delroy in the cells.

Sir Montague, sensing the officer's nervousness, sought to put him at his ease by first asking him to describe his duties as custody officer. This Leach did. Then, in answer to further questions from the coroner, he gave his account of the events involving Delroy which had occurred from the time when DC Matthews first brought Delroy into the custody suite at the police station until the time when his body was taken away by the ambulance.

"How would you describe the mood Mr Brown was in when he was brought back from being interviewed by DC Matthews?" asked the coroner.

"Very subdued, sir, almost in a daze."

"Did you think of having him examined by the police doctor?"

"No, sir, I didn't, because in my judgment there was nothing medically wrong with him. He was just a bit shaken."

"Was there anything about him which suggested to you that he might be under the influence of drugs?"

"No, sir, there wasn't. If there had been, I would have had him seen by the FME immediately."

"Thank you, Sergeant," said Sir Montague. "Any questions for this witness, Ms Patel?"

"Yes, sir, thank you sir," said the solicitor. She got up, turned to face PS Leach and began, "You've said that, in your view, there was nothing medically wrong with Mr Brown, but you've also said that, when you put him back in his cell after he had been interviewed and charged, you left the wicket in his cell door open, so that you could keep an eye on him, isn't that correct?"

"Yes, that's right."

"So, you were concerned about him?"

"Yes, I was, a bit."

"You had not seen anything to suggest that he was violent in any way, had you?"

"No, I hadn't."

"So, your concern for him arose because he appeared vulnerable, not because he appeared violent, is that correct?"

"Yes, that's correct."

"Do you consider that it was appropriate to allow a vulnerable prisoner to be visited in his cell in the middle of the night by an officer with no connection to the investigation which had led to that prisoner's being charged?"

PS Leach stiffened. "It was only to be a very short visit," he said. "I had no reason to think that it would do any harm."

"I see," said Neeta. She considered putting to the officer that he should have anticipated that this decision by him might have harmful consequences, as indeed it had done, but she decided that this would serve no useful purpose, and that she preferred not to antagonise him unnecessarily. "Very well," she continued. "When you got to the cell after the alarm rang, you saw Mr Brown lying on the floor against the wall on one side of the cell and DC McKinnon standing with his back to the wall on the other side of the cell, is that correct?"

"Yes, it is."

"So, DC McKinnon was making no effort to tend to Mr Brown at all, is that right?"

"Yes, it is, but I got the impression that that was because DC McKinnon was in shock."

"But that is only your impression, isn't it?"

"Yes, it is."

"And DC McKinnon admitted to you that he had pushed Mr Brown, didn't he?"

"Yes, but the way he put it was that Mr Brown had come at him first, and that he had only tried to push Mr Brown away from him, and that he had not pushed him hard."

"Mr Brown was a much smaller man than DC McKinnon, wasn't he?"

"Smaller, certainly. I don't know about much smaller."

"About six inches smaller and a good couple of stones lighter, wouldn't you agree?"

"That sounds about right."

"Thank you, Officer, that's all."

Neeta sat down and Sir Montague asked DC McKinnon's solicitor if he had any questions for this witness.

"Yes, sir, thank you, sir," said Jessop, getting up. He turned to the officer. "Sergeant Leach," he said, "you were concerned about Mr Brown when he came back from being interviewed because he appeared shaken, disturbed, is that right?"

"Yes, it is."

"And is it your experience as a custody officer that disturbed prisoners are sometimes prone to completely unprovoked and unexpected outbursts of violence?"

"Well, yes," replied Leach hesitantly. "That does sometimes happen."

"Thank you, Sergeant," said Jessop and sat down.

It was just after one o'clock when PS Leach finished giving his evidence and the court adjourned for lunch.

After lunch the coroner called DC McKinnon to the witness box.

McKinnon would have preferred not to have to give evidence, but he had no choice. He had the right to refuse to answer questions which might incriminate him, but he did not have the right to refuse to give evidence altogether. As he got up to walk to the witness box, the eyes of almost everyone in the courtroom turned to look at him. A hostile murmur arose from Delroy's friends and members of his family.

Sir Montague, determined to be fair to the officer, simply asked him to tell the jury where he was at about 11.30 in the evening of 6th September and to describe the events in which he became involved at that time.

In response, McKinnon recited almost word for word the account of events given in the statement by him handed to Chief Inspector Elliott by Roger Jessop. Elliott, who had a copy of that statement in front of him as McKinnon gave his evidence, was not surprised at this, but it made him uneasy.

Sir Montague recognised McKinnon's evidence as a prepared speech, but, conscious of the officer's difficult position in the proceedings, decided, at least for the time being, to ask him no further questions and to leave that to Ms Patel and Mr Jessop.

He turned first to Neeta and, at his invitation, she rose to question the officer.

"Had you had any previous dealings with Mr Brown?" she asked.

McKinnon hesitated almost imperceptibly before replying, "No, I hadn't."

"Very well," said Neeta. "What were you told that led you to believe that Mr Brown had information on a case you were working on?"

"I refuse to answer that question on the grounds of Public Interest Immunity," replied McKinnon.

A murmur of incomprehension and suspicion went round the courtroom. Chief Inspector Elliott looked up in surprise. He had not expected this. Even the coroner looked surprised.

Public Interest Immunity was a legal principle which allowed a witness in court proceedings to refuse to answer a question on the grounds that, to answer it, the witness would have to disclose sensitive information, when it would not be in the public interest to do so. Among the situations in which a question put to a witness might be met by a claim to Public Interest Immunity were those in which, to answer the question, the witness would have to disclose state secrets when this might endanger national security, to disclose the contents of communications between public servants and others when this would inhibit the proper functioning of a public service or to disclose the identity of a police informant when (as would normally be the case) this would endanger the informant's safety or discourage others from acting as informants.

A court confronted with a claim to Public Interest Immunity had a difficult and delicate balancing act to perform in deciding whether to allow the witness not to answer the question which had been put. On the one hand, while it was in the public interest that sensitive information should not be disclosed when its disclosure could have harmful consequences, on the other hand, it was also in the public interest that information should not be withheld from the court or other parties to the proceedings when this could lead to a miscarriage of justice. Where the court consisted of a judge or a coroner sitting with a jury, this was a decision to be taken by the judge or coroner and not by the jury. The court first had to decide whether the information requested in the question put to the witness was relevant to an issue before the court. If it was not, that was the end of the matter. The witness did not need to answer the question. If, on the other hand, the information requested was, or might be, material to an issue in the proceedings, the court had to decide whether more harm would be done by requiring an answer to the question or by allowing the witness not to answer it.

To make this decision, the court might have to hold a private hearing at which, in the presence of the coroner or judge, but in the absence of everyone else (including members of the jury), the witness would disclose to the court the information for which he or she sought Public Interest Immunity. Whether or not such a private hearing was held, the decision whether or not to allow a witness to refuse a question on the grounds of Public Interest Immunity was always a difficult one for the court.

Sir Montague's initial look of surprise turned to one of concern. This was not an issue in which he wished to become embroiled. He turned to the jury.

"Members of the jury," he said, "a legal point has just been raised with which we do not need to trouble you, so I would ask you to retire while I sort it out. No doubt, you'll all welcome the opportunity to take a break and stretch your legs for a few minutes."

The jurors got up and filed out of the courtroom. Some of them were grateful for the break, but others resented being asked to leave the courtroom, feeling that they were being excluded from what was going on, just when proceedings had taken an interesting turn, and harbouring a suspicion that things which they had a right to know were being withheld from them. In the minds of some members of the jury some of this suspicion attached itself to DC McKinnon.

Once the jury had left and the courtroom had been cleared of everyone except McKinnon and the two lawyers, Sir Montague turned to the officer's solicitor.

"Now, what's this all about, Mr Jessop?" he asked, a note of irritation in his voice. "Am I going to have to hear from your client in camera?"

Jessop got to his feet. He was not pleased with the answer which his client had given to Neeta's question. It was not the answer which he and McKinnon had agreed on, but, upon hearing it, his face had remained expressionless, registering no trace of surprise or displeasure. As he rose to address the coroner, he appeared completely calm and unruffled.

"I don't think so, sir," he said, with quiet assurance. "In my respectful submission, the question here is simply one of relevance. What relevance can the source or nature of the information received by my client about Mr Brown have to the issue of how Mr Brown met his death? Of course, there are public interest considerations here, too. My client naturally does not want to disclose information about other cases he was, or is, working on or about police methods or sources of information. But, in my respectful submission, the issue of disclosure does not arise, because the answer to the question asked by my friend is irrelevant to the issues which this court has to decide."

Sir Montague felt relieved. Mr Jessop's argument had a lot of force in it and offered a simple solution to the problem which confronted him. The coroner assumed that the source of DC McKinnon's information was a police informant and he wanted to avoid getting into a situation in which he would have to ask the officer questions about this informant. Like many lawyers, he accepted that the police had to rely heavily on informants to combat crime, and that the identity of these informants had to be protected, but he felt uneasy about the hidden and sordid role played by police informants in the criminal justice system, and preferred to keep his distance from the whole distasteful business.

He turned to Delroy's family's solicitor. "What do you have to say about that, Ms Patel?"

Neeta felt out of her depth. This was not a subject which she had ever been asked to argue before. "In my submission, sir," she said hesitantly, "a central issue in this case is why and how this witness and Mr Brown came to blows, and what this witness was told about Mr Brown before he went to Mr Brown's cell is relevant to that issue, because what he had been told about Mr Brown obviously dictated what the witness said to Mr Brown when he got into the cell, which, in turn, obviously determined what then occurred between them."

Sir Montague looked dubious.

Jessop rose to his feet again. "Sir," he said, "in my submission that argument fails, because it is clear that my client had insufficient time to explain his reasons for visiting Mr Brown in his cell, before Mr Brown assaulted him. Not only is it my client's evidence that Mr Brown assaulted him, before my client had a chance to say anything, but it is also the evidence of Sergeant Leach that my client was alone with

91

Mr Brown in his cell for no more than two minutes before the alarm went off. This, in my submission, clearly precludes any possibility that my client and Mr Brown could have had any discussion about my client's reasons for visiting Mr Brown, before, as my friend puts it, 'they came to blows'."

Sir Montague looked troubled, but, in the end, took the easy way out. "I think that must be right, Ms Patel," he said carefully. "I do not say that the issue raised by your question is completely irrelevant to the issues before this court, but I rule that it is insufficiently relevant to those issues for you to be allowed to pursue this line of questioning."

Neeta tried hard not to look disappointed. She felt that she had been outsmarted by her more experienced opponent, and that she had let her clients down.

Having made his ruling, the coroner summoned the jury back into the courtroom. As the jurors filed back in and took their seats, they noticed that DC McKinnon, who was still in the witness box, had a satisfied smirk on his face, while Sir Montague looked rather flushed and Ms Patel rather subdued.

Sir Montague thanked the members of the jury for their patience and invited Neeta to resume questioning DC McKinnon.

Neeta found it difficult to get back into her stride. "I put it to you, Officer," she suggested, rather feebly, "that you did have some conversation with Mr Brown before you came to blows with him."

"No, that is not correct," replied McKinnon confidently. "I did not have any conversation with Mr Brown, and I did not come to blows with him. He made a violent and unprovoked assault on me. I only used reasonable force to defend myself."

"That's not true, is it? Mr Brown did not assault you, did he?"

"He did assault me, and the injuries that I had when I was seen by the FME prove that he did."

"You could have received those injuries in some other way, couldn't you?"

"Perhaps I could, but I didn't. I received them from Mr Brown when he assaulted me."

Sergeant Leach, who was still in the courtroom, shifted uncomfortably in his seat, troubled by a brief, uncertain memory of the scene which had met his eyes when he first entered Delroy's cell after the alarm went off and a nagging awareness that he knew of another possible explanation for at least some of McKinnon's injuries.

Neeta continued her questions to McKinnon. "I put it to you that you assaulted Mr Brown first, and that you only received your injuries when he tried to defend himself from you, isn't that the case?"

"No, that's not the case. He assaulted me first, and that's when I received my injuries."

"You're much bigger and stronger than Mr Brown was, aren't you?"

"I'm bigger than he was, but I don't know that I'm stronger than he was. He seemed very strong. A lot of these people are much stronger than they look."

To Neeta this last comment sounded suspiciously like racial stereotyping, but she was wary of challenging McKinnon to explain what he meant by it, in case the response she got ended up playing to the prejudices of some of the jurors.

Instead she asked, "You pushed him very hard, didn't you?"

93

"No, I did not push him hard. I only pushed him hard enough to get him off me."

"So, how do you account for the severity of his injuries?"

"After I pushed him away from me, he stumbled and fell backwards. It was his fall that caused his injuries."

Neeta realised that she was getting nowhere. She felt that she was making a poor job of questioning McKinnon and could see no point in continuing her questions to the officer. "Thank you," she said, trying to conceal her feelings of failure. "I have no further questions."

Roger Jessop had an easier task. "Detective Constable McKinnon, how long have you been a police officer?" he asked his client.

"Five years."

"Have you ever been convicted of any criminal offences?"

A murmur of disapproval ran round the courtroom at this apparently pointless question.

"No, I haven't," replied McKinnon.

"Have you ever had any findings of guilt made against you in police disciplinary proceedings?" asked Jessop.

"No, I haven't."

"Is the evidence which you have given this court the truth?"

"Yes, it is."

"Thank you," said Jessop and sat down.

Sir Montague looked thoughtfully at DC McKinnon for a few moments, and then said, "Yes, thank you, Officer. You may step down now."

The court next heard evidence from Dr Johnson, the FME who had been called by Sergeant Leach to examine Delroy in his cell and then from the young hospital doctor who had pronounced Delroy dead on his arrival in hospital.

Both doctors said that Delroy's injuries indicated that he had received a hard blow to the back of his head, and, when questioned by the coroner, both agreed that these injuries were consistent with the deceased's having struck the back of his head on the wall of his cell.

Neeta tried to suggest to both doctors that Delroy's injuries were more consistent with his having been pushed back violently against the wall than with his having fallen against it, but neither doctor was prepared to commit herself on this, both stating that they were unable to say from Delroy's injuries whether he had fallen against the wall or been pushed against it.

After hearing evidence from the two doctors, the court adjourned for the day.

That evening Alison French went in search of Bertie O'Connor.

Three days earlier Bertie had come to see Alison at the offices of the *Brixton Chronicle*, and she had been astonished at the change in him. He looked (and smelt) clean, was wearing fresh clothes and was sober.

Alison had tried to hide her surprise. "Why, hello Bertie," she said, greeting him warmly. "How nice to see you. How are you? You're looking well."

"Do you find me changed then?" he asked, in obvious delight.

"Why, yes, I do," she said, deciding that it would not be tactful to elaborate.

"I'm on the wagon," he said proudly. "Been on it for nearly two weeks now."

"Congratulations," she said enthusiastically, a little unsure of what else to say.

"What 'bout my clothes? Do you like them?" he asked.

Standing in the middle of the *Chronicle*'s reception area, he slowly swivelled round in front of her.

Tracey, who was sitting at the reception desk, let out a giggle.

Alison looked round at her, and scowled, before turning back to Bertie.

He was wearing a clean, if crumpled, grey suit, a slightly frayed, but clean, white shirt, a green tie and a pair of well-polished black shoes.

"I got them from the Sally Ann. They're almost new," he said proudly. "An' I've now got a regular place at the hostel, too. I've not had to sleep rough for over a week."

"So, what's brought all this about, then?" asked Alison, finally giving way to her curiosity.

"I've been asked to give evidence in court," explained Bertie with pride. "You know, 'bout that fellah that died in the police station, the one I told you 'bout."

"Yes, I remember."

"An' I thought that, if one of them judges is willin' to show me the respect of bein' ready to listen to what I got to say, then I owes it to him an' to mysel' to go along an' say my piece an' not to turn up lookin' like an old dosser."

Alison looked impressed. "So, you've been asked to give evidence at the coroner's inquest, have you?"

"I have," replied Bertie with dignity. "An' I've got somethin' to tell them that I never told you. Somethin' that happened before the alarm went off. Somethin' that I've only since been after rememberin'."

"What's that, then, Bertie?" Alison asked with interest.

Bertie smiled evasively, and shook his head. "I can't tell you that now," he said tantalizingly. "I'm savin' it for when I'm in court."

"Come on, Bertie, you can tell me," she urged.

Bertie, however, was not to be moved, and, in the end, Alison gave up. "OK, then," she said, as they parted company, "I'll see you in court. I'm going to be there covering the inquest for the *Chronicle*."

But Bertie did not turn up for the inquest.

The evening before the coroner's court began to hear evidence, he had been sitting on a bench in Brockwell Park and imagining himself giving evidence in court the next day, when he was approached by two large white men, both wearing dark suits. One, who was tall and thin, with long greasy fair hair and a badly pock-marked face, was wearing sunglasses, even though it was by then almost dark. The other was shorter and stockier, with a shaved head and an ugly, jagged scar running from the bottom of his right ear to the right corner of his mouth. Bertie's first thought was that they were plain-clothes policemen, but then something, perhaps the sunglasses, told him they were not.

The shorter of the two spoke first. "Are you Bertie O'Connor?" he asked.

"That depends on who's askin'," countered Bertie, trying to conceal his nervousness.

"Let's just say we're law enforcement agents," said the man. He grinned and his scar made it look as if his grin extended from the left side of his mouth right up to his right ear. "Now," he went on, "unless you can convince me that you're not Bertie O'Connor, I'm going to assume you are. How does that sound?"

"Yeah, OK, I'm Bertie O'Connor," conceded Bertie hurriedly. "What do you want with me?"

"We just need a little word with you," said the man

ominously. He took hold of Bertie's right arm and the man in the sunglasses took hold of the old man's left arm.

Bertie found himself being hauled to his feet, frog-marched out of the park and bundled into the back of a white four-door Saab parked outside the park gates. The man in the sunglasses got into the back of the car with him. The other man got into the driver's seat. The car drove off. Bertie, who was in any event unused to travelling in cars, was too frightened by what was happening to him to take in where they were going.

After about ten minutes, the car stopped in a quiet street of terraced houses which Bertie did not recognize. There was no one about. The driver got out of the car and unlocked the front door of the house outside which they had stopped. The house was boarded up, as were the houses on either side of it. The driver looked around and then came back and pulled open the back door of the car next to the pavement. Without a word the man in the sunglasses pulled Bertie out of the car, onto the pavement, up the short path leading up to the house and into the house itself.

Inside the house there was debris and dust everywhere. The man in the sunglasses pulled Bertie along the hall and into a room at the back of the house. In the middle of the room was a single wooden chair. Under the boarded-up window was a broken-down table with only three legs. The floor was strewn with food wrappers and empty cans and bottles. The room smelt stale and damp. A naked light bulb dangled from a flex in the middle of the ceiling giving off a dim light.

The man in the sunglasses sat Bertie down roughly on the chair.

The man with the scar followed them into the room. In his right hand he had a large bottle of cheap wine. He stood in front of Bertie. "So," he said with a sneer, "you're goin' to give evidence in court tomorrow. Is that right?"

Bertie cringed away from him. "I don't really have no choice," he said plaintively. "I've had like a summons from the court. So, I gotta go, or they'll put me in jail."

"Is that so?" marvelled the man with the scar sarcastically. "And I hear you've got something important to tell the court about what happened before the alarm went off the night that black drug dealer died in Brixton nick. Is that right?"

Bertie wished that he had not told so many of his cronies about the evidence he was going to give at the inquest, but, reminded of the possible importance of what he had to tell the court, he found some of his courage coming back to him. "Yeah, that's right," he replied, with a note of defiance in his voice.

"But you told that girl at the paper that you were woken up by the alarm going off," objected his interrogator. "It was in the paper. So, you can't know anythin' about what happened before the alarm went off, can you, because you were asleep then, right?"

Bertie knew that it would be safer not to argue, but he had a stubborn streak in his character, and the status that he had attained as a result of what he knew about Delroy's death was now so important to him that he couldn't help himself.

"No, I wasn't," he insisted. "I know now that I wasn't."

"So what happened before the alarm went off when you weren't asleep?" demanded the man with the scar.

"I'm not tellin' you," said Bertie defiantly.

A dangerous glint came into his captor's eyes. "You're just a confused old wino," he jeered dismissively. "You don't really know what happened that night at all."

99

"Yes, I do," maintained Bertie.

"Well, we don't think it would be in the interests of justice for you to go wasting the court's time with your rantings and ravings," declared the man with the scar. "You might give the jury the wrong idea. You understand?"

"You can't stop me," asserted Bertie rashly.

"I think we can," said the man with the scar, his eyes narrowing. He began opening the bottle of wine. "Here, have a drink," he suggested, offering it to Bertie.

"No, thanks. I don't want one."

"I think you do," said the man, putting the mouth of the bottle to Bertie's lips.

Bertie kept his mouth firmly closed. The man with the scar stepped back a pace, and, with the back of his right hand, struck Bertie a hard blow on his right cheek. "Take the fuckin' drink," he shouted. "Where's your fuckin' manners, you Irish dosser?"

Bertie continued to keep his mouth closed. The man with the scar raised his right hand again and this time slapped Bertie hard on his left cheek. The man in the sunglasses moved in behind the chair Bertie was sitting on and, grasping Bertie by the chin with his left hand and by the forehead with his right hand, attempted to prise the old man's mouth open. At the same time the man with the scar put the bottle back to Bertie's lips and forced it hard into his mouth, breaking one of the old man's teeth as he did so.

Bertie attempted to struggle but, every time he tried to pull away from them, one of the men punched or kicked him.

Once his assailants had finished with him, they bundled him into their car again and drove him back to Brockwell

Park where they unceremoniously dumped him outside the park gates.

The next evening, when Alison went to the hostel where Bertie had been staying to look for him, she was told by the warden that Bertie had not been allowed into the hostel the previous night because, when he turned up, he was obviously drunk and appeared to have been fighting.

"But he was on the wagon," objected Alison.

"I know," agreed the warden, "but being on the wagon never lasts long with the likes of Bertie. You get used to it in this job."

Despite being told this, Alison could not understand why Bertie had gone and got himself drunk just the evening before he was due to give evidence at the inquest. He had seemed to be looking forward to his day in court so much. She found it hard to believe that it was simply that his dependence on alcohol had proved too much for him, and she wondered whether it was that the thought of standing up and giving evidence in front of a courtroom full of people had made him so nervous that he had felt the need to start drinking again. Whatever his reason for getting drunk the previous evening, she was concerned about him – especially in the light of the news that he appeared to have been involved in a fight. She knew that he was often to be found hanging around outside Brixton Station, and she went there to look for him, but he was not there, and no one she spoke to there had seen him that day or could suggest where he might be. So, in the end, she had to give up her search for him, and went home.

Alison had to wait until two days later, when that week's issue of the *Brixton Chronicle* came out, before she could get into print with a report on the inquest into Delroy's death, but accounts of the first full day of the inquest appeared the next day in many of the national daily newspapers.

Andrew Thomas, in Nottingham, saw the report of the day's proceedings in his copy of *The Times* – the newspaper which he had delivered to his home every day, but never took with him to work, and was at pains to hide from any of his colleagues who visited him at home.

In the months since his meeting with Delroy in Railton Road, Andrew had come to regret ever having volunteered for Operation Fleece. After taking part in the operation, he had not been allowed to return to his beat in the centre of Nottingham. Instead, he had first been assigned to a job in his station's operations room for three months, and then posted to a beat in a quiet part of the city, where most of the residents were white, a few Asian, but none Afro-Caribbean. These measures, he was told, were for his own safety – to ensure that he was not recognised by anyone involved in drug dealing in Brixton who might visit Nottingham. But his changed role left him feeling more isolated and more unsure of his identity than at any time since he had joined the police.

Then came the news of Delroy's death. Andrew heard it when he telephoned DS Fletcher to ask if Delroy had been arrested. Fletcher's reply was short and to the point. He said simply that Delroy had been arrested, but had died in custody in the night of the day of his arrest. When Andrew tried to find out more, Fletcher was uncommunicative, and implied that what had happened to Delroy was none of Andrew's business.

To Andrew, the news of Delroy's death came as a double blow. Not only did he feel that his participation in Operation Fleece had been rendered completely futile, because his contribution to the operation could not now result in a single conviction, but he also experienced real feelings of regret and guilt at Delroy's death. As he looked back on their meeting in Railton Road, he remembered with gratitude that Delroy had been willing to trust him when none of the other dealers had appeared prepared to do so, and that the other man had responded to his obvious inexperience with an easygoing tolerance. He could not help feeling that Delroy had shown him more trust and kindness than the white police officers running Operation Fleece, and he was forced to confront the painful thought that it was the trust and kindness which Delroy had shown him which had led, indirectly, to Delroy's death in police custody.

The strain of trying to cope with these troubling thoughts began to tell on Andrew. One evening he and a white colleague came across two young black men trying to break into a car. As Andrew went to arrest one of them, the young man taunted him, calling him a 'coconut', a term of abuse familiar to him as meaning 'black on the outside, but white on the inside'. Andrew, who was accustomed to insults of this sort and usually had little difficulty in ignoring them, reacted with uncharacteristic violence, turning the young man round and banging his face hard against the roof of the car, before handcuffing his hands roughly behind his back.

Andrew's white colleague, who had privately always thought of Andrew as rather too soft to be a police officer, looked on with startled incomprehension, before quickly moving in to calm Andrew down, muttering, "Steady on, Andy". Andrew quickly regained his self-control, but the incident left him feeling badly shaken and ashamed of his behaviour.

Already troubled by Delroy's death as he was, Andrew was disturbed to read in *The Times* of Roger Jessop's apparent attempts to persuade witnesses at the inquest to agree that Delroy had been a violent drug addict, and he became convinced that it was up to him to set the record straight. When he got to work, he went to see Inspector Latham, who was in charge of his relief, and asked him for permission to go down to London to give evidence at the inquest.

"You see, sir," he explained, "I've met the man. I know he wasn't like that, and I think I should tell the inquest what I know."

Inspector Latham tried to calm him down. "Now look here, Andrew," he said firmly, "your meeting with this man Brown lasted no more than a few minutes, did it?"

"No, sir, but…" began Andrew.

Latham did not allow him to finish. "And in that few minutes," he said, "you cannot possibly have made a full assessment of the man's character. On my reading of this newspaper report, the arresting officer, what's his name, Matthews, seems to have known Brown far better than you can possibly claim to have done and to have given the inquest a full and fair account of the man's character."

Andrew looked down at his feet, wanting to explain why he felt it was so important for him to give evidence at the inquest, but unable to find the words to express what he wanted to say.

Latham went on, "And I have to say this to you, that I don't think it would do your career any good to go rushing off down to London to give evidence at this inquest."

He paused for a moment to let this point sink home, and then asked, "You're studying for your sergeant's exams, aren't you?"

"Yes, sir," confirmed Andrew awkwardly.

"Well, this service is looking to promote officers like you," said Latham. "And I wouldn't like you to do anything to jeopardise your very good prospects of promotion."

'Officers like me, how?' wondered Andrew. 'Coconuts?' he asked himself bitterly. But all he said was, "Yes, sir. Thank you, sir," and withdrew his application to go down to London to give evidence at the inquest.

When the inquest resumed that morning the first witness called to give evidence was Dr Irene Houseman, the pathologist who had carried out the post-mortem on Delroy's body.

Sir Montague knew Dr Houseman well, and they greeted each other warmly, but, while the pathologist was giving her evidence, each addressed the other with professional formality.

It was no longer customary as it had once been for an inquest jury to view the body of the person whose death was the subject of the inquest, but, as was commonly the practice, the members of the jury at the inquest into Delroy's death were provided with a series of photographs of the deceased's body, which were referred to by Dr Houseman as she gave her evidence. These photographs, taken from a variety of angles, showed the body stripped not only of every thread of clothing, but also of every vestige of dignity. Some showed the incisions made to the deceased's head, neck and torso by the pathologist, as she carried out her post-mortem examination. When she referred the jury to these photographs in the course of giving her evidence, several of the jurors looked visibly distressed and turned quickly away from them.

While the pathologist's evidence was dramatic in its effect on some of the jurors, the gist of what she had to tell the court in answer to the questions put to her by Sir Montague was simple: Delroy had died when he broke his neck as the result of a sharp blow to the back of his head. His injuries were consistent with this blow having been caused by his head striking the wall of his cell.

Sir Montague asked Dr Houseman if she had found any evidence that Delroy was under the influence of drugs at the time of his death. The pathologist replied that she had found traces of cannabinoids in the deceased's blood, which indicated that he had smoked cannabis several hours before his death, but that, in her opinion, the concentration of the drug which she had found in his system was too low to have had any effect on his conduct immediately before his death.

When he had finished questioning Dr Houseman, Sir Montague asked Neeta Patel if she had any questions for the pathologist.

Neeta confirmed that she had and got to her feet. "Wouldn't you agree," she asked Dr Houseman, "that the deceased's injuries are more consistent with his having been pushed hard against the wall of his cell than with his having fallen against the wall?"

In asking this question, the solicitor had been expecting the same non-committal answer as she had received when she put the same question to the two doctors who had given evidence the previous day, but the pathologist surprised her.

The question was one which had been troubling Dr Houseman since she first carried out her post-mortem examination on Delroy's body. At first, she, too, had taken the view that it was not a question that she could answer, and this was the view reflected in her original report. However, as time had gone by and she had reviewed the results of her post-mortem examination, she had come to modify her opinion on this issue.

"In my view," she said, carefully, "it is impossible to say that the deceased's injuries were not caused by his falling against the cell wall, but the nature of the injury to the back of his head suggests to me that his head struck the wall with a force unlikely to have been caused by a fall, even a clumsy or awkward fall, and more likely to have been produced by the deceased's having been propelled against the wall by something other than his own weight."

As the meaning of the pathologist's words sank in, a murmur ran round the courtroom.

To Neeta, the answer to her question which she had received from Dr Houseman was so unexpected that, for a few moments, she was almost lost for words. She hesitated briefly and then, with a sudden conviction that she was going to get more help from this witness, she said, "You mentioned earlier in your evidence that you found some red marks, small bruises, to the deceased's shoulders. What, in your opinion, caused those?"

Again the pathologist phrased her answer carefully. This, too, was an issue on which she now felt prepared to offer an opinion which she had not included in her original report. "The marks you refer to were very faint – so faint that I almost missed them," she said. "Those on the deceased's right shoulder don't even show up on the photographs. I cannot say for certain what caused them, but the marks on the left shoulder suggest to me that they were caused by the deceased's being grasped by the shoulders by the hands of someone facing him. If you look at the photographs of his left shoulder, you'll see to the front a single red mark and to the back three parallel lines, characteristic of the impressions left by the thumb and first three fingers of the human hand."

Another murmur ran round the courtroom. A number of eyes turned to look at DC McKinnon, who was leaning slightly forward in his seat holding the back of the seat in front of him with his right hand.

Neeta hesitated before asking her next question, fearing that, if she pushed Dr Houseman too hard, the pathologist might resile from some of what she had just said. "Would you say, then," the solicitor asked slowly, "that it looks as if the deceased was being held by the shoulders by someone facing him when he was propelled backwards in the movement which caused him to strike the back of his head on the cell wall?"

"That is a possible explanation for what I found when carrying out my examination of the body," replied Dr Houseman, "but I cannot go further than that."

Neeta felt jubilant. "Thank you very much, Doctor," she said, and sat down.

Roger Jessop got up to try and repair the damage.

"Doctor, the opinions you have just expressed in answer to the questions put to you by my friend are not the same as the opinions expressed in your original post-mortem report, are they?" he asked.

"I have slightly modified my views on some of the issues in this case. That is true," agreed Dr Houseman.

"That suggests some uncertainty on your part, doesn't it ?"

"These are issues on which it is difficult to be dogmatic."

"Quite so. And you cannot be certain that the deceased did not die as the result of a fall?"

"I have already said that."

"Nor can you be sure that the faint marks to his shoulders were caused by someone holding him, can you?"

"No, I can't. But that is, in my opinion, the most probable explanation for them."

"But not a sufficiently probable explanation for you to mention it in your original post-mortem report?"

"As I have said, my views on some of the issues in this case have changed since I wrote that report."

"Quite so. But, even if we accept your present views on this issue and assume that they are not going to change again, you cannot say, can you, exactly when the deceased received those marks to his shoulders? He could have received them earlier, say, when he was arrested or when he was put in his cell, couldn't he?"

"That is possible, although, in my view, the marks were fresh and had been caused very shortly before the deceased's death."

Jessop changed the subject. "You found evidence that the deceased had smoked cannabis, didn't you?"

"Yes. Some hours before his death."

"And is it not correct that regular and prolonged use of cannabis can cause brain damage, behavioural problems and even psychosis or psychotic episodes?"

"I'm not really qualified to answer that question. I believe that the research findings on the subject are equivocal. I can only say that I found no sign of neurological damage in the deceased."

"What about the prolonged use of crack cocaine? I know you say you found no cocaine in the deceased's system, but what if he was a regular user of the drug who had last used it just sufficiently long before his death for it not to show up on your examination? Couldn't his use of crack have caused him to suffer behavioural problems, making him perhaps more prone to violence?"

Neeta almost got to her feet to protest at the highly speculative nature of this question, but, in the end, decided not to. Her decision paid off.

"Again," replied the pathologist, "I am not really qualified to answer that question, but I repeat that I found no sign of neurological damage in the deceased, and I can also say that I found none of the signs which I would have expected to find if the deceased had been a regular user of crack cocaine."

Jessop recognised that the answers which he was getting from Dr Houseman were not helping his client's case, but he gave no sign of this. He merely smiled pleasantly at her, said, "Thank you, Doctor," and sat down, as if completely satisfied with the answers which she had given him.

The members of the jury watched this performance with interest, and were impressed, but not deceived.

Sir Montague also thanked Dr Houseman again and then released her.

Next the court heard briefly from Dr Howard, the FME who had examined McKinnon shortly after Delroy's death. The doctor repeated his evidence to the police that he had found DC McKinnon to have bruises to the back of his head and a small bruise to his right shin and that, in his opinion, these injuries were consistent with, but not diagnostic of, their having been caused in the manner alleged by the officer.

Neeta asked the doctor, "When you say DC McKinnon's injuries were not diagnostic of having been caused in the manner described by him, you mean, do you, that they could have been caused in other ways?"

"Yes, they were simply blunt trauma injuries, which

could have been caused in a number of different ways," replied Dr Howard.

Unable to think of any other specific alternative explanations for DC McKinnon's injuries to put to the doctor, Neeta was about to sit down, when a thought occurred to her.

"You haven't mentioned any injuries to DC McKinnon's neck or throat, have you?" she asked.

"No, DC McKinnon did not complain of any injury to his neck or throat, and so I did not examine them."

"You see, in his evidence, he told this court that Mr Brown took hold of him by the throat, so, if he had told you that, I would have expected you to have examined his neck and throat."

"If he had told me that, I would have examined his neck and throat, but, as I recall, all he said was that the prisoner who assaulted him had pushed him backwards."

"And you yourself saw no injury to DC McKinnon's neck?"

"No, but, as I've said, I didn't examine it."

"Wouldn't you have noticed such an injury, if there had been one, even if DC McKinnon did not complain of it?"

"Not necessarily. It would depend on the nature and extent of the injury, which, in turn, would depend on how much pressure had been applied to the neck and for how long."

"In other words, if DC McKinnon's neck had been seized hard, you would expect there to be signs of that, wouldn't you?"

"Yes, but still possibly signs only visible on a proper examination of his neck, which, as I've said, I did not carry out."

Neeta felt she had taken this line of questioning as far as she could, thanked the doctor and sat down.

Again, Jessop sought to repair the possible damage done to his client by the answers Neeta had obtained to her questions.

"Is it your experience, Doctor," he asked, "that, when individuals are examined by you in the immediate aftermath of an assault on them, they sometimes, perhaps because they are in shock, fail to give you a full description of the assault on them and, as a result, some of their more minor injuries are missed by you?"

"Yes, that does happen sometimes, but I try to make sure it doesn't by being thorough in both my questioning and my examination of the patient."

"But it still happens sometimes?"

"Yes, it does."

Jessop thanked the doctor and sat down.

Dr Howard was the last witness to be called to give evidence and the next stage in the proceedings was for the coroner to sum up to the jury. Neither Neeta nor Jessop had any right to address the jury, but, before delivering his summing up, Sir Montague invited both lawyers to address him, in the absence of the jury, on which of the various verdicts open to an inquest jury he should leave open to the jury in this case.

In the legal argument which followed, the issue was whether the possible verdicts to be left to the jury should include one of 'unlawful killing'.

Jessop argued that there were two reasons why it would be wrong for the coroner to leave it open to the jury to reach a verdict of unlawful killing. In the first place, he said, the evidence heard by the court did not include enough evidence to support a verdict of unlawful killing to enable a jury, properly directed, to return such a verdict. Secondly, if the jury were to return a verdict of unlawful killing, that would, in effect, be a verdict that the deceased had been unlawfully killed by Jessop's client, DC McKinnon, and, for the jury to return such a verdict, would be contrary to the provision in the Coroners Rules that, 'No verdict shall be framed in such a way as to appear to determine the criminal liability of a named person'.

Neeta countered the first of these points by arguing that the testimony of Dr Houseman provided sufficient evidence that Delroy Brown had been unlawfully killed for the issue to be left to the jury. As for Jessop's second point, Neeta said that she accepted that the coroner would have to direct the jury that, if they returned a verdict of unlawful killing, they must not name any individual as responsible for the killing, but she submitted that the jury should not be precluded from reaching a verdict of unlawful killing just because that verdict would lead many people to infer that a particular person was responsible for the killing.

After listening carefully to the arguments of both lawyers, Sir Montague announced that he was persuaded by those of Ms Patel and would leave a verdict of unlawful killing open to the jury. He said that, while, in his view, the evidence that the deceased was unlawfully killed was not strong and he would direct the jury accordingly, there was sufficient evidence to support that conclusion for it to be right for him to leave the issue to the jury.

The court then adjourned for lunch.

After lunch, Sir Montague delivered his summing up to the jury.

He began by explaining to them, that, in giving their verdict, they would be asked to answer a series of questions

– What was the deceased's name? What was the disease or injury which caused his death? When, where and in what circumstances did he sustain any injury which caused his death? – and then to state which of certain conclusions they had reached about his death. The three alternative conclusions open to them were a verdict of unlawful killing, a verdict of death by accident or misadventure or an open verdict.

The coroner went on, "A verdict of unlawful killing, ladies and gentlemen, is a finding that the deceased met his death by murder or manslaughter. There has been no suggestion in this case that the deceased was murdered. You therefore only have to consider whether the case is one of manslaughter. There are, in law, different forms of manslaughter. First of all, it is manslaughter if the deceased was killed by someone who, at the time, was committing an unlawful and dangerous act. So, it is manslaughter if the deceased was killed by someone who was committing an unlawful assault on him. But an assault is not unlawful if it is committed by someone exercising his or her right to defend himself or herself. So, it is not manslaughter, if the deceased was killed by someone acting in lawful self-defence. A person is recognised to have been acting in self-defence, if, in defending himself or herself, he or she used no more force than was reasonable in the circumstances as he or she believed them to be at the time. This means that it is not manslaughter if the deceased was killed by someone who honestly believed that the deceased was about to assault him or her and who used reasonable force to defend himself or herself from that assault – even if his or her belief that he or she was about to be assaulted was an unreasonable one. It is also manslaughter if the deceased was killed by a person committing an act which that person realised was likely to cause death or serious injury – unless, once again, the person concerned was acting in self-defence. Finally, it is manslaughter if the deceased was killed by someone, who, while under a duty of care to the deceased, a duty not to expose him to harm, committed an act of gross negligence which caused the deceased's death."

Sir Montague stressed to the jury that they must only return a verdict of unlawful killing, if they were satisfied beyond reasonable doubt, satisfied so that they were sure, that the deceased's death amounted to manslaughter. That meant, among other things, that they must be sure that the deceased was not killed by someone who, at the time, was acting in self-defence.

He continued, "If you are not satisfied beyond reasonable doubt that the deceased was unlawfully killed, you should next consider whether he met his death by accident or misadventure. A verdict of death by accident or misadventure means that no one is to blame for the deceased's death. It is the appropriate verdict if the deceased was unintentionally killed by someone who was acting in lawful self-defence."

The coroner explained that, to return a verdict of death by accident or misadventure, the jury had to be satisfied, not beyond reasonable doubt, but on a balance of probabilities that this was how the deceased met his death.

He went on, "Only if you are unable to reach a verdict of unlawful killing or a verdict of death by accident or misadventure, should you return an open verdict. An open verdict, as its name suggests, means that the question of how the deceased met his death is left open, undecided. It is therefore a verdict which you should only return as a last resort."

Sir Montague directed the jury that, on matters of law, they must accept what he had told them, but that, on matters of fact, the final decision was theirs. He explained that he had a duty to sum up the evidence to them, but that, if they disagreed with him on a matter of fact, such as whether a particular witness was telling the truth, or was lying, or mistaken, they should ignore his views on the matter.

He then went through the evidence in the case, carefully summarizing what had been said by each of the witnesses who had appeared before the court. As he did so, he drew the jury's attention to the evidence supporting a verdict of unlawful killing and the evidence supporting a verdict of death by accident or misadventure. He pointed out the weaknesses in the evidence in supporting a verdict of unlawful killing, but told the jury that, ultimately, the question of whether the deceased was unlawfully killed was a question of fact for them. He instructed them, however, that, if they did reach a verdict of unlawful killing, they must, in no circumstances, name anyone as responsible for the killing.

"And now, ladies and gentlemen," he concluded, "the decision is yours."

The jury retired to consider their verdict, the court rose and Sir Montague withdrew to his room.

Of the witnesses, lawyers, spectators and journalists left behind, some remained in their seats, some stood talking in small groups in the courtroom and some wandered out into the street outside.

Elliott went out into the street to telephone his office on his mobile phone. As he turned to go back into court, he noticed McKinnon and Jessop standing in a corner of the paved area outside the building. There were other small groups on this paved area, but all of these had stationed themselves well away from McKinnon and his solicitor. In some of these groups people were standing in silence, in others they were talking to each other in low voices. Some of the conversations appeared animated. Many of those standing outside the court building were casting looks, most of them hostile and angry, in McKinnon's direction.

Elliott returned thoughtfully to his seat in the courtroom.

People drifted in and out of the courtroom. Some returned to their seats, others who had remained seated stood up and began to move around. Some who came into the courtroom stayed for some time, while others wandered into the room and out of it again almost immediately. Some moved around in groups or pairs, others on their own.

After the jury had been out for about an hour and a half, speculation began as to why it was taking the jurors so long to reach their verdict.

"Do you think it means they can't agree?" Delroy's mother asked Neeta anxiously. "Is it goin' to be an open verdict? Are they goin' to let that DC McKinnon off?"

Neeta tried to reassure her. "I don't know," she said. "But an open verdict wouldn't be so bad for us. At least it would mean that the jury were not convinced by his story."

Delroy's mother was not persuaded by this. "But they should see it as unlawful killin'," she insisted. "Anyone can see that policeman was lyin'."

After just over two and a half hours, the usher announced that the jury were coming back into court.

Everyone hurried back to their seats. As the members of the jury filed back into court, their faces were scanned by the people already there for an indication of the verdict they had reached. Some of the jurors looked flushed. Almost all of them wore self-consciously serious expressions.

The foreman of the jury was a middle-aged white man in a grey suit. He answered Sir Montague's questions in a firm, confident voice.

The preliminaries over, the coroner asked, "And what is your conclusion as to the deceased's death?"

"It is our verdict that the deceased was unlawfully killed," declared the jury foreman.

There was a moment's stunned silence. Then the courtroom erupted. There was cheering and clapping. A young black man jumped to his feet, punched the air with his right fist and shouted, "Yo". Almost everyone else got to their feet, too. Delroy's mother shouted, "Alleluia", and turned to hug Neeta, nearly taking the solicitor's breath away. Althea and Bernice embraced each other. Delroy's father at first remained in his seat looking stunned. Then he, too, slowly got to his feet. He extended his right hand to Neeta and said simply, "Thank you".

Sir Montague, himself surprised by the jury's verdict, tried to call the court to order, but had difficulty in making himself heard. After a few minutes, however, the noise subsided sufficiently for him to thank the jury and bring the inquest to a close.

In the meantime, Roger Jessop took McKinnon's arm and quickly ushered him out of the courtroom.

Elliott watched them go. He had seen juries acquit too many defendants whom he was sure were guilty not to be sceptical about the ability of juries to reach correct verdicts. Nor did he believe that the evidence heard by the jury in this case justified them in reaching a verdict of unlawful killing. And yet he could not escape the feeling that, perhaps, despite the lack of evidence to support their verdict, this inquest jury had somehow got it right. He wondered what would happen now.

Under Review

The following morning *The Times* carried an editorial on the subject of the inquest jury's verdict on Delroy's death:

INQUEST QUESTION
Quis custodiet ipsos custodes?

Juvenal posed the question usually translated 'Who is to guard the guards?'. It is a question highlighted by the verdict delivered at the end of the inquest into the death in police custody of Mr Delroy Brown – although, in this context, it is perhaps more aptly rendered, 'Who is to police the police?'.

The jury's verdict that Mr Brown was unlawfully killed is a verdict that he met his death as the result of a criminal act, but no criminal charges have been brought against any of the police officers who had

Mr Brown in their custody when he met his death. This inevitably raises questions about the efficacy of the current system for deciding whether police officers are to be prosecuted in cases involving deaths in police custody.

At present every death in police custody is investigated by a senior police officer acting under the supervision of the Police Complaints Authority. It is then for the Crown Prosecution Service to decide whether any of the police officers in the case should be prosecuted. In making this decision, the CPS applies two tests. Firstly, is there sufficient evidence for there to be a realistic prospect of conviction? Secondly, is a prosecution in the public interest?

It is said by the police (although not by the Police Federation) that these investigations have to be carried out by police officers, because only they have the necessary training and experience. But any investigation into the conduct of police officers carried out by other police officers will almost inevitably attract questions both as to its impartiality and as to its thoroughness.

The role of the Crown Prosecution Service in these cases is also open to question. The principal function of the CPS is to prosecute cases referred to it by the police. In carrying out this function, CPS lawyers have to work closely with police officers. As a result, a CPS lawyer is likely to tend to prefer the word of a police officer to the word of a member of the public. A CPS lawyer faced with an allegation against a police officer which the officer denies will probably be inclined, all other things being equal, not to believe the allegation.

The CPS maintains that it applies the same tests to all those accused of criminal offences, but the application of the first of these tests may work to the advantage of police officers. This may occur, if CPS lawyers applying the test allow themselves to be influenced by conviction rates. The conviction rate for police officers who are prosecuted is lower than for other defendants. Juries, it appears, are reluctant to convict members of the police. CPS lawyers may conclude from this that, for there to be a realistic prospect of the conviction of a police officer, the evidence against the officer must be stronger than against other potential defendants. If CPS lawyers draw this conclusion, police officers will stand a better chance of escaping prosecution than others. Surely this is wrong. Police officers should, if anything, be prosecuted more readily than others. They are in a position of authority and enjoy special powers. It is clearly in the public interest for them to be prosecuted if they abuse these powers and commit criminal offences.

It is not, however, in the public interest for a police officer to be accused of a criminal offence at an inquest, where he or she does not have the benefit of the safeguards properly afforded to a defendant in a criminal trial. Whether or not a police officer has committed a criminal offence is not an issue which should be raised at an inquest. It is an issue which should be decided by a criminal court. The system needs to be changed to ensure that this is what happens.

Mr Brown's death in police custody led to rioting on the streets of Brixton. There is no excuse for public disorder of this sort. But it underlines the depth of public concern over this issue.

The newspaper once dubbed 'The Thunderer' was no longer as influential in public affairs as it had once been, but it was still read in high places. Among its regular readers was the Director of Public Prosecutions, Sir James Rowcliffe, QC.

Sir James, a tall, handsome man of fifty-seven, with pale blue eyes and short curly grey hair, had only recently been appointed DPP. Before his appointment, he had been one of the select group of barristers known as Senior Treasury Counsel, who appeared for the prosecution in the most serious and complex criminal trials. Although a highly skilled advocate, he lacked the arrogance characteristic of many senior barristers. Instead, his keen and agile mind lay hidden behind a gentle, courteous manner which had often seduced defendants and witnesses into disclosing things which they had not intended to reveal. In his private life he was a shy man, who liked to spend his time reading, listening to music and walking in the country. His decision to apply for the post of DPP had been prompted by the sudden and unexpected death of his wife, which had left him feeling at a loss and in need of a new challenge to take his mind off his grief.

Running the Crown Prosecution Service was certainly proving a challenge. As Senior Treasury Counsel, Sir James had been instructed by the CPS, but not employed by it. As a result, he had been aware, before taking on the post of DPP, of some discontent among the staff of the organisation which he now headed, but he had not been prepared for the profound state of demoralisation in which he found the service when he took office. His predecessor had turned the CPS into a bureaucracy obsessed with filling in forms and collecting statistics, and run by managers more intent on furthering their careers by their diligence in these areas than on improving the effectiveness with which the cases referred to the service were reviewed and prosecuted. As the cost of managing and administering this bureaucracy absorbed an ever greater proportion of the organisation's resources, the number of members of staff employed by the CPS to review and prosecute the cases referred to it was reduced. As a consequence, the lawyers and caseworkers left to carry out these functions (ironically identified by the organisation's managers as its 'core business') found themselves struggling to cope with ever increasing workloads, painfully conscious that, despite their best efforts, the quality of their work was inexorably deteriorating.

At the same time, as Sir James soon recognised, the role of the CPS as an independent prosecuting authority was widely misunderstood by police, public, press and politicians alike, with the result that, not only was the organisation attacked for its failures, but it was also frequently subjected to trenchant criticism simply for carrying out properly the duties assigned to it by Parliament.

As he read that morning's editorial in *The Times* about Delroy's death, Sir James sighed. He suspected that the author of the editorial was mistaken in implying that this was a case in which the CPS had not done its job properly, but, knowing the pressures his staff were under, he was ready to concede that the case might not have been reviewed as thoroughly as it should have been and that, as a result, an error might have been made. He took the view that the best way to deal with criticism of this nature was to address the issues which it raised head on. He asked his secretary to make some enquiries for him and, when she came back with the names he had requested, he dictated a memo to Peter Rotherhithe asking for the CPS file on the case, a letter to Sir Montague Thirske requesting a transcript of the evidence given at the inquest and letters to Roger Jessop and Neeta Patel informing them that, in view of the inquest jury's verdict, he would be conducting a personal review of the evidence relating to Delroy's death.

Peter Rotherhithe was never at his best first thing in the morning, and, on finding Sir James's memo on his desk when he arrived at work the next day, he experienced a feeling of nausea and a turbulence in his bowels which caused him to pay several visits to the toilet. He had missed the press coverage of the inquest and had no idea why the DPP was calling for his file on the case, but any request by one of his superiors for one of his files always caused him acute anxiety.

When he had composed himself sufficiently, he summoned Linda Fawcett to his office. His hand shaking, he brandished the DPP's memo under her nose. "What's all this about?" he asked her aggressively. "Why is the director asking for this file? I hope you haven't let me down on this one, Linda. You know, of course, that I'll always back you up whenever I can, but, at the end of the day, if you've made a mistake, you have to take responsibility for it."

Fawcett suppressed a sigh. She had been following the press coverage of the inquest into Delroy's death and had been anticipating something like this. "I expect it's because an inquest jury has returned a verdict of unlawful killing in this case, whereas, when I reviewed the case, I advised that there was insufficient evidence against the officer who was with the deceased when he died for there to be a realistic prospect of the officer's being convicted of an offence in relation to his death," she explained patiently.

Rotherhithe looked at her in consternation. The situation, he thought, could not be worse. Of course, it was Linda who had made the decision which would now be the subject of critical scrutiny, but no doubt he would be censured for having delegated a case of such sensitivity to her, rather than reviewing it himself. "So, you got it wrong, did you?" he demanded, adding bitterly, "I thought I could trust you."

Fawcett felt exasperated. She, too, was worried at the thought of having one of her cases scrutinised by the director and, although she knew better than to expect any support from Peter Rotherhithe, she resented his immediate assumption that she had made the wrong decision in this case. "No," she said firmly, "I don't think I did get it wrong. Of course, I haven't seen a full transcript of what was said at the inquest, but, as far as I can make out, the jury's verdict was largely based on things which the pathologist said at the inquest, but did not say in her original report – which was all I had to go on. What's more, as far as I can tell, the jury's verdict came as a surprise to almost everyone, and there was a widespread view that it was not supported by the evidence adduced at the inquest."

Rotherhithe was only partially reassured. "Yes, I see," he conceded grudgingly. "Well, you'd better get me the file. I'll just have to do what I can to repair the damage."

Fawcett brought him the file and left it with him. After she had gone, he spent some time looking through it. Then he carefully drafted a covering letter to send with it to the DPP. It read:

Dear Sir James,

DC Michael McKinnon
Death in Custody of Mr Delroy Brown

As requested, I enclose my file relating to the advice requested by the police as to whether a prosecution should be brought against DC Michael McKinnon in relation to the death in custody at Brixton Police Station of Mr Delroy Brown.

As you will see, this file was originally reviewed by one of my principal crown prosecutors, Ms Linda Fawcett. In normal circumstances, I would, of course, have reviewed it myself, but, unfortunately, on this occasion, I was prevented from doing so by the pressure of other work.

I chose Ms Fawcett to review this case because she is an able and experienced lawyer, on whose judgement I have generally found myself able to rely.

Having now had an opportunity to read the enclosed file myself, I would venture to suggest that, although Ms Fawcett's decision that there was insufficient evidence against DC McKinnon for there to be a realistic prospect of his being convicted of an offence in relation to Mr Brown's death, was a proper decision for her to have reached on the basis of the evidence before her at the time, it would have been prudent for Ms Fawcett, before making this decision, to have sought some clarification of the evidence contained in the report of the pathologist, Dr Houseman, and that, if she had done so, she might have reached a different decision.

I hope that this will be of some assistance to you, and that, if I can be of any further assistance to you, you will not hesitate to let me know.

Yours very sincerely,
Peter Rotherhithe,
Branch Crown Prosecutor

Yes, thought Rotherhithe, that should do nicely. He wondered whether to show the letter to Linda Fawcett before he sent it, but decided not to. She might misunderstand his intentions in writing it. Women could be funny that way.

Sir Montague Thirske was not surprised to receive the DPP's request for a transcript of evidence given at the inquest into Delroy's death. He remained unconvinced that the jury's verdict of unlawful killing was the right one, but recognised that it was a verdict which more or less compelled the CPS to look again at its decision not to prosecute DC McKinnon. He wondered if he should have directed the jury more forcibly on the weaknesses in the case for a verdict of unlawful killing. But then again, he reflected, juries were funny things. Very often, the more you pushed them in the direction of one verdict, the more they pulled in the direction of another. He could, of course, have refused to allow them the option of returning a verdict of unlawful killing at all, as he had been urged to do by Mr Jessop, but he remained of the view that that would have been a misuse of his discretion. He instructed his coroner's officer to send the transcript requested by the director of public prosecutions to the DPP as soon as possible. He wondered what Sir James would make of it.

On receiving his letter from the DPP, Roger Jessop wrote to DC McKinnon enclosing a copy of the letter and suggesting that the officer make an appointment to see him to discuss its contents.

When McKinnon duly came to see Jessop two days later, he was in an angry and petulant mood. "I don't see how the CPS can do this," he complained bitterly. "They told me they weren't going to prosecute me, and, as far as I'm concerned, that should be the end of the matter. It took them long enough to make their decision in the first place, so why should they be able to go back on what they've told me, just because some stupid inquest jury doesn't know its arse from its elbow."

"Just calm down," advised Jessop. "I know that this is upsetting for you, but you've got to get it into perspective. All they're doing is looking at your case again. That doesn't mean they're going to prosecute you and, in my view, it remains unlikely that they'll do so."

McKinnon was not reassured by this. "Yeah, unlikely, but not impossible, right?" he argued. "Look, can't you do anything to stop them? I mean, isn't it an abuse of process or something to tell someone he's not going to be prosecuted, and then to go ahead and prosecute him all the same? I'm sure there must be a stated case on it. So, can't you get a court order or something to stop them prosecuting me?"

"That's not how it works," explained Jessop patiently. "The CPS based its decision not to prosecute you on the evidence available to it at the time, but reserved the right to reconsider the decision in the light of any new evidence which might become available to it in the future."

"So, I could have this hanging over me for the rest of my life, is that what you're saying?" demanded McKinnon angrily.

"In theory, yes, but, in practice, I think that, once this review is over, that'll be the end of it."

"And this review is all down to that new DPP, is it?" asked McKinnon peevishly. "I mean, it sounds from that letter as if looking at my case again is all his idea, doesn't it?"

Jessop, too, was a little concerned about this aspect of Sir James's letter, but tried to reassure his client. "Well, I suppose it does," he conceded, "but I wouldn't worry too much about that if I were you."

"Wouldn't you? All that stuff about conducting a personal review of the case? Sounds like he's got it in for me, just because I'm a police officer. Going to make an example of me, know what I mean?"

"I really don't think it's like that," maintained Jessop, although privately he wondered if his client's fears might not have something in them.

"Don't you? Well, I do. But I take it from what you've said that you're not going to do anything to stop him conducting his personal review of my case."

"There isn't anything I can do to stop that."

"Then, perhaps I should start taking things into my own hands."

"I don't know what you mean by that," said Jessop firmly, "but I strongly advise you against taking any action designed to influence the outcome of this review. Just try and be patient and, if the DPP comes up with anything new, let me deal with it."

"Yeah, OK, whatever you say, Mr Jessop," agreed McKinnon, his manner suddenly changing.

Jessop regarded him curiously. He wondered what had brought about this abrupt change, but McKinnon's face told him nothing. The solicitor hoped that his client was not going to do anything foolish.

Neeta Patel also sent her clients a copy of the letter which she had received from the DPP and invited them to come and see her to discuss it. They came to see her two days after Jessop's meeting with McKinnon. Delroy's parents, his younger brother Leroy, Althea, Bernice and their children all crowded into her small office. They were in a jubilant mood.

"So, does that mean they're goin' to charge that DC McKinnon with killin' our Delroy?" asked his mother, eagerly.

"No, it doesn't quite mean that," cautioned Neeta. "What it means is that the director of public prosecutions himself is going to look at all the evidence in this case and, when he's done that, he may, and I emphasise may, decide to prosecute DC McKinnon. It all depends on whether he thinks there's enough evidence against McKinnon for there to be a realistic prospect of his being convicted in a criminal trial."

"But don't the inquest jury's verdict prove that?" asked Leroy.

"Not necessarily," replied the solicitor. "The DPP may still decide he doesn't agree with the inquest jury. And, in fact, I have to say I think we were rather lucky to get them to return a verdict of unlawful killing."

"We weren't lucky," said Delroy's mother. "You done a good job, Miss Patel."

A murmur of approval ran round the small room.

Neeta blushed slightly. "Well, it's very kind of you to say that," she said, "but, you see the problem is this. For DC McKinnon to be convicted of murder or manslaughter, a jury would have to be satisfied beyond reasonable doubt, that he was not acting in self-defence when he pushed Delroy against the wall of his cell. So far, the only real evidence of that is what the pathologist, Dr Houseman, said at the inquest, and the DPP may well decide that more evidence than that is needed for there to be a realistic prospect of DC McKinnon's being convicted in a criminal trial – especially as what Dr Houseman said at the inquest was different from what she said in her original report."

"Yeah, 'cause you got her to tell the truth," said Leroy.

"No, I don't think that was it," said Neeta. "I think she honestly changed her mind. And, though from our point of view, it's obviously a good thing that she did, unfortunately the fact that she changed her mind also weakens her evidence."

"But this director of public prosecutions," put in Bernice, "he's the top man, yeah?"

"Yes," agreed the solicitor with a smile. "He's the head of the Crown Prosecution Service."

"So, the fact that he's dealin' with this case personally, that's got to mean somethin', yeah?" pursued Bernice.

"Yes, I think it means that this case is being taken very seriously."

"So there won't be no cover-up?" demanded Leroy, suspiciously.

"No," replied Neeta carefully. "I don't think there'll be a cover-up, but, as I've said, on the evidence before the DPP at present, I don't think he is very likely to have DC McKinnon charged."

Her clients looked crestfallen.

"Ain't there nothin' we can do to get him to see things our way?" asked Leroy. "Hold a demo outside his office or somethin'?"

"No," advised the solicitor. "I don't think a demonstration would be a good idea at this stage. What we really need to do is to get some new evidence to strengthen the case against McKinnon."

"An' how we goin' to do that?" queried Leroy, sceptically.

"Well, what I'd like to do is to try and get a statement from Robert O'Connor, the man who was in the cell next to Delroy's, when Delroy died."

"How's that gettin' new evidence?" objected Leroy. "Everybody already know what O'Connor gotta say. It was in the paper right at the start."

"Well, to begin with," explained the solicitor patiently, "if we get a statement from Mr O'Connor and pass it to the DPP, that, as I understand it, will be the first evidence of what O'Connor has to say that the DPP has been able to take into consideration in this case. That's because the DPP can only take into account evidence which would be admissible in court and therefore he can't take into account that newspaper account of what O'Connor told the paper."

"But hasn't the DPP had a statement by this man O'Connor from the Police Complaints people?" asked Delroy's father.

"No, as I understand it, he hasn't – apparently because no statement was taken from O'Connor by the police officers who investigated the case for the PCA."

"I wonder why not," said Leroy, with heavy sarcasm.

"Well, whatever the reason," said Neeta, "the result is that, at present, the evidence being considered by the DPP does not include any evidence from Mr O'Connor."

"An' do you think that, if we get the DPP a statement by this man, that will help our case?" asked Delroy's father, dubiously.

Neeta hesitated. "To be honest," she replied, "I'm not sure. It depends on what O'Connor has to say. If he gives us a statement which goes no further than what he was quoted as saying in the paper, then I don't think that will do us much good."

Delroy's family's disappointment showed on their faces.

"But," went on the solicitor quickly, "I believe it's possible that Mr O'Connor may know more about what

132

happened on the night Delroy died than came out in that story in the paper."

Her listeners immediately looked interested.

"What make you say that?" asked Delroy's mother.

"Something, I was told by Alison French," replied Neeta. "You know, the journalist from the *Brixton Chronicle*."

Her clients nodded. They remembered Alison.

"She and I got talking together as we were leaving the inquest," went on the solicitor. "And, during our conversation, she said that, before the hearing, Mr O'Connor had told her he was going to be a witness at the inquest, and that he was going to tell the court something he had not told her originally about what happened just before the alarm went off in Delroy's cell."

"So, why didn't he give evidence at the inquest?" demanded Leroy.

"I'm afraid he just didn't turn up for the hearing."

"But why not?" persisted Leroy.

"Ms French couldn't tell me that," replied Neeta carefully. "But she did say that he has a bit of a drink problem and that might explain why he didn't make it."

"Unless he was warned off by the police," suggested Leroy darkly.

"I don't think that's very likely," said the solicitor.

"Yeah?" Leroy challenged her. "No disrespect, Ms Patel, but I guess you don't know the police like I do."

His mother intervened. "But, if the man's got a drinkin' problem, he's not goin' to be much good as a witness, is he?" she objected, anxiously.

"I agree he's not going to make the best of witnesses," conceded Neeta. "But, at this stage, I think getting a statement from him probably represents our best chance of strengthening the case against DC McKinnon. So, with your consent, I'd like to ask Ms French if she can put me in touch with Mr O'Connor. The only thing is, if I get her involved, it's likely to mean there'll be more about this case in the *Chronicle*."

"As far as I'm concerned," said Althea, speaking for the first time, "that's not a problem. Alison's OK. I reckon she's on our side. It was her that brought what happened to Delroy out into the open in the first place."

The others agreed. Since Althea and Bernice had met Alison at the demonstration outside Brixton Police Station, the rest of the family had got to know the young journalist, and she had written further articles about the family and the events which had followed Delroy's death. As a result, the family had come to trust her and, although they had not been happy with everything she had written about them, they believed that, on the whole, she had been fair to them, and that her articles had helped them in their campaign to find out the truth about how Delroy died.

"Right," said Neeta, bringing her meeting with her clients to a close. "That's what I'll do, then, and, of course, as soon as I have any news, I'll let you know."

When Delroy's family had left, Neeta telephoned the offices of the *Brixton Chronicle*, and asked to be put through to Alison French.

The young journalist came onto the line. "Hello, News Desk, Alison French speaking."

"Hello, Alison, this is Neeta Patel."

Since their conversation following the inquest, the two young women had met several times for coffee and had got to know each other quite well.

"Hi, Neeta," said Alison warmly. "What can I do for you?"

The solicitor came straight to the point. "It's about the Delroy Brown case. Can you tell me where I can find Robert O'Connor?"

"Bertie? Why? What's brought him back into the case?" asked Alison, immediately interested.

"Nothing new," hedged Neeta warily. "I just need to get a statement from him. That's all."

"But why now?" pursued Alison, sensing a story.

Neeta hesitated, then said, "OK, I'll tell you, but only on the basis that part of what I'm going to say is strictly off the record and that you promise not to publish, or to tell anyone, any of what I tell you, unless I say you can. Do you agree?"

It was now Alison's turn to hesitate. She wondered whether, if she agreed to Neeta's conditions, she would be compromising herself as a journalist, but she was intrigued to hear what the solicitor had to tell her, and decided that half a story was better than no story at all. "Yeah, OK," she said finally.

"Right," said Neeta. "The reason why I want to get a statement from Mr O'Connor is that I've had a letter from the director of public prosecutions, Sir James Rowcliffe, saying that he's going to carry out a review of the evidence relating to Delroy Brown's death."

Alison felt an immediate thrill of excitement. This was news. "So, how much of that can I publish?" she asked.

"Well," said Neeta carefully, "I think you can publish the fact that the DPP has said that he's going to carry out a review of the case, as I think that that's going to come out anyway, if it hasn't already, but, and I must emphasise this, I don't want you to disclose that you got this information from me."

"That sounds fair enough. So does this review mean that DC McKinnon is going to be prosecuted?"

"No," replied the solicitor, firmly. "It very definitely does not mean that. It means exactly what it says. The DPP is just going to take a new look at the evidence in the case."

"But, when he's done that, he could decide to prosecute McKinnon, couldn't he?"

"Yes, he could, but this is where we come to the issue of my getting a statement from O'Connor, and I must insist that you do not disclose to anyone the fact that I'm seeking a statement from him to submit to the DPP, or the rest of what I'm about to tell you."

"Yeah, yeah," agreed Alison quickly, her interest growing.

"No, Alison, listen," insisted the solicitor. "This is important. I've got to be certain that what I'm about to say is not going to appear in the Press in any shape or form. Do you understand that?"

"Yes, OK, Neeta," said Alison, a little more soberly.

"Very well. The answer to your question is that, in my opinion, the DPP is very unlikely to have DC McKinnon charged with murder or manslaughter unless we can come up with some fresh evidence that strengthens the case against McKinnon – and that's what I'm hoping will be provided by what O'Connor knows about what happened just before the alarm went off in Delroy's cell."

"Yes, I see," said Alison thoughtfully. "The problem is that I don't know where Bertie's got to. I've made a couple of attempts to find him since the inquest, but he just seems to have disappeared. He's not been seen around any of his usual haunts since just before the inquest, and no one seems to have got any idea where he's gone."

"Oh, well," sighed Neeta resignedly. "Never mind. I suppose I'll just have to use an enquiry agent to find him."

"No, don't do that, Neeta," Alison urged her. "At least not for the moment. Give me a few days, and I'll see if I can find him for you."

Neeta hesitated. She felt that Bertie was more likely to talk to Alison than to an enquiry agent, but, at the same time, she was concerned that, if Bertie told Alison anything new, his evidence might be undermined by allegations, justified or unjustified, that the young journalist had put words into his mouth for the sake of a good story. Neeta was also anxious about what use Alison might make of anything Bertie told her. The solicitor did not want what the old man had to say appearing in the Press at this stage.

Alison sensed her misgivings. "It'll save you money," she argued, adding jokingly, "I won't charge you a penny."

"All right," agreed Neeta finally. "But I want to be with you when you talk to him. And I don't want anything he tells you appearing in your paper without my say-so."

Alison was reluctant to agree to the second of these conditions, but decided to take a long view. "OK, provided anything you and the family decide to release to the Press comes to me first."

"That sounds fair to me. Very well. It's a deal."

With some difficulty, Alison persuaded her editor to let her do what she called some research among Brixton's rough sleepers, which she said she hoped she might turn into an article for the paper.

She began looking for Bertie late the next afternoon, starting her search at the entrance to Brixton Underground Station.

The broad pavement outside the station was crowded with passers-by and people entering and leaving the Underground. On the edge of the crowd, next to Brixton Road, Alison saw a small group of people, mostly men, drinking out of cans. Some were standing with their backs to the railings running alongside the road, others sitting on an untidy stack of wooden pallets and plastic crates left lying on the pavement. Alison started to move towards them, intending to ask them if any of them knew Bertie, but, as she did so, two members of the group began arguing loudly with each other, and, fearing that the argument might develop into a fight, she quickly stopped in her tracks.

She turned towards the entrance to the station and saw, just inside it, on the left, a man and a woman sitting on the ground with their legs stretched out in front of them and their backs to a wall which formed the left-hand side both of the station entrance and a small covered arcade next to it. Their faces and hands were lined and weather-beaten and their clothes worn and faded. They looked well into their sixties, but Alison guessed that they were probably younger. She made her way towards them, but, as she was about to bend down to speak to them, the man looked up at her and gave a fierce scowl. She backed hurriedly away from them.

As she moved backwards, she almost fell over the outstretched legs of an old man who was sitting facing the pavement with his back to a pillar just inside the station. Beneath him on the ground was an old grey blanket and next to him on the blanket was a brown dog which he had on a leash made out of a piece of string. The old man was wearing a black woollen balaclava, a large overcoat tied at the waist with another piece of string and a pair of grey woollen gloves. Both the balaclava and the gloves had large holes in them.

The dog growled half-heartedly at Alison, and the old man regarded her warily. Alison stopped, and, keeping a careful eye on the dog, bent down to talk to the old man. "Do you know…" she began, but her words were drowned by a loud commotion in the ticket hall at the bottom of a flight of steps leading down into the station from the pavement to her right. A small black man with long dreadlocks was shouting at members of the station staff. Alison could not make out what is was all about. In an attempt to make herself heard above the noise, she bent down towards the old man again and shouted, "Do you know Bertie O'Connor?" The dog got up and barked at her. Several passers-by looked at her curiously. The old man cowered away from her and shook his head.

Alison stood up and looked around. At the top of the steps down into the ticket hall she noticed a man selling *The Big Issue*. He was large and heavily built with long, wiry light-brown hair and a long straggling beard. He had a red bandana tied round his head and was wearing a green combat jacket, green canvas trousers and heavy black boots. Alison bought a copy of the magazine from him, and asked him if he knew Bertie O'Connor.

"Sure I know Bertie," he replied, "but I haven't seen him about for a few weeks now."

"Do you know where I might find him?" asked Alison.

The man looked at her curiously. He shook his head. "No idea, I'm afraid," he said. "You might find someone hanging around by the mainline station who knows where he is, but you want to be careful who you go talking to. There's some crazy people around." He shook his head and added contemptuously, "They call it 'care in the community'."

Alison thanked him and set off for the mainline station,

making her way through the run-down arcade beside the Underground station.

As she went through the arcade, passing the row of shops set into the wall on her right, she saw, lying on the ground next to the bare, orange-tiled wall on her left, a black man wrapped in a heavy overcoat. She briefly considered trying to rouse him to ask him if he knew Bertie, but then, detecting no sign of movement from him and wondering, with a slight shudder, whether he might be dead, she swiftly decided to let him be.

She emerged from the arcade into Electric Lane, and turned left. The narrow street, flanked on both sides by high brick walls was almost deserted. She hurried the short distance along it into the inviting bustle of people in Atlantic Road ahead of her.

As she came out of Electric Lane, she stopped and looked up at Brixton Station standing on the raised viaduct running along the far side of Atlantic Road. The station jutted out a few feet from the top of the viaduct, the overhang supported by two rows of pillars embedded in the pavement beneath it. Outside the pillars a steep metal flight of stairs, rising diagonally from left to right, climbed from the pavement up to the station above.

Alison crossed the road and turned right along the pavement beneath the overhanging station. She passed the foot of the metal staircase on her right and, a few steps further on, on her left, she came to the entrance to an archway leading under the station. A few feet into the archway, she saw a young man sitting on the ground with his back to the wall on her right, his knees drawn up to his chest and a dirty bedspread drawn around him like a cape. He was staring vacantly at the ground ahead of him. Beside him lay a piece of brown cardboard on which had been scrawled the words, 'Homeless and Hopeless'. Lying on the piece of card were a few coins. Alison approached the young man, bent down and added a pound coin to his meagre takings. The young man did not look at her, but just murmured automatically, "God bless you."

Alison bent a little closer to him. "Do you know a man called Bertie O'Connor?" she asked gently.

The young man looked at her with an anxious expression on his face. He shook his head. "No, I'm sorry, I don't," he replied, regarding her fearfully.

Alison wondered if he was afraid she was going to abuse him or take back the money she had given him because he was unable to give her a positive answer to her question. She noticed that he was shivering.

"That's OK," she reassured him. "Don't worry." She wanted to reach out and pat him on the shoulder, but, uncertain of how he would react if she touched him, she stepped back.

The young man visibly relaxed. His chin sank back on his chest and he resumed staring at the ground in front of him.

Alison continued along the passage through the archway.

A woman came towards her pushing a supermarket trolley packed with bulging black bin bags. She was wearing a grey headscarf and a man's overcoat with its sleeves turned up. She appeared to have several layers of clothing on under the coat. The bin bags were open at the top and many of them were split. They seemed to contain mainly clothes and bundles of newspaper.

As the two women drew level with each other, Alison stopped. "Excuse me," she said.

The woman with the shopping trolley stopped, too. She seemed pleased at being spoken to. "Yes, me dear," she said encouragingly, in a strong West Country accent. "What can I do for you?"

"Do you know Bertie O'Connor?" Alison asked her.

"Yes, me dear, I do," replied the woman brightly. "Knows 'im well, I do."

"Could you tell me where I can find him?" asked Alison.

The woman's face clouded over. "No one stays," she sighed mournfully, shaking her head. She seemed to forget that Alison was there and began to walk away, pushing her trolley and murmuring to herself over and over again, "No one stays. No one stays."

Alison walked on. On her left she passed some railings and an open gate, behind which was a recess in the wall leading to a second flight of stairs up to the station. Beside the railings was an unoccupied wooden chair with some empty lager cans on the ground next to it. The roof above Alison's head at this point was much higher than it had been at the entrance to the archway and was made of glass. On the upper part of the back wall of the recess to her left and on a wall descending from the ceiling ahead of her were two large multicoloured, multicultural, murals.

Alison continued through the passage under the archway, coming out among the market stalls lining Brixton Station Road. There were not many shoppers around, and some of the stallholders were beginning to pack up for the day. Alison turned left, and went from stall to stall asking the stallholders if they knew Bertie. One man said that he did, but told her that he had not seen the old man for several weeks, and did not know where he had gone.

At the end of the road Alison turned round, and began

returning back the way she had come, but, on reaching the entrance to the alleyway under the station, she walked past it, continuing on a short distance further along Brixton Road.

She turned right into Popes Road. Here, beneath and between two railway bridges, the market was busier, with shoppers crowding round the stalls, music blaring out and traders shouting their wares and doing business with their customers. There was a strong smell of fish in the air. Alison tried to speak to some of the stallholders, but, as soon as they realised she was not buying, they quickly fobbed her off, with answers such as, "Sorry, dear, can't help you."

Alison passed under the second railway bridge and came back out into Atlantic Road.

On a street corner, on the other side of the road, a man was standing declaiming into a megaphone. "Only repent of your sins and you can begin a new life today."

Alison felt tired and dispirited. She turned right, went back along Atlantic Road and crossed over into Electric Lane.

The narrow road, hemmed in by the high brick walls on either side of it, now seemed completely deserted.

From the entrance to the arcade ahead of her and to her right, a woman appeared blocking her way. Alison recognised her as the woman she had seen sitting at the entrance to the Underground station earlier that afternoon.

"I'm Pat," announced the woman, speaking in an unexpectedly clear and confident voice, with the air of someone used to commanding attention.

"Hello, Pat," said Alison a little nervously. "I'm Alison." She wondered uneasily if she was about to be mugged. She looked around for the man she had seen the other woman with earlier, but, to her relief, she could see no sign of him.

"It's all right," said Pat, obviously reading her thoughts. "He's gone."

"Oh, fine," said Alison lamely, not knowing what else to say.

Pat looked her up and down. "So, Alison," she enquired, finally, "what's your interest in Bertie O'Connor?"

"Why?" countered Alison. "Do you know where he is?"

"You first," insisted Pat. "Why are you asking questions about him?"

Alison was struck by the other woman's air of authority, and wondered what her background was. She sensed that it would be a mistake not to stick as close to the truth as she could, but was wary of referring to Neeta's involvement in her search for Bertie. "I'm a journalist," she said, "and I need Bertie's help on a story I'm working on."

Pat looked at her speculatively. "A journalist?" she echoed. "Are you the one who wrote that story about him in the paper a few months back?"

"Yes, that's right," said Alison. "And it's really still the same story I'm working on now."

"I remember him talking about you," said Pat thoughtfully. "He said you were kind to him."

"He's a nice man."

"Yes, he is." Pat contemplated Alison for a few moments and then declared, "And I think maybe he'd like to see you again."

Alison felt encouraged. "So, can you tell me where I can find him?" she asked.

"He's moved away. He got beaten up. I don't know what it was all about. He wouldn't tell me. He just said Brixton wasn't safe for him any more."

The news that Bertie had been beaten up concerned

Alison. She wondered if his being beaten up had anything to do with what the warden of his hostel had told her about his having been in a fight. "Do you know where he's moved to?" she asked.

"Waterloo. He sleeps under the bridge."

"So, is that where I'd find him?"

"You won't find him there during the day, and I wouldn't advise you to go looking for him there at night. You wouldn't be safe."

Alison looked disappointed. "Perhaps if I went with someone?" she suggested.

Pat considered. "Well, I suppose I could take you up there to see him one night. You'd be safe with me," she said.

"Would you really? That would be great," said Alison. "Could I bring someone with me?"

"Who?" demanded Pat dubiously.

"Neeta Patel," replied Alison. She hesitated, but anticipating what she foresaw would be Pat's next question and deciding that it would be best to be honest with her, she added, "She's a solicitor."

"Why do you want to bring her?" asked Pat warily.

"It's to do with this story I'm working on," explained Alison. "It's about a man who died in the cells at Brixton Police Station, and Neeta has been instructed by the dead man's family to try and find out the truth about how he died. Bertie told me that he knows something about the events leading up to the man's death which he's never told anyone, and Neeta and I both want him to tell us what that is."

"All right," agreed Pat. "On one condition. If Bertie doesn't want to talk to you, you're to leave him alone. I'm not having him bullied. Do you understand?"

"Yes, of course. I've no wish to upset him."

"So long as that's agreed," said Pat firmly. "When do you want to go?"

"Tomorrow?"

"OK. Tomorrow it is. I'll meet you and this solicitor outside the main entrance to Waterloo Station at nine o'clock. Put on some old clothes. Don't wear any jewellery or make-up. Don't carry handbags. Don't bring any credit cards or any more than a few pounds in cash. Got all that?"

"Yes, I think so."

Once more Alison was impressed by Pat's authoritative manner and, as they parted company, she wondered how the other woman had ended up living on the streets.

A Change of Direction

On the afternoon of Alison's encounter with Pat in Electric Lane, DC McKinnon went to keep an appointment at a basement office in a narrow street in Soho.

Attached to the railings at the top of the flight of steps leading down to the office from the pavement was a small brass plate which read, 'John Bates Investigations'.

McKinnon took a quick look up and down the street and hurried down the steps.

At the bottom of the steps was a door with an Entryphone beside it. He pressed the button on the Entryphone.

"Yes?" queried a young woman's voice, disembodied and indifferent.

He bent down to speak into the Entryphone. "Michael McKinnon to see Mr Bates," he said in a confidential murmur.

He glanced back over his shoulder to make sure that no one was looking down at him through the railings above his head.

A buzz and a click announced that the door had been unlocked. He pushed it open and went in. He found himself in a dimly lit corridor. He took a few steps along it and came to a door on his right with a plastic sign on it bearing the word 'Reception'. He knocked. There was no reply. He cautiously opened the door and went in. Facing him across a room about twenty-foot square was a young woman sitting at a desk. On the desk was a word processor, but it was not switched on. There was a smell of nail varnish in the air. The young woman looked at him, but did not speak. He felt forced to say something. "My name's McKinnon," he announced. "I have an appointment to see Mr Bates."

The young woman stood up and walked round to the front of her desk. She was wearing a very short, very tight skirt. "This way, please," she said and led McKinnon to the next room along the corridor. It was a small waiting room with chairs around the walls. To McKinnon's relief, there was no one else there. "Please take a seat," said the young woman. "Mr Bates will see you in a moment." McKinnon sat down in a chair facing the doorway. The young woman left the room, closing the door behind her. On a coffee table in the middle of the room was a small pile of old magazines, mostly devoted to fast cars, motorcycles and sport. McKinnon picked up one of the motoring magazines and began leafing idly through it.

After about ten minutes, the young woman returned. "Mr Bates will see you now," she said. She took McKinnon to the third room on the right of the corridor, and ushered him in.

As McKinnon entered the room, Mr Bates got up from a chair behind a large desk facing the door to greet him.

John 'Bull' Bates was a short, powerfully built man of forty-four with close cropped fair hair and pale blue eyes. He had formerly been a detective sergeant in the Metropolitan Police, but his career as a police officer had been brought to an end five years earlier as the result of an incident during a rugby match in which he had taken part.

The match was a 4th team game played in St Albans on a cold and damp day in November. Bull was a front row prop forward in the visiting team. Both sides were made up partly of youths with no talent for the game and partly of older men, like Bull, who had once been good players, but who were now well past their prime. It was a close but scrappy match, peppered by bad-tempered outbursts on the part of some of the older players who resented finding themselves playing at this lowly level. Towards the end of the game, with the visiting team just three points behind, there was a scrum deep into the home team's half of the pitch close to the touchline. The ball was put into the other side of the scrum. The visiting team began to force the home team back. As this happened, Bull's opposite number reached down into the scrum with his right hand, seized Bull's genitals and gave them a sharp twist. Bull let out a yelp of pain, turned his head to the right and sank his teeth into his tormentor's right ear. He bit so hard that most of the other man's earlobe came off in his mouth, and blood spurted dramatically from what remained of it. The scrum collapsed and, in the confusion, Bull spat the piece he had bitten from his adversary's ear out into the mud.

Unfortunately for Bull, while his adversary's assault on Bull's genitals remained unseen by anyone, Bull's actions in biting off the other man's earlobe, though missed by the referee, were clearly witnessed by a linesman and several

149

spectators, and captured by one of the spectators on a video camera.

Confronted with this evidence, the police, advised by the CPS, had no alternative but to take out a summons against Detective Sergeant John Bates charging him with assault occasioning actual bodily harm.

Bull pleaded not guilty to the charge. He considered claiming that he had acted in self-defence, but decided against it. He had no evidence that his adversary had assaulted him first, and had little confidence that he could convince the jury that this was what had happened. There was also the risk that, if he told the whole story and was believed, the result would only be to convince the jury that what he had done to the other man was an act of retaliation, rather than an act of self-defence. He decided therefore to say nothing about the assault on him by his adversary, and to claim that he had bitten the other man's earlobe off by accident in a clash of heads in the scrum. The jury, though reluctant to convict a police officer, took just twenty minutes to reject his defence, and find him guilty.

The judge, appalled that a police officer should commit an unprovoked assault of this nature and displeased by Bull's refusal to admit his guilt, sentenced him to four months' imprisonment.

During the two months of this sentence which Bull served, he suffered two serious assaults and a string of minor assaults and indignities at the hands of fellow prisoners determined to make the most of the opportunity presented to them to exact retribution from him for his work as a police officer. In most of these incidents he would have been able to give as good as he got, but he held back in order not to risk extending his time in custody.

On leaving prison, his career as police officer over, Bull Bates set up in business as a private detective.

One of his first clients was a businesswoman who wanted to find out if one of her associates had a criminal record. Bull no longer had any legitimate way of getting this information, but he knew he could find out what his client wanted to know if he could find a way of getting access to the Police National Computer.

He thought of Simon Rowe.

Simon Rowe was a detective constable in the Metropolitan Police who had been a member of Bull's team, and was the only one of the disgraced officer's former colleagues to have kept in touch with him after his ignominious departure from the service. Police officers were notoriously loyal to one another, but keeping in touch with a former colleague dismissed from the service after being convicted of a criminal offence was not good for a serving officer's career prospects. As Bull had discovered, officers prepared to ignore such considerations were rare, but DC Rowe was one of them.

Bull and Rowe were having a drink together in a quiet corner of the pub where they usually met, well away from the police station where Rowe was based, when Bull told Rowe about his frustration at not being able to satisfy his client's very reasonable wish to discover whether her business associate had a criminal record. Instinctively, Rowe glanced around him, but Bull had made sure that there was no one in earshot before he began speaking.

Rowe knew that Bull was finding it difficult to get his business off the ground, and was anxious to help his friend if he could. "If you give me the guy's details," he suggested, "I could check him out on the PNC."

Bull gave no sign that he had been hoping that Rowe would say this, but gratefully accepted his friend's offer.

Both men knew that what they were proposing was illegal, and agreed that, if they were to provide this service to Bull's client, she should be charged a substantial fee to compensate them for the risks they would be taking on her behalf. Bull's client, who was a wealthy woman, was happy to pay the fee which he asked, and Rowe obtained the information which she wanted from the Police National Computer. Bull passed this information on to her, and split the fee which she paid him with Rowe.

A few weeks later, Bull was consulted by a young woman who believed she was being followed, but who had been unable to get the police to investigate, and asked Bull if he could find out the name and address of the registered keeper of the car which she believed was being used for this purpose. Once again, Rowe obtained this information from the PNC and Bull passed it on to his grateful client in exchange for a substantial fee – which, once again, the two men shared.

Similar transactions followed and Bull's business thrived as he acquired a reputation as a private investigator who could obtain confidential information which others could not.

Bull also developed new professional capabilities. He took courses in martial arts and photography, and learnt how to hack into computers. He assembled a collection of top of the range equipment – a camera capable of taking crystal clear long-range photographs, a camcorder, a number of different sound-recording devices and two computers with some sophisticated accessories. He made visits abroad on which he bought more surveillance equipment, including devices for tapping telephones, and a Glock 9mm semi-automatic handgun. He did not apply for a firearms certificate for this weapon, and so was not compelled to surrender it when the holding of all handguns was made illegal.

The first police officer to become a client of Bull's was DC Roy Carter.

DC Carter had found himself in trouble as the result of a police raid in which he had taken part on the home of a Mr Anwar Khan. The raid took place as a consequence of an anonymous tip-off which the police had received that Khan was involved in the importation of heroin, and which they had been ready to believe because, although Khan was known as a respectable businessman, he had been born in Pakistan. On searching Khan's home, Carter and his colleagues found no evidence to support the allegation made against the businessman, which they naturally found frustrating, and Carter became involved in a confrontation with Khan in which he expressed this frustration in forcible terms. Unfortunately for Carter, Khan was a well-educated and articulate man whose response to this incident was to lay a formal complaint against the officer, accusing him of racial abuse. His allegation was supported by his wife and teenage daughter who had both been present when their home was raided by the police. He also claimed to have a tape recording made by his wife of most of what Carter had said to him.

DC Carter feared that his career as a police officer was over and spoke about his fears to his colleague, DC Rowe, who suggested that former Detective Sergeant Bates might be able to give him some advice on how to deal with the officers investigating the complaint made against him. Carter did not have much confidence that Bull would be able to help him, but went along to see the private investigator anyway.

Bull was sympathetic. "I can see why you're worried," he commiserated. "I've been there. I know what it's like."

"What would you advise me to do?" asked Carter.

"Just leave it with me for a few days," Bull told him. "I'll think about it."

Carter was disappointed, but tried not to show it. "Thanks for your time," he said as he left. He did not expect to hear from Bull again.

Two weeks later Carter received a letter from the complaints unit informing him that the complaint made against him by Khan had been withdrawn. The letter did not say why. Carter telephoned the investigating officer to ask what reasons Khan had given for withdrawing his complaint. The investigating officer was curt. "He didn't give any reasons," he said. "If I was you, I'd thank my lucky stars and leave it at that."

It was only when Bull telephoned Carter a few days later to suggest that the officer come round to see him for 'a little chat' that it occurred to Carter to wonder whether Bull might have had something to do with Khan's change of heart.

Bull provided the officer with little enlightenment. "Well, Roy," he greeted him, "I understand that Mr Khan has withdrawn his allegations against you."

Carter's suspicions that Bull had had something to do with this development were growing. "Would you, by any chance, know why?" he asked.

"Well," said Bull, "apparently he and his very attractive wife and daughter are now no longer sure of what exactly it was that you said to him, and have discovered that the tape on which they thought they had recorded your conversation with him is, unfortunately, completely blank."

As he spoke, Bull's gaze travelled down from Carter's face to a small cassette tape lying in front of him on his desk.

The officer stared at the tape. "Is that it?" he asked a little hoarsely.

"Hard to say," replied Bull blandly. "One blank tape is pretty much the same as another, isn't it?"

"Can I have it?" Carter's voice was still hoarse.

"I don't think you need it, Roy," said Bull, closing his right hand firmly round the cassette, and looking the other man straight in the eye.

Carter hesitated and then asked abruptly, "What did you do to get him to drop his complaint?"

Bull affected surprise. "Me?" he said. "I didn't do anything. Just picked up the good news on the grapevine." He gave a genial smile, and added, "So, you see, you don't owe me anything."

Carter looked incredulous. "What, nothing? You don't want anything from me?"

Bull slid his left hand under his desk and pushed a small button set into the underside of the desktop. "Well," he said, "there is just one small favour you could do for me."

He leant back in his chair.

"What's that?" asked Carter warily, an uneasy premonition coming over him.

"Nothing much really," Bull reassured him. "It's just that I need to get hold of copies of a couple of statements which have been made to colleagues of yours about one of my clients who has been accused of fraud by his former business partner, and is due to be interviewed about this allegation by your colleagues."

Carter felt sick. "But that's illegal," he protested weakly.

"Well, technically, of course, it is," conceded Bull. "But

the allegations made in those statements are going to be put to my client during the interview anyway, aren't they? So, there's not going to be any harm done to anyone is there?"

He slowly turned the cassette over in his right hand.

"Yeah, yeah, OK, I'll do it," agreed Carter hurriedly.

When Carter returned to Bull's office with the photocopied statements he had been asked for, Bull handed him a bulky brown envelope. "Just a little token of my client's appreciation," he said, smiling amiably.

Carter was surprised. Performing the 'small favour' asked of him by Bull had proved much easier than he had expected, and he had never imagined that he would be paid for it. "Any time," he said gratefully.

Bull took the officer at his word, and DC Carter became the private detective's second source of information within the Metropolitan Police – allowing DC Rowe to begin running fewer risks on his friend's behalf.

Other police officers against whom complaints had been made by members of the public learned about Bull's mysterious powers, and came to avail themselves of his services. Complaints referred to Bull were invariably withdrawn. His clients never discovered how this was achieved, but were very grateful to him for what he had done for them, and found it difficult to refuse him the 'small favours' he asked of them in return.

Bull was always thorough in his work. He secretly recorded all the conversations in which police officers agreed to carry out the favours he asked of them. He thought of this as his insurance policy – just in case any of these officers should be tempted, or placed under pressure by their superiors, to cooperate with any future enquiry into his activities. The microphone used to record these conversations was concealed in an elegant little black china bull, which stood on his desk and was often the subject of mild curiosity on the part of his clients, some of whom wondered if it was a present given to Bull by a woman in his life.

DC McKinnon was referred to Bull by a fellow officer who, although McKinnon was unaware of this, was one of Bull's satisfied clients. When McKinnon asked how Bull could help him, the other officer was reticent. "Just go and see him," he advised, putting his hand on McKinnon's shoulder. "He'll sort you out."

Before going to see Bull, McKinnon made some enquiries about the former detective sergeant, and found out about the circumstances of his dismissal from the police service. This exercise did not inspire him with confidence in Bull, but he did not know where else to turn.

When McKinnon was shown into Bull's office, Bull was not surprised to observe the officer regarding him with an air of suspicion tinged with ill-concealed contempt. He had seen the same attitude in other police officers when they first came to him for his help. It did not worry him. He knew that he had been a better police officer than almost all of them would ever be.

"What can I do for you, Mr McKinnon?" he asked, genially.

He had already made enquiries about his visitor, and knew the situation that McKinnon was in, but saw no reason to let him know this.

Despite his misgivings about Bull's ability to help him, McKinnon decided to come straight to the point. "I'm job," he said. "I'm getting grief from the CPS, and I've heard you're a man who might be able to help me."

Bull looked at the officer thoughtfully. "Always pleased to help someone from the job," he said, enjoying, as usual, the irony of the situation. "What exactly is the problem?"

McKinnon launched himself into his story with venom. "Fucking black crack dealer went for me in his cell. I pushed him away. He knocked his head on the cell wall, broke his neck and died. Clear case of self-defence. CPS said they weren't going to do me for it. Then a fucking inquest jury that doesn't know its arse from its elbow brings in a verdict of unlawful killing, and now the DPP says he's going to look at the case against me again. I reckon he's got it in for me just because I'm a copper – you know how it is."

Once again Bull contemplated McKinnon thoughtfully. He wondered how much the officer knew about him, but something McKinnon had said interested him more. "The DPP," he mused, almost to himself. "That would be the new DPP, Sir James Rowcliffe, wouldn't it?"

"Yeah, fucking prick. Him and his fucking criminal protection society. Why don't they get on with prosecuting some real criminals?" McKinnon demanded. "And my fucking solicitor's no fucking good either. Won't do nothing to stop them."

But Bull was not listening. He was remembering his trial for assault. James Rowcliffe, then already Queens Counsel but not yet knighted, had appeared for the prosecution at the trial. It was unusual for such a senior barrister to represent the prosecution in the trial of a defendant charged with the relatively minor offence of assault occasioning actual bodily harm, but the Police Federation had arranged for a QC to represent Bull, and the CPS had therefore decided to instruct a QC to prosecute the case. Bull remembered Rowcliffe's kind, courteous manner and soft caressing voice and the effortless way in which, in cross-examination, he had induced Bull to contradict himself repeatedly, and had seduced him into making admissions which he had never intended to make.

As he thought about James Rowcliffe, then prosecuting counsel and now director of public prosecutions, an idea began to take shape in Bull's mind. He turned his attention back to McKinnon. "I think I may be able to help you," he said. "Just leave it to me."

McKinnon regarded Bull sceptically. "Why? What are you going to do?" he asked.

Bull tapped the side of his nose with his right forefinger. "Don't ask," he said. "You don't want to know."

McKinnon did want to know, but realised that Bull was not going to tell him any more, and he did not pursue the question further. Shortly afterwards, he left, dispatched on his way with a promise from Bull to be in touch with him soon. McKinnon did not expect much to come of this promise.

That evening Bull's idea took the private detective on a short walk from his office in Soho to nearby Leicester Square.

When Alison French and Neeta Patel arrived outside the main entrance to Waterloo Station at just after nine o'clock the following evening, they found Pat already waiting for them.

Alison was wearing an old grey sweatshirt, a pair of faded blue jeans, a battered pair of blue and white trainers and a green anorak with a broken zip. Neeta had on a worn fawn polo-necked sweater, an old pair of brown slacks with a small tear over the right knee, a scuffed pair of brown walking shoes and a faded navy blue raincoat. In accordance with Pat's instructions, neither was wearing any make-up or jewellery or carrying a handbag.

Pat regarded the two younger women critically. Alison and Neeta had felt rather proud of their outfits, but, under Pat's gaze, both felt uncomfortably self-conscious.

"Do we look OK?" asked Alison nervously.

"You look like a couple of social workers," replied Pat disparagingly.

Alison and Neeta felt disconcerted.

Pat laughed at their discomfiture. "Never mind," she said. "You'll do."

She led them away from the station and through an underpass into a concrete open-air arena, around the top of which, well above their heads, ran the wall which defined the large roundabout at the southern end of Waterloo Bridge.

As they emerged from the underpass into the arena, they passed four men sitting on the ground with their backs against a wall drinking from cans of lager. One of the men let out a loud wolf-whistle, and another shouted, "Give us a kiss, darling."

Pat turned and glared at the men.

The response was immediate. "Sorry, Pat," called out one of the four contritely. "Didn't realise it was you."

Pat did not reply, but turned away from the men, who began to recriminate with each other in loud, drunken whispers.

It was beginning to get dark.

Pat took Alison and Neeta to their left towards an area to the side of the arena covered by the end of the bridge. It was like a huge cavern, its roof held up by bulky concrete supports.

The women passed a group of people huddled around a small fire.

Under the bridge it was dark and gloomy. As their eyes became accustomed to the murky light, Alison and Neeta saw, spread out on the ground around them, sleeping bags, small piles of blankets, large cardboard boxes and several small huts, no more than three-foot high, made out of pieces of wood, plastic sheeting and cardboard. There was a dank smell in the air – a mixture of sweat, urine, damp and decay. In one of the sleeping bags a figure lay curled up, moaning softly. A few feet away, a man and woman sat side by side on one of the piles of blankets, staring in front of them, not speaking. From somewhere in the darkness came a distressed cry. A cigarette end glowed, illuminating the weather-beaten face of a man sitting alone with his back against one of the pillars supporting the bridge. From inside one of the small huts came a faint light and a low murmur of voices. A man shuffled past with a can of Special Brew in his hand. Two young girls, who looked no more than fourteen years old, sat huddled together in a cardboard box staring out fearfully into the gloom. From further under the bridge came a loud curse, followed by the sounds of a scuffle.

Alison and Neeta exchanged nervous glances.

Pat, moving slowly but purposefully, led them to a dark corner behind a concrete pillar. As she approached it, she called out in a low voice, "Bertie? Are you there, Bertie?"

At first there was no reply, but then came a thin voice, asking nervously, "Who's that? Is that you, Pat?"

"Yes, Bertie, it's me," called back Pat reassuringly.

As they rounded the pillar, Alison and Neeta could just make out the silhouette of a man seated huddled with his back to the pillar and his knees pulled up to his chest. He had what looked like an old quilt drawn round his shoulders. His head craned anxiously towards them.

"I've brought someone to see you, Bertie," said Pat gently.

She dropped to her haunches facing him and flicked on a small torch, holding it with its beam directed downwards so that they could all see one another without being dazzled by its light. Alison and Neeta crouched down beside her. Monstrous shadows formed around them.

Bertie saw Alison. A brief look of recognition crossed his face, quickly replaced by one of apprehension.

Alison was shocked at the change in him. He looked aged and shrunken. His cheeks were hollow and his eyes dull. She wanted to give him a hug, but held back. "Hello, Bertie, it's me," she greeted him softly.

"Hello, Miss French," he said spiritlessly.

His eyes shifted to Neeta and regarded her apprehensively.

Alison tried to allay his anxiety. "This is Neeta," she told him. "She's a friend of mine."

Pat shot her a questioning look, challenging the adequacy of this explanation of who Neeta was.

Alison understood her concern, and nodded to her in acknowledgement. She had no intention of misleading Bertie, but wanted to get round to telling him why she had brought Neeta with her in her own way. She turned back to him, and asked, "How are you, Bertie? I've been worried about you."

"No need," he said listlessly, not looking at her, but staring at the ground. "I'm OK."

Alison resisted saying anything about the obvious deterioration which had taken place in him since she last saw him, and instead asked, "But why didn't you turn up for the inquest?"

Bertie shook his head, shying away from the question.

Then, still staring at the ground, he asked in a flat voice, "How did it go? I s'pose it went off all right without me."

"No, Bertie, I'd say you were missed," Alison told him, trying to rally his spirits. "The jury brought in a verdict of unlawful killing, but the inquest left important questions unanswered, and we're hoping you could help answer them. Neeta here is the solicitor for the dead man's family, and they desperately want to know what really happened to him."

She looked at Pat, who nodded.

Bertie shook his head again, this time more vigorously. "I'm havin' no more to do with courts, judges, police, lawyers an' all," he declared, a defiant anguish in his voice. He shuddered.

Alison wondered what he was afraid of. "Don't worry," she reassured him. "We're not here to ask you to appear in court. All Neeta here would like you to do is to give her a statement about what you know."

Bertie glanced at Neeta, then looked down at the ground again. "I'm sorry," he said, quietly. "I can't help you."

Alison tried again. "Can't you at least tell us what it was you were going to tell the inquest about what happened before the alarm went off?" she pressed him gently. "You don't have to give us a statement if you don't want to. Just tell us what you know."

Neeta winced at the suggestion that it would be enough for Bertie to tell them what he knew without giving them a statement, but she said nothing, recognising that it was Alison whom he trusted and who was most likely to get him to tell them what he knew.

Pat caught Alison's eye and gave her a look warning her not to push Bertie too hard.

Bertie hesitated, struggling with conflicting emotions, and then said, "It wasn't much really. It was just…"

His words were drowned out by a commotion breaking out in the darkness nearby. Voices were shouting abuse at each other. There was the sound of glass breaking and then a scream. Running footsteps clattered away into the night, pursued by a shout of, "I'll get you for that, you fuckin' bastard." Then it was quieter again.

Alison leaned forward towards Bertie. "You were saying, 'It was just…'," she prompted him eagerly.

Bertie looked at her vacantly for a moment, and then resumed, "Oh, yeah. It was just that I heard a voice shoutin', that's all."

"And was that before the alarm went off?" asked Alison.

"Yeah, that's right," said Bertie.

"And what was it shouting, this voice?" pursued Alison.

"It wasn't much," repeated Bertie. "It was just, 'Leave me alone, Mr McKenna', somethin' like that."

Alison and Neeta exchanged looks as they took in the significance of what he had just said.

"Was that all?" asked Alison. "Or was there anything else?"

Bertie looked deflated. "No," he replied dispiritedly, "that was all. I s'pose it doesn't help much."

"But it does," exclaimed Alison, excitedly. "It proves that…"

Neeta interrupted quickly. She did not want Bertie to be told anything about what he had heard which might affect the way in which he gave evidence in any future trial or lay him open to the charge that he had been coached in what to say. "Yes, Mr O'Connor, it's a great help, it really is," she told him. "And it would be an even greater help if you could put it into a statement for me."

A look of panic came into Bertie's eyes. "I'm not makin' no statement," he cried. He turned to Alison. "You told me I wouldn't have to make no statement," he reproached her, with undisguised anguish in his voice.

Pat intervened. "That's right," she said firmly. "You told him he wouldn't have to make a statement, and, if he doesn't want to make a statement, he's not going to make one."

Neeta contemplated trying to make Bertie change his mind, but, looking at his face and Pat's, she knew it would do no good.

Bertie gave Pat a grateful look, and then turned back to Alison. His eyes pleading with her not to think badly of him, he clumsily tried to change the subject. "So, how is it you know Pat, then?" he asked.

Alison found the look in the old man's eyes almost unbearable. "I went looking for you around Brixton Station," she told him, trying not to let him see the effect he was having on her, "and I met Pat there."

"She's a clever woman, is Pat," declared Bertie proudly. "Used to be a top civil servant. Did you know that?"

Involuntarily, Alison and Neeta both looked at Pat.

Pat gave them a wry smile, enjoying their surprise. "Well, I wouldn't say 'top'," she said, "but, yes, I was what they called a 'senior civil servant' in the Ministry of Agriculture, Fisheries and Food."

"But, how…?" blurted out Alison, before adding quickly, "I'm sorry. It's none of my business."

Pat remained unruffled. "It's all right. I don't mind telling you," she said. "I'm a manic depressive," she continued, in a matter-of-fact tone. "About ten years ago, I hit a high, and started doing strange and irresponsible things. When I came out of hospital, my head of department was very sympathetic, but suggested that I think very seriously about whether I was really suited to a career in the civil service. I felt very ashamed of the things I'd done and very guilty at having let my colleagues down. So, I did the honourable thing, and resigned. Then I discovered how difficult it is to get work if you have a history of mental illness. I got depressed, and hit the bottle. I fell behind with my mortgage payments, my house was repossessed, and I ended up on the streets. But then, on the streets, I found that there were people ready to look out for me – complete strangers, some of them in a much worse way than me, making sure I didn't come to any real harm. Slowly, I began to get back on my feet. I found a place in a hostel, where the staff referred me to a really good doctor, who put me on lithium, and made me realise I have to stay on it. So now, most of the time I'm stable, though I have had some more short stays in hospital, and, when I'm well, I have my hostel place, which is a roof over my head, and my social security payments, which cover my food and other basic needs. That means I can spend my days on the streets among my friends, the people who looked out for me when I was at my lowest, and I try to do what I can to see that those in the greatest need of help get it. I've got to know my way around the system pretty well, and I'd say I'm more use to society now than I ever was as a civil servant."

Neither Alison nor Neeta could think of what to say to this. Both had been impressed by Pat's story, but neither could really understand why she had not tried to get back to a more conventional way of life, and they were afraid that anything they said would sound insincere or patronising.

Pat was not surprised or offended by their silence. She realised that it must be difficult for two professional young women to understand the path her life had taken. "Come on," she said. "I think we should be going."

Alison turned back to Bertie. "Is there anything we can do for you – to repay you for the help you've given us?" she asked. "I mean, could you use a few quid for a hot meal or something?"

Bertie did not reply, his pride struggling with the thought of what the money could buy him.

Sensing his dilemma, Alison quickly pulled a ten-pound note out of one of the pockets of her jeans, leaned forward and pressed the money into his right hand. It was the only money she had with her. "Here, take this," she urged him. "I'll charge it to expenses." Then, giving him no chance to protest, she got swiftly to her feet. "Goodbye, Bertie," she said gently. "Look after yourself – and make sure you come and see me the next time you're in Brixton." She turned quickly to leave, stumbling slightly and fighting back her tears.

Neeta and Pat said their goodbyes to Bertie and followed Alison out into the arena.

The three women crossed the dark open space in silence.

Pat accompanied Alison and Neeta to the entrance to Waterloo Station, where she announced, "This is where I leave you. I hope what Bertie told you was what you wanted to hear."

"Well, it's certainly a help," said Neeta, "although I'm not sure how much use we'll be able to make of it, if he won't make a statement."

"I'm afraid that's your problem," said Pat brusquely.

"Yes, of course it is," agreed Neeta quickly. "And I don't want you to think we aren't grateful for all you've done to help us track Bertie down. We really do appreciate it."

"You're welcome," said Pat, adding, with a sly grin at Alison, "so long as you don't offer me any money."

Alison reddened and felt tears pricking her eyes again, but Pat reached across, squeezed her arm and said, "Don't worry. You did the right thing."

Sir James Rowcliffe owned a large house on the edge of Hampstead Heath. Since the death of his wife he had lived there alone. He had a son and a daughter, but both were grown up and had homes of their own. The house felt cold and empty, and he did not enjoy living there by himself, but it held so many memories for him that he shied away from selling it and moving to a new home. Taking on the post of director of public prosecutions had aggravated his loneliness, for it had distanced him from the easy camaraderie of life at the Bar, and had placed him at the head of an organisation, many of whose most senior members resented the appointment of an 'outsider' to the post of DPP and, while almost grovelling in their day to day behaviour towards him, showed him no warmth or inclination to spend time in his company after work.

As he found himself spending more and more long, lonely evenings in his big, empty house, he took to filling his time by going for walks on Hampstead Heath. On one of these walks he found, in an isolated spot high on the heath, a wooden bench from which there was a panoramic view over London. This became his favourite haunt and, in the early summer, as the weather grew warmer, he began to spend many evenings there, reading or simply contemplating the view. Sometimes as he sat in his eyrie, he would see someone out for a stroll or taking a dog for a walk, but often he saw no one at all.

One fine evening, at the end of July, about a week after Alison and Neeta's visit to see Bertie, Sir James was sitting on his bench on Hampstead Heath reading *The Warden* by Anthony Trollope. It was a novel he had read many times, but it remained one of his favourites, and, although, since he had taken up the post of DPP and had become acquainted with the political machinations of those in the higher echelons of the CPS, he had begun to find the intrigues of Trollope's clerics a little tame, he still found much in it to enjoy. He had recently lost his original copy of the book, and the one he was reading was a new paperback. On its front cover was a photograph of a well-known actor playing the Reverend Septimus Harding in a recent television adaptation of the book.

As he was reading, Sir James became aware of a figure climbing the hill towards him. At first, he took little notice, but then realised, with some dismay, that the intruder, a boy of about fourteen, was heading straight for him.

"Cor, some hill that, eh?" pronounced the boy as he reached Sir James. "Still, it's a good view, innit?"

Sir James said nothing. He noticed that the boy, who was quite good-looking in a rather effeminate way, had brightly dyed blonde hair, an earring in his right ear and what looked suspiciously like traces of mascara around his eyes.

"Mind if I join you?" enquired the boy, sitting down beside him without waiting for an answer. He was panting slightly.

Sir James hoped that the boy would leave as soon as he had got his breath back. He returned to his book.

"Is it a good book?" asked the boy.

Sir James did not want to talk to him, but sensed that the boy, too, might be lonely, and did not wish to be rude to him. "I like it," he replied briefly, but not unkindly.

The boy leaned forward and craned his head round to look at the front of the book in Sir James's hands. "Is it about religion, then?" he asked, taking his cue from the photograph on the book's cover.

Sir James gave a slight sigh. "More about the church, really," he replied. "And politics."

But the boy was not really listening. "I used to be into religion," he declared, "but then I looked around at all the bad things there is in the world and I thought, right, they say God is all good and all powerful, but, if that's true, right, why does he let all them bad things happen? I mean, I'm not tryin' to be funny nor nothin', but it don't make sense, do it?"

Sir James was a little taken aback by this outburst and was momentarily unsure of how to respond to it.

As he hesitated, the boy suddenly held out his hand to him and announced, "I'm Jack, by the way."

Uneasily, Sir James took the hand proffered to him and shook it. "Hello, Jack," he said, but did not introduce himself.

Jack seemed not to notice this omission. "So, what do you think about what I just said then?" he asked.

Sir James did not feel like getting into a theological discussion with him. "Well, Jack," he replied, "it's a very difficult question. What I can tell you is that cleverer minds than ours have tried to find an answer to it, but have not been able to come up with one that they all agree on."

Jack leaned back on the bench, as if considering this. "Is that right?" he marvelled. Casually, he reached out with his right arm, and draped it along the top of the back of the bench behind Sir James.

Sir James looked around. He was beginning to feel uncomfortable, and decided that this conversation had gone on long enough. "Yes, it is," he said shortly. "Now, if you'll excuse me, I really must be going." He prepared to leave but, with instinctive courtesy, did not immediately stand up to go.

Jack did not seem put out by Sir James's decision to bring their encounter to an end. "Yeah, I gotta be on me way, too," he declared, getting quickly to his feet. Then, suddenly, he turned back, and leaning forward, placed his mouth close to Sir James's right ear and murmured into it in a low voice, "Remember, if you can't be good, be careful."

Sir James started back in surprise, and Jack turned quickly away from him, and made off down the hill. Sir James watched him go. "What an extraordinary boy," he muttered to himself. He looked around uneasily, but could see no one else about. He thought of returning to his book, but the light was beginning to fade. A cool breeze had sprung up. The leaves on a small clump of bushes down the hill to his right rustled. Sir James shivered slightly, got up, and began to walk slowly down the hill.

The first thing Sir James noticed when he arrived for work at CPS headquarters in Queen Anne's Gate the following morning was that there was something odd about the way in which the members of his staff whom he met on his way to his office greeted him. Few looked him in the face, and those who did wore expressions of embarrassment or malicious curiosity.

It was when he got to his office that he discovered the reason for this phenomenon.

On his desk lay a copy of that morning's issue of *The Sun* newspaper, considerately placed there by one of his aides. On the front page were three colour photographs of his encounter with Jack the previous evening. The first picture showed the two shaking hands, the second, Jack sitting with his arm apparently around Sir James, and the third, Jack bending over Sir James and speaking into his ear, but looking suspiciously as if he were giving him a kiss on the cheek. In all three photographs Jack's face had been blanked out, but his brightly dyed blonde hair and even his earring could clearly be seen.

The piece accompanying these photographs did not carry one of *The Sun*'s famously jocular headlines, for, on this occasion, the newspaper was bent on demonstrating the seriousness of its intent. The piece read simply:

THE DPP AND THE RENT BOY

These pictures were taken yesterday evening on Hampstead Heath – a well-known meeting place for homosexuals. The man in the pictures is the Director of Public Prosecutions, Sir James Rowcliffe, who lives alone. The boy with him is known to police as a rent boy. The boy's face has been blanked out because he is only 14 years old. As head of the Crown Prosecution Service, the DPP is responsible for seeing that paedophiles are brought to justice. What is going on here, Sir James? asks The Sun.

Sir James gazed at the paper in anger and disbelief. Surely, whoever was responsible for this did not think that he or she could get away with it. He also felt angry with himself. How could he have been so stupid? How could he have let himself be set up so easily? With an effort, he forced himself to think calmly about the situation. This thing must be nipped in the bud straight away, he decided.

He summoned his secretary, and instructed her to arrange a meeting for him with the heads of the various directorates of the CPS for eleven o'clock that morning.

His secretary would not look at him.

Sir James tried to remonstrate with her. "This is all nonsense, Marion," he told her, gesturing at the copy of *The Sun* on his desk. "You know that, don't you?"

"Yes, of course, Sir James," she murmured in obvious embarrassment. "I'll just go and start organising that meeting for you."

Sir James was dismayed. He liked and trusted Marion and had always got on well with her. If she did not believe him, who would?

His meeting with the senior members of his staff did not go well.

"You'll all have seen this morning's edition of *The Sun*," he began briskly, looking around the oval table at them.

No one looked back at him. Some of those seated round the table examined their fingernails. Most just gazed down at the surface of the table.

Sir James took a deep breath. "Yesterday evening," he told them firmly, "I was sitting quietly reading a book on Hampstead Heath, which, as some of you will know, is next to my house, when I was approached by this boy." He gestured at the copy of *The Sun* on the table in front of him. "I had never seen him before, and had no idea who he was. He engaged me in a brief conversation, and then, just before he left, made a stupid comment in my ear. That's all there is to it. The whole thing is clearly an elaborate set-up."

There was silence around the table.

After a few moments, the director of communications spoke. "Of course, I'm sure we all accept everything you say, Sir James," he said smoothly, his tone conveying the exact opposite of his words. "But the problem here is one of image and timing. As you are aware, the service has recently come in for a good deal of criticism, and the time and effort, which you will naturally wish to put into dispelling these most unpleasant insinuations, will unfortunately distract attention from the efforts of everyone in the service to counter these wider criticisms."

A murmur of agreement ran round the table.

"So, what are you suggesting?" demanded Sir James indignantly. "That I should resign?"

The others around the table shifted in their seats.

"Well, of course, Sir James," replied the director of communications with patent insincerity, "I'm sure I speak for everyone present, when I say that we should all be very sorry to see you go – especially in such very unfortunate circumstances – but I do think that that would perhaps be in the best interests of the service."

A second, slightly louder, murmur of agreement ran round the table. Two of those there had already mentally begun drafting their applications for Sir James's job.

Sir James was outraged, and, for once, his legendary calm deserted him. "But to resign in these circumstances would be tantamount to conceding that these despicable innuendos are true," he exploded angrily.

"We do understand your position, Sir James," said the director of communications, "but we also have to think of the good of the service. We are only too aware that, throughout your brief time as director, you have always placed the interests of the service first, and we would ask you to do so again on this occasion. And, of course, relieving yourself of the onerous responsibilities of the post of director would enable you to devote all your energies to repudiating these scandalous allegations."

Sir James had heard enough. With quiet dignity he got up from his seat. "Thank you for your support, ladies and gentlemen," he said politely, inclined his head in a slight bow, and left the room.

That afternoon he received a summons to call on the Attorney General. He was disappointed, but not surprised, to find that the government's chief law officer viewed matters in much the same way as his own director of communications. The government, it appeared, was extremely grateful to him for the way in which he had carried out the role of director of public prosecutions, but felt that it would be unfair both to him and to the Crown Prosecution Service to expect him to remain in post, 'while these unfortunate matters remain unresolved'.

The Attorney General tactfully left the room while Sir James wrote his letter of resignation.

"Bad business," he commiserated when he returned. "But we all have to be so devilishly discreet these days. It's the price of public office, I'm afraid."

He was relieved that Sir James had agreed to go quietly.

Reset

"Men, dem all de same," complained Delroy's mother bitterly on hearing of Sir James's resignation. "Why him can't keep him t'ing inna him pants?"

The rest of the dead man's family also reacted to the news with dismay.

They feared that, with Sir James's departure from the post of director of public prosecutions, the fresh review into the circumstances of Delroy's death which he had instigated would be dropped or quietly forgotten.

All agreed that they needed to make an urgent appointment with Ms Patel to discuss this turn of events with her.

Neeta had not been in touch with Delroy's family in the week or so since she and Alison had been to visit Bertie – largely because she was still trying to make up her own mind about where Bertie's revelation took them.

She had discussed the problem with Alison over a cup of

coffee when the young journalist had accompanied her back to her home on their return from Waterloo.

Alison was puzzled that Neeta was not more elated by what Bertie had told them. "I know it's not much," she said. "Just someone shouting, 'Leave me alone, Mr McKenna', but, the way I see it, that someone has got to have been Delroy shouting at McKinnon. Or do you think it's a problem that Bertie says the name he heard being shouted was McKenna rather than McKinnon? That could just be a mistake on Bertie's part."

"No, I don't think that's a major problem," conceded Neeta carefully. "I agree that the inference, that what Bertie heard was Delroy shouting at McKinnon, is a strong one. Delroy may have got McKinnon's name wrong or Bertie may have heard or remembered it wrong, but the names are so similar that I don't think we'd have too much difficulty in getting it accepted that it was McKinnon who was being shouted at. Of course, we'll have to check whether there was anyone in the cell area that night called McKenna, but that shouldn't be too difficult, and I'm reasonably confident that we'll get confirmation that there wasn't. Obviously McKinnon's lawyers would make as much as they can of the discrepancy in order to try and discredit Bertie's evidence, but it might even operate in our favour. Sometimes juries seem to prefer evidence which doesn't fit together too neatly. They seem to trust it more."

"OK, then," went on Alison enthusiastically, "as I see it, what Bertie heard proves that McKinnon was lying when he said that Delroy just came at him, and that there was no conversation between them. It also proves that Delroy had at least some idea of what McKinnon's name was – which suggests that McKinnon was also lying when he said he'd had no previous dealings with Delroy. And, most important of all, the fact that Bertie heard Delroy shouting 'Leave me alone' strongly suggests that McKinnon and not Delroy was the original aggressor – which undermines McKinnon's claim that he only acted in self-defence."

"Yes," agreed Neeta, "I think I'd go along with all of that, but the problem is that Bertie is unwilling to appear in court, and won't even make a formal statement about what he heard."

"But can't you and I give evidence about what Bertie told us?" queried Alison impatiently. "After all, you're a solicitor, and that must count for something, mustn't it?"

Neeta gave a wry smile. "I'm afraid it's not as simple as that," she explained. "Any evidence by us of what Bertie told us would be classified as hearsay, and would be inadmissible in a criminal trial. The judge would simply refuse to allow us to give that evidence. And I'm afraid that the fact that I'm a solicitor makes absolutely no difference. Even if I were a High Court judge, I would not be allowed to give that evidence."

"So, is that it then?" asked Alison in dismay. "Is there no way we can get what Bertie heard taken into account?"

"I'm not sure," said Neeta thoughtfully. "There are some provisions in sections 23 and 24 of the Criminal Justice Act 1988 which we might be able to use to get around the problem. These provisions allow hearsay evidence to be admitted in criminal proceedings in certain circumstances, but the difficulty is that they only apply to evidence which is recorded in a document. So, if Bertie had given us a written statement, and had then become unavailable to give evidence at court, the prosecution might have been allowed to produce that statement in court, but, of course, Bertie refuses to give a statement."

"So, how do these provisions help us then?"

"Well, I'm not sure yet that they do. But it's possible that, if you and I make notes of what Bertie told us this evening, our notes might become admissible in evidence."

"But that doesn't make sense. You're saying that we wouldn't be allowed to tell the court what Bertie told us, but we would be allowed to hand in as evidence our notes of what he told us. Why's that?"

"Well, it turns on the wording of section 24. Let me read it to you."

Neeta pulled a large legal textbook from one of her shelves, leafed quickly through it and then went on, "Ah, yes, here it is. Listen. *'A statement in a document shall be admissible in criminal proceedings as evidence... if the following conditions are satisfied (1) the document was created or received by a person in the course of... a profession or other occupation... and (2) the information contained in the document was supplied by a person... who had... personal knowledge of the matters dealt with'."*

"I see," exclaimed Alison excitedly. "Our notes will be documents created by us in the course of our professions, and the information they contain will be information supplied by Bertie who had personal knowledge of the matters dealt with. Great! So, that's our problem solved. Hey, Neeta, you're brilliant."

"Hang on. I'm afraid it's not that simple. Section 24 goes on to say that, if the statement was prepared for the purposes of criminal proceedings or a criminal investigation, it is not admissible in evidence unless the person who made it is unavailable to give evidence because he or she is dead, too unwell to attend court as a witness or out of the country or cannot be found or be expected to have any recollection of the matters in question. Now, at the moment, none of those conditions applies to Bertie."

"Yes, but wait a minute. Our notes won't be classified as statements prepared for the purposes of criminal proceedings or a criminal investigation, will they?"

"I don't know. I think that's something that could be argued both ways."

"OK," said Alison, trying a new tack, "the reason that Bertie is unavailable to give evidence seems to be that he's frightened. Won't that do?"

"I'm afraid not. It would do, if Bertie had made a statement to a police officer, but, as all he's done is to speak to a solicitor and a journalist, it won't."

"This isn't half complicated."

"And it gets worse. Even if we manage to persuade a judge that our notes of what Bertie told us are admissible evidence, the judge still has the right to keep them from the jury if he thinks it would be in the interests of justice to do so, and my instinct is that that is exactly what most judges would do."

"So, is there any other way of getting round the problem?"

"Well, if we ever manage to get McKinnon charged, the CPS could get a subpoena requiring Bertie to attend court, but, if he still refused to turn up or to give evidence, there's not much anyone could do about it. The judge could lock Bertie up for a few days for contempt of court, but that's about it."

Alison shivered at the thought of Bertie being sent to prison. "What if I ran a story about what Bertie told us?" she suggested. "That would bring it all out into the open and maybe force the CPS to prosecute McKinnon, and then perhaps we could try to get Bertie to change his mind about giving evidence of his own accord."

"No, I don't think that would be a good idea," said Neeta quickly. "If the evidence is inadmissible, the DPP won't be able to take it into account in deciding whether to prosecute McKinnon – even if it is published in the press. Your story would only show our hand to McKinnon and his lawyers, and might even place Bertie in danger. We know Bertie's already been beaten up once, which may have something to do with this case. As you yourself said, he seems to be frightened of giving evidence for us. What's more, if McKinnon is ever placed on trial, and what Bertie told us is ruled to be inadmissible against him, his lawyers would have a strong argument for getting the case against him thrown out on the grounds that he could not get a fair trial after this inadmissible evidence had been splashed all over the papers where it could be seen by potential jurors who might be influenced by it."

Alison looked disappointed. "But…" she began.

"No," interrupted Neeta. "I must insist that you don't run a story on this now. You gave me your word. Remember?"

"Yes, yes, OK. You don't have to remind me," said Alison, a little chastened. She had not imagined that being a journalist was going to be as complicated as this.

Neeta tried to raise her spirits. "Come on," she said. "Let's sit down on opposite sides of my kitchen table, and make our notes about our visit to Bertie this evening, what we said to him, and, most importantly, what he said to us. We'll have a better chance of getting them admitted if we can show that we made them as soon as possible after the events which we've recorded in them. And I think it's best, if we make them independently without discussing them with each other. Is that OK with you?"

"Yes, sure," said Alison, glad to be doing something which she might eventually be able to use in a story for her paper.

When Neeta learned of Sir James Rowcliffe's resignation the following week, her reactions were mixed. On the one hand, she shared the fears of Delroy's family that the review of the evidence relating to Delroy's death which Sir James had promised would be compromised by his departure, but, on the other, she experienced a sense of slightly guilty relief at the realisation that the hiatus in the review of the case by the CPS likely to be caused by this turn of events would give her more time to decide what to do next.

Delroy's parents came to see her with their son Leroy, but neither Althea nor Bernice came, as, although they had kept in touch with Delroy's family, both now had new partners and had moved on with their lives.

The meeting was an emotional one.

Leroy was vociferous. "It's a fit-up," he raged. "Anyone in this country asks too many questions about the pigs, he gets fitted up. There ain't no justice."

Neeta tried to pacify him. "I don't think that the events leading up to the DPP's resignation can have had anything to do with the review he promised to carry out into Delroy's case," she said.

"Yeah?" Leroy challenged her. "No disrespect, Miss Patel, but I don't think you really know how the police operate around here. You gotta be black to know how it really is."

Neeta wondered if he thought that she and members of her community suffered no racial prejudice or discrimination, but she realised that his experience would have been different from hers, and she said nothing.

"But there's them photos in the paper," wailed Delroy's mother plaintively. "An' him givin' up his job show he must've been up to no good, don't it?"

Her husband intervened. "There's no point askin' why the man's gone," he said quietly. "Fact is he's gone an' we gotta decide what to do next. Isn't that right, Miss Patel?"

Neeta looked at him gratefully. "Yes, I think it is," she agreed. And I think our best course of action is to carry on as if nothing had happened. Our position is that, while he was DPP, Sir James Rowcliffe promised us that he would carry out a personal review of the evidence relating to Delroy's death, and we expect that promise to be honoured by his successor as DPP."

"An' if it ain't?" demanded Leroy. "What then?"

"Well, I don't think that situation will arise," Neeta reassured him. "But, if it does, we can go for what's called a judicial review, and apply for a court order for the new DPP to do what Sir James Rowcliffe promised he would do."

Leroy was not convinced. He harboured strong doubts whether a review carried out by the new DPP on the orders of a court would be carried out with the same energy as a review carried out by Sir James on his own initiative would have been.

Similar misgivings were shared by all the others in the room, including Neeta, but no one voiced these anxieties. There seemed no point.

Neeta decided it was time to change the subject. "And now," she announced, "I have some news for you."

Her clients looked at her expectantly.

"It's not all good," she warned them hurriedly, "but it's something that may help us."

She described the meeting which she and Alison had had with Bertie and what he had told them.

As Delroy's mother heard what had probably been her son's last words, she let out a small sob.

But Leroy was exultant. "Yeah," he exclaimed, punching the air with his right fist. "Now we got the bastard. Now we can really nail him."

"Wait a minute," Neeta cautioned him. "I told you the news is not all good. The problem is that this man, O'Connor, is refusing to make a statement about what he heard or to give evidence in court."

"Then you gotta make him," said Leroy indignantly. "You gotta make him – even if you gotta get a court order to do it."

"I'm sorry, Leroy. It isn't that simple," Neeta told him patiently, and she explained the limitations on what could be done to get Bertie to give evidence in court.

"So, why don't this man, O'Connor, want to help us?" asked Delroy's father quietly.

"He didn't say, but the woman who took us to see him told Alison French that he moved away from Brixton because he was beaten up, and both Alison and I got the impression that he's very frightened of something – though we don't know what."

"I knew it!" exploded Leroy angrily. "It's the pigs, innit? They know how to operate the system, and they've put the frighteners on him, innit?"

His father intervened. "Hang on there, Leroy," he said quietly. "We gotta think 'bout this t'ing calmly. Don't do no good gettin' ourselves work up 'bout it."

He turned to Neeta. "Isn't there not'ing else you can do 'bout this, Miss Patel?"

"There may be," said Neeta carefully, "but it's all a bit complicated, and I don't want to give you any false hopes."

She tried to explain as simply as she could how they might be able to use the legal provisions she had discussed with Alison, but, to her no great surprise, she was met with looks of blank incomprehension.

"Sounds like a lotta mumbo jumbo to me," complained Leroy when she had finished. "Why don't we just ask Alison to put what this geezer told you in her paper? I bet that'd get things movin'."

Patiently, Neeta explained why she did not think this would be a good idea.

Like Alison, Leroy was inclined to question Neeta's views on this subject, but his father intervened. "We'll do whatever you advise, Miss Patel," he assured her. "I'm sure you know best."

Neeta thanked him with mixed feelings. She appreciated his confidence in her and the freedom of action which this gave her, but she worried whether she could live up to his expectations of her.

"There is one more thing," she said. "I'd strongly advise you not to tell anyone about what Mr O'Connor told Alison and me. It might place Mr O'Connor in danger, and make it even less likely that we can somehow persuade him to give evidence in court."

The family agreed and, led by Delroy's father, they got up to leave.

Sir James's resignation also brought about another meeting between DC McKinnon and Bull Bates.

This was an altogether happier affair than the meeting between Delroy's family and their solicitor.

Bull let McKinnon do most of the talking.

The officer alluded only indirectly to what had

happened since their last meeting. "I got to hand it to you," he said admiringly. "You really are as good as I was told you were."

"I'm glad you think so," replied Bull laconically.

"I certainly do," enthused McKinnon.

His attention was caught by the little black china bull standing on Bull's otherwise sparsely covered desk. He had seen it before, but, for the first time, it seemed to him somehow an incongruous thing for a man of Bull's bulk to have on his desk.

His mind returned to the reason for his visit. "How did you know he was a pervert?" he asked. "And why hasn't it come out before?"

Bull said nothing, but gave just the trace of a smile.

A sudden suspicion began to dawn on McKinnon. "I suppose he really is a nonce, isn't he?" he asked.

Again Bull said nothing, but allowed himself a slight, deliberately enigmatic, smile.

McKinnon's eyes widened. "But how…?" His question tailed away.

Bull just shook his head.

McKinnon was impressed. "Well! Well! Well!" he murmured in muted tones, as he took in the full extent of what had been done on his behalf.

Then a sobering thought occurred to him. "How much do I owe you?" he asked, betraying some anxiety.

Bull leaned back expansively in his chair. "As I told you, Michael, I'm always happy to help someone from the job," he declared genially. "So, to you, there's no charge." He paused to allow his words to register and to inspire an appropriate feeling of gratitude. "But there is a small favour you could do me…"

McKinnon experienced immediate misgivings, but tried to conceal them. "Yes, of course," he agreed with apparent enthusiasm.

Bull was not deceived, but nor was he deterred from his usual course. Unnoticed by McKinnon, he slid his left hand under his desk.

Despite the obvious risks, Sir James Rowcliffe, demanded that the Metropolitan Police locate Jack, and interview him about the criminal activity which *The Sun* had implied that Sir James had engaged in with the boy, and the Metropolitan Police, confronted with this unusual demand, somewhat reluctantly did as Sir James had asked.

Jack told the officers who interviewed him that he had been approached in Leicester Square by a man who had offered him twenty-five pounds for his help in playing a practical joke on a homophobic friend of the man's. The man had told him what to do, and had said that he would be taking photographs of Jack's encounter with his friend, which he would use to embarrass his friend, if his friend came out with any homophobic remarks in the future.

The boy said he was very sorry for the trouble which he had caused to Sir James, who had seemed to him like a 'nice geezer'.

He regretted that he was unable to describe the man who had put him up to his encounter with Sir James, as it had been very dark when they met and the man had stayed in the shadows throughout their conversation.

Jack did not mention the very much larger sum of money promised, and paid, to him by the man on his completion of what had been asked of him or the threats made to him by the man of the very unpleasant consequences which he would suffer, if he should help the police or anyone else to identify him.

The officers interviewing Jack had an uneasy feeling that he had been thoroughly coached in what to say to them, but they had no way of knowing if this coaching had been by the man who Jack said had given him his instructions or by Sir James or someone acting on Sir James's behalf, and they decided that they could take the matter no further.

The Sun, confronted with the account given by Jack to the police, and threatened with libel proceedings by a man known to have friends among the judiciary, took the unusual step of printing a front-page apology to Sir James. Its wording, hammered out in negotiations between the lawyers acting for the two parties, was not entirely to Sir James's satisfaction, but was eventually accepted by him on the advice of his legal team.

It read:

CORRECTION AND APOLOGY

The Sun apologizes to Sir James Rowcliffe, the former Director of Public Prosecutions, for the unjustified implication of improper conduct by Sir James contained in a recent front-page article. The Sun now accepts that the boy referred to in that article made an unsolicited approach to Sir James, that their only meeting lasted only a few minutes and that no improper conduct took place between them. The Sun is sorry for the distress caused by the article to Sir James, his family and friends and, as an expression of its regret, will pay a substantial sum to a cancer charity nominated by Sir James.

This apology took up the same amount of space on the front page of *The Sun* as the original article about Sir James had done, but was not accompanied by any colour photographs, and was of much less interest to the paper's readers than the original article had been. There were even some of the paper's readers who believed that the apology was an unwarranted one forced on their favourite newspaper by a powerful establishment figure with friends in high places. 'No smoke without fire', they were convinced.

Sir James returned to his career at the Bar.

He was not offered, and did not for a moment consider seeking, reinstatement as director of public prosecutions.

Pending the appointment of a new DPP, the Crown Prosecution Service's director of operations, Paul Weatherall, was installed as acting director of public prosecutions.

Weatherall, a man in his late fifties was, unlike Sir James, a career prosecutor. Before the establishment of the Crown Prosecution Service, he had been employed by the Metropolitan Police solicitors' department as a prosecuting solicitor, and, when the CPS came into being, he, like others in similar positions, suddenly found himself in the right place at the right time. The inauguration of the Crown Prosecution Service involved the creation of a whole new hierarchy of well-paid posts, and, in the face of negligible competition, Paul Weatherall who, until then, had enjoyed a distinctly mediocre career, had no difficulty in procuring a place high in that hierarchy. Once there, he discovered that almost all the top posts in the CPS were filled by others like himself, and that, as a result, exceptional ability was not a prerequisite for advancement within the organisation. Steadily and unobtrusively, he gained further promotion, eventually rising to become director of operations.

Even before Sir James's resignation, Weatherall had begun to covet the post of director of public prosecutions, and he now saw his appointment as acting DPP as his opportunity to establish his credentials as the best man for the job. In pursuing this objective, his strategy was, as it had been throughout his career in the CPS, to delegate as many contentious decisions as possible to others, so that, if and when things went wrong, no one could reasonably hold him responsible for what had happened.

One of his first decisions on being appointed acting DPP was that he was going to have as little as possible to do with cases involving deaths in police custody. He had worked closely with the police throughout his career, and preferred, if he could do so, to avoid confronting the possibility that police officers might sometimes be guilty of serious misconduct. He also recognized that these cases tended to generate a great deal of controversy, and that, if he was seen to have handled one of them badly or insensitively, it could mean the end of his hopes of becoming more than acting DPP.

He surveyed the file relating to Delroy Brown's death at Brixton Police Station with distaste, and viewed Sir James's undertaking to carry out a personal review of the case with irritation. What had the man been thinking of? Here was proof, if further proof were needed, that appointing someone from outside the CPS to be DPP was a mistake. These people always took too much on themselves. If they were civil servants, they would know how to delegate properly.

A belt and braces approach, that was what was needed in this case, he decided. He would first send the file back to Peter Rotherhithe for the branch crown prosecutor or one of his senior lawyers to carry out a further review of the case and then send it to senior treasury counsel for an outside opinion. That way no one could accuse him of failing to have the file reviewed properly. At the same time, he could not envisage senior treasury counsel concluding that there was sufficient evidence against DC McKinnon to justify prosecuting the officer for manslaughter. He anticipated, therefore, that he would be able to advise against the prosecution of DC McKinnon, but be able to say that he was doing so on the independent advice of senior treasury counsel – with the result that no one would be able to claim that his decision reflected any bias by him or the CPS in favour of the police.

A very satisfactory solution to a potentially hazardous problem, he concluded.

The File

Peter Rotherhithe's dismay at receiving the file relating to Delroy Brown's death back from the DPP's office was somewhat assuaged when, on reading the memo from Weatherall which accompanied the file, he homed in on the use by the acting DPP of the phrase, 'for further review by you or one of your senior lawyers'. "One of my senior lawyers," he mused. "Yes, I think this is one for Stuart."

Stuart Fox was a fifty-year-old solicitor who had worked for the Crown Prosecution Service for almost ten years. He was a big, well-built man, with a bold-featured face, incongruously marred by an almost permanent expression of acute anxiety. Before joining the CPS, he had spent nearly fifteen years in private practice carrying out conveyancing work. He had a keen mind and an extensive knowledge of the law, but had not had a successful career either in private practice or in the CPS. He was a careful and thorough lawyer who was good at identifying problems, but slow in his work and hesitant in making decisions. He had been driven out of private practice by the ever-increasing pressure to get through more and more work to make more and more money for the firm which employed him. He had become worried that the volume of work he was being expected to get through made it ever more likely that he would miss something important or make mistakes. "Don't worry," his firm's senior partner had told him. "That's what we have professional indemnity insurance for." But this gave him no comfort. He clung stubbornly to the notion that his clients were entitled to expect him to get things right, and that they should not be expected to make do with the right to make a claim on the Solicitors Indemnity Fund when he got things wrong.

He had joined the Crown Prosecution Service in the hope that, freed from the commercial pressures of private practice, he would be able to concentrate on practising the law rather than on making money, but he found his new employers aping the private sector by embarking on the assiduous compilation of a range of largely meaningless 'performance indicators', which forced him to spend more and more time filling out forms required for statistical purposes and less and less time on legal casework. After he had been in the CPS for two years, he had, in accordance with the service's usual practice, been promoted to the grade of senior crown prosecutor, but he knew that there was no prospect of his rising any higher in the organisation. He was not, he knew, 'management material', and he had no aspirations to a managerial post, but he wished that the qualities which he knew he brought to his work were afforded more respect within the CPS. As it was, he found his line managers sidling up to him for his advice when they had a difficult point of law to resolve, but clearly scornful of what they saw as his failure to get his priorities right.

"Where do you hope to be in five years' time?" Peter Rotherhithe had once asked him.

"Doing the same job, but doing it better," he had replied, to Rotherhithe's obvious incomprehension.

He was, he knew, despised for his lack of ambition. He would not have minded this so much, were it not for the fact that every day he found deficiencies in the management of the CPS making it harder for him to do his job properly.

Amid these general anxieties, one of his cases in particular was nagging away at him.

The file was one which he had reviewed several weeks previously, and the facts of the case were straightforward. Two uniformed police officers out on patrol had stopped two young black men whom they said they believed to be in possession of cannabis. The officers had told the young men of their suspicions, and that the officers were going to search them. The young men had protested that they had no cannabis on them, and had resisted being searched. A fight had developed, in the course of which the officers had received minor injuries. The young men had then been arrested and taken to Brixton Police Station, where they had been found to have no cannabis in their possession, but had been charged with assaulting the officers in the execution of their duty.

Fox's initial reaction on reading the file had been to allow the case to proceed, but, just as he was about to sign it off, his mind had been jogged by a faint memory, which had sent him off in search of two other files, which he had recalled reviewing in the previous few weeks. His suspicions had proved correct. The facts of the three cases were almost identical, and all three involved the same two police officers. Only the names of the young black men involved and the locations of the alleged offences were different.

Troubled by this discovery, Fox had attempted to discuss the latest case with Linda Fawcett and Peter Rotherhithe, but both had told him firmly that he did not have sufficient grounds on which to discontinue the case. Rotherhithe had dismissed the similarity between the three cases as 'a coincidence', and, when Fox had pointed out that, in all three cases, the only grounds given by the officers for attempting to carry out a search had been that the young men were out at night in an area where the possession and use of drugs were widespread, Rotherhithe had told him firmly that the officers patrolling these areas knew the areas far better than he did, and that it was not for him to second-guess their 'operational decisions'. In any event, Rotherhithe had added, even if the officers had been a little 'over-zealous', that was no excuse for the young men concerned to have assaulted them.

Fox, already struggling to keep on top of his work, had not had the strength to argue, and had allowed the case to proceed, but he had felt ashamed of his weakness, and his sense of shame had increased when he had learned earlier that day that the two young black men charged in the case had been found guilty of assaulting the police officers in the execution of their duty, and were likely to receive prison sentences.

Slowly his guilt began to turn to anger. It was all Peter Rotherhithe's fault, he told himself. Why had Peter not allowed him to discontinue the case? Why did the man have no backbone?

The irony of his asking his last question was not lost on him. It was, he reflected bitterly, a question he should be asking about himself.

Filled with these feelings of shame and anger, he became aware of Peter Rotherhithe hovering in front of his desk. He looked up from the file which he was trying to review with a strained expression on his face.

"Ah, Stuart," Rotherhithe greeted him with false bonhomie. "I've got something here which I think is just up your street. A tricky little death in custody case which Linda reviewed when it first came in, but which the acting director wants us to have another look at. It's a case, I think, which calls for that famous thoroughness of yours. Raises some interesting questions on the law of self-defence, which I'm sure that you, with your excellent knowledge of the law, will really enjoy getting your teeth into."

Fox found Rotherhithe's patronising manner towards him grating on him even more than usual. He reached out automatically for the file which his BCP was brandishing enthusiastically in his right hand. "Yes, all right, Peter," he said, taking it. "I'll look at it as soon as I can." He put the file down on his desk and returned to the work he had been doing.

Rotherhithe looked down resentfully at the top of Fox's head. 'What a miserable chap Stuart is,' he told himself. 'Never shows any appreciation of my efforts to channel some of the more interesting work his way. Next time I won't bother.' He attempted to appear unperturbed. "Perhaps if you could do that by Friday," he suggested loftily.

Fox did not look up. "Yes, all right, Peter," he snapped back tersely.

He was reaching the end of his tether.

Rotherhithe looked at him curiously, but said nothing.

At seven o'clock that evening, long after all his colleagues had left the office, Fox remained working at his desk. He was very tired and was making very slow progress. He finished reviewing a file, and glanced at his watch. "I'll do just one more and then I'll go," he decided.

He picked up the file Peter Rotherhithe had given him earlier. He was too tired to take much interest in its contents. Mechanically he worked his way through it. He was critical of the brevity and superficiality of Linda Fawcett's review, but had to admit that he would have come to the same conclusion as she had done. He read laboriously through the transcript of the evidence given at the inquest, and wondered why he was being asked to re-review the case. He recognised that Dr Houseman's evidence strengthened the case against DC McKinnon, but he could not see that the pathologist's evidence made the case against the officer strong enough for there to be a realistic prospect of his being convicted of a charge of manslaughter. Surely even the acting DPP could see that. 'Presumably, getting me to re-review the file is just another CPS public relations job,' he thought bitterly. 'As if I haven't got enough to do already.'

He was just about to put his conclusions about the case down in writing when he found himself considering two bulky little brown envelopes tucked away at the back of the file. Each envelope contained a cassette tape – one a copy of the recording of the interview of Delroy Brown by DC Matthews and DC Jones and the other a copy of the recording of the interview of DC McKinnon by Chief Inspector Elliott. Fox hesitated. Elsewhere in the file were full, typed summaries of both interviews which he had already read. Was there any point in listening to the tapes of the interviews? He knew that none of his colleagues would have bothered to do so, but he, as always, felt driven to do things more thoroughly than anyone else. From his briefcase he pulled the small portable cassette player on which he listened to classical music on his train journeys to and from work, put the small earphones into his ears, and began to play the first tape.

As the voices of DC Matthews and Delroy Brown droned on, fatigue began to get the better of Fox. He found it difficult to concentrate on what the two men were saying and began to doze off.

Suddenly, he was wide awake again. He stopped the machine, rewound the tape a short way and began to replay what he had just heard.

"Yes," he exclaimed aloud. "I was right. It's 'Ice', not 'Eyes'."

He played a little more of the tape, and then stopped the machine again abruptly. He began scrabbling through the papers in the file, until he came to the typed summary of the interview of DC McKinnon by Chief Inspector Elliott. There he found what he was looking for. Quickly he removed the tape from his cassette player, and replaced it with the tape of the interview of DC McKinnon. His hands were shaking slightly. He set the machine to fast forward. Several times he stopped it, listened, stopped it, set it to fast forward, stopped it and listened again until, finally, he found what he was searching for.

"Yes," he cried again, clenching his right fist in excitement. He now saw this case in a new light.

He took the earphones out of his ears and put the cassette player to one side. He pulled the file close to him, hunched over it, and began to write on the inside of its front cover in small, neat and slightly crabbed handwriting:

This case needs further investigation. McK says he went to B's cell, 'because I had received info that B had info abt a case I was working on', but at the inquest McK refused to elaborate on this, claiming PII. In i/v B had offered to give police info about a man called 'Ice' (not 'Eyes'). When McK was i/v'd, he denied knowing a man called 'Eyes'. He seems to have been very keen to do this — it is the only question he answered in the whole i/v. Why? Is it because he does know 'Ice'? Info McK expected to get from B could have been about a case which had nothing to do with 'Ice' — but this seems unlikely. B offers to give police info about 'Ice', and, within hrs, McK goes to B's cell to get info abt a case he is working on. Too much of a coincidence for info not to have been same info. When McK went to B's cell to get info from him, B had already told Matthews that he was only prepared to divulge it to a senior officer — so it's almost certain he would have refused to give it to McK. Did this lead to a confrontation between the two men? Is this why they came to blows?

Fox paused, quickly scanned what he had written, and then went on:

McK's reliance on PII as reason for refusing to say more abt info he had received re B suggests that McK's info came from an informant — but can this be the case? Seems clear from i/v of B that he only decided to offer police info re 'Ice' while he was being i/v'd — so how could informant have known that B was willing to give info to police? Matthews and Jones say they did not tell McK abt B's offer, but they must have done — no other way McK could have known abt it. If McK did not get his info from informant, what other PII grounds could he have had for refusing to say any more about it? Is it that there's an ongoing police investigation re 'Ice' which would be prejudiced, if its existence came out into the open? In my view Chief Ins Elliott shld be asked to look into this. We don't need to know the details — just whether McK was involved in investigation re 'Ice'. This may blow police investigation re 'Ice' — but a man has died here and that may be the price we have to pay to find out why.

Fox put down his pen, then picked it up again, and added, as an afterthought:

And, while we're at it, we shld ask Elliott to make further efforts to get a state't from O'Connor. O'C is the nearest thing we have to an eyewitness (an earwitness?!), and, without state't from him, evid is incomplete.

He read through what he had written with a sense of elation, tinged with malicious glee. He revelled in the knowledge that he had discovered something which everyone else seemed to have missed, and he relished the thought that the conclusions he had reached about this case would be unwelcome both to his superiors in the CPS and to the police. The questions he had raised would undoubtedly complicate any public relations exercise which the CPS hierarchy had in mind, and would not make Peter Rotherhithe popular with those above him. He remembered Peter's jibe about his 'famous thoroughness', and gave a sardonic smile. He imagined that Peter would find his thoroughness less amusing now. As for the police, Fox was sure that Chief Inspector Elliott would not be pleased at being asked to re-open the case, but that was just too bad. He thought of the many occasions over the years on which memos which he had sent to police officers, asking them to investigate a case further or to obtain additional evidence for him, had been ignored or dismissed. Well, this time the police would have to do as he asked.

He looked at his watch. It was nearly nine o'clock. Fatigue and elation had induced in him a sense of euphoria. Thoughts about the case filled his head. He did not feel like going home to his flat.

He was seized by an impulse to go and see the place where it had all begun – where Delroy Brown had made his sale to PC Andrew Thomas.

He got out his London A-Z map, and discovered that Railton Road was a long road running roughly parallel to the railway line between Brixton and Herne Hill stations.

He got up from his desk.

He felt unwilling to leave the case file behind. He wanted to take it with him, to be able to re-read and savour his review of the case when he got home. Taking the file with him could do no harm, he convinced himself. He would bring it back to the office when he came into work the next morning. Hurriedly, he stuffed it into his briefcase, and left.

The file had given him no idea of exactly where in Railton Road the deal between Delroy Brown and PC Andrew Thomas had taken place, but he reasoned that it was most likely to have been at the Brixton end of the road. He went to London Bridge Underground Station, and took the Northern Line to Stockwell and then the Victoria Line to Brixton.

There were still a few people about in Brixton Road as he emerged from Brixton Underground Station, but these rapidly thinned out as he turned into Atlantic Road, and, by the time he reached the point at which Atlantic Road merged into Railton Road, he found himself almost alone.

The street ahead of him was poorly lit, and looked dark and uninviting. He began to wish he had not come, but was unwilling to let himself give up and go home. He decided that he would go just far enough along the road to give himself a feel of the place, and then turn back.

Suddenly, he was startled by a high-pitched shriek. He stood rooted to the spot. There was another shriek and then a frantic scrabbling sound. He realised, with relief, that it was just two cats fighting in a nearby garden. He took a deep breath. He could feel his heart pounding. He looked up and down the street. There was no one in sight.

He felt a sudden need to sit down for a few minutes, and looked round for a bench or low wall to sit on. He noticed, a little further on, to his right, what looked like a children's play area, which he thought might include seats or benches for parents to sit on, and he began walking towards it.

Gingerly, he crossed the road, leaving behind him a large development of what appeared to be council housing.

The play area was shrouded in darkness, and he could not make out from outside whether it contained any seats or benches. Cautiously, he went in through the entrance and began picking his way around the area, peering into the darkness, but he found nothing to sit on, and was about to turn back, when he heard a shout coming from behind him.

He turned and saw three black teenagers approaching him, one slightly ahead of the others. All three wore baggy trousers, loose-fitting puffer jackets, baseball caps and trainers. The one in front was small and wiry. The other two were bigger. Both were tall, but one was fat, the other more muscular.

"Hey, you," called out the small boy aggressively. "You a bastard? You a white bastard?"

Fox knew immediately that they were going to kill him.

The three teenagers did not share Fox's knowledge of how their encounter with him would end. They knew only that this middle-aged white man in his three-piece suit was trespassing on their territory, and they intended to frighten him off, and perhaps to induce him to hand over his valuables to them, before he left.

Slowly and menacingly they moved towards him. The tall, fat boy was brandishing a knife in his right hand. Its blade glinted in the dark.

Transfixed by his knowledge of his impending fate, Fox stood his ground. He was suddenly filled with rage at the way his life had turned out, and determined not to go without a fight.

With his right hand he reached into the inside pocket of his jacket, pulled out his wallet and threw it on the ground just in front of him.

Instinctively, the small boy moved forwards and bent down to pick it up.

This was Fox's cue. He dropped his briefcase, brought both his hands down on the back of the boy's head, forcing it downwards, and, at the same time, brought his right knee hard up into the boy's face.

There was an audible crunch as the boy's nose broke under the impact. He gave a scream of pain and staggered backwards with both hands to his face.

The other two boys only hesitated for a moment before moving in on their friend's assailant.

Stuart Fox's body was spotted early next morning by a man out walking his dog. He had died of multiple stab wounds. His briefcase and wallet had gone, but, in the right-hand pocket of his waistcoat, the police found his laminated CPS security pass.

This discovery provoked a chorus of unsympathetic comments from the uniformed officers on the scene.

"Oh, CPS, is he? What a shame!"

"Not in the public interest to prosecute whoever's done this, I'd say."

"No, you're right. The killer's done the public a favour."

"Yeah. One bastard less on the villains' side."

The officer appointed to head the investigation into Fox's death suppressed a grimace of irritation. He understood that many of his officers resented the exercise by CPS lawyers of their powers to discontinue cases brought by the police, but this kind of hostility towards the CPS only made it harder for the two organisations to work together effectively. "Come on, lads," he remonstrated with them. "Let's just get on with it." He wondered how on earth this CPS lawyer's body had ended up in a children's play area on Railton Road.

Five days later a large, bulky brown envelope arrived at the offices of the *Brixton Chronicle* addressed to Alison French.

Alison noticed that the package was postmarked two days previously, and that the postmark was a local one. Curious to find out what the envelope contained, she tore it open. Inside was a white cardboard folder. It was grubby and battered, and spread across its top right-hand corner, was an uneven dark reddish-brown stain. It did not look like coffee.

The front cover of the folder was divided into rectangular boxes and columns of various shapes and sizes – most with small, printed headings to them and some also with things written in them. Across the top of the folder, in large black letters, were printed the words 'Crown Prosecution Service' and, just below this, written in capital letters with a blue felt-tipped pen, was the description 'Advice File'. Alison was fascinated. It was the first time that she had ever seen a CPS file.

She noticed that, printed in one of the boxes, were the words 'Preferred Advocate', and that next to these someone had written the name 'L. Fawcett', but that this had been crossed out, and had had inserted above it 'S. Fox'.

The second name rang a bell in Alison's mind, but, for a moment, she could not place it. She was sure she had come across it recently, but where?

As she searched her memory for enlightenment, her eyes wandered down the cover of the CPS file in front of her, and there, with a sudden thrill, she saw a name which she had no difficulty in recognising. Under the heading 'Defendants', on a label stuck on the front of the file was typed the name, 'DC Michael McKinnon'.

Alison stared at the familiar name, and noticed that, next to it, under the heading 'Offences', was typed 'Murder/ Manslaughter'.

Her mind reeled. Did this mean that DC McKinnon had been charged with killing Delroy Brown? Surely, if he had been, she would have heard about it.

Perhaps the contents of the file would make things clearer, she thought.

She opened it.

At the top of the inside cover of the file was a large box containing the printed heading 'Initial Review', and, in this box, in a clear bold hand, someone had written simply, 'Insuff. Evid. See advice to Ch Ins Elliott. NFA.' The review was signed 'L. Fawcett', and dated about six months earlier.

Further down were about twenty closely written lines in a completely different handwriting. These spilled out of the box intended for the second review of the case, and filled the rest of the inside of the front cover of the file. Their opening words, 'This case needs further investigation', immediately caught Alison's attention, and she quickly read on. She could not understand all of what followed, but its gist was clear, and filled her with growing excitement. The review was signed 'Stuart Fox' and dated six days previously.

As Alison looked at the signature, she realised, with a shock, where she had come across the name Stuart Fox before. Of course, it was the name of that CPS lawyer who had been found murdered the previous week. One of her colleagues had done a short piece about the murder in the last issue of the *Chronicle*. She pulled out her copy of the paper, and found the story. Yes, that was right. Stuart Fox had been found murdered in a children's playground in Railton Road the previous Wednesday morning, the suspected victim of a street robbery.

Alison felt both exhilarated and apprehensive. She knew that she had a story that would be the envy of almost any journalist in the country, but she feared that she lacked the experience needed to cover it.

Carefully, she read through all the documents on the CPS file, and listened to the two interview tapes it contained.

Hearing Delroy's voice gave her an eerie sensation and, as the recording of his interview progressed, and she detected his initial cheery confidence turning to fear, a slight shiver ran down her spine.

When she was confident that she had a clear grasp of her material, she went to see her editor.

Brian Reid was only six years older than Alison and had only been the editor of the *Brixton Chronicle* for a few months. As he listened to what his trainee told him, and looked at the file she had brought him, he, too, felt a little out of his depth, but he was a bright and enterprising young man and his immediate instinct was to run with this story if he possibly could. "Listen, Alison," he said, "this is a great story, but we're going to need help in deciding how to play it. I'm going to call our lawyers and get one of them down here to advise us on what use we can make of this." He tapped the CPS file now lying on his desk. "In the meantime, I don't want you to talk about this to anyone, inside the office or out. Do you understand?"

"Yes, of course," agreed Alison immediately. She had been thinking of telephoning Neeta to tell her about this development, but had already decided against it. She remembered Neeta's refusal to allow her to write a piece for the *Chronicle* about what Bertie had told them, and did not want to give her the opportunity to voice any objections which she might have to this story.

At twenty past four that afternoon, Brian Reid called Alison back into his office. With him was a slim young man in a dark-blue pinstriped suit. Reid performed the introductions. "Alison, this is John Ross from our solicitors. John, this is Alison French, the colleague of mine who's handling the story which we need your advice on."

The young lawyer got up from his seat to greet Alison. They shook hands and then both sat down opposite Reid.

The *Chronicle*'s editor got straight down to business. "I've already explained the situation to John," he told Alison. He turned to Ross. "So, John, it's over to you."

"Thank you, Brian," said the young lawyer briskly, pleased at the opportunity to demonstrate his knowledge of his subject. "Certainly an interesting situation you've got here. There's no doubt at all in my mind that what you've been sent is a genuine CPS file. We don't know for sure where it's come from, but it was probably stolen from this poor chap Fox when he was mugged. It might have been sent to you by a disgruntled CPS employee, but I think that's less likely. If it was sent to you by someone working for the CPS, then he or she has committed an offence under the Official Secrets Acts. However, wherever the file came from, it is not an offence under the Official Secrets Acts for you to publish its contents. If the file was taken from Fox when he was mugged, whoever took it is guilty of stealing it. Equally, if it was sent to you by a CPS employee, then that employee is almost certainly guilty of its theft. That raises the question of whether you, in taking possession of the file and not handing it in to the police, are guilty of theft or handling stolen goods."

Alison looked anxious.

"Don't worry," Ross reassured her. "To be found guilty of either theft or handling stolen goods, you would have to be proved to have acted dishonestly, and, so far, in my view, there's no question of your having done that, but to be on the safe side, what I suggest you do is copy this file and its contents, and return the original to the police or the CPS without delay."

"OK," said Reid, "we'll do that straight after this meeting. I think we'll turn it over to the CPS rather than the police, if that's all right with you."

"Yes, that's fine," confirmed Ross. "Though, either way, I'd suggest you make sure that you get some proof of what you've done – send it recorded delivery or something like that."

"Will do," agreed Reid. "Any other problems?"

"Well," replied Ross, with a rueful smile, "as usual, the main thing you have to watch out for is the libel laws. What that means in this case is that you must be very careful not to publish anything that suggests that this DC McKinnon is guilty of murder or manslaughter or that he lied to the coroner's court. If you did that, your only real defence to a major libel suit would be to prove that what you had published was true – and, on what you've got here, I think you'd find that difficult. So, what I suggest is that before you go to press, you let me check your copy to make sure it doesn't contain anything libellous."

"Agreed," said Reid. "Anything else?"

"No, I don't think so." Ross grinned. "Isn't that enough for you?"

Reid grinned back. "More than enough, I suspect. Thank you, John. We'll be in touch."

"I'm sure you will," said the lawyer wryly.

After he had gone, Alison made copies of the CPS file and everything on it. Then she put the original file in a large brown envelope which she addressed to Peter Rotherhithe, and marked 'Private and Confidential'.

It was now just after six o'clock. Alison went to see Reid and asked him how he wanted her to return the file to the CPS. He told her to give it to him to put in his safe overnight, and to send it to Rotherhithe's office by courier first thing the following day.

When the courier arrived the next morning, Alison gave him the package for Rotherhithe, with strict instructions to get a signed receipt from the person he handed it over to, but not to tell anyone at the other end who had sent it. "I don't suppose anyone will ask you," she told him, "but, if they do, just play dumb. OK?"

"Yeah, sure, Miss French," the courier assured her with a grin. "Playing dumb is one of my specialities." He did a lot of work for the *Chronicle*, and had a soft spot for her.

Alison spent most of the next day and a half working on her story. She wished she could include in it what she and

Neeta had been told by Bertie O'Connor, for it seemed to her that Stuart Fox's theory, that DC McKinnon and Delroy Brown had come to blows because Delroy had refused to give McKinnon the information Delroy had about this man 'Ice', was supported by Bertie's revelation that Delroy had shouted out 'Leave me alone' at McKinnon. She also found that knowing what Bertie had told them, but having to write her story as if she did not, made putting the story together much more difficult than it would otherwise have been. She felt, however, that she had no choice in the matter. She had promised Neeta that she would not publish what Bertie had told them, and she also knew that, if she did include it in her story, Bertie's safety might be put at risk.

She drafted and redrafted the story until just an hour before her deadline, both Brian Reid and John Ross finally declared themselves satisfied with what she had written.

The next morning her story appeared on the front page of the *Brixton Chronicle* accompanied by photographs of Brixton Police Station and the children's play area where Stuart Fox's body had been found. It read:

NEW QUESTIONS OVER PRISONER'S DEATH
Murdered Prosecutor's Call for Fresh Enquiry
Exclusive Special Report by Brian Reid and Alison French

Senior Crown Prosecutor Stuart Fox, found stabbed to death last week, wanted police to re-open their enquiries into the death in police custody of local man Delroy Brown, official documents passed to the Chronicle reveal.

Mr Brown, whose death was first reported by the Chronicle, died on 6th September last year, while being held at Brixton Police Station on a charge of supplying crack cocaine.

An inquest jury found that Mr Brown was unlawfully killed, but, to date, no one has been charged with causing his death.

Mr Fox, whose death was reported in the Chronicle last week, had been asked by the acting director of public prosecutions to review Mr Brown's case.

Mr Fox wanted the police to investigate whether there was a link between Mr Brown's death and an earlier offer by Mr Brown to supply the police with information about a man known as 'Ice'.

Mr Brown made this offer to DC Matthews and DC Jones, just before he was taken to the cell where he died only hours later.

Mr Brown died while alone in his cell with DC Michael McKinnon, a police officer based at Brixton Police Station.

DC McKinnon told the inquest into Mr Brown's death that he went to the cell because he had heard that Mr Brown had information about a case he was working on, but the officer refused to answer questions on this subject.

In his review, Mr Fox raised the question of whether it was Mr Brown's offer to supply the police with information about 'Ice' which led DC McKinnon to believe that Mr Brown had information about a case DC McKinnon was working on.

Mr Fox noted that Mr Brown told DC Matthews and DC Jones that he was only prepared to give his information about 'Ice' to a senior officer. The prosecutor concluded that 'it's almost certain' Mr

Brown would have refused to give this information to DC McKinnon.

Mr Fox then raised the further question of whether it was a refusal by Mr Brown to give DC McKinnon information about 'Ice' which explains why there was a confrontation between the two men and why they came to blows.

However, as reported in the Chronicle, DC McKinnon told the inquest that he had no chance to speak to Mr Brown before Mr Brown made an unprovoked attack on him. He said that he used only reasonable force to defend himself from this attack, and that Mr Brown then fell, sustaining the injuries which caused his death.

Nonetheless, Mr Fox recommended that the Police Complaints Authority look into the question of whether DC McKinnon was involved in an investigation into 'Ice' which might explain the officer's visit to see Mr Brown in his cell.

Mr Fox, whose death is being treated by the police as murder, died within twenty-four hours of completing his review of Mr Brown's case. In an unexplained link, the prosecutor's body was found in a playground in Railton Road – the street where Mr Brown is alleged to have committed the offence which led to his arrest.

Mr Fox's death is the second recent blow to those campaigning for a fresh investigation into Mr Brown's death.

Last month, Sir James Rowcliffe, who, as director of public prosecutions, had promised a fresh review of Mr Brown's case, resigned suddenly following the publication of a story about him in The Sun, which The Sun has since retracted.

It was, perhaps, a pity that Sir James Rowcliffe was not a reader of the *Brixton Chronicle*.

Within hours of the publication of Alison's story, she received a telephone call from Neeta Patel.

Neeta's tone was cold. "Quite a surprise you've sprung on us," she said.

"Yes, I suppose it was," agreed Alison awkwardly.

Neeta reacted angrily. "Do you have any idea what you've done?" she demanded.

"Sorry?" queried Alison, taken aback. "What do you mean?"

"I mean," retorted Neeta, "that you and your wretched paper have placed my clients in serious danger. I've just had Bernice and Althea on the phone, both terrified out of their wits."

Alison still did not understand. "Terrified? Terrified of what?"

"My god," said Neeta, her anger subsiding a little. "You really don't get it, do you? Listen, it's like this. You've told the whole world that Delroy was a police informant. That, in Brixton, places everyone in his family in serious danger."

"I didn't say he was a police informant. I only said he'd offered to give the police information. I didn't say he'd given them any."

"That's not a distinction anyone around here is going to make. If this man Ice is in any way involved in serious crime, then even offering to give the police information about him is something that he and his friends are going to punish."

"But what's the point of doing anything to anyone in Delroy's family? Delroy's already dead, so it can't have any effect on him – and he's the only one who's even offered to give the police any information about Ice."

"It's to discourage others from doing the same thing. The word gets round and the message goes out, 'Grass on us to the police, and we'll get you – and, if we can't get you, we'll get your family'."

Alison was appalled. "But that's completely unfair," she said.

"Fairness has nothing to do with it, I'm afraid," Neeta told her, suddenly conscious of how much longer than Alison she had been working in Brixton. "As far as these people are concerned, it's war out there – and different rules apply."

"I'm sorry," said Alison. "I had no idea."

Neeta recognised that the young journalist was telling the truth. "All right," she sighed. "Nothing we can do about it now, anyway. We'll just have to hope that Ice and his friends have other things on their minds."

Alison was shaken by what Neeta had told her, but later, when she thought about it, she realised that, even if she had known before she wrote her story that there was a risk that it would place Delroy's family in danger, she would still have written it.

She was growing into her profession.

Before the end of the day, however, she received another unpleasant surprise.

Just before five o'clock that evening she got a call on the *Chronicle*'s internal telephone line from Tracey in reception.

"There are three police officers here to see you," Tracey told her. She sounded nervous. "They say they have a search warrant. They said they wanted to speak to Brian, but he's already gone. So, now, they're saying they want to speak to you."

"Tell them I'll be right down," said Alison. She put the telephone receiver down and got up from her desk. She felt her stomach churning and her hands shaking.

She went downstairs.

Standing in the reception area were three men, two of them in police uniform.

"I'm Detective Sergeant Stone from Brixton Police Station," said the one in plain clothes, holding out a Metropolitan Police warrant card in his right hand. In his other hand he had a piece of paper. "I have a warrant here to search these premises for stolen goods," he went on. "I believe you have in your possession a file belonging to the Crown Prosecution Service. It will save us all a lot of trouble if you would just hand it over to me now."

Alison was stunned. "B... but we haven't got it," she stammered. "The CPS have got it back. I sent it to them by courier."

"When was that?" demanded Stone.

"The day before yesterday, first thing in the morning."

"And where exactly did you send it?"

"To the branch it came from. It was in an envelope addressed to the branch crown prosecutor, Mr Rotherhithe. I've even got a receipt for it signed by someone in his office. Shall I get it for you?"

Stone frowned. He took a mobile phone out of his pocket. "Just wait here a moment, if you wouldn't mind," he said, and stepped out of the front door.

The two uniformed officers stayed with Alison and Tracey. No one spoke. Through the large plate-glass window at the front of the *Chronicle*'s offices, Alison could see Stone speaking on his mobile phone. He was making impatient gestures with his free hand.

After a few minutes he rejoined Alison and the others. "They're going to phone me back," he said.

There was an awkward silence, broken, after a few moments, by Stone.

"You have no idea, you people, do you?" he said, accusingly. "Writing about informants on your front page, putting people's lives in danger, interfering with a murder investigation – none of it matters to you, does it? Just so long as you get a good story."

Alison said nothing. She was tempted to ask him which murder investigation he meant, but did not want to make the situation worse.

Stone's mobile rang, and he stepped outside into the street to answer it.

He returned almost immediately, a furious expression on his face. "I'm sorry to have troubled you, Miss French," he announced with cold formality. "I understand the file has been found. Apparently Mr Rotherhithe is away at a conference this week, and the envelope containing the file had been left on his desk unopened to await his return."

With a flick of his head he gestured to the two uniformed officers to leave.

He followed them out.

"Typical CPS," he muttered vehemently as they got outside. "First they don't know they've lost the file and then they don't know they've got it back again."

Repercussions

"Alison French?" enquired the voice on the telephone. It was a man's voice, deep and resonant.

Alison did not recognise it, but guessed from its timbre that the speaker was black.

"Yes, that's me," she confirmed cautiously.

"Hi," said her caller. "My name's Ben Weekes. I'm a youth worker at the Caribbean Centre. I wonder if I could have a word with you about your front-page story last week."

"Yes?" Alison prompted him.

Her tone remained wary. It was exactly a week since the *Chronicle* had carried her report on the questions which Stuart Fox had raised about Delroy's death, and, since then, she had encountered a wide variety of reactions to the story. She had found the local black community particularly sharply divided over what she had written, with some members of the community enthusiastically welcoming its publication, while others were vociferous in their criticism of it – condemning its identification of Delroy as a police informant as an insidious attempt to undermine support for a full investigation into the circumstances of his death. She wondered what line this caller would take.

"It's about this guy Ice," he said. "I'm phoning on behalf of someone who wants to give you some information about him."

Alison was immediately on her guard. If Neeta was right about the risks run by Delroy in offering to supply information about Ice to the police, any offer to provide such information to a journalist like her seemed unlikely to be genuine.

"What sort of information?" she asked sceptically.

"I can't talk on the phone. Could we meet somewhere, do you think?"

Alison suspected a trap – an attempt, perhaps, to lure her somewhere where she would suffer some violent retribution for referring to Ice in her story in the *Chronicle*. But, despite her fears, she could not help feeling intrigued.

"Maybe," she replied cagily. "How about 'The Punchbowl'?" she asked, naming a pub a few doors down from the *Chronicle*'s offices in Coldharbour Lane.

"Ah, yes, that epitome of Caribbean culture," commented her caller ironically. "All right, then. When shall we make it?"

Alison felt a little reassured. A man who used a word like 'epitome' seemed somehow less likely to be liable to do her harm. "Lunchtime today? About one?" she suggested.

"OK. I'll see you there, then. How will I recognise you?"

"Why don't you come and collect me here?" proposed Alison, again playing for safety. "We're only just down the road from The Punchbowl."

"As you wish."

There was something in his voice which made Alison suspect that he was laughing at her. As she put the telephone receiver down, she hoped that she had not made a mistake in agreeing to meet him.

She had already found the past week a very difficult one.

Over the week she had had a stream of telephone calls. Many of her callers had been critical of her story in the *Chronicle* and, when she had tried to defend what she had written, some had become fiercely argumentative.

Two of the calls had been frightening.

The first of these took her completely by surprise. She had answered the telephone as usual, to be met, without warning, by a man's voice telling her with cold vehemence, "You got a big mouth, bitch, an' if you don't shut it, it's goin' to be shut for you. So lay off them lies you been spreadin' 'bout drug dealers and informants, stuff you don't know nothin' 'bout. Got it?" Then the line went dead.

For a moment she just held the receiver in her hand, staring at it, as if transfixed. Then she began trembling, slammed down the receiver, and burst into tears.

She continued to feel badly shaken for the rest of the day.

The second call had come the next afternoon. This time, when she picked up the receiver, she was told with the same icy intensity, "If you don't stop writin' all them lies, bitch, I'm goin' to give you a nice little baby to keep you home where you belong – an' am I goin' to have fun doin' it. Know what I mean?"

This call came as less of a shock to Alison, but still unnerved her. She was sure that both calls had been made by the same man. She was also convinced that, although the

219

caller gave the impression of being black, he was in fact a white man trying to sound like a black man.

She remained on edge, expecting him to call again.

Then she was summoned to Brixton Police Station to be interviewed by officers investigating the murder of Stuart Fox.

She went to the police station accompanied by John Ross.

The interview was conducted by DS Stone.

Alison did not find it a pleasant experience.

Stone began by asking her how she came into possession of the CPS file relating to Delroy's death.

"It just arrived in the post in a brown envelope," Alison told him.

"And when was this?"

"The Monday morning before you came looking for it."

"Yes, I see." Stone did a quick mental calculation. "That would be five days after Mr Fox's body was found." He made a note. "Do you still have the envelope?"

"No, I'm afraid I don't. I just threw it away."

Stone looked grave. "Well, that, I have to say, is a very serious matter. That envelope might well have had on it fingerprints belonging to the person who sent you the file, and that person might be the person who murdered Mr Fox, or, at the very least, someone who might have led us to the murderer. So, by throwing it away, you have destroyed what could have been vital evidence in a murder investigation."

"Now, just hang on," intervened Ross. "There's an awful lot of 'mights' there. What about the file itself? Have you tested that for fingerprints?"

"The lab has subjected it to some preliminary tests, yes," replied Stone. "But, so far, no useable prints have been found on it. And there again, Miss French may well be to blame. In handling the file instead of bringing it straight to us, she may well have wiped off prints which it had on it when she got it."

"Again, that's pure speculation, isn't it?" objected Ross. "Isn't it a fact that paper and cardboard do not take fingerprints very well, and that that's the most likely reason why none have been found on the file?"

"I can't say I agree with you there, sir. I've dealt with quite a number of cases where fingermarks have been found on paper – cheques and so on," said Stone. "And then there's the question of handwriting." He turned back to Alison. "The name and address on the front of the envelope, were they handwritten, Miss French?"

"Yes, they were," replied Alison. "Printed in blue biro, I think," she added, trying to be helpful.

"Yes, well, not as useful as handwriting, of course," conceded Stone. "But it still might have helped us to identify the person who sent you the file."

Ross ostentatiously raised an eyebrow. "Really, Sergeant, that's clutching at straws, isn't it?"

Stone ignored this. "And then there's DNA. If the person who sent the file to Miss French licked the back of the stamp or the flap sealing the envelope, we might have been able to get his DNA from there."

Ross said nothing. As a solicitor who did not specialise in criminal law, he didn't know much about DNA evidence and, although he was sceptical about the possibility that it might have been obtained in the way in which Stone had suggested, he didn't feel able to challenge the officer on the issue.

Stone, satisfied at having finally silenced Ross, moved onto a new subject. "Who was the envelope addressed to?" he asked Alison. "Anyone in particular?"

"Yes, me," replied Alison uneasily.

"I see," said Stone, stressing the words in a way which suggested that he found this information particularly significant. "And why would that have been, do you think?" he asked, contriving to imply that the fact that the envelope had been addressed to Alison indicated that there was some connection between her and the person who had sent her the file.

"I suppose it's because of the articles I've written for the *Chronicle* about Mr Brown's death."

"Yes, I see." Stone sounded unconvinced. "And what about the postmark? I don't suppose you remember anything about that, do you?"

"Yes, I do," Alison replied eagerly. "It was a local postmark, and it was dated two days before I got the file – the Saturday, that would be."

"Yes, well, I'm sure that's very helpful," said Stone dismissively, his tone implying the opposite to his words. "But it really would have been much more satisfactory if we had been able to examine that envelope ourselves."

"I'm not convinced that that would have made any real difference to your enquiries, Sergeant," interjected Ross robustly. "Now, I don't think there is anything else my client can usefully tell you. So, unless you have any further questions for her, may I suggest that we bring this interview to an end. Ms French and I both have other things to do, and I'm sure you do, too."

Stone bristled. "I don't think you and your client realise what a serious position she is in. This is a murder investigation, and I'm seriously considering charging her with obstructing police."

Ross was not inclined to take this threat seriously, but, nonetheless, adopted a more conciliatory tone. "Now just a minute. Ms French has come here voluntarily to give you all the help she can. So, if there is anything else you want from her, I suggest you just ask."

"Well, since you mention it, there is just one thing," replied Stone with a grim smile. "I wonder if Miss French would be kind enough to let us have a set of her fingerprints, so that, if any prints are found on the file, we can check if they are hers – purely for elimination purposes, you understand."

Alison looked enquiringly at Ross.

The lawyer looked about to object, but then seemed to change his mind, and nodded.

"Yes, OK," agreed Alison.

Stone took them to the custody area. As they entered it, Alison noticed a sour, sickly smell in the air. A heavy steel door clanged shut, making her start. At a large counter to their left the custody officer stood writing something in a large book. Other officers moved around calling to each other in loud self-important voices and jangling bunches of keys.

Stone greeted the custody sergeant briefly, and then led Alison and Ross to a short corridor with cells on either side of it. Most of these had their doors open and were empty. Alison wondered which of them Delroy had died in, and suppressed a shudder.

At the end of the corridor, Stone ushered Alison and Ross into a small side room, where he took Alison's fingerprints, taking each of her fingers in turn, and pressing them down on the pad of black ink and then onto the fingerprint form. Alison hated the process, and, as it went on, she felt her face reddening, and the muscles in her hands and arms tightening. She got the impression that Stone was enjoying her discomfiture, and making the procedure last as long as he could. When it was over, she was given the opportunity to clean her hands, but could not get all the ink out of the grooves in her skin. She felt bitterly humiliated.

"Can I go now?" she asked in a small, angry voice.

"Yes, of course," replied Stone, with a satisfied grin. "And may I say how grateful we are to you for your cooperation, Miss French," he added, with exaggerated courtesy.

"I'm sorry about that," said Ross when he and Alison got outside. "It just seemed like the quickest way to get him off your back."

"Yeah, sure," said Alison, concealing her feeling that he had let her down.

She had wanted to tell DS Stone about the threatening telephone calls she had received, but had not had the courage to do so. She did not think he would have been sympathetic.

Later that afternoon, as Alison sat at her desk, wishing that she had never come to Brixton, never met Bertie O'Connor and never heard of Delroy Brown, she received a telephone call from Giles Markham.

Giles had been a student on the same postgraduate course in journalism as Alison, and, to the surprise of everyone who had been on the course with him, he was now a trainee journalist on the *Daily Mail*. He had not done well on the course. His first degree had been in law, and he wrote in a formal and long-winded style which he was reluctant to modify. "I want to be a serious journalist, not some tabloid hack," he had told his tutor loftily. Rumour had it that he had only got his job on the *Daily Mail* because he had an uncle who knew the paper's editor.

Alison had not had much to do with Giles when they were students together, and was surprised to receive a call from him.

"Hi, Alison," he greeted her effusively. "Great story! Everyone here is talking about it."

"Really?" she said, surprised, but gratified.

"Absolutely. And when I mentioned to my editor that you'd been on my course, he was really interested. Asked me to find out what else you've been doing. Said there might be an opening for you here."

"So, what do you want to know?" asked Alison eagerly, excited by the prospect of a job on a national newspaper, and cheered by the vision of an opportunity to get away from Brixton.

"Why don't we meet for a drink?" suggested Giles. "Then you can really put me in the picture."

They arranged to meet that evening in a Fleet Street wine bar described by Giles as 'my usual watering hole'.

Alison got to the wine bar just after seven o'clock that evening, to find it packed with a large number of middle-aged men in suits in varying states of wear and a few smartly dressed women. To get in, she had to squeeze through people standing in the doorway. Inside the air was thick with smoke, and reverberated to the noise of loud conversation and clinking glasses.

She stood just inside the doorway, looking around for Giles, and then caught sight of him edging his way towards her through the groups of drinkers crowded into the bar.

"Hi, Alison, good to see you," he greeted her enthusiastically. He kissed her clumsily on the cheek – something he had never done before.

There seemed to Alison something forced about the

cheerfulness of his greeting and a tired and dispirited look in his eyes.

He went to the bar to get them both a drink. While he was gone, two people sitting at a small table near the door left, and Alison quickly laid claim to their seats.

"Clever girl," Giles congratulated her when he returned. "Never easy to get a table in this place you know. That's because so many of the top lawyers and journalists come here, you see."

He sat down.

"So, how are you Giles?" Alison asked him. "How are you getting on at the *Mail*?"

A pained look briefly crossed his face. "Well, of course," he said, "it's very difficult for me to get my stuff printed because there are so many top journalists on the paper, but you learn so much just being round these people. They're always giving me little tips – the really useful things that no one ever tells you at uni." He did not elaborate.

"Yeah, that must be really great," agreed Alison, although she was not sure that she would enjoy working for a newspaper which never ran anything that she wrote – even if it was a national daily.

"Most of them come in here," Giles told her. "If you hang about for a bit, I'm sure you'll see a few well-known faces."

Alison looked around. She could not see anyone she recognised. She noticed a big, fat man standing by the bar who seemed to be staring at them. Giles waved to him, but the man just turned away from them and leaned across the bar to speak to the barman.

"So, how about you?" asked Giles hurriedly. "Apart from this big story you've come up with, how are you getting on down there in Brixton?"

"Not too badly," said Alison. "I've brought along a copy of my CV and some of my cuttings for you to have a look at."

She opened her handbag, took out a sheaf of papers and gave them to him.

Giles stuffed them into his inside coat pocket without looking at them. "Thanks," he said. "I'll make sure my editor gets them." He took a drink. "Now tell me all about this big story of yours. How did you get onto it?"

"Somebody sent me the CPS file on the case in the post."

"Gosh, that was lucky. And this file, do you still have it?"

"No, I've only got a copy of it. We had to give the original back to the CPS."

"Do you think you could lend me what you've got? I'm sure I'd find it really useful to look at your source material, and see how you've used it."

Alison looked disconcerted, and Giles added quickly, "And I'm sure my editor would be really interested in that, too."

"You know I can't do that," Alison protested quietly. "My boss would never agree to it."

"Oh, come on, Alison. He doesn't need to know, does he?"

A suspicion dawned on her. "You wouldn't, by any chance, be planning to do a story of your own around this file, would you?"

Giles reddened. "Please, Alison," he pleaded. "You've no idea how hard it is to get noticed when you're working on a big paper like the *Mail*. All I need is a break – and you could give me that, just by letting me have a look at that file. I'm sure there must be more stuff in there that you weren't able to use, but that I could do something with."

227

He saw that she showed no sign of relenting, and added quickly, "We could do the story together, if you like, with your byline on it, too. How does that sound?"

"I'm sorry, Giles, I just can't do it."

Alison got up to go. She realised that there had never been any question of her being offered a job on the *Mail*.

It was the next morning that she received her telephone call from Ben Weekes and agreed to meet him at one o'clock the same day.

At five to one she got a call from Tracey downstairs at the *Chronicle*'s reception desk.

"Alison, there's a man here to see you," breathed Tracey down the line, placing a slight, but unmistakable, emphasis on the word 'man', "a Mr Ben Weekes."

Alison went downstairs.

As she entered the *Chronicle*'s reception area, she saw a tall black man standing looking at the display of front pages from back issues of the paper mounted along the wall to her right. On hearing her come in, he turned towards her. He had ebony skin and short, tightly curled black hair. He was wearing a dark blue sweatshirt, faded blue jeans and black trainers. Alison guessed him to be about twenty-five or twenty-six.

"Mr Weekes?" she enquired, approaching him, with her right hand extended. "I'm Alison French."

He took a step forward to meet her and shook her hand. He had a warm, firm grip. "Hi," he said, giving her a friendly smile. "Please call me Ben. I'm more comfortable with that."

Alison found him very attractive. There was something about his eyes which she could not quite define, but which drew her to him.

"OK, thank you," she said, trying to sound as businesslike as possible, "and please call me Alison."

"Right, thanks."

Ben gestured towards the front door with the palm of his right hand. "Shall we go?"

"Yeah, sure."

When they got to the door, he held it open for her, and, as she went through the doorway and turned into the street ahead of him, she caught a glimpse of Tracey giving her a long wink through the big plate-glass window in front of the *Chronicle*'s offices.

Ben followed her out onto the pavement, and they walked the short distance along Coldharbour Lane to The Punchbowl.

The pub was crowded with young people from the shops and offices nearby.

"What'll you have?" asked Ben, as they got inside.

"A Stella, please," said Alison.

"Not a G and T?" he queried, with a gently mocking smile. "And what do you think I should have? A large rum, perhaps?"

She smiled back, but did not rise to the bait.

"No," he pronounced with a grin. "I think I'll have Stella, too."

They made their way towards the bar.

Alison remembered Ben's ironic description of The Punchbowl as 'that epitome of Caribbean culture' and, looking round her, was suddenly uncomfortable, conscious of what he meant.

Along the wall to her right was a crudely painted mural of a deserted beach planted with palm trees and looking out over an empty blue sea into a sunny sky. From the ceiling

229

above her hung fishing nets, while the front of the bar counter, which faced her, was shaped to look like the side of a wooden boat. Standing on the floor at the right-hand end of the counter was a large, highly polished wooden barrel with the word 'Rum' stencilled on it in big black letters, and propped on the bar was a blackboard, on which, inscribed in coloured chalk, was the legend 'Rum Cocktails Our Speciality', followed by a list of names including, 'Cuba Libre', 'Between the Sheets' and 'Ether Nunny'.

A Bob Marley song, commandeered to serve as background music, filtered half-heard through loudspeakers, its muted but insistent strains evoking, as if in protest at its setting, a poignant longing for a distant land and a different way of life.

Alison felt her face reddening.

"I'm sorry about this," she said awkwardly. "You were right."

"How do you mean?" he asked.

"That crack of yours about this place as 'that epitome of Caribbean culture'," she replied, not looking at him.

"Oh, I see," he said wryly. "Yes, it is a bit much, isn't it? Still, don't worry. I don't let it bother me."

She was grateful to him for trying to alleviate her embarrassment, but still felt uncomfortable.

"Would you like something to eat?" he asked her.

"No, I'm all right, thanks," she replied, her appetite dulled by her discomfiture.

Ben bought their drinks and they looked around for somewhere to sit.

Along the side of the room opposite the mural was a row of wooden booths, each made up of two high-backed benches placed face to face across a rectangular table set at right angles to the wall. One of the booths was empty, and they made their way over to it. Alison slid along the bench on the right-hand side of the table until she was sitting next to the wall, and Ben eased himself into the seat opposite her.

They sat facing each other, enjoying an illusion of privacy.

"So, how long have you been working for the *Chronicle*?" asked Ben.

"Just over half a year. And you? How long have you been at the Caribbean Centre?"

"About two and a half years."

Both took sips of their drinks.

Alison decided conversation between them would be easier if they got onto the reason for their meeting.

"You said you had some information for me about this man Ice."

Ben looked around and then leaned forward towards her. "Not me, personally," he said in a low voice. "It's this lad who comes along to the youth club I run. Last night some of the other lads there were talking about your piece in the *Chronicle*, and afterwards he came up to me and asked if I could fix up for him to meet you. Said he had something important to tell you about this guy Ice."

"What's this boy's name?"

Ben shook his head. "I don't know."

Alison found this hard to believe. So far she had been inclined to trust Ben, but now she began to wonder if he was being honest with her.

"You don't know?" she challenged him, her voice edged with suspicion.

"He isn't a lad I know all that well," explained Ben patiently. "He doesn't come to the club on a regular basis, just turns up occasionally. I only know him by his street name."

"And what's that?"

Again Ben glanced around him. "I'd rather not say. If word got out that he was going to talk to you about Ice, he could be in real danger."

Alison seized on this. "In that case, why does he want to speak to me at all?"

"He didn't say," replied Ben, shaking his head.

"This doesn't make any sense to me," pronounced Alison. "How do I know it isn't some sort of trick?"

"All I can say is, I believe this lad is genuine."

"So, why do you think he wants to talk to me?"

Ben took another quick look around. "Well, I'm only guessing, but the word is that this guy Ice is a dealer who uses kids to sell crack on the streets for him, and my theory is that this lad is one of the kids who works for him, but wants out. Problem is, from what I've heard, when other kids have tried to give up working for Ice, the guy's had them beaten up so badly they've ended up in hospital. So, if I'm right, this kid has to find some other way out, and maybe he figures that, if what Ice is up to gets into the papers, the guy will be forced out of business, and won't have any more use for the kids he's got working for him."

"If that's the case, why doesn't this boy go to the police? He could speak to them in confidence on the basis that he wasn't prepared to go on the record, but they could use what he told them to collect the evidence they need to get this man Ice locked up. I know giving information to the police is dangerous, but it can't be as risky as going to the press."

"I did ask him if what he wanted to tell you wasn't something he'd do better telling the police, but he just mumbled something about them being the last ones he'd go to."

"And did he say why that was?"

"He didn't need to. It's just the way most black kids round here feel about the police. And I bet, if you'd been stopped and searched as often as they have, you'd feel the same way."

Alison felt rebuked. "And what about you?" she asked, challengingly. "How do you fit into all this? I mean, your main job is supposed to be to help these kids to stay out of trouble, isn't it? So, if this boy could be putting himself in danger by talking to me, shouldn't you be trying to keep him away from me, rather than helping him to get in touch with me?"

"Yeah, I know," said Ben looking worried. "I've thought about that. But the impression I get from this lad is that he's determined to go to the papers with what he knows – whatever that is – and the way I see it is that he's safer doing that through me than trying to do it through anyone else."

"And how about you? Aren't you putting yourself in danger in getting involved in all this?"

"Yeah, I've thought about that, too, and I won't pretend the risks don't scare me, but, like you said, it's my job to help these kids and that's what I've got to try and do."

"What about the information this boy wants to give me? Do you have any idea what it is?"

"No, I don't. He wouldn't say."

"So, it could be no more than you've already told me – that this guy Ice is a drug dealer who uses kids to sell crack for him."

"Yeah, it could be that, but I don't think it is. That's stuff that's been doing the rounds for some time, and this lad definitely seems to think that what he has to tell you is not something which is already common knowledge."

"Well, I know from the CPS file that Delroy Brown told the police that this guy Ice was into more than just dealing in drugs. Maybe this boy wants to give me some information about the other things he's into."

"Maybe." Ben sounded dubious. "I did get the impression that what he wants to tell you has something to do with Delroy Brown, but, and I don't know why, I don't think that's it."

Alison considered this. "OK," she said at last. "Where and when does he want to meet me?"

"He says we're to be at Brixton Station tomorrow evening at seven o'clock and he'll phone me then on my mobile, and tell me where we're to go from there."

"I'm not sure I like the sound of that. I'll tell you what. I'll go along with it for now, but, if he suggests we go somewhere I'm not happy with, then I'm backing out. OK?"

"Yeah, sure. Makes sense to me."

They arranged to meet outside Brixton Underground Station at a quarter to seven the following evening, and then to walk the short distance to the mainline station together.

Outside the pub, Alison turned to Ben, and asked, slightly awkwardly, "Just one more thing. This guy Ice, do you know, is he black or white?"

He looked at her curiously. "Black," he replied, "probably Jamaican."

"Right, thanks," said Alison abstractedly. She was thinking about her two anonymous phone calls. Had she been wrong in her conclusion that the man making the calls had been white? Of course, Ice being black did not mean that her caller could not have been white, but it seemed to make that more unlikely.

She found these thoughts disturbing. Her earlier sense that she knew something, however little, about her anonymous caller had given her some small comfort, but now she felt this deserting her.

Ben, watching her, asked critically, "So, what? Do you think that this guy Ice being black makes him more dangerous?"

"No, no, it's not that," she reassured him hurriedly, although she was suddenly uneasily aware that she did find the thought of being up against a violent black criminal somehow more frightening than the thought of being up against a violent white criminal.

She told Ben about the anonymous calls and her belief that the man making them had been a white man pretending to be black. "But now, I'm not so sure," she explained, "and it's just being back to knowing nothing about him that's getting to me."

Ben nodded. "Yeah, I can see why that would upset you."

They had stopped outside the *Chronicle*'s offices. Alison could see Tracey watching them with interest through the windows. "OK, then," she said, her hand on the door. "See you tomorrow."

"Yeah, OK," said Ben. "See you tomorrow."

He began to walk off down the street.

Alison watched him for a few moments and then went inside.

"Enjoy your lunch?" asked Tracey, with a mischievous grin.

"Yes, thank you," replied Alison formally, determined not to encourage her.

"It's all right for some," said Tracey with exaggerated envy in her voice. "I could do with a gorgeous fella like that calling to take me out to lunch some time."

"It was work," Alison told her primly.

But Tracey remained unabashed. "Yeah, and nice work if you can get it, that's what I say," she commented, with a grin.

"Very funny," said Alison sarcastically. "Now," she asked, firmly changing the subject, "are there any messages for me?"

Reluctantly Tracey recognised that her fun was over. "Just one," she said. "That solicitor, Ms Patel, phoned. Asked if you could call her back."

Alison went upstairs to her desk and telephoned Neeta.

"Hi, Alison," Neeta greeted her. "Thanks for ringing me back."

"That's OK. What can I do for you?"

"Well, it's like this. You remember when we came back to my place after we went to see Bertie, and we discussed how we might get what Bertie told us admitted in evidence against McKinnon?"

"Yeah, and you suggested that we might be able to do it by getting in our notes of what he said to us."

"Yes, that's right. Well, after giving the subject some thought, I've decided to seek counsel's opinion, that is to get the advice of a barrister, on the subject. And…"

Alison interrupted her, "You'd like to send this barrister a copy of my notes."

"Yes, if that's OK with you."

"Yeah, of course. Shall I drop them in to you tomorrow morning?"

"That would be great. If you can make it about eleven, we could have a cup of coffee together."

"Yeah, I'd like that. So, I'll see you there at about eleven, then."

"I'll look forward to it."

Both women were glad of the opportunity to repair any damage done to their relationship by Alison's last article in the *Chronicle* about the Delroy Brown case and Neeta's angry criticism of the article in their last telephone conversation.

The next morning, as they sat drinking coffee in Neeta's office, Alison asked, "So, if this barrister thinks our notes of our conversation with Bertie could be used in evidence against McKinnon, what happens next?"

"Well, then we'd both have to make formal statements producing our notes as exhibits, and setting out how they meet the requirements set out in those sections of the 1988 Criminal Justice Act which I discussed with you."

"And would you draft my statement for me?"

"I'd probably ask the barrister to do that, just to be on the safe side."

"And then what?"

"Well, once we'd both signed our statements, I'd send them with copies of our notes to the CPS as part of my efforts to persuade them to reconsider their decision not to prosecute McKinnon."

"But wouldn't that give away where Bertie is? And couldn't that lead to him being bothered by police officers sent to interview him by the Police Complaints Authority – or worse?"

"Yes, I have thought about that."

"And not only would that be letting Bertie down after he told us that he didn't want any more to do with the police, but it might result in his moving on and going into hiding somewhere where we couldn't find him, if we need him."

"Yes, I agree, but I think there's a way round the problem. What I propose to do is to send the CPS edited, or, to use the jargon, redacted, versions of our notes, with all references to where we met Bertie deleted from them."

"Will the CPS accept that?"

"I don't see why not. It'll be pretty clear to them that what has been blacked out is the location where we met Bertie, and they should understand why that's been done."

"Sounds good to me."

"Well, I hope it will work."

Neeta turned carefully to the other subject which she wanted to raise with Alison.

"Anyway," she asked, with deliberately friendly interest, "how are you getting on? What sort of reaction did you get to your story last week?"

"Oh, mixed, you know," replied Alison, grateful for this signal that Neeta no longer harboured any ill feelings towards her over the story. "I've had a lot of phone calls about it – some congratulating me on it, some saying I should never have written it."

Neeta nodded understandingly.

Alison did not say anything about the anonymous telephone calls she had received. Nor did she mention Ben.

She asked tentatively, not looking at Neeta, "And how about you? Have you heard any more from Althea or Bernice since last week?"

"Yes, I have. As a matter of fact I had a phone call from Althea just after you rang me yesterday afternoon."

"And how was she?" Alison asked anxiously, still not looking at Neeta. "They haven't had any trouble as a result of my story, have they?"

"No, I'm glad to say they haven't. In fact they seem to

have stopped worrying that there will be any reprisals against them, and to have decided that maybe your story was a good thing after all, as it should put pressure on the CPS to reconsider their decision not to prosecute McKinnon."

Alison felt relieved. "That's excellent. I'm really pleased to hear that."

"Yes, I thought you would be."

Neeta hoped that Delroy's family's optimism would not prove misplaced.

Alison spent the rest of the day working at the *Chronicle*'s offices, but found it hard to concentrate on what she was doing. She kept thinking about the arrangements which she had made for the evening ahead, contemplating them with a mixed sense of excitement and apprehension.

She found herself looking forward to seeing Ben again, but remained unsure of how far she could trust him. Was he what, and who, he appeared to be? She made what enquiries she could to try and find out more about him, but, in the short time available, got no further than obtaining confirmation that there was a youth worker by the name of Ben Weekes on the staff of the Caribbean Centre.

At half past six, she tidied her desk, carefully re-applied her make-up, and prepared to leave for the Underground station. She found that she was feeling increasingly nervous at the prospect of what she might be letting herself in for, remembering the anonymous telephone calls, and imagining some of the more unpleasant things that might happen to her. She felt her heart beating, and noticed that her hands were shaking slightly. She was tempted to telephone Ben, and tell him that she could not keep her appointment with him, but she did not do so, persuading herself that she could always back out later – after she had seen him.

She had not told any of her colleagues about what she planned to do that evening. She did not want people in the office gossiping about her seeing Ben again. What she did in her free time, she told herself, was none of their business. But, as she got ready to leave the office, an uneasy thought occurred to her. What if she went missing? No one would know where to start looking for her. Hastily, she scribbled a note describing her plans for the evening, sealed the note in an envelope addressed to Brian Reid and slipped the envelope into her appointments diary.

She said goodnight to two of her colleagues who were still at work at their desks, went downstairs, and stepped out of the *Chronicle*'s offices into Coldharbour Lane.

Outside, the sky was grey with thick clouds, a thin but persistent rain was falling, and a blustery wind was blowing east along the street from Brixton Road. There were few people around. A tin can, caught by the wind, clattered across the road. A sheet of newspaper flew up and attached itself to the windscreen of a passing car, forcing the vehicle to a sudden stop. The driver, a large black man wearing glasses, got out cursing and removed the obstruction, then got back into the car, wiped his glasses on the front of his shirt and drove off at speed.

Alison pulled the collar of her coat up around her neck, and began making her way down the street, walking into the wind. She put her head down to prevent the rain driving into her face, and felt water seeping into her hair and running down her neck.

She passed The Punchbowl, experiencing, despite her recently acquired distaste for the place, a twinge of envy for those warm and dry inside it.

At the end of the street she turned right and walked along Brixton Road towards the Underground station.

She felt cold and bedraggled.

She saw Ben waiting for her just inside the entrance to the station. He raised his right hand in a greeting, and, as she realised that he had seen her, she felt a quiver of chagrin at the thought of what she imagined she must look like to him. She quickly took a handkerchief out of her handbag and dabbed at her face with it, hoping that her make-up had not run.

As she reached him, he gave her a sympathetic grin. "My, you've really caught it, haven't you?" he commiserated.

She noticed, to her irritation, that he seemed completely dry, untouched by the rain.

"You could say that." She tried not to sound peevish. "How about you? You seem to have missed it."

"Yeah, got here about quarter of an hour ago, just before it started."

Automatically, she looked at her watch. It was ten to seven. That meant he had arrived ten minutes early for their appointment, she noted, experiencing, but trying to resist, this as an indication that he had been looking forward to seeing her again.

"Shall we go?" she suggested.

"Yeah, might as well," he agreed.

There was an awkwardness between them.

They left the Underground station, turning right along Brixton Road.

Neither spoke.

It was getting dark, the grey skies precipitating an early dusk.

Passing under a railway bridge which crossed the road high above their heads, they saw looming ahead of them the side of the viaduct carrying the railway lines bound for the mainline station.

They crossed the entrance to Atlantic Road, and turned right along the pavement between the road and the viaduct.

The rain had stopped, but the wind was still blowing hard.

The shops built into the arches under the viaduct and those standing along the pavement opposite it were all closed, some secured with metal shutters which rattled in the wind.

The street was deserted.

Ahead of Alison and Ben lay the dark silhouettes of the mainline station jutting out from the top of the viaduct, the big metal staircase sloping up to the station from the pavement below it and, high above both, a second viaduct crossing the street mounted on massive pillars.

An empty cardboard box, caught by the wind, came careering past them from behind, making Alison start. Ben put out a hand to steady her, then quickly took it away again.

They went in under the arcade formed by the overhanging station, experiencing, as they did so, an uncomfortable sensation of being hemmed in by the rows of dark pillars on either side of them.

Alison turned to her right to go up the metal staircase leading up to the station above, but Ben touched her on the left elbow, and, as she turned to look at him, shook his head and said, quietly, "No, we need to go up the other stairs – the ones up to the Orpington platform."

Somewhere, far away, they heard a police siren wailing.

They turned left into the broad arch-roofed passageway under the station. The air around them felt damp and cold. Pale yellow light lit the way ahead of them.

Instinctively, they both quickened their steps.

They came to the recess in the left-hand wall of the passageway, turned into it, climbed one flight of stairs and then, after making a turn of a 180 degrees to their left, went up a second flight of stairs to reach the top of the staircase. There they came to a short pathway leading to their right and, taking this, they walked past the ticket office onto the station platform.

Alison looked at her watch. It was exactly seven o'clock.

The small station was bleak and dingy, its platforms exposed to the strong, cold wind.

Along to Alison's and Ben's left stood a dark, motionless figure and, across the railway track from them, two more. Alison knew from previous visits to the station that they were only life-sized statues, but this evening she found their presence somehow unnerving.

There seemed to be no one else on the station.

A young black man appeared on the platform opposite them. He appeared to be talking into a mobile phone. Alison looked enquiringly at Ben, but he shook his head.

A sudden warbling tone very close to her made Alison start. It was Ben's mobile phone. She watched him intently as he answered it.

"Yes," she heard him saying, "I'm OK… No, really, I'm fine… I'm sorry, this just isn't a very good time. I'll call you back later. Bye." There was a note of ill-restrained irritation and impatience in his voice.

He ended the call, keeping the phone in his hand. "My mum," he explained apologetically. "She always rings at the worst times."

Alison giggled, relaxing a little.

The young black man who had been on the platform opposite them had disappeared again.

"This boy we're waiting to hear from," Alison asked, "do you think maybe now you could tell me his name – his street name, I mean?"

Ben hesitated, looking troubled. "Yeah, OK, but not for publication, all right?"

"Of course I'm not going to publish it," she said indignantly, the strain of the situation betraying itself in her voice. "What do you take me for?"

"OK, OK." Ben held up his hands, as if to ward off an attack. "He goes by the name of Jay."

She was tempted to ask him more about Jay, but did not want to make him feel under pressure to say more about the boy than he was ready to.

They relapsed into silence.

Alison, her hair still damp from the soaking it had received in Coldharbour Lane, shivered in the cold wind.

Ben's mobile phone rang again.

He answered it and, almost immediately, she saw his face grow tense, and heard gradually rising anxiety in his voice. She could not hear what his caller was saying, but heard Ben say, "Yeah... But why?... How?... Does he know it's you?... OK, don't worry, we will. Look out for yourself. Bye."

He ended the call, put the phone quickly in his pocket, and, turning to Alison, put his right arm around her shoulders. "That was Jay," he said, beginning to usher her back the way they had come. "He says Ice is onto us, and we've got to get out of here quick."

As they hurried down the stairs from the station, Ben stumbled and almost fell, but the arm which he had round Alison's shoulders helped him to steady himself and, as he regained his balance, he gave her a gentle, encouraging squeeze.

On emerging through the open gate at the foot of the staircase into the passage under the station, they were confronted by two large white men in dark suits. One, who had taken up a position in the middle of the passageway, was stocky with an ugly scar running from the right-hand corner of his mouth to the bottom of his right ear, while the other, who was standing to his left, was taller with long, greasy fair hair and a pock-marked face and, despite the poor lighting in the passageway, was wearing sunglasses.

Alison, although initially frightened at the sight of the two men, remembered that Ben had told her that Ice was black, and felt some relief, assuming that these two men, though still possibly dangerous, were not there looking for her and Ben.

The stocky man with the scar on his face spoke. "Hey, you black bastard," he sneered menacingly. "What you doin', fuckin' with a white woman?"

"Ignore him," muttered Alison under her breath.

The man heard her. "Shut the fuck up, bitch," he snarled. "You're just as bad as he is. Why can't you stick to your own kind? White guys, like us, not fuckin' good enough for you? That's why you're tryin' to stitch up that copper, innit? Just 'cause he's white, and that drug dealer that died was black."

"Leave her alone," said Ben quietly.

"You gonna make me?" demanded the man aggressively.

"No, we don't want any trouble," said Ben, keeping his voice calm.

The taller man in the sunglasses intervened. "But that's just it, innit? You are makin' trouble. You're not wanted around here and we're goin' to make sure you fuck off outta here."

"Yeah, that's right," growled the other man.

He took a step towards Ben.

Ben raised his fists defensively, adopting a classical boxer's stance.

The man in the sunglasses began moving towards Alison.

Alison instinctively took a step backwards, raised her right knee and then pivoting round on her left foot, straightened her right leg and with her right foot, kicked him hard in the groin.

The man let out a yelp and doubled over in pain, and Alison, swivelling round again, landed a kick on his chin, sending him crashing backwards onto the ground, his sunglasses flying off and clattering along the passageway.

Ben and the shorter man, both taken completely by surprise, stood briefly motionless, looking on, until Ben, recovering first, delivered two hard punches, a left and then a right, to the other man's jaw.

The man staggered backwards, his legs gave way under him and he collapsed to the ground.

Ben stepped across to Alison, put his right arm around her shoulders and said urgently, "Come on. Let's go."

They hurried, half running, past Alison's victim lying on the ground moaning, out of the passageway, along Atlantic Road and back onto Brixton Road.

At the entrance to the Underground station they stopped, pausing to regain their breath.

"Where did you learn to fight like that?" asked Ben, regarding Alison with undisguised curiosity.

Alison looked sheepish. "It's really down to my dad. When he heard I'd got this job in Brixton, he went over all protective, and said he wouldn't let me take it, unless I learned how to defend myself properly first. Well, there wasn't any way he was going to stop me taking the job, but, just to keep him happy I took some kick-boxing lessons. And I really enjoyed them, found them a great way of exercising, but I never thought I'd have to use what I'd learnt in them to defend myself. How about you? Where did you learn to box?"

"At a club, when I was a kid. All the kids around where I grew up went there," said Ben, adding with a self-deprecatory smile, "I was going to be the first black British heavyweight champion, you know."

Alison smiled back. "So, do you still box?"

"No, I gave it up years ago."

"Why was that?"

"Just wasn't good enough. Our coach said I didn't have the killer instinct."

"I'm glad," said Alison, and suddenly burst into tears.

Instinctively, Ben put his arms around her.

Alison felt angry with herself for giving way to her tears, but found his embrace very comforting.

"Would you like me to see you home?" he asked.

"Yes, thanks, I would," she said gratefully.

When they got back to the flat which she shared with two other young women in Streatham, she invited him in for coffee.

Her flatmates were both out.

Neither Ben nor Alison felt like discussing the events of the evening, so, as they sat side by side on the settee in the living room of the flat talking over their coffee, they took the opportunity to find out more about each other.

They discovered that they had both taken degrees in English – Alison at Nottingham University and Ben at Warwick University.

"What was your course like?" asked Alison.

Ben considered. "A bit disappointing really, I suppose. I mean, when I was doing English for A level, I really liked it, but at uni it was all a bit…" He paused, searching for the right word.

"Post-modern?" suggested Alison, laughing.

Ben laughed, too, and then, in one of the happier outcomes of a discussion on Post-modernism, he bent forward and kissed her.

Alison, her emotions heightened by what they had been through during the evening, found herself responding to his kiss with unexpected passion and, when at last their lips separated, she looked at him and asked, quietly, "Would you like to stay?"

"Yes, if you'd like me to," he replied softly.

She nodded, and they kissed again.

On Ice

"What did you make of those two last night?" Alison asked Ben, as they sat sharing breakfast in the kitchen of her flat the following morning.

Bright sunshine was pouring through the window and, with the smell of freshly made coffee filling the room and Ben sitting opposite her, she felt ready to examine the dark, unreal and violent events of the evening before.

"You mean Butchered Face and the Sunglassed Kid?" quipped Ben trying to make light of their ordeal, although he still felt badly shaken by it, acutely aware that, if it had not been for the element of surprise in Alison's response to the threat which had faced them, they could both have been badly beaten up – or worse.

"Yeah," said Alison with a wan smile. "Were they just a couple of racist thugs, or was there a connection between them and the call you got from Jay?"

Ben's reply surprised her. "Thugs, yes, they were thugs,

but racist thugs, I'm not so sure. I reckon that was just an act. And believe me, I've come across enough of the real thing to be able to tell the difference. No, to me, all that stuff the guy with the scar was coming out with sounded like something out of a bad film about the American South. Did you notice he even put on a bit of an American accent?"

Alison nodded. "There was something else about him, too," she said sombrely. "From his voice, and especially the way he said the word 'bitch', I'm pretty sure he's the one who made those two anonymous phone calls I got."

Ben reached across the table with his right hand, and gave her left hand a sympathetic squeeze.

"So," she asked, "what exactly did Jay say when he phoned you last night?"

"It was something like 'Ice is onto you. You gotta get out of there.'."

"And what about Jay himself, did he say Ice was onto him, too?"

"No, he said Ice had found out that we were going to be at the station, and knew why we were there, but not who our contact was."

"So, how could Ice have found out what we were going there for? I never told anyone where I was going – let alone why I was going there."

"Me neither."

They thought about this, and then Ben suggested, "Maybe someone overheard us talking in The Punchbowl."

"Yeah, I suppose that's possible," conceded Alison. "OK, but how would Ice finding out about what we were up to explain those two thugs going for us last night. I mean, those two were white, and you told me Ice is black."

"Well, I've never met the guy," said Ben defensively. "He's never been round to my place for tea. But, from what I've heard about him, I'm sure he's black. And it's not just because he's a crack dealer. There are plenty of white crack dealers, too. No, it's a more general thing. Nobody's ever said to me, in so many words 'Ice is black', but the people I've heard talking about him, the way they've spoken about him, make me sure he is. So, I guess those two last night were just a couple of heavies he sent to scare us, or rather, to scare you."

"But, why exactly?"

"Well, the way I see it is this. Ice and his friends want you to stop writing about Delroy Brown's death because where you're going with it looks likely to expose Ice and his criminal activities, but they don't want you to know that that's why they want you to drop the story, so they make it a racist thing. The phone calls, they wanted you to think that they were from black friends and supporters of Delroy's who are angry that you're portraying him as a drug dealer and police informant, while last night the two of them wanted to present themselves as white racists who don't like you trying to hold a white police officer responsible for the death of a black criminal."

Alison was still not completely convinced. "But, if Ice is black, is it really likely that he'd be in with a couple of white guys like those two?"

"I agree it'd be unusual, but I don't think it's impossible."

Alison digested this. "OK," she said. "What do we do now?"

Ben looked concerned. "Don't you think we should back off? I don't know about you, but what happened last night scared the shit out of me."

"Yeah, I know what you mean, but I can't let it go. First those phone calls and then what happened last night – it's like those guys have thrown down a challenge to me, and I want to find out more about them, and why they're trying so hard to scare us off."

Ben gave a sigh of resignation. "All right," he agreed. "But, if it's Ice you want to know about, I think you should leave trying to find out about him up to me."

Alison looked about to object, but he went on, "There are places I can go where you can't, people I can ask about him who wouldn't talk to you."

"Like who?" she queried sceptically.

"Like my Uncle Desmond, for a start," he said with a grin.

She wondered if he was pulling her leg.

"Well, he's not really my uncle," explained Ben. "He's a cousin of my dad's, a bit of a waster – the 'white sheep of the family' my dad calls him. He knows lots of the sort of people who are likely to know Ice, and he may even have come across the guy himself. What's more, he's always had a bit of a soft spot for me, so he may tell me what he knows about the guy – but he's not going to do that if you're there."

"OK," agreed Alison reluctantly, "but you've got to tell me everything he tells you."

"I will."

That afternoon, in search of his father's cousin Desmond, Ben called in on Cool Cabs, a small minicab company based in Atlantic Road.

Cool Cabs was a company with problems, for it was both embroiled in a bitter turf war with one of its rivals and plagued by attacks on its cabs by gangs of street robbers operating in the area. The turf war took the form of a violent vendetta between the drivers working for Cool Cabs, who all identified themselves as Caribbean, and the drivers drawn from the West African community who worked for Home Run, a competing concern based around the corner in Coldharbour Lane. The street robbers, working in twos and threes and posing as customers, but armed with knives and sometimes with handguns, preyed on the cabs operated by both companies, especially late at night. For both reasons, there were times when Cool Cabs and its employees found themselves involved in what was a cut-throat business in more than just a figurative sense.

The company operated from a ground-floor office which had formerly been a shop, and had a large plate-glass front window – now protected by a heavy wire-mesh shutter. Above the window a neon sign, spelling out the name Cool Cabs in green and yellow letters on a black background, flickered uncertainly, as if unsure whether it was meant to be illuminated during the day.

Ben pushed open the door to the office and went inside.

Facing him, as he entered the room, was a sturdy counter topped by a reinforced glass partition and, to the right of this, a heavy steel door. Behind the counter sat a man taking telephone calls and issuing instructions into a microphone, the voices of drivers out in their cars crackling back at him over the radio.

Around the edges of the half of the room on Ben's side of the counter were half a dozen plastic chairs, and, sitting on two of these, two large black men, who, as Ben came in, casually got to their feet.

There was no one else in the room.

Ben began to make his way towards the door beside the counter.

The two large men silently moved in front of him to stand with their backs to the door, blocking his way.

"Me Ben Weekes," he told them, speaking in a strong Jamaican accent which Alison would not have recognised. "Me here to see me Uncle Desmond."

Without speaking, the two men moved aside. One of them nodded to the man behind the counter.

There was a loud click as the door was unlocked. Ben pushed it open and entered a narrow corridor leading to the back of the building. On his immediate left was a door to the area behind the counter and, a little further along, on the same side of the corridor, the entrance to a narrow flight of descending stairs.

Ben went down the stairs, coming to a dimly lit cellar measuring about ten metres long by about four metres wide and serving, officially, as the company's drivers' restroom and, unofficially, as a social club for their friends and hangers-on.

In the centre of the room was a billiard table with a long canopy light suspended above it, and, on a bracket high on the wall to Ben's left, was a large television set. Around the sides of the room stood a dozen or so plastic chairs, three well-worn armchairs and a very old settee. Spread out on the chairs lay a couple of newspapers and discarded on the floor were several empty lager cans. There was a strong, sweet smell of stale cannabis smoke in the air.

Two men were playing at the billiard table. Another was sitting watching television. All three glanced up as Ben came in, and then went back to what they were doing.

Ben saw his father's cousin sitting by himself at the far end of the room in one of the armchairs.

Desmond Weekes was a small man of about fifty with long greying dreadlocks. He had once done some occasional driving for Cool Cabs, but had had a brush with the law, which had led the police to discover, despite much prevarication on his part, that he had never had a driving licence of any sort, and the company would no longer employ him. He continued, however, to enjoy the use of its leisure facilities.

That afternoon, as on many other afternoons, he was sitting quietly in his favourite corner of the cellar smoking cannabis and gazing benignly into space.

Ben walked over to him, and, after they had exchanged greetings, pulled up a chair opposite him, and sat down on it.

Desmond, with New World courtesy, offered his visitor his cigarette, but Ben, wishing to keep a clear head, regretfully declined the offer.

The two men talked, their conversation conducted in low voices and punctuated with much shaking of his head on Desmond's part and much anxious looking around by both men, as they checked that no one was listening to what they were saying.

On leaving Cool Cabs, Ben had to go to work at the Caribbean Centre, and did not finish there until eleven o'clock that evening.

After work, he went to Alison's flat, where she answered the door and let him in. Her flatmates were in the living room watching television, so she took him into the kitchen, closing the door behind them.

She made him some coffee, and he told her about his visit to see his father's cousin.

"It seems," he reported sombrely, "that this guy Ice is really bad news. Apparently his real name is Winston Henry and he's a Jamaican Yardie, a local gangster, who came to this country about two years ago. The word is that he killed three men in a gang war, and had to leave Jamaica in a hurry to escape retaliation, and to avoid arrest for murder. It's also said that these aren't the first men he's killed, and that he got the name Ice from the way he carries out his killings. Apparently, he likes to shoot his victims at point-blank range, looking into their eyes as he pulls the trigger, and is notorious for showing no emotion as he kills them."

Alison shuddered. "Sounds a bit melodramatic to me," she objected. "Are you sure your Uncle Desmond isn't spinning you a bit of a yarn?"

"These Yardies are real psychos," Ben told her grimly. "And, for your information, I'm not just taking Uncle Desmond's word for this. I phoned a cousin of mine who's in the Jamaican police, and he confirmed that there's a man called Winston Henry who's wanted for murder over there, and who's believed to have fled the country."

"So, why don't the Jamaican authorities apply to have him extradited back to Jamaica?"

"Because they don't know where he is. My cousin said they have their suspicions that he's in the UK, but not enough evidence that he's here to apply for his extradition. Apparently, it's quite likely he came to this country using a passport in a false name. It seems he has quite a few aliases. He's known among other things, according to Uncle Desmond, as Carlton Healy and Donovan Haynes."

"OK, so what did Uncle Desmond have to say about what Henry/Healy/Haynes has been up to since he came here?"

"All sorts. He's been dealing crack as I'd heard, but he's also been running prostitutes, and collecting protection money from local businesses, and, apparently, his latest thing is armed robbery. The word is that he's carried out two unsuccessful attempts to hold up security vans, and is expected to have another go at that. Apparently he likes the challenge."

"And what about our friends, Butchered Face and the Sunglassed Kid? Are they part of his gang?"

"Uncle Desmond wasn't sure. He said there have been rumours that Ice has got a couple of white guys working for him, but only rumours. He said, if they're true, Ice would go to a lot of trouble to make sure he wasn't seen with these guys, as he wouldn't want word to get round that he'd got in with a couple of whites. It'd be bad for his reputation."

"And what else did you find out? Did you discover where Ice lives or where he hangs out?"

Ben regarded Alison with a mixture of irritation and concern. "No," he said, almost sharply, "I didn't. Apparently he moves around a lot. When he first came here he used to hang around in the centre of Brixton, driving an old D-reg navy blue BMW with a dark red driver's door, but he doesn't seem to do that any more – too conspicuous, I suppose."

"So, there's nowhere we can go to try and get a sighting of him?" she asked disappointedly.

"No," he replied brusquely, "there isn't."

"Oh well," she said, with a small sigh of resignation. "Still, what you've just told me will make a great story – I mean, about Ice being Winston Henry, and about his being wanted in Jamaica for murder. Of course, I'll have to get confirmation of my facts from the Jamaican police press office or the Jamaican High Commission over here – but I shouldn't have thought that will be too difficult. And then I could end my piece with the question: 'Is this man now in Brixton?'."

Ben looked at her in consternation. "Don't be crazy," he said. "You can't publish all that stuff."

"Why not?" she demanded, reddening.

"Haven't you heard a single thing I've said?" he retorted, his anger rising. "This guy, Ice, is obviously very dangerous – far more dangerous even than I first thought. What you did last night, right, that was brave, but taking on Ice by writing up what I've told you in your paper, that wouldn't be brave, that would be stupid, downright stupid."

"Don't call me stupid," Alison snapped back at him.

Ben, sorry to have offended her, adopted a more conciliatory tone. "I'm sorry. I'm not saying you're stupid. I'm saying writing all this stuff up in your paper would be stupid. You could easily get yourself killed. And it's not just yourself you'd be putting at risk. Think about it. Last night, two men, who probably work with Ice, see you and me together. Today I go and talk to Uncle Desmond. Then you write up all this stuff about Ice. The obvious conclusion Ice and his friends are going to draw from those facts is that Uncle Desmond talked – and that could quite easily be the end of Uncle Desmond. Now, that may not matter to you, but it matters a hell of a lot to me. You really have to understand how dangerous these people are. This isn't a game."

"I never thought it was," said Alison sulkily, but showing some contrition. "OK, give me a bit of time. I need to think about this."

"You do that," he said coldly, his anger rekindled by her refusal to acknowledge that this was an issue on which he had the right to expect her to do as he said.

He got up to go. "Don't worry," he told her. "I'll see myself out."

"No, don't go," she said, tears pricking her eyes. "I'm sorry. If you really don't think I should publish any of this stuff, I won't. I promise."

He relented and stayed.

For the next two or three days, Alison spent a lot of time trying to think of a way in which she could get to write up what she had discovered about Ice, while, at the same time, not exposing herself, Ben or Desmond to the dangers that Ben had warned her about. She thought of making an anonymous call to the Jamaican High Commission in London to tell the staff there that Winston Henry had been seen in Brixton. That might lead the Jamaican authorities to apply for his extradition, and, if they did that, he would be arrested, everything she knew about him would come out into the open, and she could write it up, without her being in any danger from him, and without his knowing where she had originally got her information from. This seemed to her a good idea, but, aware that it was by no means perfect and unsure how Ben would react to it, she decided to wait a few days before broaching it with him.

Then she saw the car.

It happened when she was out covering a story about an old woman who had not won the lottery. The woman had had her handbag snatched by two teenage boys as she was on her way to buy a lottery ticket. She said that she played the same six numbers in every draw, and that, in the draw for which she had been unable to buy a ticket because her handbag had been stolen, her numbers had all come up. Only two people had bought tickets with the winning numbers on them for that draw, and these two had won £3,000,000 each. The old woman said that she was now too frightened and depressed to leave her flat, and so Alison had been sent out to interview her there.

The flat was on the third floor of an ugly concrete tower block on a decaying council estate. Several of the other flats in the block had their windows boarded up, its lifts were not working, and its stairwells were spray-painted with graffiti and smelled of urine. In a corner of a landing on the second floor Alison saw three discarded hypodermic syringes and some small burnt pieces of tin foil. The flat had large brown patches on the inside of its outer walls and smelled of damp.

The old woman made Alison some tea and fussed over her. "You're the first one as 'as been to see me in months," she said, before adding ruefully, "Might've been different if I'd won the lottery."

She looked wistfully at a photograph of a young family on her mantelpiece and, seeing Alison following her gaze, explained, "My daughter and her family. They don't live far away, but money's very tight, so they can't get over to see me much."

Alison was glad to get away. She was already beginning to discover that indiscriminate compassion was not a luxury she could afford in her profession. She also wanted some time to come to terms with an unsettling realisation which had come to her during her interview with the old woman. It had happened when Alison had asked the woman if she could describe the boys who had snatched her handbag, and the woman had replied, "It was two white boys what done it." At that, Alison suddenly became conscious that, until that moment, she had automatically pictured the two boys who had carried out the robbery as black. She was horrified. If anyone had described her as racist, she would have protested angrily, and now could point to her relationship with Ben to refute any such allegation, and yet…

As she walked to the bus stop to catch her bus back to the office, she was so perturbed by the thought that she was, after all, racially prejudiced, that she almost did not see the car – or what was left of it. But, suddenly, there it was in front of her at the side of the road – the wreck of an old navy blue D-registration BMW with a dark red driver's door, apparently taken from another car of the same type.

Alison experienced an immediate thrill of excitement. This must be the car that Ben's Uncle Desmond had told him about – the one that Ice used to drive around in. There couldn't be another one like it in Brixton.

The BMW appeared to have been involved in a head-on collision, and then to have been extensively vandalised. Its front was badly crushed in, all its windows had been broken, and all its wheels had been removed, leaving it perilously balanced on piles of bricks. Alison wondered how long it had been there. She looked inside it. There were wires hanging down from the dashboard and signs that someone had tried to set fire to the upholstery.

She felt disappointed. When she had first seen the car, she had thought that perhaps there might be something in it which might tell her more about Ice, but now there seemed little hope of that. Still, there was no harm in looking, she told herself.

She looked around. The only people in sight seemed to be a group of teenage boys kicking a football around on a patch of grass about fifty metres away from her. She could not tell if anyone was watching her from the windows of the surrounding blocks of flats.

Gingerly, she tried to open the door of the BMW but at

first the door remained stubbornly shut, and the car swayed alarmingly on its piles of bricks. Then, suddenly, the door came open, and the car, after giving one final lurch, settled back into its original position.

The boys stopped kicking their ball, and stood watching her curiously.

Alison, catching sight of them out of the corner of her eye, decided to ignore them in the hope that they would lose interest in her and what she was doing.

She leaned cautiously into the car, carefully testing the effect of each of her small movements on the vehicle's stability. It seemed to be holding steady.

She was not sure what she hoped to find. Something with the name Winston Henry on it, she thought. But then what? What she would really like would be a photograph of the man, but the idea of a criminal like Ice carrying around snaps of himself struck her as absurd, and even the chances of finding a document with a photograph of him on it seemed remote. No, what she should be looking for, she decided, was a document with his name and an address on it – a discarded letter, a used envelope, something like that. At least then she would know where he lived – which would be useful information to pass on to the Jamaican High Commission.

The car's glove compartment was open but empty. The pockets in its doors contained a couple of empty cigarette packets, the torn remains of small cardboard Rizla cigarette paper boxes and a few chewing gum and sweet wrappers, but nothing else.

Alison had the sensation that someone was standing nearby watching her. She quickly looked up and saw, through the broken windscreen, that two elderly women had stopped on the pavement a couple of metres away from the BMW, and were staring at her. When they realised that she had seen them, they quickly began shuffling away.

Alison felt embarrassed. This was pointless, she told herself. She stepped back to get out of the car, but the hem of her coat snagged on the end of the metal runner under the driver's seat closest to her, causing the car to rock unsteadily. She leaned forward carefully to free herself, and, as she did so, caught sight of a small, crumpled ball of yellow paper under the seat.

She picked up the piece of paper and flattened it out. It was small – about nine centimetres across by about twelve centimetres long – had the number HO/RT1 printed at the top, and seemed to be some sort of official form. At first, Alison thought that it was white on the front and yellow on the back, but then she realised that what she had in her hands were two copies of the same form – a white one filled out in biro and, under that, a yellow carbon copy of it.

She examined what was written on the form – and a shiver ran down her spine.

Filled in at the top of the form was the name Carlton Healy, which she immediately recognised as one of the aliases used by Ice and, below that, a Brixton address.

Her hands trembling with excitement, she put her find into her handbag, and walked quickly to her bus stop.

That evening, with some trepidation, she showed the form to Ben, as they were sitting in the kitchen of her flat sharing a take-away curry.

"Do you know what this is?" she asked, taking the form from her handbag and trying to make her question sound as casual as possible.

Ben glanced up from his plate. "Yeah, it's a producer," he replied, not taking much interest. "How did you get that? I thought you said you didn't have a car."

She avoided the question. "What's a producer?" she asked.

He looked at her curiously. "Why do you ask? You must know, if you've been given one."

"I wasn't given it," she said awkwardly, anticipating his next question.

To her surprise, however, he did not ask her where she had got the document, but instead retorted, with feeling, "Lucky you! I've been given enough of the bloody things."

"But what is it? I know you said it's a producer, but what exactly is that?"

"It's a form the police give you if they stop you while you're driving and you don't have your documents with you – you know, your licence, your insurance certificate and your MOT certificate. You've then got seven days to produce them at a police station – or they summons you."

"But why do you keep getting stopped by the police in the first place? Are you really such a bad driver?" she teased him.

"No," he said grimly, "it's because my car is a VW cabriolet, which, though not new, is still in very good condition – and because I'm black. You see, your average copper in Brixton sees a young black guy driving a smart car, and thinks immediately that the driver must be a drug dealer, or the car must be nicked, or both – so he pulls the car over on the pretext of wanting to see the driver's documents. In the first three months after I bought my car, I got stopped more than ten times. So I wrote a letter of complaint to the chief superintendent at Brixton Police Station and, after that, things got a bit better, but I still get stopped fairly often. It's just that now I always make sure I've got my driving documents with me, so I don't have to go through the hassle of being given a producer."

Alison was indignant. "But that's wrong," she protested. "It's racist."

As she said the last word, however, her indignation turned to discomfort, and she felt herself reddening.

Ben did not seem to notice this. "Yeah, it is, but it's what happens," he said laconically. He reached across for the piece of paper in Alison's hand. "So, if you weren't given this by the police, where did you get it?"

Reluctantly, she gave it to him. "I found it," she said nervously.

He looked at the producer, and, as he saw the name written at the top of it, he gave a slight intake of breath, and his expression hardened. "Where?" he asked sharply.

"I didn't go looking for it," she replied hurriedly. "I was out on a job this afternoon, and I saw that car, you know the one that your Uncle Desmond said Ice used to drive. It was in a real mess, and had obviously been dumped, so I thought I'd just have a quick look around inside it – and I found that under the driver's seat."

Ben regarded her with exasperation, tinged with a grudging respect. "You really won't let it go, will you?" he said.

Alison was relieved that he did not seem to be taking what she had done as badly as he might have done. "Look," she pointed out excitedly. "It's got his address on it."

Ben inspected the producer again. "This address doesn't exist," he told her. "I know this road quite well. It's near where I live. The houses in the road only go up to about number 50 or possibly number 60 – and this gives Healy's address as number 98."

Alison felt crestfallen.

Ben began separating the two copies of the producer.

"And there's something I don't understand here," he mused. "When a copper gives you one of these, you get the top copy, the white one, and he keeps the yellow one – that's the one the police use to summons you – but this…" He glanced down at the bottom of the form. "PC McKinnon…"

"What did you say?" exclaimed Alison, jumping up from her seat and coming round the kitchen table to stand behind him, looking over his shoulder. "PC who?"

"PC McKinnon," repeated Ben, surprised by her reaction. "He's the officer who's given Ice this producer. Look, there's his name down at the end. So what's so special about it?"

"Don't you see?" she cried, patting his shoulder impatiently with her right hand. "How this all started was that Delroy Brown, who'd told the police he'd got some information about Ice, died when he got pushed up against the wall of his cell by a police officer called McKinnon – probably because he wouldn't tell McKinnon what he knew about Ice."

Ben mulled this over. "Yeah, but just a minute," he objected, "that McKinnon was a detective in the CID at Brixton, wasn't he? But the copper who's issued this producer is obviously a uniformed officer – a traffic cop based in Croydon, I think, to go by the number he's given here as his shoulder number. So, they can't be the same person. They must just be two coppers who happen to have the same surname. After all, it's not such an uncommon name as all that."

Alison remained unconvinced. "It's too much of a coincidence," she argued, returning to her seat opposite him. "Look, this producer was issued in the November of the year before last, but the incident in which Delroy Brown died happened in September last year. So, isn't it possible that in the ten or so months between the two events, PC McKinnon, the traffic cop based in Croydon or wherever, could have become DC McKinnon, the detective with the CID at Brixton?"

"Seems a bit improbable to me."

"Yeah, but not impossible right? So what we need to do now is to find out when DC McKinnon started working for the CID at Brixton and what he was doing before that."

Ben found Alison's enthusiasm infectious. "OK," he agreed, surprising himself. "And I think I know someone who may be able to give us that information."

"Who's that?" she asked.

Ben looked slightly uncomfortable. "A girl called Marie," he replied, his eyes avoiding Alison's. "We went to school together and I know that, about a year and a half ago, she was doing some sort of administrative job in the Criminal Justice Unit at Brixton Police Station – that's a civilian team that liaises between the police and the CPS."

"So, you're thinking of going to see this Marie to ask her what she knows about DC McKinnon?" asked Alison carefully.

She wondered how he knew so much about what his former schoolmate had been doing only a year and a half previously, a good seven or so years since they would have been at school together.

"Yeah, that's right," he replied quickly. "It'd be easy. She only lives a couple of streets away from my place."

"Why don't we go and see her together?" Alison suggested casually. "I think I'd like to meet this Marie."

Ben looked about to object, but then obviously changed his mind. "OK," he agreed uneasily. "I'll see if I can arrange it."

Their meeting with Marie took place three evenings later at the three-bedroomed terraced house which Ben shared with his mother and father and two younger sisters.

Alison had been amused to find out that Ben still lived with his parents, but had quickly discovered that the subject was one which he did not like to be teased about.

When he showed her into the living room of his home, Marie was already there talking to his mother.

The two women were sitting next to each other on the settee and Alison noted, with a slight pang of jealousy, that they seemed to know each other well.

As Alison and Ben came into the room, his mother got up to welcome them, and, once he had performed the introductions, she invited them to make themselves comfortable in two armchairs facing the settee, while she sat down again next to Marie.

The three women eyed each other speculatively, Alison curious about the nature of Ben's relationship with Marie, while Ben's mother and Marie tried, from their different perspectives, to discern the extent of his involvement with Alison.

Ben caught his mother's eye, and looked briefly, but meaningfully, in the direction of the living room door.

She got the message. "Well, then," she announced, with obvious reluctance, "I'll leave you young people to get on with whatever it is you all got to do."

As she left the room, Alison and Marie continued to size each other up.

Marie was a small, young woman with a round face and a mass of long shiny curly black hair. She had light brown skin with freckles of a darker brown over her nose and under her eyes.

She was, Alison had to admit to herself, with another pang of jealousy, very pretty.

Their conversation did not begin well.

Marie was the first to speak. "So," she challenged Alison with heavy sarcasm and in a strong Caribbean accent which Alison suspected was being put on for her benefit. "You the gracious white lady that's been standin' up for all us poor oppressed black folk by kickin' up a fuss about that black man that died in the police station?"

Alison reddened. "I just tried to report the truth about what happened to him, that's all," she retorted. "The colour of his skin doesn't come into it."

"Ah, but that's where you're wrong," Marie contradicted her. "The colour of his skin, it matters – it matters a whole lot. You see, he wasn't just black, he was a drug dealer, and the more you go on about him, the more white people think that's what black people do – they deal drugs. And those white people, they forget about black people like me and Ben and Ben's mum and dad that's just tryin' to lead honest, decent lives."

Alison felt uncomfortable. She wanted to say that she had never made a point either of the fact that Delroy was black or that he had been arrested for supplying drugs, but, before she could do so, Marie went on, "It's the same with all this stuff about the police all bein' racist. They ain't all racist. When I worked at the police station, some of them were really nice to me – treated me just the same as everyone else. And they got a hard job to do round here. They gotta protect us from all these drug dealers and the like, whether they're white or black."

Alison was tempted to ask her what she made of all the times the police had stopped Ben in his car, but thought better of it.

Ben intervened. "Please, Marie…" he pleaded.

"Yeah, OK," she said, relenting a little. "So long as she realises it ain't all that simple." She looked at Alison. "So, what is it you want to know?" she asked.

Ben felt that things might go better if he asked the questions which he and Alison wanted to put to Marie.

"It's about DC McKinnon," he began.

"Oh, him," interrupted Marie. "Now he was a surly beggar. But he was the same with everyone."

"Yeah, well, what we'd like to know to start with, is when did he start working at Brixton?" said Ben.

Marie thought. "It was a couple of months after I started there, so that would make it in the January of last year. I'm sure it wasn't before that and I don't think it can've been much after that – February at the latest."

"Just over eighteen months ago, then?" suggested Ben, exchanging a glance with Alison.

"Yeah," agreed Marie, "that would be about right."

"And what was he doing before that?" asked Alison, unable to contain herself any longer.

Marie appeared to resent her intervention. "He was in uniform," she replied sullenly. "With the traffic unit in Croydon, I think."

Alison gave Ben a triumphant look.

"But isn't that unusual?" he queried. "Being transferred from being a uniformed officer with a traffic unit to being in CID?"

"Yeah," agreed Marie, "I'd say it is. I don't remember anything like it happening to any other officer while I was there."

"So, what exactly did he do in the CID at Brixton?" asked Alison.

"He was on the drugs squad," replied Marie coldly. "He was supposed to have an informant who passed him a lot of information about dealers in Brixton, and who wouldn't talk to anyone else – and that's how he got transferred to the CID."

Alison tried to ignore her hostility. "And what was the general opinion in the police station about what went on between McKinnon and Delroy Brown the night Brown died?" she pursued.

Marie shook her head. "I ain't goin' to talk about that," she declared. "Fact is I think I've said too much already." She got up to go.

"Sure," said Alison. "And I really am very grateful for all you've told us."

"I didn't do it for you. I did it for him," said Marie pointedly, her head gesturing towards Ben.

He showed her out. Alison could hear them murmuring together in low voices on the doorstep. She wondered what they were saying and whether they were talking about her.

"So how long did you go out with her for?" she challenged Ben when he returned.

He looked embarrassed. "Only for about six months," he said sheepishly. "And it's all been over between us for about a year and a half – long before I met you."

He took Alison back to her flat in his car. It was the first time she had been in it. She wondered if they would be stopped by the police. She almost hoped they would, so that she could give the officers who stopped them a piece of her mind.

On the way they discussed what Marie had told them.

"Now at last I think we have the explanation for why McKinnon went for Delroy when Delroy refused to let

McKinnon have the information that Delroy had on Ice," pronounced Alison with satisfaction.

"Why?" prompted Ben. "What's your theory?"

"OK, listen. This is how it goes. Marie has confirmed that, before McKinnon joined the CID as a member of the Drugs Squad at Brixton, he was a traffic cop, right? We also know from her that he got himself into the CID by getting information about dealers like Ice from an informant. Now that, I reckon, explains how he came to give that producer to Ice. His new informant obviously tipped off McKinnon the traffic cop that Ice was a dealer. So McKinnon, as part of his campaign to get himself into the CID, stopped Ice on the pretext of asking for his driving documents but with the real intention of catching him in possession of drugs. However, Ice obviously didn't have any drugs on him because McKinnon clearly didn't arrest him, but only gave him a producer. Now that must have rankled with McKinnon. So when he heard that Delroy was offering to give the police information about Ice, McKinnon went to Delroy's cell to get that information to use to get back at Ice for making a fool of him the first time they met. But Delroy had told the officers who interviewed him that he was only prepared to give his information about Ice to a senior officer, and, according to that CPS lawyer, Stuart Fox, he would almost certainly have refused to give it to McKinnon. And, if McKinnon felt that Delroy was denying him the chance of getting back at Ice, that would explain why McKinnon got angry and went for Delroy."

Alison sat back in her seat with her arms folded in front of her. "What do you think?" she asked.

"Hmm," pondered Ben dubiously. "I don't know." Then, suddenly slamming on the brakes and bringing the car to a screeching halt, he shouted, "No! No! No! No! No!"

Alison was thrown forward in her seat, almost striking her head on the windscreen, before being thrown back by her seatbelt. A car travelling behind them swerved sharply to avoid running into the back of Ben's car. The driver hooted loudly and, as he drove past them, thrust his right fist out of his window with its middle finger extended upwards.

Alison looked at Ben in astonished concern, tinged with anger. "What's the matter?" she demanded. "No wonder you get stopped by the police if that's how you drive. What do you mean, 'No! No! No! No! No!'?"

Without answering, Ben put the car back into gear, and drove it into a small side street on their left, where he stopped, switching off the engine.

He turned to Alison. "I'm sorry," he apologised. "It's just that it suddenly came to me that you're wrong – about as wrong as you could be. Look at the chronology. About two years ago, Ice comes to the UK, apparently using the false name Carlton Healy, and almost certainly entering the country in breach of the immigration laws. Three or four months after he gets here he is stopped in his car by PC McKinnon, the traffic cop. Now, there are some things about this stop which have been bothering me ever since you first showed me that producer. First of all, why didn't McKinnon keep the yellow copy of the producer? Without it, there's no way the police could prosecute Ice if he failed to produce his documents – which is the whole point of the exercise. Secondly, the address which Ice gave McKinnon doesn't exist. Now, perhaps McKinnon didn't know that, but, in my experience, if he wasn't familiar with the address, he would almost certainly have called in on his radio and asked for a PNC check to be made on it, and, when he was told that the address was a false one, he could, and normally would, have arrested Ice. And lastly, if

Ice has a Jamaican accent, as I bet he does, McKinnon would almost certainly have radioed in for a check to be made on his immigration status – and, if he'd done that he'd presumably have found out that Ice was an illegal immigrant, for which again, he could, and normally would, have arrested him. But McKinnon obviously didn't arrest Ice, because, if he had done, Ice would no longer be here – he'd have been deported. So the question is: Why didn't McKinnon arrest Ice?"

He paused for her to take in what he had said, and then continued, "And what happens next? About two months later, McKinnon is transferred to the Drugs Squad in Brixton – because, apparently, he has access to an informant able and willing to supply him with high-grade information about Brixton's drug dealers. Now, who better to do that than one of those dealers themselves? And who does McKinnon know, who we know is a drug dealer?"

"Ice," exclaimed Alison, "so you're saying that Ice is…"

"McKinnon's informant," pronounced Ben triumphantly. "That's the trade-off. McKinnon doesn't arrest Ice as an illegal immigrant (which would have meant Ice being deported back to Jamaica to face almost certain trial for murder and possible death at the hands of his enemies), and, in exchange, Ice becomes McKinnon's informant – as a result of which McKinnon's career enjoys a considerable boost."

"But your Uncle Desmond told you that Ice is still committing all sorts of offences himself. Not just drug dealing, but running prostitutes, demanding protection money and even armed robbery."

"Yeah, well, up to a point he'd probably have to go on engaging in criminal activities in order to continue to be accepted in the circles which give him access to the information he's passing to McKinnon."

"Yeah, OK, maybe up to a point, but from what your Uncle Desmond has told you, Ice has gone way beyond that point – and surely McKinnon must know that."

"I think he must, but, if he knows, or suspects, the full extent of what Ice is up to, I think he's got a problem. I can't believe that, in those circumstances, he should go on using Ice as an informant, but, if he turns Ice in, it's not going to do his career any good. So that may be one reason why McKinnon is allowing Ice to get away with what he's been doing, but there may be another. McKinnon may be getting a cut of the proceeds of the offences Ice is committing – it wouldn't be the first time a copper has been corrupted by an informant."

Alison looked sombre. "So, when Delroy Brown turns up offering to give the police information about Ice, McKinnon has to do something about it. So he goes to Delroy's cell, not to get Delroy to give him the information he has about Ice, but…"

"To make sure that Delroy does not give that information to any other officers."

"And," went on Alison, shaking her head at the thought of Delroy's plight when McKinnon appeared in his cell, "Bertie O'Connor, the man who was in the cell next to Delroy's, has told me and Neeta Patel, Delroy's family's solicitor, that he heard Delroy shout out, 'Leave me alone, Mr McKenna' or something like that. So it looks as if Delroy not only knew Ice, but also knew McKinnon, and was probably aware of the association between the two – which explains why he'd told the officers who'd interviewed him that he was only prepared to give the information he had about Ice to a senior officer. Poor Delroy. When he saw McKinnon coming into his cell, he must have been terrified, for, knowing what kind of man Ice is, he probably thought right from the start that McKinnon was there to kill him and shut him up once and for all."

She stopped, thought for a moment, and then added, "But do you think that's right? Do you think that, when McKinnon pushed Delroy up against the wall of his cell, as the pathologist Dr Houseman suggested at the inquest, McKinnon intended to kill Delroy?"

Ben considered this. "It's possible," he said slowly. "But I think it's unlikely – and would be difficult, if not impossible, to prove. No, I think it's more likely that McKinnon just intended to rough Delroy up a bit, frighten him into keeping his mouth shut."

"But," said Alison, "according to the coroner at the inquest, that would still make Delroy's death manslaughter."

"Yeah," agreed Ben. "For which McKinnon should be prosecuted."

They sat for a few moments in silence, both thinking about the final confrontation between Delroy and McKinnon and the implications of what they had just worked out.

Finally, Alison spoke. "I wonder," she speculated, "if Jay knows all this or, at least, about McKinnon's relationship with Ice, and that's why he didn't want to take what he knows about Ice to the police."

"You could be right," said Ben, "and if you are, the poor lad is in very serious danger." He thought for a moment and added, "And, if Ice even suspects that we're close to discovering his relationship with McKinnon, so are we."

Alison took his hand. "I think we should take all this information to Neeta Patel. She will know what to do."

"Yeah, OK," agreed Ben, restarting his car.

Tip-Off

"I'm sorry, I don't think I can help you," said Neeta Patel.

Alison and Ben, who were sitting facing her across the desk in her office, looked at her in dismay.

It was the morning after their meeting with Marie and they had just finished explaining to the solicitor why they had come to her for her advice.

"Why not?" Alison's voice was taut with disappointment.

Neeta, who had listened to what Ben and Alison had told her with growing concern, hesitated before replying, the silence punctuated by a heavy patter of rain on her office window.

The telephone on her desk rang, making both her visitors start.

Neeta answered it. "Can you hold my calls, please? I'm with clients."

She put the receiver down and turned back to Alison and Ben. "First of all," she said, "let me make it clear that

I think you do need legal advice. You don't have much evidence to support this theory of yours, but, if you're right, and I'm inclined to think you probably are, then I agree that the situation you've got yourselves into is a serious and complicated one, and you and this boy Jay are almost certainly in real danger."

"Then why can't you help us?" asked Alison, close to tears.

"My problem," explained Neeta, "is that what I face here looks to me like what we lawyers call a conflict of interests. What I mean by that is that I don't think I can advise you in this matter, because it is one in which I already represent Delroy Brown's family, and what is in their best interests may not be in yours. Why I say that is this. My duty to Delroy's family is to pass on to them what you've told me, and probably to give it any publicity which may help to persuade the DPP to prosecute DC McKinnon for causing Delroy's death. But, from your point of view, the more people I tell what you've told me, the greater the danger you're in is likely to be."

Alison looked worried. "So what are you going to do?" she asked.

"Well, the Law Society says that in situations like this, I have to stop acting for both parties. That is, I have to send both you and Delroy's family to different firms of solicitors."

"But," protested Alison, "if we go to another firm of solicitors, how do we know we can trust them? I mean, it might turn out that they represent Ice or one of his friends."

Neeta tried to reassure her. "Don't worry. If, in the course of consulting a solicitor, you disclose something which it is in the interests of another of his or her clients to know, but which you don't want that person to be told, then the solicitor has to respect your wishes, and has to refer both you and the other person concerned to different solicitors. So, even if, by bad luck, the solicitors you go to already act for Ice, they can't pass on to him anything you tell them, unless you say they can."

Ben was sceptical. "That's all very well in theory, but can we be sure it's how things would work out in practice?"

Neeta had to admit to herself that he had a point. She knew of some local solicitors who were rumoured to be too close to the criminals they represented and others who were simply too indiscreet to be trusted with what Alison and Ben had told her. There was also the time factor. Alison and Ben could be in imminent danger, and needed advice without delay.

She took a deep breath. "Very well. I'll see what I can do for you, but you've both got to accept that there may come a time when I have to send you elsewhere. Understood?"

Alison and Ben looked at each other and nodded.

"Yes, thanks," said Alison, speaking for both of them. "That's fine."

"Right," said Neeta briskly. "What I'm going to suggest to you to begin with is more common sense than legal advice. First of all, don't tell anyone else, anyone at all, what you've just told me. Second, and this applies mainly to you, Alison, try to do all you can to give the impression that you've lost interest in this story, that it's run its course, and that there's nothing more to say about it."

"OK," agreed Alison quietly. She half wished that this were true.

"Next, I suggest that you avoid being seen together."

Alison and Ben exchanged glances.

Neeta smiled. "I'm not saying that you have to stop seeing each other. Just be discreet about it. And, if either of you is out on your own, I'd advise you to stick to places where there are plenty of people about, and not, for example, to hang around on deserted railway stations! I'd also suggest that you avoid being out at night."

"That's going to be impossible for me," objected Ben. "I have to work most evenings."

"All right. I understand that, but try to make sure that, whenever possible, you have other people with you when you're travelling home from work, and try to do as little of the journey as you can on foot. Use your car, if you can, even if you're only going a short distance."

"Yeah, OK," agreed Ben. "I get the idea."

"And that boy, Jay – I think you should try to get him out of London. Is there any way you can do that?"

"I've got some relatives up in Liverpool who would probably be prepared to put him up," said Ben. "The problem is, though, that since he rang me that night on Brixton Station, I haven't seen him, and I haven't been able to get in touch with him. I've got his mobile number, but, whenever I've tried to call him, I've got no reply, only his answering service."

"Why don't you leave a message for him?" suggested Alison.

Ben shook his head. "I don't want to do that, just in case his phone has fallen into someone else's hands."

There was an uncomfortable silence. Alison shivered.

"Well," said Neeta, "I suppose all I can suggest is that you keep trying his number."

Ben nodded.

"Now," went on Neeta, "we come to the difficult bit. I think we've got to take what you've told me to the police."

Alison and Ben looked apprehensive.

"Not the Brixton police," Neeta reassured them quickly. "I agree that you can't go to them. I'm not saying that, if there is a relationship between DC McKinnon and this man Ice, all the officers in Brixton will be in on it. In fact, I think that, in the nature of things, very few of them will be. But I accept that, if there is such a relationship, we have no way of knowing which other officers at Brixton are in on it, and which are not. There's also the risk that, even if we speak to an officer who's not in on it, he or she may pass on what we've said to an officer who, though the first officer is unaware of this, is in on it. So, I think we need to go to someone on another force."

"But who?" asked Alison.

"Well, what I'd like to do, with your consent, is to take what you've told me to Chief Inspector Elliott of the complaints unit of the Surrey police. He's the officer who carried out the original investigation into Delroy Brown's death for the Police Complaints Authority, which means that he already knows about this case, but, at the same time, he should be completely independent from the police at Brixton. I also see going to him as a possible way of reconciling your interests with those of Delroy's family, since the only way you're really going to be safe from this man, Ice, is if the police investigate and arrest him, while, at the same time, if it's Elliott who carries out the investigation, and he finds a link between Ice and McKinnon, that should further the campaign by Delroy's family to get McKinnon prosecuted. How does that sound?"

"Yeah, good," said Ben.

Alison was not so sure, but had nothing better to suggest. "Yeah, OK," she agreed.

It did not take Neeta long to get Elliott on the telephone.

"Good morning, Chief Inspector," she began. "My name is Neeta Patel, and I'm the solicitor representing the family of Delroy Brown, the man whose death at Brixton Police Station last year you investigated for the PCA."

"Yes, Ms Patel, I remember you from the inquest." Elliott's tone was cordial, but guarded. "What can I do for you?"

"Well, there have been some important developments in the case, and I'd be grateful if you would very kindly let me visit you at your office to discuss these with you."

Elliott suspected that the 'important developments' referred to by Neeta were no more than the discoveries made by Stuart Fox and the dead prosecutor's recommendation that the police dealing with the case investigate whether DC McKinnon had been involved in enquiries into this man, Ice. Elliott had learned of these developments unofficially, but had received no formal request from the CPS to carry out an investigation such as that recommended by Fox, and had no inclination to do so. He could not see the point. McKinnon had said all along that he had gone to Brown's cell because he believed that Brown had information on a case he was working on, and it had always been possible, even likely, that Brown would have refused to give McKinnon the information he wanted. Fox's discoveries made this scenario more probable, but hardly gave McKinnon a motive for assaulting Brown. Elliott also felt very reluctant to become involved in an investigation into the work being done by officers of another police force on an ongoing case. He suspected, however, that this was exactly what Ms Patel wanted to try and make him do in the hope that the outcome of his investigation would put pressure on the CPS to prosecute DC McKinnon.

"Why don't you set out these 'important developments' as you call them, in a letter to me?" he suggested.

Neeta wrinkled her nose in irritation. "The matters which I wish to discuss with you are not matters which I would be happy to commit to paper at this stage."

Elliott's interest increased a little, but he still felt inclined to suspect a ruse designed to engineer him into agreeing to a meeting with the solicitor. "All right then," he countered, "perhaps you could tell me a little more about what it is that you want to come here to talk to me about."

"It really isn't something I want to speak about over the phone." A note of exasperation was beginning to creep into Neeta's voice.

Feeling that this confirmed his suspicions, Elliott was brusque. "In that case, I really don't think I can help you."

"Very well, then," sighed Neeta. "You give me no choice. The position is this. When Mr Brown was interviewed, he offered to give the police information about a man known by the street name Ice. I now have strong grounds for believing that this man Ice is a dangerous criminal wanted for murder in Jamaica and currently involved in the commission of serious offences, including drug dealing and armed robbery, over here – and that he is a police informant working for DC McKinnon."

There was a moment's silence at the other end of the line. Then Elliott said quietly, "Please do not say any more, Ms Patel. If it is convenient to you, I will see you here at two o'clock this afternoon. In the meantime, please, I would urge you not to repeat any of what you have just told me to anyone, whether a police officer or civilian, and, if, as I imagine, you have received this information from someone else, I would urge you to ensure that that person does not repeat it to anyone else either."

Alison and Ben left Neeta's office separately, Ben first and Alison a few minutes later.

Ben collected his car from the side street where he had parked it and drove home. When he got back, he made several attempts to telephone Jay, but continued to get only the boy's answering service.

Alison caught the bus back to her flat in Streatham. She sat on the top deck of the bus next to a window. She felt tired and on edge. Some teenagers in front of her began jostling each other and shouting, and she scowled at them irritably, wondering why they were not at school. When she got home, she shut and locked the door of her flat firmly behind her. She telephoned Brian Reid to apologise for not being at work and to say that she was not going to be in for the rest of the day. "I'm sorry," she told him. "It's a personal problem that I need some time to sort out. I'll take the day as annual leave, if you like."

Reid heard the strain in her voice. "That's all right," he said. "Take as long as you need. Is there anything I can do to help?"

"No, thanks. It's something I have to sort out myself." Alison felt close to tears. She wished she could have told Brian the whole story.

That afternoon Neeta and Alison met at Waterloo Station, and travelled to Guildford by train together. As the train left the station, Neeta tried to engage Alison in conversation, but found her unresponsive. The two women lapsed into silence, and Alison stared unseeing out of the window as the train took them through the south London suburbs and out into the Surrey countryside.

Ben, meanwhile, set out for Guildford in his car. As he drove out of Brixton, he found himself constantly checking in his mirrors to see if he was being followed.

He wondered what he would do if he discovered he was. Outside London, on the A3 just south of Tolworth, a police car came up behind him at speed with its two-tone siren sounding and its blue light flashing. Ben, imagining briefly that he was about to be intercepted by friends of DC McKinnon's intent on preventing him talking to Chief Inspector Elliott, experienced a moment of panic, and tensed in his seat, his grip tightening on the steering wheel, but the police car swept past, disappearing down the road ahead of him. He gazed after it, feeling shaken and unnerved. A cold trickle of sweat ran down the side of his body from his right armpit.

When he got to Guildford, he drove to the city's railway station to pick up Neeta and Alison. Arriving there about twenty minutes before their train was due, he parked in the station car park, took out his mobile phone, and made another attempt to telephone Jay.

This time he got through.

When Neeta and Alison emerged from the station a few minutes later, they saw Ben standing by his car, and walked over to join him. All three got into the car, and Ben drove them the short distance to Surrey Police Headquarters.

"I've just managed to contact Jay," announced Ben on the way. "He's agreed to leave London, but not to go and stay with my relatives. He says he has friends who can put him up, though he didn't say where. I don't think he trusts me completely."

"Well, so long as he's safe," said Neeta. "That's the main thing."

"Yes, it is," agreed Alison, "but did he say what it was he wanted to tell me about Ice?"

"Yeah, he did," said Ben, "but it wasn't quite what I was

expecting. He said he reckons Ice is bribing the police to keep them off his back."

"So, does that mean that your theory that Ice is working for McKinnon as an informant is wrong?" queried Alison.

"Not necessarily. Listen. What Jay has actually seen is this: he's twice seen Ice talking to a big white man who Jay suspected was a copper and who he has since seen coming out of Brixton Police Station. Both times, Ice and this suspected copper kept looking around them, as if they wanted to make sure no one was watching them, and both times Ice handed over what looked like a brown envelope to the other man. Jay assumed the envelope contained cash, and that's why he believes Ice is bribing the police. But there are a couple of other possibilities which fit in with my theory. It could be either that what Ice was handing over was not money, but information, or it could be that it was money, but not a bribe so much as a cut of what Ice is making from his criminal activities."

"But why is Jay telling you all this now, when he wouldn't tell it to you before and had us going through all that cloak and dagger stuff at Brixton Station?"

"Yeah, I asked him about that, and he said he wanted to meet you to give you the information personally, because he wanted to make sure that it got through to you. Like I said I don't think he trusts me completely."

"So, what's changed?"

"Well, he didn't say exactly, but he knows I took you to Brixton Station to meet him, and I got the impression that he took that as a sign of good faith which meant that he could trust me to pass on to you what he told me."

"Yes, I see. I suppose that makes sense."

"And he's given me another bit of information which I think will interest your Chief Inspector Elliott."

"What's that?"

"Wait and see," replied Ben tantalisingly.

Alison felt irritated, but unable to summon up the energy to press him to answer her question.

Ben, preoccupied with his own thoughts, did not notice her subdued mood. "By the way," he said, "when we see Elliott, I'd rather we didn't tell him Jay's name – at least, not unless we really have to."

The two women agreed.

When Chief Inspector Elliott was informed that Neeta had arrived to see him, he was a little disconcerted to hear that she was not alone, but he gave instructions for all three members of her party to be shown to his office.

When they were ushered in to see him, he got up from his seat behind his desk to greet them.

Of Neeta's two companions, he remembered seeing the young woman with Delroy Brown's family at the inquest, and concluded that she must be the solicitor's assistant. He assumed that the young black man must be the source of Neeta's information about Ice, and deduced that he was a member of Brixton's criminal fraternity.

Neeta thanked him for agreeing to see them, and introduced Alison and Ben. "This is Ms French. She's a journalist on the *Brixton Chronicle*. And this is Mr Weekes, who's a youth worker at the Caribbean Centre in Brixton."

Elliott stiffened. "I'm sorry," he said. "I can't possibly discuss the matters you mentioned on the phone this morning in the presence of a member of the press, and I have to say, Ms Patel, that, in my view, it is very irresponsible of you to have brought Ms French here, and I hope you have not disclosed to her any of what you told me when you rang me this morning."

Neeta was briefly taken aback, but quickly recovered. "Chief Inspector," she said firmly, "the information which I gave you on the telephone this morning was all given to me by Ms French and Mr Weekes – and I think, perhaps, you should be grateful that Ms French has authorised me to discuss what she has uncovered with you, rather than rushing into print with it."

Disconcerted, but attempting to conceal his discomfiture, Elliott became conciliatory. "I'm sorry," he apologised. "I had no idea."

This, he could see, was going to be difficult. He wanted to find out what Alison and Ben knew about DC McKinnon and this man Ice, but he did not want to risk finding himself being quoted in a newspaper, either on the subject of Delroy Brown's death in custody or on anything to do with anyone who was, or might be, a police informant.

"Please, why don't you all sit down?" he suggested, gesturing to three chairs placed facing him across his desk, one of which had just been brought in by his secretary.

His visitors accepted his invitation, and he resumed his seat opposite them.

He looked at Alison. "Ms French," he said, "I do hope you will forgive me for misunderstanding your status in this matter, but the issues which Ms Patel has indicated that you wish to discuss with me are very, very sensitive indeed, and, before we go any further, I must insist that anything I say here today is, so far as your profession is concerned, very strictly off the record. Do you understand that?"

Alison nodded. "Yes, of course," she replied awkwardly. She felt a long way out of her depth.

Elliott got the impression that she was afraid of him. This, he thought, was no bad thing, since it should discourage her from quoting him in her newspaper. Still, he reminded himself, you could never be too careful in dealing with the press, and this, he felt, was an occasion on which to concentrate on listening and asking questions, and to exercise great caution in divulging any information he had or expressing his opinions on anything he was told.

"Right, then," he suggested, "perhaps it would be best if you started by telling me everything you know about this man Ice, and what it is that has led you to believe that he is a police informant employed by DC McKinnon."

Alison and Ben looked at Neeta, who nodded and began recounting what they had told her.

When she had finished, Elliott looked grave. It was clear to him that there was enough in what Alison and Ben had unearthed about DC McKinnon and Winston Henry or Ice to require thorough investigation and that, if Ben's theory about the nature of the relationship between the two men proved correct, the repercussions would be very serious indeed, but, at the same time, he wanted to make sure that his visitors did not harbour an inflated notion of the strength of the case which they had put to him.

"Thank you," he said carefully. "I am very grateful to you for bringing these matters to my attention, and I assure you that I take them very seriously, but as you, Ms Patel, will appreciate, so far as DC McKinnon and this man Henry are concerned, there's very little in what you've told me that amounts to evidence which could be used against either man in a court of law."

"Yes," agreed Neeta, inclining her head forward slightly. "I know. But then, that's precisely why we've come to you – so that you can investigate what we've told you, and find out the truth about Henry and his relationship with McKinnon."

Elliott wondered how much the solicitor knew about how the police operated, and whether she realised the problems he would face in carrying out the investigation she proposed. Yes, he could check up without much difficulty on whether there was a man called Winston Henry wanted for murder in Jamaica and known by the street name Ice, but after that, the going would get much harder. If Henry was a police informant working for McKinnon, that fact would, if the system was working properly, be known to only two officers, McKinnon himself and a senior officer, probably DCI Greaves, both of whom could decline to discuss the issue on security grounds. Nor was that the only problem. Just ascertaining whether Henry was in the country might not be easy, and, even if it was established that he was, locating his exact whereabouts might still prove difficult. Then, if he were traced, there would be the problem of investigating his alleged criminal activities. The obvious way of doing this would be to conduct a surveillance operation against him, but, if he was living in Brixton, to mount such an operation without the knowledge of the Brixton Police would present considerable difficulties, and could have undesirable, and perhaps even dangerous, consequences.

To Neeta he said simply, "That may not be as easy as you seem to think, Ms Patel. Even finding Henry could be problematic."

Ben leaned forward in his chair. "Not necessarily," he said.

Everyone else in the room looked at him.

"Why do you say that?" asked Elliott sharply. "Do you know something about this man that you haven't told me?"

Ben explained. "As Ms Patel has already mentioned to you, this afternoon, while I was waiting for her and Ms French at the station here, I spoke on the phone to the lad who originally asked me to contact Ms French on his behalf, and he not only told me about the transactions which he has witnessed between Ice and the man he believed to be a police officer and we think was McKinnon, but he also gave me some information which should save you the trouble of having to go looking for Henry."

"And what was that?" Elliott's scepticism was obvious.

"He told me that Ice is planning to hold up a security van in a place that is in your area."

There was a moment's silence.

Elliott had learned from hard experience to treat with great caution third-hand information about offences which were said to be being planned by others, especially when, as in this case, that information came from someone with whom he had had no previous dealings, and was said to emanate from a source whose reliability was, so far as he was concerned, completely untested, and, although he knew that such tip-offs occasionally provided the basis for successful police operations, he doubted whether this particular piece of information would prove as helpful as it sounded.

"That's very accommodating of him," he said drily. "And exactly where and when is he going to carry out this robbery?"

Ben consulted a piece of paper he was holding. His hands were shaking slightly. "This Friday afternoon, on a Castle Road in a place called Chipstead, just off the A23."

"I know the place you're talking about," interrupted Alison excitedly. "It's a narrow road which runs down from the top of a hill into the valley below. I used to go riding there when I was a kid."

Ben, a little disconcerted by her intervention, acknowledged it with a brief nod, but continued with what he was saying to Elliott. "And, according to my road map, it's in Surrey, which means it's on your patch, yeah?"

Elliott suppressed a smile at Ben's use of the word 'patch'. He wondered which television programme the young man had got it from. "I think so," he said, looking slightly embarrassed. He got up and walked over to a map on the wall on his right. "You see, a lot of places in that area that people think of as being in Surrey, are actually in the London boroughs of Sutton and Croydon, and so come under the Met." He examined the map, running his right forefinger over a small area of it. "No, you're quite right. It's quite close to our boundary with Croydon, but it's in our area."

"So, you can go and get him, yeah?" said Ben.

Elliott regarded him thoughtfully. "This Friday afternoon, you say?"

"Yeah, that's what he said."

"And today is Tuesday. So, if your information is correct, we don't have much time to act on it. Did your informant tell you any more about this robbery?"

Ben shook his head. "No. All he said is what I've told you, and my impression is that that's all he knows."

"But it's enough, isn't it?" asked Alison eagerly. "I mean, on what Ben – Mr Weekes – has told you, you can just keep a watch on the road, and then, when Ice tries to hold up the security van, you can just move in and arrest him, can't you?"

She felt cheered by the thought that, by the end of the week, Ice could be in custody and no longer in a position to harm her or Ben.

Elliott sighed inwardly. "I'm afraid it's not as easy as that. These things take a lot more organising than you seem to realise, Ms French. And, before I start committing officers and money to the sort of operation you describe, I'm going to have to make some enquiries of my own into some of the things you've told me and satisfy myself that such an operation is justified."

"You will be discreet, won't you?" urged Neeta. "You won't do anything which might increase the danger Ms French and Mr Weekes are in?"

"Don't worry," Elliott reassured her. "I'll tread very carefully." He turned to Ben. "But I do need to know some more about this informant of yours. To begin with, what's his name?"

"I don't know. I only know his street name."

"And what's that?"

"I'd rather not say."

"Why not?"

"I don't want to put him in any more danger than he's already in."

Elliott considered. Without even the boy's street name, he would be unable to make any enquiries about him which might indicate whether or not the information he had given Ben was likely to be reliable. At the same time Elliott sympathised with Ben's position, recognising that there was a real risk that, if word got out that the police were looking for the boy, as it almost inevitably would, the danger to him from Henry and his associates was likely to increase. There was also the time factor. Even with the boy's street name, Elliott thought he was unlikely to be able to find out much about him in three days.

"All right," he said.

Ben, who had been watching him anxiously, gave a brief sigh of relief.

Alison was beginning to see Elliott as an ally. "If you do mount an operation to arrest Ice on Friday, can we be there to see it?" she asked.

Elliott looked horrified. "No, you can't, Ms French," he said firmly. "As I would have thought you would appreciate, any police operation involving the intervention by officers in a robbery in which firearms are likely to be used carries with it exceptional dangers, and is no place for civilians. You must stay away. Do you understand?"

Alison appeared about to argue, but then replied meekly, "Yes, OK, I understand."

Elliott examined her face searchingly, but decided that his message had got through.

"Right," he said. "And, while we're on the subject of your safety, I'd strongly advise both you, Ms French, and you, Mr Weekes, to stay away from Brixton, and indeed out of London, until at least this Saturday. Can you do that?"

Alison nodded. "Yeah," she said. "I should be able to get time off work and to go and stay with my parents in Epsom."

"What about you, Mr Weekes?" asked Elliott, turning to Ben.

"I don't know. I've got relatives in the north of England I could go and stay with, but I don't think I can get away from work at such short notice."

"Look," said Elliott, "I appreciate that you don't want to inconvenience your colleagues or to let down the people who use your centre, but, coming from your background, you must know how dangerous people like this man Henry can be, and, in this instance, you must put your own safety before your job and your obligations to others. Do you understand?"

Ben looked worried. "Yeah," he mumbled, "I'll try and sort something out."

"See that you do," said Elliott. "Now, unless any of you have anything else you want to raise, I suggest that we call this meeting to a close. I need to get to work on this."

His visitors murmured their agreement and prepared to leave.

When they had gone, Elliott sat at his desk for a few moments thinking. Then he picked up his telephone.

Half an hour later, he had confirmation that there was a Jamaican by the name of Winston Henry, who was known by the street name Ice, and who was wanted in Jamaica for murder, and believed by the Jamaican police to be in the UK.

He telephoned Brixton Police Station, and made an appointment to see DCI Greaves there at nine o'clock the following morning.

Then he got a file from a filing cabinet in the corner of his office, and took from it a list of the security firms operating in Surrey. He telephoned the first company on the list.

"Good afternoon. My name's Elliott. Can I speak to your head of security, please?"

"May I ask what it's concerning?"

"It's confidential."

"OK. Putting you through to Mr Lawrence, now."

Elliott introduced himself. "I'm Chief Inspector Elliott of the Surrey Police. I'm engaged in a very sensitive enquiry and I must ask you to keep the contents of this call strictly confidential. Do you understand?"

Sam Lawrence was a former sergeant with the Metropolitan Police. "Yes, of course, sir," he said.

"Thank you. Now what I need to know from you is this: Are you going to have any security vans operating in the area between the M25 and Croydon on Friday afternoon?"

Elliott was deliberately keeping the area he was interested in vague.

"Yes, I think we have two vans out in that area then," said Lawrence. "Just let me check." There was a pause. "Yes, that's right. Why? Do you think one of them may be a target?"

"I can't say. But I need to know the routes those vans will be taking."

Lawrence hesitated. "Well, sir," he began awkwardly, "I don't know that I can…"

"No, no," Elliott reassured him quickly. "Of course, I don't expect you to give me that information over the phone. What I'd like to do is to come and see you. I'll bring my warrant card with me as proof of my identity."

Lawrence was relieved. "Yes, that sounds fine, sir. When would you like to make it?"

"Two o'clock tomorrow afternoon all right with you?"

"Yes, sir, that'll be no problem."

"Thank you. I'll see you then. I'll be in an unmarked car and plain clothes, and I'd ask you not to tell anyone else that I'm a police officer or why I'm visiting you. If you could just tell your staff that you're expecting a Mr Elliott, and that they're to let me in, I'll produce my warrant card to you when we meet. OK?"

"Yes, sir, I'm happy with that."

Elliott made similar calls to the rest of the security firms on his list. He learned that four more of the companies would have vans out in the area he was interested in that Friday afternoon. The security managers of all four companies agreed to see him, and he made arrangements to visit them the following afternoon.

The next morning he kept his appointment with DCI Greaves at Brixton Police Station.

He began by explaining the reason for his visit. "As you'll be aware, the CPS are carrying out a review relating to the death here of Delroy Brown, and I'm looking again at some aspects of the case."

He knew that this was a misleading way of putting the matter, but rested secure in the knowledge that both the statements he had made were true.

"Yes, I see." Greaves' response was guarded. "And how exactly can I help you?"

Elliott decided on a direct approach. "Do you remember that the last time I came to see you, I asked you if you had come across a man who goes by the street name, 'Eyes'?"

Greaves knew from Alison's article in the *Brixton Chronicle*, where this question was leading, but decided to brazen the situation out. He looked Elliott straight in the face and replied firmly, "Yes I do. And I told you I'd never heard of anyone known by that name."

"What about Ice? Have you come across a man known by that street name?"

"Ice?" Greaves gave a slight cough. "Well, of course, that's a different matter. Yes, I understand that there is a man in Brixton who uses that name."

"A recent article in the local press raised the question of whether, at the time of Brown's death, DC McKinnon was involved in an investigation into the activities of this man Ice. Was he?"

"No, he was not."

Greaves leaned back in his chair looking confident.

Elliott eyed him speculatively. "Then is, or was, this man Ice by any chance employed by DC McKinnon as a registered informant?"

This was a question that Greaves had not been expecting. He bristled with indignation. "Now, look here, Tony, I don't know how you do things in your neck of the woods, but here it's our policy never to confirm or deny whether a particular individual is, or is not, an informant."

Elliott knew that this was the proper line for Greaves to take, but he felt convinced that, in the context of the reason he had given for his visit, if Ice was not a police informant, Greaves would have said so. He wondered how much Greaves knew about Ice.

"Are you aware that this man, Ice, is an illegal immigrant who is wanted for murder in Jamaica?" he asked.

Greaves looked taken aback. "No, I didn't know that."

"What about his activities in this country? Do you know what he's been doing since he arrived here?"

"I've heard him mentioned as a small-time drugs dealer, but there's never been the evidence to prosecute him."

"I see. Nothing else?"

The muscles in Greaves' face tightened. "Not that I'm aware of. Why? What else has he been up to?"

"I don't know," replied Elliott truthfully. He saw no need to mention the so far unsubstantiated allegations made to him about the other criminal activities Henry had been engaged in.

Greaves glowered at him. He seemed about to ask another question, but said nothing.

"Right," said Elliott. "Well, I think that's all. Thank you very much, Dennis. You've been most helpful."

Greaves gave him a searching look. "Any time," he said stiffly.

Elliott got up to go. "Just one more thing," he said. "You will treat the contents of this conversation as confidential, won't you?"

"Yes, of course," snapped Greaves sourly.

Elliott left feeling some sympathy for him. He guessed that Greaves had been persuaded to agree to the recruitment of Henry as a police informant without knowing the truth about the man's background, and he knew that, if that was the case, Greaves could now face some difficult questions – particularly if Henry was proved to have continued to engage in serious criminal activity while employed as an informant.

As soon as Greaves was sure that Elliott had left the building, he summoned DC McKinnon to his office.

McKinnon, who knew nothing of Elliott's visit, arrived with no idea of why his DCI had sent for him.

"Sit down," said Greaves grimly. "I want a word with you."

"Sir?"

Greaves lost his temper. "Don't you fucking 'sir?' me," he shouted. "Do you know who I've just had in here?" He did not wait for an answer. "That overeducated fucking arsehole, Tony Elliott – you know, the chief inspector from Surrey who's investigating the Brown case for the PCA. And do you know why he was here? To give me a fucking grilling about your friend Ice."

McKinnon tensed in his seat.

"And what do you think he asked me?" demanded Greaves a little more calmly, but still belligerently. He looked expectantly at McKinnon.

"Was it about that stuff in the local paper, sir?" ventured McKinnon cautiously.

Greaves made a dismissive gesture with his right hand. "Is, or was, this man Ice," he recited in a high-pitched imitation of Elliott's voice, "by any chance employed by DC McKinnon as a registered informant?"

"But how…?" There was a strained note in McKinnon's voice.

"Yeah, I'd like to know that, too. Anyway, I told him to mind his own fucking business."

McKinnon looked relieved. "Yeah, well, that's right, sir. That's what you've got to do, isn't it?"

Greaves regarded him contemptuously. "But, then what do you think Chief Inspector Elliott told me?" he demanded, his voice rising again.

McKinnon shook his head. "I don't know, sir."

"You don't know, sir," sneered Greaves savagely. "Let me put this another way. What do you know about Healy that you should've told me, but haven't?"

"Nothing, sir, I swear," protested McKinnon earnestly.

"Nothing, sir, I swear," echoed Greaves in a mocking falsetto. His voice became grim again. "What about the fact that he is an illegal immigrant who is wanted for murder in Jamaica?" he demanded accusingly.

"He isn't, sir, is he?" replied McKinnon quickly. "I didn't know that. Honest I didn't."

Greaves regarded him intently. "I hope for your sake that that's true. But even if it is, if what Elliott says about Healy is correct, you're still in deep fucking shit. Why didn't you know this stuff? Didn't you make the proper checks?"

"Yes, sir, I did." Beads of sweat were beginning to stand out on McKinnon's forehead. "I can only think that Healy isn't his real name, and that's why this information about him hasn't come out."

Greaves looked sceptical. "That's not fucking good enough, and you know it. And there's another thing. Elliott seems to think that there's something about Healy's current activities that I ought to know. Can you tell me what that is?"

"I'm sorry, sir, I have no idea."

"Don't fuck with me. You must know what he's up to. That's part of your job."

"Yes, sir, I know, sir. But, as far as I'm aware, all he's into is what I've told you about – a bit of small-time dealing. You know, the sort of thing he's got to do to keep in with the people he's giving us. He knows the score. I've told him that, if he gets into anything heavy, we can't stop him going down for it. We can have a word with the judge which will get him a reduction in his sentence, but that's all. I'm sure he understands the position, sir."

"Are you?" Greaves sounded unconvinced. "Well, just to be on the safe side, I want you to make some enquiries into exactly what he's up to these days. And make that your top priority, because, if he's engaged in serious criminal activity, I want us to pull him in before Elliott or anyone else does. Understand?"

"Yes, sir."

"Right then, well, get on with it."

When Elliott got back to his office in Guildford, he found on his desk a short, faxed report on Winston Henry from the Jamaican Constabulary in Kingston.

The report included a copy of Henry's Jamaican criminal record. This showed him to have eleven convictions for a variety of offences including larceny, robbery, the possession of cocaine, the possession of an offensive weapon, unlawful and malicious wounding and the unlawful possession of a firearm. Eight of these convictions were for offences which he had committed while he was still a juvenile, and the last was for an offence of robbery which he had carried out eight years earlier when he was twenty-seven and for which he had been sentenced to five years' imprisonment. The report stated that, although Henry had been convicted of no offences since his release from prison, he was believed by the Jamaican police to be heavily involved in organised crime. It confirmed that a warrant had been issued for his arrest on three charges of murder, indicating that the alleged victims were believed to have been rival drug dealers. It concluded that Henry was regarded as extremely dangerous and, if apprehended, should be approached with great caution.

When he had read the report, Elliott glanced at his watch. He had about an hour before he had to leave for his appointment with Sam Lawrence. He got a packet of sandwiches, an apple and a bottle of water out of his briefcase and had lunch at his desk. As he ate, he made careful notes of his conversation with DCI Greaves.

At about the time Elliott was finishing his lunch, Bull Bates received a visit from DC McKinnon.

McKinnon had telephoned Bull within minutes of leaving DCI Greaves' office.

"We need to talk," he said, a note of panic in his voice.

Bull felt contempt for McKinnon's inability to control or disguise his fear, but not wishing to provoke McKinnon into doing or saying anything which might lead to an investigation of his own activities, he agreed to see him.

As the two men sat facing each other in Bull's office, Bull noted with distaste that McKinnon was sweating profusely.

"Right, what's the problem?" he demanded.

"We're in deep fucking trouble," replied McKinnon,

wiping his forehead with a large, not too clean, white handkerchief.

Bull did not like McKinnon's use of the word 'we'. "Why?" he asked, his eyes narrowing.

"You remember that little toerag, Delroy Brown, who bought it after he fell and banged his head when he went for me in his cell?"

Bull nodded.

"Well," said McKinnon, "just before I went to see him, he'd been offering to give the officers who'd nicked him information about a man who, as it goes, is a snout of mine."

"Why didn't you tell me this before?"

McKinnon shifted uneasily in his seat and looked at the floor. "Didn't seem relevant," he said, without conviction. "And you know how it is with informants, you don't tell anyone about them unless you have to. It's like second nature, isn't it?"

He wiped his forehead again.

"And why does this mean we're in trouble?" asked Bull, although he was beginning to form an idea of the answer.

"My DCI says that this prick, Elliott, who investigated Brown's death for the PCA is stirring things up again, claiming that my snout's an illegal immigrant who's wanted for murder in Jamaica and suggesting that he's been committing serious offences here, too."

"Is that true?"

"I don't fucking know, but, if it is, everybody's going to think I knew, and that I topped Brown to stop him talking."

Bull regarded him speculatively. McKinnon was a big man, but Bull did not think him capable of calculated, cold-blooded murder. He was too weak, too fearful. But then again, there were plenty of killers who killed out of fear, many doing so in a moment of blind panic. McKinnon looked capable of that.

A thought crossed Bull's mind. "Any possibility you were followed here?"

"Of course not. What do you think I am?"

"OK, OK." Bull patted the air above his desk with both hands in a gesture of reassurance. "Let's look at this. It doesn't matter what anyone thinks. What matters here is evidence. And I take it from what you say that there's no evidence that you knew all this stuff about your informant."

"That's right. But what I'm worried about is this. Say Elliott nicks my snout and finds evidence that he has been committing serious offences here, my snout could try and weasel his way out of it by saying that I knew what he was doing, and that I agreed to it as part of his cover."

Bull wondered if this was true, but felt fairly sure that McKinnon would not tell him if it was. He decided that it didn't matter.

"Well, I think someone needs to talk to your informant, and make sure that doesn't happen," he said.

McKinnon looked anxious. "But what…?" he began. He struggled to find the right words. "…What if he's the killer that Elliott says he is?" he asked at last.

Bull found it hard to disguise his contempt. He had no time for officers like McKinnon. If they didn't have the bottle to stand up to the real villains, they shouldn't be in the force.

A thought occurred to him. "You haven't, by any chance, said anything to him about me, have you?" he asked.

McKinnon looked uncomfortable and stared at the floor. "Well," he mumbled, "when some stuff about him came out in the local paper, and he was getting a bit worked up, I did tell him that you were my backup, my protection, you know."

"I see," said Bull grimly, adding with heavy sarcasm, "And I suppose you gave him my name and address."

"No, no, not your address."

"But my name?"

McKinnon nodded dumbly, his eyes once again fixed on the floor.

Bull's face darkened. "Well, now suppose you give me his name," he said, with a hard edge to his voice.

"The name he gave me was Carlton Healy," mumbled McKinnon, chastened.

"But?" barked Bull impatiently.

"That may be an alias. I've heard his real name is Winston Henry. He's known by the street name Ice."

"And where does he live?"

"I don't know. I used to have an address for him, but he left there."

"So, where does he hang out?"

"Brixton."

McKinnon saw the look of annoyance on Bull's face. "I'm sorry," he added quickly. "I honestly can't be more precise than that. I know he runs a couple of small-time dealers on Railton Road, but that's about it. The way we do business has always been that, if he has something for me, he gives me a buzz. I don't even have his number."

Not for the first time, Bull wondered what on earth McKinnon was doing in the CID.

"These dealers, do you have their names?" he asked.

McKinnon shook his head.

"OK," said Bull. "Now, what I need you to do is this. You've got to find out everything you can about where I'm most likely to find this man Henry in the next few days. You've got that, everything?"

"Yeah, OK."

"And you'd better come up with something, for both our sakes."

McKinnon wondered what Bull planned to do with this information, but thought it better not to ask.

"Yeah, sure, Bull," he said, getting up to leave.

It was the first time he had used Bull's nickname.

Chief Inspector Elliott's visits to the first three security firms he had arranged to call on proved uneventful. At each of the firms, he was given details of the routes to be taken by the vans being operated by the company in the area between the M25 and south Croydon on the coming Friday afternoon, but none of these routes included Castle Road, Chipstead. With only two firms left to visit, Elliott began to think that he was on a wild goose chase, and that he had been right to distrust Ben's tip-off.

His view began to change during his visit to the fourth firm he called on, a small company called Surrey Security.

Surrey Security was based in a square two-storey concrete building on an industrial estate behind an electrical superstore on Purley Way in Croydon. The building stood in a yard surrounded by a high steel mesh fence topped with barbed wire. Notices on the fence warned that the premises were protected by CCTV and patrolled by security guards and dogs. The only way into the yard was through a large double gate at the end of a short turning off one of the roads through the estate.

When Elliott drove up to the gate, he found it locked. Fixed to a post on the right of the gate at about waist height was a button-operated Entryphone. He wound down his car window, and pressed the button. He heard the Entryphone click on, and, at the same time, he saw a closed-circuit television camera on the top of a fence post a few yards to his right swivel slightly to train itself on him.

"Mr Elliott to see Mr Anderson," he said, dipping his head with the double aim of speaking into the Entryphone and concealing his face from the camera.

The gates swung open, and he drove into the yard.

He parked his car in a marked parking space, and walked over to the entrance to the building. It, too, was locked. Embedded in the wall beside the door was another Entryphone. He saw that this one had a small camera integrated into it. He turned his face away from it, pressed the button, and repeated, "Mr Elliott to see Mr Anderson."

The door clicked, and he pushed it open.

He found himself in a small lobby, where he was met by a large bald man of about sixty, in a grey suit, who introduced himself as Alan Anderson, the company's security manager.

Elliott glanced around to make sure that they were alone, produced his warrant card and said, "I'm Tony Elliott. Thank you for agreeing to see me."

Anderson took the warrant card, but hardly looked at it. He seemed nervous. He gave the card back to Elliott, and the two men shook hands.

Elliott felt sure that he had seen Anderson before, but he could not remember where or when. He thought the other man looked somehow wrong in a suit.

Anderson led him up a narrow flight of stairs, and showed him into a functional and sparsely furnished office with heavy steel bars across the window, a filing cabinet in one corner and a large safe in another. A few feet in front of the window was a desk with two chairs facing each other across it. On the desk was a telephone, but nothing else. Elliott wondered if it had been cleared for his visit.

Anderson moved towards the chair behind the desk, and, gesturing to the other one, invited Elliott to take a seat.

They both sat down, and, once they were seated, Anderson leant forward across his desk with his hands clasped together in front of him.

"You said on the phone that you needed to know the routes some of our vans will be taking on Friday afternoon. Is that right?" he asked.

"Yes, that's right." Elliott consulted his notebook. "The three you said you're going to have out in the area between the M25 and this part of Croydon."

Anderson looked at him expectantly, as if waiting for him to explain why he wanted this information, but, eliciting no response, got out of his seat and walked over to the safe. He unlocked it and took out a green file, from which he pulled three sheets of paper which he handed to Elliott.

"Here you are," he said. "Those have got their routes in them."

Elliott took the three sheets of paper and looked at the top one. It was a printed form headed 'Vehicle Itinerary' and completed in neat black handwriting. Below the heading, next to the printed words 'Date', 'Vehicle' and 'Crew' were entered that Friday's date, a vehicle registration number and two men's names. The middle section of the form was divided in two by a vertical line. To the left of this line, beneath the printed heading 'Collection From' was written the word 'Gatwick' with a warehouse number next to it and below this the names of three supermarkets in Caterham, Banstead and Wallington, while to the right of the line, below the printed heading 'Delivery to' were written the name of a company in Croydon opposite the Gatwick entry and the name of a high street bank, also in Croydon, opposite the names of the three supermarkets. Below these two columns, in a box running across the whole of the page and headed 'Route', was written a sequence of place names and road names and numbers.

It was the name Chipstead that first caught Elliott's eye, but it was the words 'Castle Road' which followed this that really captured his attention. He blinked, looked again, and then glanced back at the rest of the form. The name of the company taking the delivery from Gatwick was vaguely familiar to him but for the moment he could not place it.

As casually as he could, he put the form down on Anderson's desk and began examining the second one. As he did so, he caught a glimpse of Anderson's face, and thought he saw him open his mouth as if to say something, but then close it without speaking.

Elliott completed his scrutiny of the two remaining forms. He found it hard to focus on their contents, but satisfied himself that neither of them mentioned Castle Road, Chipstead.

"Thank you very much," he said, as he put the third form down on Anderson's desk.

Anderson looked anxious. "Did you find what you were looking for?" he asked.

Elliott was evasive. "I'm afraid I have another visit to make before I'll know that," he replied, almost truthfully.

He began to get up to go.

Anderson got up, too.

"Well," he said, with what seemed to Elliott a forced heartiness, "if there's anything else I can do to help you with your enquiries, you will let me know, won't you?"

Elliott wondered if it was his imagination or if Anderson had placed a rather odd stress on the words 'help you with your enquiries'. It also occurred to him that Anderson had shown less curiosity than the other security managers he had visited about why he had asked for the information he had requested. Was this significant? he asked himself.

"Yes, I will. Thank you," he said. "And thank you for your cooperation this afternoon."

"Not at all. Always pleased to help the police in any way we can." Anderson seemed to have regained his composure.

The two men shook hands, and Anderson showed Elliott out.

As Elliott drove to the gate, he glanced in his rear-view mirror, and saw Anderson standing in the doorway of the building watching him go.

Twenty minutes later, at just after six o'clock, he arrived at the last of the security firms he had arranged to visit, a small company in Sutton. The firm's security manager had told him on the telephone that the firm would have only one van operating in the area between the M25 and south Croydon that Friday afternoon, and Elliott noted from the firm's paperwork that this vehicle's itinerary would not take it into Chipstead.

As he left Sutton and began heading back to Guildford, he considered the decision that now faced him. The information that Surrey Security was going to have a security van passing through Castle Road, Chipstead that Friday afternoon inclined him to the view that he would have to act on Ben's tip-off, and mount an operation based on the assumption that Henry was planning to attempt to rob the vehicle. He would have to involve armed officers in the operation, and, although their attendance could be secured quickly, it would need to be justified. None of this would matter if the operation was successful, but, if Henry failed to turn up, and no attempt was made to rob the security van, he would have some difficult questions to answer.

He wished he knew more about Ben's informant and how this informant had got his information.

His mind went back to his visit to Surrey Security, and he suddenly remembered, in rapid succession, both where he had seen Anderson before and why the name of the company due to take delivery of the consignment from Gatwick was familiar to him.

He decided that he needed to see the place where Ben had said the robbery was going to take place, and, taking advantage of a roundabout, he turned his car around, and headed for Chipstead.

Castle Road was, he discovered, a narrow country road, only wide enough for a single vehicle. It snaked in a series of bends down a steep hillside. Lining both sides of the road were trees and shrubs, between some of which could be seen green fields broken up by the occasional hedge, copse or small wood. Traffic was only allowed to travel along the road in one direction, down the hill, and was so sparse as to be almost non-existent – partly, it seemed, because almost all the traffic travelling between Chipstead High Road at the top of the hill and Outwood Lane at the bottom appeared to be using the neighbouring Hazelwood Lane, which, though still narrow, was a little wider than Castle Road, and carried vehicles in both directions. He could see, however, that the driver of a vehicle the size of a security van might well prefer to take it down Castle Road, rather than to have to manoeuvre it past vehicles coming in the other direction up Hazelwood Lane.

He drove down Castle Road several times, each time returning up the hill by way of Hazelwood Lane.

The light was beginning to fail, and the trees which overhung Castle Road shrouded it in darkness, giving it an almost sinister air.

It would, Elliott knew, be less forbidding in full daylight, but still, he thought, the ideal place in which to hijack a passing vehicle.

Hijack

The next morning Elliott arrived at his office just after eight o'clock.

He did some research which confirmed that what he thought he remembered about Alan Anderson and about the company taking the delivery from Gatwick was, in both cases, correct, and he set about gathering some further information on both subjects.

At nine o'clock he telephoned Anderson, and made an appointment to call on him about an hour later – the earliest he estimated he could get to Surrey Security's premises by car if he set off immediately. He got the impression that Anderson had been expecting his call.

As he drove up the A3 there were times when he felt tempted to exceed the seventy-mile-an-hour speed limit, but he restrained himself, and still arrived at Surrey Security's premises only shortly after ten o'clock. Anderson was at the door to meet him, and, after asking his receptionist to make them both a cup of coffee, took Elliott up to his office.

"We've met before, you know," said Elliott pleasantly, as the two men settled into their chairs.

"Have we, sir?" Anderson looked slightly discomfited, feeling at a disadvantage.

"Yes, it was about fifteen years ago, just after I'd joined the service. Some of us were taken on a visit to Epsom nick, and you were the custody sergeant on duty that day."

"Goodness. You must have a good memory," said Anderson, continuing to feel unsettled, wondering where this was leading.

"Well, not bad, but it's more that you made quite an impression on me."

"Good, I hope, sir."

"Oh, yes, very good. A couple of young officers had brought in a man of about their own age, who was clearly the worse for drink and apparently bent on winding them up, and the officers were beginning to lose their tempers, when you intervened, calmed the whole situation down, and even had the three of them laughing together. Then you sent the young man off with a flea in his ear and, when he'd gone, you had a friendly word with the two officers on how to handle similar situations in future. I was very favourably impressed."

Anderson visibly relaxed. "That's very kind of you, sir."

Elliott could have added, but did not, that Anderson had gone up further in his estimation as a result of the checks he had carried out into the former sergeant. These had revealed that Anderson's career in the police service had been an exemplary one, and that he had retired from the service without a blemish on his record, and, as a consequence,

Elliott was as sure as he could be that, if the anticipated robbery involved someone on the inside working for Surrey Security, that person was not Anderson.

"Now, the reason I'm here," he began, but Anderson, leaning forward across his desk, interrupted him.

"I know. It's about the Gatwick run, isn't it?"

Elliott was not surprised. "Yes, it is," he agreed. "So, what can you tell me about that?"

"Well, the company we're delivering to on that job are bullion dealers, major bullion dealers."

Elliott knew this already, and had had it confirmed by his research, but did not say so, instead asking, "So what you're delivering to them on Friday is bullion, is it?"

"Yes, gold bars, which are going to their depository."

"Worth how much?"

"Well, as I understand it, the price of gold varies from day to day, but I know our clients paid over a million pounds for this consignment."

"I see. And how often do you make deliveries of bullion from Gatwick to these clients?"

"Once a week, every Friday, regular as clockwork."

Elliott winced. "And are all these consignments of a similar value?"

"No, they vary quite a bit. This will probably be the most valuable one we've handled to date."

"And who here knows what these runs involve?"

"Just me and the crew of the van. I use the same crew every week."

"So, what can you tell me about the crew? Do you trust them?"

"Absolutely. They're my two best men. Nick, he's in his forties, married, two kids, ex-army, as solid as they come.

And Darren, he's in his twenties, engaged to be married next year, been with us since he left school. His dad was with us for twenty years until he was forced to retire after being done over in an attempted robbery. We made sure he was properly compensated by our insurance company, and the whole family was very grateful to us. Both men fully understand that they must not talk about this run to anyone, not other members of staff, not members of their families, not anyone."

"What about holidays? Is there a relief crew?"

"No, the way we do it is, if either Nick or Darren is on holiday, I stand in for him."

"Right. What about the route? Do you use the same route every week?"

Anderson looked uncomfortable. "Well, normally we'd vary the route each week. Standard practice."

"But?"

"Well, up to about six months ago we were varying the route on this run every week in the normal way, but one Friday afternoon the boys got stuck for over an hour in really heavy traffic on the A217. It spooked them. They felt really vulnerable to attack. And the clients were really annoyed that their delivery got to them so late. They were making noises about transferring to another, more reliable company. And that was a real worry, as they're our best clients, a real catch for a small company like ours. So, I discussed the situation with the boys, and they suggested – I think it was Nick who came up with the idea – using these quiet country roads. There's so little traffic on them that hardly anyone would see our van, and my boys could be pretty sure of keeping on schedule."

Anderson looked embarrassed. He knew what was coming next. It was a point he had been uneasily suspecting he would arrive at ever since he had received Elliott's first call to him two days earlier.

Elliott, sorry to add to the older man's obvious discomfiture, but needing to take their discussion forward, said gently, "But you do see the danger in this arrangement, don't you?"

Anderson nodded unhappily, as Elliott went on, "Say someone gets wind of these consignments. Maybe someone at the airport gives something away or maybe it's someone who works for, or used to work for, your clients or even for you. Then someone who's picked up this information decides to watch for one of your vans leaving the airport on a Friday, and follows it, and then, the next week, follows it again, thereby discovering that it always takes the same route. At that point the quiet country roads you've been using cease to be less of a danger to you than the heavy traffic on the main roads, but become the ideal place in which to ambush your van."

Although he had seen this coming, Anderson's face had gone ashen. "And I take it that you have intel that that's what someone is planning to do this Friday," he said, his voice subdued.

"Well, what we've had," said Elliott carefully, "is a tip-off that a man whom I'm interested in for other reasons is planning to hit a security van travelling down Castle Road, Chipstead on Friday afternoon, and your vehicle seems to fit the bill. Now I have to say that I know very little about the source of this tip-off, and I was inclined to treat it with some scepticism, but now I know what your van is due to be carrying, I think I have to take it seriously."

"So, what do you want me to do? I'd rather not cancel the run, as that would cause my clients a great deal of inconvenience, and might even cause them to take their business elsewhere. But I'm more than happy to change the van's route to any route you care to suggest."

"No, I want the run to go ahead as usual, taking the route it always does, but with my officers taking the place of your crew."

"All right," agreed Anderson uncertainly, wondering what his bosses and his clients would think of what he was agreeing to, and how they would react if things went wrong. But he was acutely aware of the dire consequences his misplaced compromise over his vehicle's route could have had for him, his colleagues, his company and his company's clients, had Elliott not intervened. He therefore felt indebted to the officer, and this, together with the loyalty he still felt to the police as the result of his many years in the service, had made up his mind for him. "How do you want me to handle things here?" he asked.

"Well, to begin with," said Elliott, "you're not to say anything about this to anyone. Then the way I'd like to do things is this: About half an hour before your van is due to set out on its run, four of my officers will arrive here, all in plain clothes and in an unmarked vehicle. Two of these officers will escort your crew members, Nick and Darren, to a secure room which I'd like you to prepare for the purpose. These officers will temporarily deprive your men of their mobile phones, and will remain with them until this operation is over. I know you say you trust your men, but this is a precaution which I have to take in the interests of the safety of my officers. I hope you understand that."

Anderson nodded. "Yes, sir, I do," he said.

"Right," continued Elliott, "in the meantime, the other two officers, who will be armed, are to be kitted out in your company's uniforms and given full instructions on the procedures they are to follow on the run. These officers have carried out similar roles in the past, and will have a fair idea of what will be expected of them. Needless to say, the kitting out and instruction of these officers is to be carried out somewhere where they are out of both the sight and hearing of everyone on your staff apart from yourself. Then, when the time comes for this van to leave, these officers will drive it out of your yard in the usual way. Are you happy with that?"

"Yes, I think so," said Anderson carefully, "but, if you wouldn't mind running over it all, just once more, I'd be very grateful."

"Of course," agreed Elliott, and did as he had been asked. Then, satisfied that Anderson fully understood what he needed to do, he got up to go.

At about the same time, Alison and Ben were arriving in Epsom in Ben's car to stay with Alison's parents.

Alison had telephoned her mother the evening before to say that she would like to come down and stay with her parents for a few days, and her mother, who regretted how little she saw of her only daughter these days, had been delighted to agree.

Alison had then said that she would like to bring a friend with her, at which her mother, not wishing to share her precious time with her daughter with anyone outside her family, had been less pleased, but to which she had replied, "Yes, of course, darling," adding, "Male or female?"

"Male. His name's Ben."

Alison's mother experienced a feeling of apprehension. Alison had not brought home many boyfriends, but her mother had not liked any of them. None of them, in her opinion, had been good enough for her daughter, and, in trying to justify herself to Alison, she had invariably said, "But it's only you I'm thinking of. I only want the best for you."

Now she asked, "And what does this Ben do for a living?"

Alison knew that what her mother wanted to hear was that Ben was a doctor, a dentist, a lawyer, an accountant, a merchant banker or, at a pinch, a teacher, so she replied cautiously, "He's a youth worker," and then, in the awkward silence which followed, she blurted out, knowing that this was something she had to tell her mother before they arrived, "and he's black."

"I don't know why you think you have to tell me that," responded her mother just a little too quickly. "I hope you're not suggesting that I'm racially prejudiced, because, as you should well know, nothing could be further from the truth."

Later, however, recounting this conversation to Alison's father on his return from work, she added piously, "But I do worry about all those little brown babies. Poor mites. Not one thing or the other."

Her husband, Norman, a mild-mannered GP, regarded her quizzically. "I hope, Mary," he said, "you're not going to turn all *Guess Who's Coming to Dinner?* on us."

"You can scoff," retorted his wife, "but there were a lot of good points made in that film that were not answered in the way it ended."

Norman gave a brief inward sigh. "You know," he said, "there are a lot more brown babies around now than there used to be, and most people just accept them for who they are." He paused, then added, "Anyway, it's a little bit early to be worrying about little brown babies, isn't it? Ali has never mentioned this young man before, so I don't suppose they've known each other for very long."

His wife reddened slightly and set off on a new tack. "Well, you can't deny that they're different," she said.

"Who?" queried her husband, not having kept up with the change of tack. "Little brown babies?"

"No, silly. Black people. For one thing, they smell different."

Norman wondered where on earth his wife had got this idea from. Apart from anything else, she had come into contact with far too few black people in her very sheltered existence to make any generalisations at all about them. But all he said, mildly, was, "I think I read somewhere that, to the Japanese, all we white Europeans smell pretty foul."

"You and the things you 'think you read somewhere'," retorted Mary dismissively. "Anyway," she added triumphantly, "I didn't say black people smell bad – only different."

Norman could see nothing to be gained by continuing with this conversation, and his wife, satisfied that she had, by her final remark, exonerated herself from any possible charge of racial prejudice, was also happy to let the subject drop.

When Alison and Ben arrived at her parents' house the next morning, her father was out at work, but her mother was waiting for them.

The house was a large five-bedroomed detached one, a little way away from the centre of Epsom. It was separated from the road by a six-foot wall into which was set a pair of iron gates. Between the wall and the house was a large, gravelled drive, to either side of which were areas of lawn and flowerbeds which continued along the sides of the house into a large garden at the back of the building.

The gates were open and, as Ben drove through them, Alison's mother ventured a few steps out of the front door onto the drive to meet them.

Ben, who had asked Alison what he should bring her parents to express his appreciation of their hospitality, came bearing, as she had suggested, a bottle of fifteen-year-old single malt whisky for her father and a large bunch of flowers for her mother. Later, however, when he saw the extensive array of flowers in the flowerbeds in the back garden, he wondered if Alison had been mistaken in the gift she had suggested he bring her mother. More flowers seemed the last thing Mrs French needed.

But Mary, despite herself, appreciated the gesture.

She also found herself thinking that Ben was very good-looking – for a black man. He had, she thought, beautiful eyes and a lovely smile, though she quickly told herself that these attributes were insignificant in the larger scheme of things. She noticed that he was wearing an aftershave which she rather liked. It had a fresh, clean scent, unlike the rather musty aftershaves which so many men wore and which she disliked, but then she found herself thinking of it as camouflage. She also noticed that he was well dressed, his clothes casual but smart, his shoes well polished. She assumed that this was not the way he usually dressed, and that he had dressed as he had in order to impress her. But then it occurred to her that none of the other boyfriends that Alison had brought home had made any attempt at all to impress her. Rather, they had either patronised or ignored her.

It was all very unsettling.

She told Alison that lunch was not quite ready and suggested that her daughter take Ben up to his room. "It's the big one at the end of the corridor next to your dad's and my room," she said.

"Wow," whispered Alison to Ben, as she led him up the wide staircase. "You really are getting the VIP treatment. Whenever I've had friends to stay here before, she's put them in the small spare room next to my room, but the one you're getting is much grander. It's even got its own en suite bathroom. Or maybe," she suggested, as the thought occurred to her, "it's that she thought putting a distance between our rooms was necessary to safeguard my virtue." She giggled.

Ben gave a subdued smile. "Maybe," he said, but he could not help wondering whether giving him a room with an en suite bathroom was a way of lessening his need to use the family bathroom. Some white people could be funny about things like that, and he had an uneasy suspicion that Alison's mother might be one of them.

It was a beautiful early autumn day, and Alison had expected her mother to serve lunch in the garden, as she usually did on such occasions, but Mary, conscious that her garden was overlooked by the houses on either side, and not wishing to be the subject of unnecessary gossip on the part of her neighbours, decided that it would be better for them to eat in the dining room with the patio doors open so that they could enjoy the garden.

At lunch, motivated both by curiosity and by what she conceived to be her duty as a good hostess, she set about getting Ben to tell her about himself.

"Have you lived in this country all your life?" she began.

Alison winced, but was relieved that at least her mother had not asked Ben where he came from.

"Yes," replied Ben easily. "London born and bred."

"And, what about your parents? Have they always lived here, too?"

"No, they both came here from Jamaica in the early sixties."

"And what do they do?"

"Dad's a qualified engineer but he works as a draughtsman, and Mum's a nurse."

"And how do you get on with them, your parents?"

"Great. We're all very close. They've given me everything I have and I respect them."

Mary felt a twinge of surprise and envy. She was fairly sure that she had never heard any member of her daughter's generation express respect for their parents. At the same time it came to her out of the blue that she had read somewhere in a magazine that people coming from close-knit families were statistically much more likely to make loyal partners and loving parents than those who had not been so fortunate in their upbringing, but she pushed this memory away, irritated at its obvious irrelevance.

"In fact, I still live with them," added Ben.

Mary looked at her daughter. She had made strenuous efforts to persuade Alison to remain living with her parents and to commute up to her job in London, even offering to pay for her daughter's annual train ticket, but Alison had been insistent that she needed her independence.

So now her mother said pointedly, "Well, it's nice to hear that not everyone finds living with their parents unbearable."

Alison sighed. "It's not the same, Mum. Ben's parents only live a twenty-minute walk from where he works."

As lunch ended, and Mary began to collect up the plates, Ben offered to help her, but she quickly and firmly declined his offer. Then, as she moved towards the kitchen with a pile of plates in her hands, a small gust of wind came in through the patio doors, and slammed the kitchen door shut in her face, causing Ben to leap quickly to his feet and open it again for her.

Mary reddened slightly. "Thank you, dear," she said.

"It's a pleasure," said Ben, treating her to a smile.

After lunch, Alison proposed that she and Ben drive over to Box Hill, a local beauty spot, and, to her mother's surprise, asked her if she would like to accompany them, but, although Mary would have dearly liked to accept this invitation, she felt that it would be safer not to, though she could not quite put her finger on the danger she felt she would be avoiding.

By the time Alison and Ben got back from Box Hill, her father had returned from work and Alison introduced him to Ben.

Norman thanked Ben for the whisky and offered him a glass, which Ben, although not a whisky drinker, accepted out of politeness. Norman poured them both a glass and, after they had settled into armchairs in the lounge, he asked Ben about his work. So, Ben began telling him about the many problems faced by the young people who used his centre: the poverty, the substandard and overcrowded housing, the overt and covert racism, the poor schooling, the lack of employment, the pressure to join gangs, the easy availability of drugs and the ever present threat of violence. Norman listened sympathetically and with interest, and was able to tell Ben of his experiences, when, as a young doctor working as a GP in the East End, he had encountered many of the same problems as Ben was describing to him. He was saddened to hear that so little seemed to have changed, and he felt a pang of guilt for having left the East End for the easier life of a GP in Epsom, when he had met and fallen in love with Mary, and had quickly recognised that she would not be happy living in the East End, and that it would be cruel to make her do so. He admired the enthusiasm and energy with which Ben spoke about trying to improve the lives of those he worked with, and he hoped the young man would not lose his idealism. He wondered whether Ben's relationship with his daughter would last, feeling sure, with a sense of pride, that, if it did, she would not hold the young man back.

Over dinner the two men continued with their discussion, while Alison and her mother said little but listened, both taking in the growing rapport between Alison's father and her boyfriend. But, while for Alison this was a largely positive experience, tinged with only the occasional slight pang of jealousy, for her mother it was the source of more complicated and conflicting emotions.

While talking to Norman before dinner, Ben had noticed a grand piano which took up a large part of the lounge and when they returned there after their meal, he walked over to the instrument and asked, "Mind if I take a look?"

"By all means, do," said Norman. "Do you play?"

"I used to before I went to uni."

"You never told me that," said Alison, accusingly. "And anyway, you haven't got a piano in your house, have you?"

"There was a music teacher at school who really encouraged my playing, and arranged for me to be able to stay on after school whenever I liked to practise on the school piano. At one time, when I was about fifteen, I was doing that almost every afternoon."

Alison's experience of trying to learn the piano had not

been a happy one, involving, as it had, bitter battles with her mother, as Mary had tried to make her do her practice. "So how far did you get with it?" she demanded, a little peevishly.

"I took Grade 6, and my teacher said I should get a distinction, but the examiner seemed to take a dislike to me from the minute I got into the room, and I came away with a merit. My teacher who had been listening to me playing through the door was furious, and wanted to appeal, but I didn't think there was any point and after that I just sort of lost interest."

"That's a pity," said Norman. "So, what sort of person was this examiner?"

"A large middle-aged white lady in a flowery dress," said Ben ruefully and with just a touch of bitterness.

"I see," said Norman thoughtfully. "Well, how would you feel about playing something for us now?"

Ben looked hesitant, but Alison said, "Go on," and so, slightly gingerly, he sat down at the piano and lifted the lid of the keyboard.

Mary, who had been in the kitchen loading the dishwasher, came into the room and was none too pleased to see Ben at the piano, which, though she rarely played it these days, she regarded very much as her preserve, but she said nothing, taking a seat with her head slightly bowed.

However, as Ben began to play, her head came up quickly, as she heard something that she had not expected.

Ben did not see this, but his fingers stumbled on the keyboard. "I'm sorry," he apologised. "I'm afraid, I'm out of practice," and he made to get up from the piano stool.

But Mary stopped him, saying quietly, "Please go on."

Ben began the piece again and this time, though making

a few mistakes, he played it through to the end, earning a little round of applause from Norman and Alison.

But Mary knew that they had not heard what she had heard. "You know," she said to Ben earnestly, "you mustn't give up playing. You have the touch. That's rare and it can't be taught. I am, or was, a competent pianist, but I don't have it."

"What do you mean, 'the touch', Mum?" asked Alison slightly impatiently, feeling at the same time both proud of Ben and a little jealous of him.

"It's a sensitivity to the instrument which gives a special quality to the playing of those who have it," said her mother quietly, "and Ben has it."

That night Mary slept badly, tossing and turning in her bed, her mind filled with conflicting thoughts and emotions, as it replayed the events of the day.

The next morning, after they had had breakfast, and Norman had left for work, Alison announced that she wanted Ben to take her on a picnic. This time she did not invite her mother, and Mary, though she would not have accepted an invitation to join them, felt a twinge of disappointment, but set about preparing them a lavish picnic lunch.

"So, where are we going today?" Ben asked Alison.

"It's a surprise. You'll see when we get there."

Ben, although tempted to press Alison for more information as to their destination, decided to play along with her. "OK," he said, as he began turning his car in the drive. "Which way do you want me to go?"

"Go left and follow the signs to Banstead."

"Is that where we're going?"

"It's on the way."

They drove along roads taking them through leafy suburbs, interspersed with brief stretches of countryside.

It was another fine day, the trees in their autumn colours and the remnants of an early morning mist lingering in dips in the landscape but gradually lifting, as the sun grew warmer.

To begin with they spoke little, as Ben concentrated on the road, and Alison kept an eye on a map to make sure they were going the right way.

Both also found themselves thinking back over the events of the day before, but, conscious that their perspectives on these events would be different, were hesitant to share their thoughts with each other.

At one point, Ben ventured, "I like your father."

"And he obviously likes you," said Alison, before they lapsed once more into silence.

When they had driven through Banstead, Ben noticed that the road which Alison had directed him to take next was signposted as leading to Chipstead.

He pulled his car into the side of the road, and stopped.

"I don't think this is a good idea," he said firmly. "You know Elliott told us to stay away. He said it would be dangerous. He said there would be firearms involved."

"It's all right," Alison reassured him. "I know this area really well. You remember I said I used to go riding in Chipstead. Well, I'm sure I can find a place for us to watch the action from where no one will be able to see us, and we won't be in any danger."

Ben remained unconvinced. "If we're somewhere where we can see what's going on, I don't see how those involved won't be able to see us," he objected.

"Trust me," pleaded Alison, "or at least come and see

the place I've got in mind. Then, if you don't agree with me that it's safe, I promise we'll leave. Look, it's still only just after ten, and this hold-up is supposed to take place this afternoon, so we've got plenty of time to have a good look round, size the situation up, and, if you say so, leave, long before anything is likely to happen."

Ben hesitated. He believed that he understood the dangers of the situation which they were contemplating getting into far better than Alison did, and, feeling protective towards her, he was reluctant to let her expose herself to the risks involved. On the other hand, he feared that, if he refused to do as she wished, she might put this down to a lack of courage on his part, and, as a consequence, perhaps think less of him as a man.

"All right," he said slowly, "but, if I don't think it's safe, I'm holding you to your promise. Agreed?"

"Agreed."

They drove down into Chipstead valley, and then, as Elliott had done several times two days earlier, up Hazelwood Lane, edging their way carefully past vehicles travelling in the opposite direction down the narrow, winding road.

At the top of the hill, Alison directed Ben to turn right along Chipstead High Road, and then, a little further on, left into a car park next to a rugby club. There were only three other cars in the car park. Two were empty, while the third had two young men in it sitting in the front seats looking bored. Alison wondered if they were plain-clothes police officers, and looked round for Elliott, but, to her relief, could see no sign of him. She knew she should not be surprised. It was, after all, still early, and he would, she imagined, have things to organise which would keep him busy elsewhere until later.

Ben parked the car, and, as he and Alison got out, she gave him the rucksack containing their lunch, and slung over her shoulders a smaller rucksack containing the other things she thought they might need. Then she led him back onto Chipstead High Road, where they turned left, and walked along until they came to a junction with Elmore Road on their left and Castle Road on their right. There were signs at the entrance to Castle Road declaring it to be a single-track road and unsuitable for heavy goods vehicles. Even in daylight the trees overhanging the road gave it the appearance of a dark tunnel, and Ben and Alison were unable to see far along it. Alison suggested that they go back for the car, and drive it down the road to familiarise themselves with it, but Ben refused.

"You don't know what's down there," he said. "There may well be police officers taking up their positions or, worse, Ice and his friends staking the place out."

Alison looked disappointed, but did not argue. She had to admit to herself that Castle Road looked a lot more forbidding than she remembered it, and she wondered whether this was just because, when riding in the area as a girl, she had not paid much attention to it, or whether it was because she was now envisaging the road as the scene of an armed robbery.

"OK," she said, more brightly than she felt. "Then I'll show you where I think we can hide."

Ben regarded her sceptically, but followed her as she led him further along Chipstead High Road, until they came to a thickly wooded area on the right-hand side of the road.

"Here we are," she said, beginning to climb over a low fence separating the wood from the road, glad that she'd had the foresight to wear jeans for the day.

Ben held back. "Aren't you trespassing?" he asked.

"Probably," she replied with a grin, "but we journalists have to do that all the time to get our best stories."

Ben was not convinced, but clambered gingerly over the fence after her. He was not really dressed for what was now being expected of him, for, although he had taken Alison's advice to him before they set out to wear jeans and an anorak, his jeans were an expensive pair of Levi's and his anorak was a smart one not designed for clambering over fences and through thick woodland. However, he followed Alison gamely as she pushed her way through the trees and bushes, and, though ruefully noting a tear in his jeans just below his right knee and, a few moments later, another in the sleeve of his anorak at his right elbow, he remained close behind her as they approached the far side of the small wood.

Alison stopped and pointed through the few trees and bushes remaining in front of them, across a field to a line of trees and bushes on the far side.

"There," she said. "That's Castle Road down there."

Ben was not impressed. "Well," he said, "I agree that we're pretty well hidden here from anyone down there, but equally, we're not going to be able to see much of anything going on down there. I mean, I can just about make out a road on the other side of those trees, but anything happening there is going to be more or less completely obscured by them."

Alison opened her rucksack, and took out a pair of field glasses belonging to her father. "Here, try these," she said.

Ben took the powerful field glasses out of their case, and trained them on the line of trees and bushes on the other side of the field. At first, all he could see was a blur, but, as he adjusted the glasses, he could clearly see stretches of the road through the gaps between the bushes and trees.

"And I've got these," said Alison, producing from her rucksack a pair of opera glasses belonging to her mother. "They're not as powerful as the binoculars, but I reckon I'll still be able to see quite a lot with them."

Ben, who was still looking through the field glasses, said, "I agree that the view through these is fantastic, but, you know, I can still only see the top section of the road, because, after that, it takes a sharp turn away from us, and I can't see anything beyond that bend."

Alison took the field glasses from him, and looked for herself. "I see what you mean," she said disconsolately, but then, brightening up, suggested, "You know what, I reckon that bend could be one of the best places on the road to stage a hold-up. Say, Ice, or whoever it is, starts by parking his vehicle just around the bend, and then, say, he gets word from an accomplice who's following the security van that it has started coming down Castle Road. He then brings his vehicle sharply round the bend into the view of the oncoming van, taking the men in the van by surprise and blocking their way. They will also have the additional worry of not knowing what else might lie round the bend, which might make them a bit more likely to do what they're told, and, finally, if the guy staging the hold-up needs to make a quick getaway, either when he's completed the robbery or because something has gone wrong, he can swiftly disappear, by driving off round the bend."

Ben looked at her thoughtfully. "You sound as if you have some experience of planning armed robberies," he said, with a grin.

"OK, very funny, but, seriously, that could be how it happens, couldn't it?"

"I suppose it could, and, if it doesn't and the hold-up takes place somewhere further down the road where we can't see anything of it, we won't be any worse off staying here than if we hadn't come at all. At least we're safe here, and we can enjoy the picnic your mum's made us – if not in the most comfortable surroundings."

"Great. So, shall we have our lunch now? I know it's only just gone eleven, but we want to be sure we finish eating before there's anything to see – and it's not as if we've got anything else to do."

"Yes, let's do that."

Half an hour later they had finished their lunch, and settled down to wait, taking it in turns to scan the stretch of Castle Road opposite with the field glasses for signs of movement.

For over three hours nothing much happened. About an hour after they finished their lunch a tractor pulling a trailer trundled down the road, but there was no other traffic.

Their wait was not a comfortable one. Early on Ben sat down on a tree stump which was not as dry as it looked and got the seat of his jeans and his underpants damp. Then, he developed cramp by crouching on his haunches too long, and got bitten on his legs by ants which had found their way under the bottom ends of his jeans. He realised he had been rash to assume that, if they saw nothing, they would be no worse off than if they had not come at all.

Alison had also been bitten, receiving some kind of insect bite to her neck, and began feeling cold and tired.

They got their first inkling that they had not suffered this discomfort in vain when Ben spotted some movement at the bend at the bottom end of the stretch of road they were watching. For a moment he could not make out exactly what this was, but then quickly realised that it was a black four-by-four backing up rapidly round the bend. At the same time he saw a security van bearing the name Surrey Security travelling down the road towards the bend and coming to a sudden halt a few yards back from the four-by-four.

"Look," he said, grabbing Alison's arm.

She trained her mother's opera glasses on the scene below.

A large black man got out of the four-by-four and started walking towards the security van. He had something in his right hand which looked like a long gun.

The two men in the security van recognised the weapon as a semi-automatic and, though they were themselves armed, and the windscreen of their vehicle was supposed to be bulletproof, both ducked down below the dashboard, and the man in the passenger seat spoke urgently into a hand-held radio.

Almost instantly a loud hailer boomed out from somewhere behind the security van, "Armed police. Put down your weapon."

The large black man stopped in the middle of the road, and hesitated for a moment, as if suspecting a trick on the part of the crew of the security van, but then dropped his gun, turned, and ran back towards the four-by-four holding both arms high above his head. He got into the vehicle, and quickly backed it up a couple of feet as if lining it up to drive it off down the road.

"He's not going to get away, is he?" said Alison. "The police are bound to have blocked off the bottom end of the road by now, aren't they?"

The same thought had obviously occurred to the driver of the four-by-four, for, instead of driving off down the road, he swung his steering wheel round sharply, and drove at a gap between two trees at the side of the road nearest to Ben and Alison. At first the vehicle seemed to get stuck on a low bank of earth bordering the road, and also to be held back by a bush growing between the two trees, but the driver rolled it back a few feet, and then flung it back at the gap between the trees, this time successfully getting over the bank and flattening the bush which had stood in his way.

To Ben's and Alison's relief, the four-by-four did not come in their direction, but drove along the side of a small wood running at right angles to the road at the bottom of the field before disappearing through a gap between the wood and a hedge running roughly parallel to the road.

Where the motorcyclist came from, Ben and Alison did not see, but suddenly a short, heavily built man dressed from head to foot in black leather appeared driving a motorcycle in hot pursuit of the four-by-four, and disappeared after it through the same gap. They assumed he was a police officer, and hoped he would catch the driver of the four-by-four.

A police car came screaming up the road from the bottom of the hill and round the bend with its two-tone horn sounding, its blue light flashing and four uniformed police officers inside. It attempted to follow the route taken by the four-by-four and the motorcyclist, but got stuck on the bank between the road and the field, apparently unable to move forwards or backwards. The driver began calling for urgent assistance on his radio, while the other three officers scrambled out of the car, and began running across the field. Two headed for the gap which the four-by-four and motorcycle had gone through, but the third began making his way up the field towards the wood where Ben and Alison were hiding. Convinced that they were well concealed, they could see no reason for him to be coming in their direction, but they decided that they preferred not to risk a possible confrontation with him, grabbed their rucksacks, got back out of the wood the way they had come as quickly as they could, and began walking back along Chipstead High Road.

As they approached the entrance to Castle Road, they saw uniformed police officers and marked police vehicles everywhere. Some of the vehicles had their blue lights flashing. Alison spotted Elliott with his back to them in the middle of a group of uniformed police officers and others whom she assumed to be plain-clothes officers. She and Ben began to move towards him, and, as they did so, passed several uniformed officers escorting two white men in handcuffs to a police carrier. They recognised the men as the two who had attacked them in Brixton Station, although the one who had been wearing sunglasses then was not wearing them now. The recognition appeared to be mutual, for both men scowled aggressively at them, causing Alison to take a step backwards. She and Ben guessed that the men had been caught following the security van in another vehicle, and arrested as suspected participants in the attempted robbery.

As they got close to Elliott, Alison and Ben heard crackling over a police radio, a voice saying, "Yes, sir, he's dead. Single bullet to the head. No sign of the motorcyclist or the weapon used."

Before she could stop herself, Alison found herself blurting out, "Who's that? Is it Ice? Is he dead?"

Elliott wheeled round furiously. "What the hell are you two doing here?" he demanded angrily. "I told you to stay away. How did you get here? Did you come by car?"

Alison nodded, while Ben stared shamefacedly at the floor.

Elliott called over a uniformed officer, and told him to escort Ben and Alison to their car. "And make sure you see them leave," he added grimly.

Then, without another word, he turned sharply on his heel, and walked off.

Post-Mortem

When Alison and Ben got back to her parents' house later that afternoon, she announced to her mother that Ben was cutting short his stay with them, and was heading back to London.

"Oh dear," said Mary, who had been rather hoping to get Ben to play the piano again for them that evening. "Nothing wrong at home, I hope."

"No, nothing like that. He's got to get back to cover for a colleague who's supposed to be on duty this evening, but has called in sick," Alison lied.

Mary, who in some ways knew her daughter well, was fairly sure that Alison was not telling her the truth. She noticed that both Alison and Ben looked subdued and tired. She wondered whether they had quarrelled, and, if they had, whether this would mean the end of their relationship. To her surprise, she found that her first reaction to this possibility was one of regret, but then she told herself that, if their relationship was ending, it would probably be for the best. After all, Alison was a very pretty girl, and would surely attract other nice young men, one of whom would make her a more… suitable husband.

Before Ben got into his car to drive off, he and Alison exchanged a brief, almost formal, kiss, which Mary, watching from the lounge, found it difficult to interpret. It did not occur to her that her presence at the window might have had some influence on the manner of their parting.

About an hour after Ben had left, the phone rang. Alison went to answer it, but her mother got there first. "It's the police," she said in a low voice, keeping her hand over the mouthpiece. "A Chief Inspector Elliott. He says he wants to speak to you."

"Yes. It's OK. I know what it's about," said Alison, taking the receiver from her mother.

Mary lingered, but her daughter waved her away with her hand.

"Alison French speaking," she said tentatively into the phone.

"This is Chief Inspector Elliott." The officer's voice was formal. "I need to speak to you and Mr Weekes about this afternoon's events, and I would be obliged if you could both come and see me here in my office first thing on Monday morning."

Alison thought for a moment. "Could we make it Monday afternoon?" she asked diffidently.

"Very well. Two o'clock all right?"

"Yes, thank you. That will be fine."

"Do I need to contact Mr Weekes, or will you do that?"

"No, I'll tell him. Thank you."

As Alison replaced the receiver, her mother reappeared, saying, "I hope you're not in any trouble."

"No, don't worry, Mum. I'm just helping the police with their enquiries," said Alison.

Her mother took the bait. "Oh dear," she said. "Isn't that what they say about people who are being questioned by the police because they're suspected of having committed a crime?"

"Well, sometimes it is, but that's not the position I'm in," said Alison, with more confidence than she felt. "The police want to talk to me about a case which I've been covering for the paper, because they think some of what I've found out may be useful to them in investigating the case."

"That sounds interesting," said Mary, looking at her daughter expectantly.

"Yes, it is, but I can't say more. It's confidential."

Later that evening, when Alison was sure that her mother was engrossed in her favourite television programme, she telephoned Ben to tell him about their appointment with Elliott, and then telephoned Neeta.

"Ben and I have been summoned back to see Chief Inspector Elliott again on Monday afternoon," she told her, "and we wondered if you could come with us."

"Yes, I think I can manage that. You're in luck because I've got a case on Monday morning which I was expecting to be a trial lasting all day, but my client's just told me he wants to change his plea to guilty, so the hearing will be a five-minute one, just long enough for him to enter his plea and for the case to be adjourned for reports, and that leaves me without any other appointments for the rest of the day."

"Thank you. I can't tell you how relieved I am to hear that."

"I'm pleased to be able to help. So, did Elliott tell you why he wants to see you and Ben again?"

"No, but we know why," said Alison, and described the afternoon's events.

Neeta listened fascinated, both wishing that she had been with Ben and Alison that afternoon and very glad that she had not. However, feeling that what was expected from her was a professional response, she said, "Well, I have to say I think you've both been very foolish, but I can't see that you've done anything for which you could be charged with an offence, so, although I am happy to come along with you if you like, I don't think you need me there, and I think that's why Elliott hasn't been in touch with me to suggest I accompany you. He strikes me as the kind of officer who does things by the book, and not one who tries to interview suspects without their solicitor when he knows they have one."

"Well, that's certainly reassuring, but I'd still prefer you to be there, if you don't mind."

Neeta, who was intrigued to hear what Elliott would have to say about the afternoon's events, was happy to agree, and they made arrangements for Ben and Alison to pick her up at Guildford Station between one o'clock and half past one the following Monday afternoon.

Elliott was angry and disappointed at the outcome of that afternoon's operation. It was true that he had clearly foiled an attempted armed robbery, and had taken into custody two men who had clearly been involved in the commission of the offence, but the man whom he believed to be his main target in the operation was dead, and the fact that that man had been shot dead in the course of the operation would place the whole operation under intense scrutiny. He was satisfied that the man had not been shot by any of his officers, and, indeed, that none of his officers had discharged their weapons during the operation, but the fact that a man had died in the course of a police operation meant that the matter would have to be investigated by the Police Complaints Authority.

He decided that at least the file on the case which he submitted to the PCA should be beyond reproach, and he determined therefore both to make this file as full as possible and to put it together as quickly as possible. He gave instructions that none of the officers who had been involved in the operation that afternoon was to leave work until they had written up their notes and made witness statements giving full details of what they had seen and done. He also instructed the police photographers who had taken extensive photographs of the scene to let him have prints of their photographs by the end of the weekend. He arranged for a full post-mortem to be carried out on the dead man the following week, and, in the meantime, he had the man's fingerprints taken, and had the bullet removed from his brain by the pathologist, and submitted for an urgent ballistics' examination. He made an urgent request to the Jamaican Constabulary in Kingston for a photograph of Winston Henry and a full set of his fingerprints. Finally, he and other members of his team made a number of attempts to interview the two men who had been arrested at the scene of the operation, though both men refused to say anything.

On Monday morning he reviewed the evidence he had assembled so far. The officers who had pursued the four-by-four and the motorcycle on foot reported in their statements that they had found the four-by-four stationary in the corner of a field with the driver's door open. Why it had stopped was not clear. There was no sign of the motorcycle or its rider.

A few yards from the four-by-four the officers had found the dead body of the man who had been seen driving the vehicle. He had a bullet wound to his head which appeared to be the cause of death. Formal identification of the dead man had not yet been carried out, but the fingerprints taken from him and photographs taken of his face matched the fingerprints and photograph of Winston Henry which had been faxed to Elliott by the Jamaican Constabulary. In addition, the few articles found in the dead man's possession included a forged driving licence in the name of Carlton Healy. The pathologist who had taken the bullet from the dead man's head had told Elliott that he had little doubt that it was the cause of death, and a preliminary ballistics report revealed that it had been fired at close range from a Glock 9mm semi-automatic pistol. Early investigations had found no evidence of the weapon having been used in the commission of other offences, which, Elliott knew, would make tracing its source even more difficult than usual, and which was also of concern to him as revealing the presence in circulation of yet another dangerous illegally held firearm.

The prime suspect in the killing of the man Winston Henry was clearly the motorcyclist, but, to his frustration, Elliott had to acknowledge that he had almost no clue as to this suspect's identity. Virtually all he had was a description of the man as short and squat and dressed in black leathers. Even the evidence as to where the motorcyclist had appeared from was conflicting, though the consensus of most of those who had seen him seemed to be that he had emerged from the woodland along the edge of which the four-by-four had been driven away from the scene of the attempted robbery.

Beyond this very limited information about the suspect, all Elliott had been able to do was to eliminate some possibilities. He had quickly established that the motorcyclist was not one of the officers engaged on the operation, and he felt almost certain that the man was not a police officer of any description. He had ruled out McKinnon as the suspect, both because, as a tall man, he did not fit the description of the suspect and because a quick telephone call to Brixton Police Station had revealed that, at the time in question, McKinnon had been with other officers in the CID room there writing up his notes on an arrest he had made earlier that day.

Elliott's hunch was that Henry had been murdered by a contract killer hired by a rival criminal, possibly because he had been discovered to be, or was suspected to be, a police informant. The officer had hoped that the two men arrested at the scene of the attempted robbery, who were clearly associates of Henry's, might be able to provide him with information about the dead man's activities which might help him to pursue this line of enquiry. The men had been stopped in a white Saab which was following the security van and in which had been found semi-automatic weapons and oxyacetylene cutting equipment. As a result, Elliott had told them that he anticipated that, when his enquiries were complete, they would be charged with attempted armed robbery, but that, if they provided him with information about Henry's activities and about anyone who might have wanted to have Henry killed, Elliott would write a letter to the judge before whom they appeared which would ensure that they would receive lighter sentences than they would otherwise get. But the two men had refused to say anything.

Elliott also felt that he needed to try and discover how Henry's killer had known where to locate his victim that Friday afternoon, but he knew that this, too, was likely to be difficult. He supposed that, if Ben's informant had known about Henry's plans, at least one or two others would have known about them too.

Neeta's unexpected arrival with Ben and Alison that afternoon was greeted by Elliott with some reserve.

"I did not expect to see you here this afternoon, Ms Patel," he said. "And I really don't think Mr Weekes and Ms French need your assistance on this occasion. If I had thought they needed you here, I would, of course, have invited you myself. Let me explain." He turned to Alison and Ben. "I do not deny that I am extremely annoyed at your behaviour on Friday afternoon, which, as you are fully aware, was directly contrary to my clear and explicit instructions to you, but that is not why I have asked you here today. My reason for calling you in, is to ask you to make witness statements about what you saw that afternoon. As you are aware, the events at which you were present culminated in a man's death. That death is now the subject of a murder enquiry, and, as part of that enquiry, I require you to make statements about what you witnessed in relation to the events surrounding the victim's death." He turned back to Neeta. "And that, I hope you will agree, is not something on which your clients require the advice of a solicitor."

"In principle, of course, you're right," said Neeta, "and, if you had told Ms French at the outset why you wanted to see her and Mr Weekes, I would almost certainly not have felt any need to accompany them to this meeting, but, now that I'm here, I hope that you will not mind if I stay, just in case anything arises on which they feel they would like my advice."

"As you wish," said Elliott stiffly.

He turned back to Ben and Alison but before he could speak, Alison asked, "So is it Ice who was killed?"

346

"I'm sorry," replied Elliott, "but I cannot discuss with you, or tell you anything about, the offence which I am investigating, particularly as you are witnesses in my investigation, and it is essential that you do not hear anything from me that might affect your evidence."

Alison opened her mouth as if about to argue, but, seeing Neeta look towards her and shake her head, she closed it again without speaking.

"Right," continued Elliott. "Now the way I'd like you to make your statements is this. I want you to make them separately, because, although I know you will have talked to each other about the events in question since they occurred, I would like, as far as possible, to get your independent recollections of what you saw. Don't worry about the possibility that your accounts may differ from one another. It is well understood that people often remember things differently, and no one will think that one of you is lying. Secondly, in order to ensure that your statements include all the information we need them to, I'm going to ask each of you to make your statement with the assistance of one of my officers to whom I'd like you to dictate what you want to say, and who will probably ask you questions as you go along, and incorporate your answers into your statement. Are you happy with that?"

"What if your officer asks me a question which I'm not sure if I should answer? Can I ask Ms Patel for her advice about that?" asked Alison.

Elliott looked at her disapprovingly. "I really don't think there's any possibility of that situation arising," he said, "but, if you wish Ms Patel to sit in with you while my officer takes your statement from you, I don't have any objection to that – though, if both you and Mr Weekes want Ms Patel to assist you in that way, you'll have to make your statements one after the other, so the whole process will take twice as long."

"I don't mind that," said Alison, "and I'm sure Ben won't either. What about you, Neeta?"

The solicitor privately shared Elliott's view that there was no need for her to sit in while statements were taken from her clients, but said, "No, that's fine with me."

Alison's statement was taken from her by a young woman police officer in plain clothes in a small, bare room furnished with just a table and four chairs. The officer was brisk and businesslike, but, although her manner to Neeta, while polite, was frosty, she did all she could to put Alison at her ease. She wrote down what Alison said in large, bold, neat handwriting, and Alison did not find the process as stressful as she had expected, for, although she felt that some of the questions she was asked seemed to betray a disapproval by the officer of what she and Ben had done, she did not feel at any point that the officer was trying to put words in her mouth, as she had feared might happen. Nor did she at any time feel the need to consult Neeta. Nevertheless, she was glad when she had read the statement through and signed it, and the process was over.

Ben's statement was taken from him in the same room by another officer in plain clothes, but this time a young male officer who treated both Ben and Neeta with what appeared to Ben rather exaggerated courtesy, particularly in comparison with the treatment which he had received at the hands of the young, uniformed officers he had encountered in Brixton. Neeta thought the officer seemed more interested than his colleague had been in Ben's and Alison's story and less inclined to be critical of their actions. The handwriting in which he wrote down Ben's statement was small and untidy, and, when Ben came to read through the statement, he found some of it almost illegible. "Don't worry," said the officer, obviously sensing his difficulty, "it'll get typed up." Ben signed the statement, and the officer said, "Thank you, sir," and shook hands both with him and with Neeta.

On reading through Ben's and Alison's statements after his visitors had left, Elliott noted with satisfaction that, although there was little in them which was new to him, there was also nothing in them which provided the basis for any criticism of the police, and, although the two statements differed in some minor details from each other and from the statements of his officers, these discrepancies were not large enough to undermine the coherence of the picture presented by the evidence as a whole. Elliott felt indeed that these minor discrepancies added to the credibility of the statements of all concerned, as statements which were too similar to each other were often suspected to be the product of collusion between the witnesses making them. The only thing in the two statements which was new to him was the information that the two men who had been arrested in the course of the operation had previously attempted to assault Ben and Alison. He might, he thought, have to ask the young couple to give further statements about this incident, but, for now, he did not think that this was necessary.

Elliott decided he needed to re-interview DC McKinnon, both in relation to Delroy Brown's death and McKinnon's relationship with Winston Henry, and also to ascertain whether McKinnon had any information which might assist him in identifying Henry's killer. He telephoned DCI Greaves to arrange the interview, and was told that McKinnon had taken the following day off in order to see his solicitor, but that Greaves would make sure that he was available for interview the day after that. Elliott grimaced and pursed his lips. He assumed that McKinnon had heard about the previous Friday's events, had anticipated being called in for interview, and had made arrangements to see his solicitor in order to be prepared for the interview.

It was therefore no surprise to Elliott that, when he arrived at Brixton Police Station to carry out the interview, he found McKinnon accompanied by Roger Jessop, nor that, as soon as they sat down in the interview room, the solicitor said, "I have here a statement made by my client, which we hope will expedite matters."

Elliott took the statement and read:

STATEMENT
Statement of Michael McKinnon
Age: Over 21

I make this statement of my own free will. I understand that I do not have to say anything, but that it may harm my defence, if I do not mention, when questioned, something which I later rely on in court. This statement may be given in evidence.

Dated 18th September   Signed M. McKinnon

I wish to make a further statement about the events leading to the death in his cell of Mr Delroy Brown in order to clarify the reason why I went to Mr Brown's cell on the occasion on which he subsequently assaulted me, and, as a result, met with the accident which led to his death, and also to clarify certain related matters.

The re-opening and prolongation of the enquiry into Mr Brown's death continue to cause me great distress, and, as a consequence of the emotional state which I am in as a result, I believe that it is in the best interests of all concerned for me to provide this clarification in a written statement, rather than in the course of an interview.

I deny that I committed any criminal or disciplinary offence in my dealings with Mr Brown or in relation to any of the other matters covered by this statement.

I consent to this statement being used in the investigation into Mr Brown's death or any disciplinary proceedings which may follow that investigation.

Dated 18th September   Signed M. McKinnon

In my original statement about this matter, I referred to information which I had received about Mr Brown, and which led me to visit him in his cell just before his death. I now wish to clarify that I obtained this information from a conversation between two of my colleagues, DC Mathews and DC Jones, and that it was to the effect that Mr Brown was offering to provide us with information about an individual called 'Eyes'. This was of concern to me, as I believed that the man Mr Brown had apparently referred to as 'Eyes' might in fact be a man with the street name 'Ice', who was known to me as Carlton Healy and who worked for me as a registered informant. If this was the case, and the man Mr Brown had offered to supply us with information about was Healy, this suggested that Healy might be committing, or have committed, serious offences which would make it inappropriate for me to continue using him as an informant. I therefore went to see Mr Brown in his cell in order to ascertain whether the man he had apparently referred to as 'Eyes' was indeed Healy, and, if so, what information Mr Brown had about Healy's activities. However, as I said in my original statement, before I had a chance to say anything, Mr Brown jumped off the bed, and came at me in a frenzy.

I did not disclose this information relating to the man known to me as Carlton Healy in my original statement, not only because I did not believe it to be relevant to the enquiry into Mr Brown's death, but, more seriously, because I feared that, if it became known that Healy was a police informant, his life would be in danger. However, I understand that there is now no longer any need for me to protect Healy's identity as a police informant, as he recently died in the course of an operation conducted by another police force.

I have recently learned that the real name of the man known to me as Carlton Healy was Winston Henry, and that he was being sought by the police in Jamaica on three charges of murder. I was unaware of these facts when Henry/Healy agreed to work for me as a registered informant. At that time I carried out all proper checks on him, and found nothing then, or prior to Mr Brown's death, or indeed at any time until very recently, to suggest that Carlton Healy was not his real name, or that he had any criminal convictions, or was facing any criminal charges

I also understand that Henry/Healy met his death while attempting to carry out an armed robbery, and is suspected of having attempted to carry out other similar offences in this country. At no time prior to his death

*was I aware of his involvement in any serious offence,
and, if I had learned of his suspected involvement in
any such offence, I would immediately have ceased to
use him as an informant. As far as I was aware, the
only offences in which Henry/Healy was involved while
working for me as an informant were minor drugs
offences.*

Dated 18th September   *Signed M. McKinnon*

"Thank you for that clarification," said Elliott,
emphasising the last word with just a hint of sarcasm, "but
there remain a few questions which I would like to ask you
about this matter, and so, if you don't mind, I'd like to
proceed to the interview which you were asked to attend
for today."

McKinnon looked about to say something, but, before
doing so, looked questioningly at his solicitor. Jessop shook
his head, and McKinnon said nothing.

There was a tape recorder on the table beside Elliott, and
he turned it on. He stated that they were in an interview
room at Brixton Police Station, gave his name, the date and
the time, and asked McKinnon and Jessop to state their
names for the tape. Both did so, and Elliott announced that
this was a second interview of DC McKinnon in connection
with the death of Delroy Brown at Brixton Police Station
on 6th September the previous year. He formally cautioned
McKinnon, referred to the statement by McKinnon just
given to him, and read the statement out. Then, addressing
himself to McKinnon, he said,

"You say in your statement that, before employing the
man you knew as Carlton Healy as a registered informant,

you carried out all proper checks on him. Could you specify what those checks were?"

McKinnon once again looked questioningly at his solicitor, and this time Jessop nodded.

McKinnon said, "Having taken the legal advice of my solicitor, I do not wish to add anything to the statement I have just given you, sir."

Remembering the first time he had interviewed McKinnon, Elliott had expected this, but pressed on, in the slender hope that some of the questions he asked might be ones that McKinnon perceived it to be in his own interests to answer or that McKinnon's refusal to answer specific questions might just be used against him in a future trial by a skilful cross-examiner.

"Were you aware that the man was an illegal immigrant?"

"I have nothing to add to my statement, sir."

"What about his associates? Can you give me any of their names?"

"I have nothing to add to my statement, sir."

"At the time of the death of the man you knew as Carlton Healy, but whom we now know to be Winston Henry, we arrested two men called Ray North and Joseph, or Joe, Peters, who appeared to have been engaged with him in attempting to carry out an armed robbery. Do you know these men or anything about them?"

"I have nothing to add to my statement, sir."

"Do you know of anyone who might have wanted to kill Henry or to have him killed?"

"I have nothing to add to my statement, sir."

"Do you have any information at all that might assist us in identifying Henry's killer?"

"I have nothing to add to my statement, sir."

Elliott felt frustrated. He could not see how answering his last questions could, in any way, have led McKinnon to incriminate himself in relation to the death of Delroy Brown. His first assumption was that McKinnon's refusal to answer these questions was due to a slavish adherence by him to the advice he had received from Jessop before the interview. But, then again, he thought, McKinnon could have looked to his solicitor for the nod advising him that he could answer these questions without incriminating himself, and had not done so. Elliott began to wonder whether McKinnon was afraid that the more Elliott learned about Henry, Henry's associates and those involved in Henry's death, the more likely it was that Elliott would discover something about McKinnon's relationship with Henry which McKinnon was anxious to hide – something perhaps that McKinnon had suspected that Delroy Brown knew. That would have given McKinnon a motive to threaten Brown, rough him up or perhaps even kill him.

Elliott looked thoughtfully at McKinnon, and then, abruptly, brought the interview to an end. It was clear that McKinnon was not going to answer any more questions, and therefore, whatever Elliott's suspicions, there was no way they were going to be either confirmed or refuted by prolonging his questioning. He had, he decided, better things to do with his time.

For the next few days, Elliott concentrated on trying to gather all the information he could which might help him to identify Winston Henry's killer, seeking to find out all he could about Henry's activities, his associates and anyone with a motive for wanting him dead. He realised that this was information which his own team would have difficulty in unearthing, and that his best chance of obtaining it lay in enlisting the assistance of the Brixton Police in doing so. He telephoned DCI Greaves.

Greaves was conscious that his supervision of DC McKinnon was likely to come under critical scrutiny after the revelation of the truth about McKinnon's informant, and he was, therefore, despite his lingering resentment of Elliott, determined to do all he could to redeem himself by doing all he could to assist Elliott in his efforts to identify Henry's killer. He called all his officers together, and told them that they were to do everything they could to obtain the information Elliott had asked for, exerting every ounce of pressure that they could on their informants and on anyone else who would talk to them.

Greaves' officers did as they had been instructed, but, despite the forceful and sometimes threatening encounters which some of them had with their informants and others, they came up with very little. One informant linked Henry to an unsolved case involving the attempted hijacking of a security van, but professed to know nothing of the other participants in this offence. Two men were named as working as drug dealers for Henry and brought in for questioning, but, although, on being promised that they would not be prosecuted for these offences, they admitted dealing drugs for Henry, they claimed to know nothing else about his activities, his associates or anyone who might have a motive for wanting him dead. They and everyone else the police spoke to denied all knowledge of the two men, Ray North and Joe Peters, who had been arrested as Henry's accomplices. All the officers reported that, despite the fact Henry was dead, everyone they spoke to appeared very fearful of talking to the police about him or anything to do with him.

While Elliott was awaiting the results of these enquiries by the Brixton Police, he received a letter from Neeta Patel enclosing two witness statements, one by herself and the other by Alison French, which Neeta said in the letter were 'self-explanatory', and which she asked to have taken into account in the consideration of any possible criminal charges against DC McKinnon arising from the death in custody in Brixton Police Station of Delroy Brown.

The two statements, which both appeared to have been drafted by Neeta, were in almost identical form. Each woman began her statement by giving her name and her profession – in Neeta's case as a solicitor of the Supreme Court and in Alison's as a journalist employed by the *Brixton Chronicle* – and each went on to report that, in the course of her profession, she had, together with the other woman and a third woman known to them as Pat, had a meeting with a man known to her as Robert, or Bertie, O'Connor. Each then gave the time and date of the meeting and stated that, at that meeting, Mr O'Connor had supplied them with information about the death in custody at Brixton Police Station on 6th September the previous year of Delroy Brown, and that, as Mr O'Connor had been in the cell next to Mr Brown's at the time of Mr Brown's death, this was information on a matter of which Mr O'Connor had personal knowledge. Each then stated that she had made notes of what Mr O'Connor had said to them, and now produced these notes, made in the course of her profession, as an exhibit for admission in evidence in accordance with the provisions of sections 23 and 24 of the Criminal Justice Act 1988 in any criminal proceedings arising from Mr Brown's death.

Elliott read through the two statements several times, trying to make sense of them. He could not see how Neeta and Alison could give evidence of what O'Connor had said to them, as this was obviously hearsay and surely therefore excluded from evidence by one of the most basic rules of criminal evidence. He remembered vaguely having attended a seminar in which sections 23 and 24 of the 1988 Criminal Justice Act had been discussed, but he could not ever remember them being relied on in any of the many cases in which he had been involved over the past ten years or so. He got down a copy of the Act from his bookshelf and began studying the two sections. It was a little difficult to work out how they fitted together, but, in the end, he thought he could see how it could be argued that Alison's and Neeta's notes of what O'Connor had said to them were admissible under these sections. He retained, however, a strong gut instinct that somehow the basic rule against hearsay would result in these notes being excluded from evidence. Neeta Patel struck him as a bright young lawyer, smarter than many of the defence solicitors he had come across, but he suspected that, on this occasion, she was being just a bit too clever. In any event, he would leave the issue to be sorted out by the Crown Prosecution Service. That's what it and its lawyers were paid for.

He wondered what it was that O'Connor had said to Neeta and Alison that Neeta was going to such lengths to get into evidence. He began looking at the copies of the women's notes which were attached to their statements. Both sets of notes were almost identical in form, and Elliott wondered if the two women had made them together, as police officers almost invariably did when writing up their notes about an incident in which more than one of them had been involved, but what immediately caught his attention in the notes were the words, 'Leave me alone, Mr McKenna'.

No wonder, he thought, that Neeta wanted O'Connor's evidence that these words had been called out by Delroy Brown admitted in evidence, for they clearly undermined McKinnon's claim that he had only acted in self-defence in response to an unprovoked attack made on him by Brown.

For Elliott, however, the proper way of getting O'Connor's evidence before a court was for O'Connor to make a witness statement, and then to appear in court to give his evidence in person. He felt frustrated that his officers had not been successful in getting O'Connor to give them a statement, and he wondered if he should make another attempt, perhaps in person, to get the man to do so. He thought about this for some time, but finally decided against it. Not only had O'Connor refused to give a statement to Elliott's officers, but he had also categorically told Alison and Neeta, whom he appeared to like and trust, that he was not prepared to make one. Moreover, even if Elliott managed to get a statement from him, it seemed more than likely that O'Connor would not turn up at court to give evidence – which would render his statement useless. After all, the man had not turned up to give evidence at the coroner's court, even after indicating a willingness to do so. Elliott had seen too many cases which had taken months to prepare collapse because a key witness had failed to turn up at court to give evidence for this to be something he wanted to risk in this case. Finally, there was the issue of O'Connor's credibility. Even if he did turn up at court, would his word be taken against the word of a police officer? Elliott doubted it.

He wondered if he should interview McKinnon again and put O'Connor's evidence to him, but was not convinced that this would be worth doing. McKinnon would either simply deny O'Connor's claim that Brown had called out 'Leave me alone, Mr McKenna', or refuse to answer questions about it, probably the latter. Nor, if no evidence of O'Connor's claim had been placed before the court, could any use be made at trial of any refusal by McKinnon to answer questions about it. That section of the interview would be excluded from evidence.

He decided to wait and see whether the Brixton Police unearthed anything about Winston Henry which raised questions about McKinnon's relationship with Henry which it was worth putting to McKinnon in an interview. If that happened and led Elliott to interview McKinnon again, he could include questions about O'Connor's claim in the same interview.

Then Greaves reported, with obvious regret, how little his officers had managed to discover about Winston Henry.

Elliott was disappointed and frustrated. He knew how difficult it could be to get anyone in a place like Brixton to say anything about a man like Henry, alive or dead. He decided that there was no point in interviewing McKinnon again, and could think of nothing else he could do to investigate McKinnon's role in Delroy Brown's death. He put Neeta's and Alison's statements and the copies of their notes attached to these, McKinnon's statement and a transcript and a tape of his interview with the officer all in a large envelope and sent them to the Crown Prosecution Service.

Several weeks later, just before Christmas, he received a letter from the CPS. It was, he noted with some surprise, signed by the new director of public prosecutions, and it read :

Dear Chief Inspector Elliott,

Death in Custody of Mr Delroy Brown
Detective Constable Michael McKinnon

As you will be aware, following an earlier review by the Crown Prosecution Service, my predecessor requested Treasury Counsel to advise on whether criminal proceedings should be brought against Detective Constable McKinnon in relation to the death in custody at Brixton Police Station on 6th September last year of Mr Delroy Brown.

I have now received Counsel's Opinion on this matter and his advice may be summarised as follows:

1. Mr Brown died as the result of striking his head on the wall of his cell in the course of a confrontation between him and DC McKinnon.

2. The initial reason given by DC McKinnon for visiting Mr Brown in his cell was vague and might even be characterised as evasive, but, in his second statement, DC McKinnon explains his reason as being to determine whether Mr Brown had information about an informant of DC McKinnon's which might have made it inappropriate for DC McKinnon to continue using this man as an informant. He also explains the reason for his failure to reveal this earlier as being in order to protect the safety of his informant. Both these explanations are plausible, and no evidence has been produced to contradict them.

3. DC McKinnon's account of what happened when he entered Mr Brown's cell is that Mr Brown launched an unprovoked attack on him, and that DC McKinnon, using what he says was only reasonable force, pushed Mr Brown away from him, as a result of which Mr Brown fell striking his head on the wall as he did so.

DC McKinnon's case is therefore that he acted in self-defence, and a charge of murder or manslaughter against DC McKinnon can only succeed if the prosecution can disprove this defence beyond reasonable doubt.

4. DC McKinnon does not offer any explanation for Mr Brown's alleged assault on him, but there is some evidence that Mr Brown was under the influence of cannabis at the time, and/or that he was in a disturbed state of mind at the prospect of a lengthy prison sentence.

5. The only evidence tending to undermine DC McKinnon's account of events and his claim that he acted in self-defence is the evidence given by the pathologist Dr Houseman at the coroner's inquest into Mr Brown's death and the evidence of Mr Robert O'Connor. Both of these are problematical.

6. At the inquest Dr Houseman gave evidence that, in her opinion, the nature of the injury to the back of Mr Brown's head suggested to her that 'his head struck the wall with a force unlikely to have been caused by a fall, even a clumsy or awkward fall, and more likely to have been produced by the deceased having been propelled against the wall by something other than his own weight'. She also gave evidence that she had found marks on Mr Brown's shoulders which suggested to her that he had been grasped by the shoulders by someone facing him. This implies, but does not prove, that DC McKinnon took hold of Mr Brown by the shoulders and pushed him hard against the wall, which in turn suggests, but does not prove, either that DC McKinnon was the aggressor or that, in defending himself, he used more force than was reasonable. However, the above opinions expressed by Dr Houseman at the inquest were

362

not opinions expressed by her in her original report, and, even at the inquest, they were put forward by her very tentatively. She agreed, in answer to a question from DC McKinnon's solicitor, Mr Jessop, that she could not be certain that Mr Brown did not die as the result of a fall.

7. *The evidence of Mr Robert O'Connor is even more problematical. It is alleged that Mr O'Connor, who was in the cell next to Mr Brown's at the time of Mr Brown's death, heard Mr Brown call out, 'Leave me alone, Mr McKenna', when DC McKinnon was in his cell. If this is true, it suggests, but does not prove, that, in his confrontation with Mr Brown, DC McKinnon did not act in self-defence, but was the aggressor. However, Mr O'Connor has refused to make a statement to police about this incident, and the only evidence of what he says he heard is the hearsay contained in the notes exhibited to statements by the solicitor, Ms Patel, and the journalist, Ms French, discussed further below. Even if Mr O'Connor were to give a statement to police confirming that he heard what he is said to have heard, it seems highly probable that he would fail to attend court to give evidence at any trial of DC McKinnon. He appears to have expressed a willingness to give evidence to the coroner's court, but failed to attend the inquest. There must also be significant doubts about Mr O'Connor's credibility as a witness. At the time of the incident to which his evidence relates Mr O'Connor had been arrested for being drunk and disorderly, and was therefore clearly under the influence of alcohol. In addition, his alleged claim that he heard Mr Brown call out 'Leave me*

alone, Mr McKenna', was not included in the original account of the incident which he gave to the Brixton Chronicle, and (although this is a minor matter) gets the officer's name wrong.

8. Ms Patel, the solicitor acting for Mr Brown's family, argues that, although what Mr O'Connor told her and the journalist Ms French he heard Mr Brown call out is prima facie inadmissible in evidence as hearsay, they can give evidence of it by producing in evidence under sections 23 and 24 of the Criminal Justice Act 1988 notes of a conversation they had with Mr O'Connor. Although this is a superficially plausible argument, there are a number of objections to it, of which the most important is that section 25 provides that a statement which is admissible under section 23 or 24 is not to be admitted in evidence where the court is of the opinion that it is not in the interests of justice to do so. Counsel is clear that the evidence of Ms Patel and Ms French would be excluded under this provision, because, given both the importance of what they say Mr O'Connor said to the case against DC McKinnon and the issues around Mr O'Connor's credibility referred to above, it would be found unfair to DC McKinnon for what they say Mr O'Connor said to be admitted in evidence without DC McKinnon being able to have Mr O'Connor cross-examined on it.

9. At the inquest into Mr Brown's death, the jury found that he had been unlawfully killed, and this was, by implication though not in law, a verdict that DC McKinnon was guilty of his murder or manslaughter. However, it is Counsel's opinion that there was

insufficient evidence before the inquest to justify this verdict, and, indeed, that, with respect to the learned coroner, it is not a verdict which he should have left to the jury.

10. Even taken at its highest, the evidence of Dr Houseman and Mr O'Connor, while tending to undermine DC McKinnon's claim that he acted in self-defence, is not sufficient to disprove that claim beyond reasonable doubt.

11. There is therefore insufficient evidence against DC McKinnon for there to be a realistic prospect of his being convicted of any offence arising out of the death of Mr Delroy Brown.

I endorse Counsel's conclusions, and I therefore advise that no further action be taken against DC McKinnon in this case.

This advice is given without prejudice to the question of whether any disciplinary action should be taken against DC McKinnon by the Police Complaints Authority or by the Metropolitan Police, as this is not a question upon which it is within my remit to advise.

Yours sincerely,
Douglas Watts, QC
Director of Public Prosecutions

Elliott was not surprised at the conclusion reached by Treasury Counsel and the DPP, and could see no grounds on which to quarrel with the reasoning by which it had been reached, but he was left with an uneasy feeling that he had not got to the truth of exactly why and how Delroy Brown had died. That was, however, he reflected ruefully, often the way with police work.

He did not expect his investigation into the murder of Winston Henry to fare any better. His instinct remained that it was a contract killing ordered by a rival criminal, a type of case in which it was notoriously difficult to obtain convictions. His best hope was that a police informant would assist his team in identifying the killer or the individual who had ordered the hit, but informants rarely dared to help police in these cases, and, in the rare case in which the police did acquire information enabling them to identify the perpetrators of the killing, the witnesses they needed to prove the case almost invariably refused to testify, whatever the promises made to them, or threats made against them, by the police.

Neeta also received a letter from the Crown Prosecution Service, but hers was much shorter, stating simply that, following a review of the case, and on the advice of Treasury Counsel, it had been decided not to prosecute DC McKinnon for any offence in relation to the death of Mr Delroy Brown, as there was no realistic prospect of his being convicted of any such offence.

Like Elliott, Neeta was not surprised at this decision. She had been advised by Counsel that the notes she and Alison had made of what Bertie had told them were unlikely to be accepted by the CPS as evidence which would be admitted in any criminal proceedings against DC McKinnon, and she had only submitted this evidence to Elliott in the hope that, taken with what was now known about McKinnon's relationship with Ice, it might promote further police enquiries which might ultimately lead to a prosecution of McKinnon, but she had been fully aware that, in this, she was clutching at straws.

She knew that she would find the DPP's decision difficult to explain to Delroy's family, and to get them to accept.

She telephoned them, and made an appointment for them to come in and see her.

Once again, it was only Delroy's parents and his brother who arrived to see her.

As Neeta had expected, her clients could not understand how the DPP had come to the decision he had. As they tried to take it in, Delroy's parents sat looking subdued, finding it difficult to know what to say, but Leroy demanded angrily, "Can't you do nothin' 'bout this? Can't we appeal?"

His mother rebuked him sharply. "Don't you go talkin' to Miss Patel like that, after all she done for us."

Neeta was conciliatory. "No, that's all right. I understand your being upset and angry. I would be too, if I were in your position. So, to answer Leroy's question, no, you can't appeal against the DPP's decision, but there are a couple of things you could do, at least in theory. You could apply to the High Court for a judicial review of the decision, asking the Court to overturn it, and order the DPP to think again. However, you would only succeed in this if you could prove either that there was something wrong or unfair about the way in which the DPP reached his decision or that it was a decision that no reasonable DPP would have made. So, even if the Court itself would have made a different decision, it will not overturn the DPP's decision unless you prove one of those two things, and I think you would find that difficult, if not impossible. The second thing you could do is to sue the Metropolitan Police for damages for wrongfully causing Delroy's death."

"We don't want no money," said Malcolm Brown quietly. "All we want is recognition that what that officer did to Delroy was wrong."

"Yes, well, an award of damages against the police would do that, too, and one advantage of suing the police for damages would be that, unlike a criminal case where the prosecution have to prove their case beyond reasonable doubt, you would only have to prove your case on what's called a balance of probabilities, that is, that it's more likely than not, that it was wrongful action by DC McKinnon that caused Delroy's death."

"Well, we can sure prove that," said Leroy triumphantly.

"Perhaps," said Neeta carefully, "but these cases are harder to win than you might think, and there are a couple of other things. First, I'm sorry to say that I couldn't conduct the case for you, as I have no experience of what is called civil litigation, though I could help you find another solicitor to take it on for you. Secondly, you'd need to apply for legal aid to cover the cost of the case, and, to get that, you'd have to show that the case passed what's called the 'merits test', that is that it had a good chance of success."

"I can't see that bein' a problem," said Leroy.

"That's all very well," interjected his mother, "but, how long's all that goin' to take? Haven't we had enough upset and worry with all this legal stuff?" She turned apologetically to Neeta. "No disrespect to you, Miss Patel, I know you done your best for us, but all this settin' ourselves against the police, it's keepin' me awake at night. We always been a respectable family. I got to say I had enough."

"An' I don't like the idea of goin' for damages," added her husband. "It'd be like blood money."

"But…" objected Leroy.

"No, Leroy," his father interrupted him. "It's over, an' that's my final word on the matter." He turned to Neeta. "Thank you for all your help. We know we couldn't've had a better solicitor."

"That's right," agreed his wife.

"Thank you," said Neeta. "I only wish I'd been able to get you the result you wanted."

"Don't worry 'bout that," said Leroy. "They're right. You done us proud. You got that inquest jury to say that what that McKinnon did to my bro' was unlawful killin' and, for the rest, no one can win against the Feds, 'specially when they got the CPS and all that lot on their side. Sorry if I sometimes spoke outta turn."

"That's OK, Leroy," said Neeta. "You've never said anything that I thought wasn't justified."

The family got up to leave and Neeta got up to open the door of her office for them.

When they had gone she closed the door behind them and, as she did so, she found herself holding back a tear.

DC McKinnon did not wait to see whether disciplinary proceedings would be taken against him.

When Elliott had asked DCI Greaves for the help of the Brixton Police in gathering information about Winston Henry, Greaves had called McKinnon into his office to ask him what he knew about Henry's activities, his associates and anyone who might have wanted him dead.

McKinnon had been expecting this, and knew that he could not simply refuse to answer his DCI's questions, as he had refused to answer those put to him by Elliott in a formal interview under caution. He consulted Roger Jessop before going to see Greaves.

Greaves gave him a cold reception. "Right, what do you know about your man Henry's activities since he's been working for you?" he demanded.

"Nothing I haven't already told you about, sir. As far as I knew, all he was doing was a bit of dealing on Railton Road, where he had a couple of others working for him."

"I see," said Greaves sceptically. "And what about his associates, what do you know about them?"

"I only know those two, and I don't even know their names."

"Don't fucking give me that. You can't have an informant working for you as long as you had him working for you, and not know who at least some of his associates are."

"No, sir. It's true, sir. He would only ever meet up with me when we were both on our own. I have occasionally seen him with other men when I've been out and about, but, when that happened, we both took care to ignore each other, so I never got a close look at any of the men he was with, and I never saw him with anyone I knew."

"What about anyone who might have wanted him dead?"

"Well, there's only the dealers he's informed on. One of them might have worked out that Healy, I mean Henry, grassed him up, but they're all inside."

Greaves looked grim. "After the shit you've dropped me in over this man, are you really asking me to believe you can't give us some more fucking help in identifying his killer?"

"Yes, sir. I'm sorry. That's all I know."

Greaves lost his temper. "You fucking liar. Get out of here, you prick."

McKinnon got up quickly and left.

As soon as he had gone, Greaves picked up the phone, and made arrangements for him to be unceremoniously transferred back to the Traffic Division in Croydon.

McKinnon had not been popular with his colleagues in Croydon before his transfer to Brixton, and he now antagonised them further by attempting to boast about his time in the CID, and generally adopting an air of superiority towards them. Soon most of them were ostracising him, and treating him with the same contempt as he treated them. He became determined to leave the police, but equally determined not to do so until he knew whether he was to be prosecuted over Delroy's death, for, if he was to appear in the dock, he wanted to do so as a serving police officer and preferably in uniform. That, he knew, would considerably enhance his chances of being acquitted.

It was therefore only when he received formal notification from the CPS that he was not to be prosecuted that McKinnon handed in his resignation, and thus, at the same time, ensured that no disciplinary action could be taken against him.

He wondered if he could join Bull as a private investigator, but, when he telephoned Bull, he got a frosty reception.

"What do you want? The informant you were worried about is dead. So you don't need me any more."

McKinnon did not think there had been anything about Winston Henry's death in the papers, but decided against asking Bull how he knew of it. Instead he said, "I've left the job, and I wondered if you could use me in your operation. You know, what with my experience in CID."

Bull snorted with contempt. "I work alone, and now that your problem is resolved, it's in both our interests that we don't have anything further to do with each other. So, don't contact me again. If you do, it will have unpleasant repercussions for you. You understand?"

McKinnon was not sure he did. He could think of a number of possibilities, none of which he cared to contemplate further. He decided to do as Bull said.

A Summary Trial

Early in the new year Peter and Thomas Lloyd appeared for trial at Camberwell Green Magistrates' Court.

There were a number of reasons why their case had taken more than a year to come to trial. In the first place, the charges against them had been changed. The offences with which they had originally been charged by the police were all what were called either way offences, that is offences which could be tried either in the magistrates' court or in the Crown Court. Their solicitor had advised them that they had a better chance of being acquitted by a jury than by magistrates, and, accordingly, at their first appearance before Camberwell Green Magistrates' Court, they had elected to be tried at the Inner London Crown Court. Their case had then been adjourned for six weeks for the police and Crown Prosecution Service to prepare the necessary paperwork for the committal of the case to the Crown Court. However, at the adjourned hearing, the CPS prosecutor had withdrawn the original charges, and had replaced them with three charges against each of the young men of assaulting a police officer in the execution of his duty. These offences were summary charges which could only be tried by a magistrates' court. Ostensibly, the reason for the change was that the CPS regarded the lesser charges which they had now preferred as sufficient to reflect the seriousness of the conduct of which the defendants were accused, but significant considerations for the CPS in making the change were that the cost of a magistrates' court trial would be significantly less than that of a trial before the Crown Court, and also that its lawyers believed, like the young men's solicitor, that the defendants were more likely to be convicted by magistrates.

Confronted by this change in circumstances, the solicitor representing Peter and Thomas had requested, and been granted, a further two-week adjournment to take his clients' instructions. During this adjournment the solicitor, an elderly man approaching retirement who had too often experienced just how difficult it was to win cases like this in the magistrates' court, had advised Peter and Thomas to plead guilty. Early guilty pleas would, he told them, earn them a lesser sentence than they would receive on conviction after a trial. His clients and their parents, however, appalled by the thought of the effect that criminal convictions would have on the young men's career prospects, had rejected this advice, and had told the solicitor they no longer wished him to act for them. At the next hearing, therefore, Peter and Thomas had appeared unrepresented, and, at the request of the duty solicitor, had been granted a further two-week adjournment to instruct a new solicitor.

When Peter and Thomas had next appeared in court they had been represented by Neeta Patel, and had pleaded not guilty to all charges. However, the court had not been able to fix a trial date, as the CPS had misplaced their file, and the prosecutor had therefore been unable to give the court the dates on which all the prosecution witnesses would be available to attend court. A further two-week adjournment had been granted to the CPS to enable them either to find their file or, at the very least, to get what were called the 'dates to avoid' of all the prosecution witnesses.

At the next hearing, a trial date had been fixed, but it was several months away, as it had been estimated by the parties that the trial would take two full days, and it had proved impossible to find an earlier date on which two whole court days would be free, and all the prosecution witnesses would be able to attend.

Then, shortly before the trial was due to take place, two of the police officers due to give evidence had unexpectedly become unavailable to attend court on the trial date because they had been called to give evidence in another case in the Crown Court on the same date, and the case had once more been adjourned for several months to a new trial date.

This time the trial went ahead.

Camberwell Green Magistrates' Court was an imposing, thirty-year-old white building which looked from the front like a large inverted letter T, consisting of a three-storey oblong lower section, with, above it, a squarer three-storey office block, set slightly back from the facade of the lower section and rising over its centre. On the first floor of the lower section were four courtrooms, the doors to which opened onto a large concourse. Courts 1 and 2 were remand courts, which worked through long lists of short hearings, such as applications for bail, the sentencing of convicted offenders and procedural hearings, like those committing cases to the Crown Court or fixing the dates of summary trials, while Courts 3 and 4 were where most of the summary trials were held. Peter and Thomas's trial was to take place in Court 3.

The arrangement of the work handled by the four courts meant that, at the beginning of days on which they were sitting, there were usually large numbers of defendants, solicitors, barristers, police officers, probation officers and others milling about outside Courts 1 and 2, but fewer people outside Courts 3 and 4. However, on the morning on which Peter and Thomas's trial was due to begin, there was a much bigger crowd than usual outside Court 3.

Neeta had arrived early and had gone up to the CPS room to speak to the lawyer who would be conducting the prosecution case against her clients. She discovered that it was to be David Lane.

Lane was a solicitor of about the same age as Neeta, and had joined the CPS less than a year earlier in the hope that the experience he gained with the organisation would be useful to him in what he hoped would be his future career as a defence solicitor, but he was regretting this decision. It was not that he had any qualms about prosecuting defendants rather than representing them, but that he felt that he was not being given sufficient time to prepare properly the cases he was being asked to conduct in court. He had only been given the file relating to the case against Peter and Thomas Lloyd late the previous evening, and had first got an opportunity to study it on his train journey home. What he had found in the file troubled him. In particular, he was concerned to find there a set of photographs of the injuries received by the defendants in their struggle with the police, which were to be produced in evidence by the defence, and which showed in the most graphic manner how much worse these injuries were than those received by the police officers. He also noted with unease that the two defendants were college students without any previous convictions.

Neeta had come up against Lane in a few short hearings in the remand courts, and had found him likeable and pleasant to deal with. She also judged him rather inexperienced, which today, she felt, was no bad thing. She asked him if he could give her copies of the statements made by the prosecution witnesses in the case. This was not something she was entitled to, but was a courtesy usually extended by CPS lawyers to defence solicitors, partly to save time in court, and Lane duly obliged.

"Could we have a word, when you've had a look at them?" he said.

"Sure," replied Neeta, wondering what he wanted to talk to her about.

She went to the canteen used by lawyers and other professionals working in the courts, and sat in a corner working her way quickly through the statements Lane had given her, underlining parts of them and feverishly scribbling notes in their margins and in her large blue notebook.

As soon as she had finished, she went down to meet up with her clients. She did not want them to think she was late.

Peter and Thomas were waiting outside Court 3 with their parents. The concourse was already beginning to fill up. There was a growing group of the young men's friends and supporters gathering outside Court 3, and a little way away from them, stood two police officers in uniform, the first of the prosecution witnesses to arrive.

With Peter and Thomas was their friend Mark Wright, whose actions had sparked off their confrontation with the police. Neeta had told him that she might need to call him to give evidence as a defence witness, and, although terrified at the prospect, he had agreed to do so. All three young men had slept badly the night before, and Mark had been violently sick. Neeta had gone carefully through their evidence with them the day before, and there was nothing she needed to talk to them about now, but she tried to do all she could to calm them down and reassure them.

David Lane appeared on the concourse, and beckoned to Neeta. She went over to him.

"How would you feel about a bind-over?" he asked.

Neeta was surprised. "Is that an offer?" she countered.

"I have to clear it with the officers and my line manager, but, in my view, it would be an appropriate way of dealing with the case," said Lane.

"Well, of course, I'll have to take instructions from my clients, and get back to you," said Neeta.

This unexpected turn of events presented her with a difficult dilemma, as she explained to her clients. "If you agree to be bound over, it means that you admit that what you did was a breach of the peace, you promise not to commit another breach of the peace for a fixed period, usually a year, and you become liable to pay a fine if you break this promise. The advantage of doing this is that a bind-over does not count as a conviction, so you do not get criminal records, but a record is kept of it by the court and the police, so, to that extent it's worse than an acquittal. Now, I think I can get you acquitted, but I must make it clear that I am by no means certain I can do so. It all depends on what the police officers say when I cross-examine them. I'll be honest and say that I'd like to fight this case, and to try and get you acquitted, but I'm not the one who will get a criminal record if I fail."

Peter, Thomas, and their parents looked worried.

"What do you advise, Ms Patel?" asked their father.

"I'm sorry," said Neeta, "I can't really add anything to what I've already said. I'm afraid that the decision is down to you. I'll leave you to discuss it among yourselves."

She moved a few yards away from them, where she was joined by Alison who had come to report on the case for the *Brixton Chronicle*.

Meanwhile David Lane had gone over to put his proposal to the police officers involved in the case, all but one of whom had now arrived.

He got a hostile reception. "In my view," said the senior officer, a sergeant, "a bind-over is never an appropriate way in which to deal with an assault on police. If the word gets round that we're soft on those who assault police officers, every officer on patrol will be a sitting duck, and we'll soon lose control of the streets."

"But," argued Lane, "these defendants are college students without any previous, who've just made the mistake of trying to stop a friend being arrested and who, to be honest, have come off much worse than you in terms of the injuries they've suffered."

"That's too bad," said the officer, "but they should never have got involved in the first place, and maybe this will teach them to show a bit more respect for police in the future. And anyway, the conduct of these defendants led to major rioting."

Lane thought privately that it would be more accurate to say that the conduct of these police officers had led to major rioting, but he said nothing. He left the officers and went to telephone the head of his branch of the CPS, Peter Rotherhithe.

He described the circumstances of the case, put forward his proposal to deal with the defendants by way of bind-overs, explained why he thought this was an appropriate way of disposing of the case, and asked Rotherhithe's permission to do so.

"What do the officers say?" asked Rotherhithe, although he knew from past experience what the answer would be.

"They're against it," said Lane.

"Well, there's your answer then," said Rotherhithe roughly.

It was his standard answer in situations like these for, although, in the days when he used to appear in court, he had never been a courageous advocate, and had taken every opportunity offered to him to compromise cases rather than to fight them, he was unsympathetic to any of his staff who tried to do the same, determined, in his current role, to do all he could to remain on good terms with the police.

Lane went back down to the concourse outside the courtrooms, where he beckoned Neeta over from her conversation with Alison.

"I'm sorry," he said shamefacedly, "my boss won't go for it."

Neeta experienced mixed emotions. She felt angry at what she felt was another slap in the face for her clients, and anxious that she might let them down, but, in a way, she was glad that the decision had been taken out of their hands, and, as for her annoyance at the change in Lane's position, she saw no point in taking it out on him. Besides, she always made a point of trying to remain on good terms with the CPS lawyers, as, from time to time, she had found herself able to use her good relationship with them to win some small concession from them for one of her clients. So, all she said to Lane was, "I see. Well, thank you for trying."

She went over to Peter, Thomas and their parents to tell them the news. They, too, reacted with mixed emotions, but Peter said defiantly, "Doesn't matter. We were going to fight it anyway."

An usher called them into court.

It was a wood-panelled courtroom. Facing them, as they went in through the door at the back of the room, was the raised magistrates' bench and, below this, also at a raised, but lower, level, and in an enclosed area, the court clerk's desk. To the right, and at the same level as the clerk's desk, was the witness box and, opposite this, the prosecutor's bench, also partly enclosed. At the back of the court facing the magistrates' bench was the dock, and, in front of this, facing in the same direction, and at the lowest level in the room, the seats and desks for defence solicitors and barristers. To the sides of the court and facing across it, were, on the right, benches for witnesses who had completed their evidence, and, on the left, benches for members of the press. At the back of the court, behind the dock and behind a glass screen, were a few seats for spectators, and, high above this, an open gallery which could accommodate more spectators, if needed. Today, both these areas quickly filled up with Peter and Thomas's friends and supporters.

David Lane, Neeta, Alison, Peter and Thomas all filed into court, while those who were to give evidence in the case remained outside the courtroom, waiting to be called as witnesses. Peter and Thomas were directed into the dock by the usher and the others all went to their places.

The court clerk called "Court rise!" and they all stood up.

Neeta had discovered before coming into court that the case was to be tried, not by a panel of lay magistrates, but by Martin Rickard, a metropolitan stipendiary magistrate, or 'stipe', that is a legally qualified and paid judicial officer.

"That's good news for us," she had told her clients. "Old Rickard is tough, and can be a harsh sentencer, but he's always fair, and, what's most important to us, he's a good lawyer, who will understand any points of law that come up without having to ask the advice of his clerk, which lay magistrates would have to do."

Rickard came in, said "Good morning," and sat down. He was pleased to see that Neeta Patel was representing the defendants, for he regarded her as a competent lawyer who would put her clients' case effectively without wasting the court's time.

Everyone took their seats, and the magistrate looked down at Neeta and said, "Ms Patel, I understand your clients have pleaded not guilty to all the charges. Does that remain the position?"

Neeta got to her feet. "Yes, sir," she said, and sat down again.

"Mr Lane?" said the magistrate enquiringly, turning to the CPS lawyer.

Lane got to his feet. "Sir," he said, "both defendants face charges of assaulting three police officers in the execution of their duty. These charges arise out of an incident in which PC Harris was attempting to arrest another individual for a public order offence, and these defendants intervened, and assaulted PC Harris and two other officers who went to his assistance." He paused briefly and then said, "With your permission, sir, I call PC Harris."

The magistrate nodded, and an usher brought PC Harris into court, where he took his place in the witness box.

The officer took the oath, and was then asked by Lane

if he recalled an incident in which he had been involved at about 11.30 on the evening of 8th September of the year before last. PC Harris asked if he could refer to his notes, and Lane asked him when he had made them. The officer said that he had made them roughly three hours after the incident, which, he said, was the first opportunity he had had to make them, and the magistrate agreed that he could refer to them.

The officer took his notebook out of his left breast pocket, and began reading from it in a slow, monotonous voice.

"At about 11.30 p.m. on 8th September of the year before last, I was the front-seat passenger in a marked police carrier being driven south along Brixton Road by Sergeant Norris. As it was a warm evening, I had the window next to me open. In the back of the vehicle were six other officers from my unit. We were in the area because there were fears of unrest following the death in custody of a prisoner at Brixton Police Station, and we had been tasked to assist in dealing with any public disorder which might arise from this. As a consequence, we were all either in riot gear or had it to hand. As we proceeded along Brixton Road, all appeared quiet with almost no one about, when I noticed three youths, the defendants and a smaller white youth, walking towards us along the pavement. Then suddenly, as they drew closer to us, the white youth raised his right arm in the air, made a 'V' sign at us, and shouted 'Wankers' in our direction."

A ripple of amusement ran through the spectators.

The magistrate glared at them, and then, turning to the officer, said, "Go on."

PC Harris continued, "I asked Sergeant Norris to stop our vehicle, and I got out and approached the three youths.

I asked the white youth to explain his behaviour, to which he replied, 'Fuck off, I haven't done anything'. I said, 'Mind your manners, young man, or I will have to arrest you'. He replied, 'But I haven't fucking done anything'. So, in view of his continuing aggressive behaviour and bad language, I said, 'Right, I'm arresting you for disorderly behaviour contrary to section 5 of the Public Order Act'. I put my hand on his arm to make sure that he did not run away, and began to caution him, but he shouted out, 'Piss off, let go of me', and tried to pull away from me. I therefore restrained him using an approved hold, at which the two defendants seized my shoulders violently from behind, and began to drag me hard away from the white youth. I continued to try and hold onto him, and a violent struggle developed between me and the three youths in which I received a number of cuts and bruises. At this point, the officers in the back of the carrier, who could see me being assaulted, came to my assistance, and, between us, we managed to restrain the defendants in spite of the fact that they were very violent. As a result of their intervention, however, the white youth, who I had been trying to arrest got free and ran off. In the meantime, some black youths on the other side of the road, who had been watching the whole thing, began shouting abuse at us and throwing stones and other missiles at us. A crowd gathered, serious public disorder began to develop, and it was only the arrival of other officers which prevented us from being overwhelmed by the mob. We managed to get the defendants into the back of the carrier, and took them to Brixton Police Station, where they were briefly detained, before being bailed to return there at a later date."

The magistrate looked grim. He turned to Neeta and said, "Cross-examination, Ms Patel?"

Neeta got slowly to her feet. She knew that how she handled the cross-examination of PC Harris would determine the outcome of this case. She turned to the officer and began, "You've referred to a group of young black men who witnessed this incident, but, apart from them, the young white man, the defendants and you and your colleagues, was anyone else present at the beginning of the incident?"

"No, as I've already said."

"And the young black men on the other side of the road, did they appear upset by the young white man's behaviour towards you?"

The officer looked scornful. "No, why would they? It wasn't aimed at them. In fact, they seemed to be enjoying it. These people have no respect for the law."

Neeta made a tick in her notebook, and carefully wrote down the officer's answer. She wondered whom his generalisation applied to. Young black men? Black people in general? But she let it pass. PC Harris might be a racist, but she had other issues to pursue with him, which, at least for today, were more important. She moved onto her next question.

"You're a member of the Territorial Support Group, is that right?"

The officer stood up a little straighter and said, "That's correct."

"And that means that you're called upon to deal with major incidents of public disorder, demonstrations, riots and so on, in which you get people hurling abuse at you, is that right?"

"Not just abuse, a lot more besides."

"And that must sometimes be distressing for you, I suppose."

The officer again looked scornful, pulled his shoulders back and said, "Not really. It's what we're trained for."

Neeta made another tick in her notebook and once again carefully wrote down the officer's answer.

There was a quiet rumble of discontent among Peter and Thomas's supporters. They could not understand what Neeta was doing. First, she had let this officer get away with a blatantly racist remark, and now she was encouraging him to boast about his police work.

Alison's reaction, however, was different. She had been watching the prosecuting lawyer and the magistrate. She noticed that both were paying very close attention to the exchanges between Neeta and PC Harris, and that, each time Neeta paused to write down one of the officer's answers particularly carefully, the magistrate seemed to be making a note of it, too. She began to feel that she was witnessing an elaborate game, and, although she couldn't work out what it was, she got a distinct impression that Neeta was winning.

Neeta began a new line of questioning. "You've referred to the young white man with the defendants as being smaller than them. Would it surprise you to hear that he is five-foot six inches tall?"

"No, sounds about right."

"And you're how tall?"

PC Harris stood up straight. "Six-foot two."

"So, quite a bit taller?"

"Yes, but the defendants are nearly as big as me. They must be about six-foot."

"Let's just concentrate on the young white man for the moment. Was he carrying a weapon?"

"Not so far as I could see."

"And you've said that you and your colleagues were all equipped with riot gear?"

"Well, I only had on my body armour and my baton attached to my belt."

"But you had your helmet and shield close at hand?"

"Well, yes."

"So, when this small young man made a 'V' sign at you and shouted 'Wankers' at you, did you feel alarmed?"

"No, of course not."

"Did you feel harassed?"

"No." The officer's reply came out quickly, but, as soon as he had given it, he suddenly lost his air of confidence, as he realised, too late, where this line of questioning was leading.

Neeta continued, "And, of course, you weren't distressed?"

The officer tried to recover the situation. "I wouldn't say that."

"But, Officer, how can you say that you were distressed by a small young man making a 'V' sign and shouting 'Wankers', when you've told this court that you have not been distressed by having abuse and other things hurled at you during major incidents of public disorder?"

"That's different," mumbled the officer. "This was an insult to the uniform."

"So, are you really saying that, when large crowds of people are shouting abuse at you and your colleagues, and throwing things at you, that is not an insult to the uniform?"

"No, that's just people getting carried away by the situation."

"I see," said Neeta, feeling annoyed with herself. She had, she thought, asked two questions too many. She decided that it would be a mistake to leave her cross-examination of PC Harris there, even though there was nothing else she really needed to ask him. She said, "I put it to you that, when you warned the young white man about his behaviour, you did not say, 'Mind your manners, young man, or I'll have to arrest you'. What you in fact said was, 'Watch your mouth, you little toerag, or I'm going to nick you'."

"That is not correct. I would not use language like that to a member of the public, however much I was provoked," said the officer piously.

A murmur of disbelief tinged with ridicule ran through the spectators, and even the magistrate looked sceptical.

Neeta took a little comfort from the small dent which the officer's last answer had made to his credibility, and said to the magistrate, "No further questions, thank you, sir."

The next prosecution witness to give evidence was Sergeant Norris. He described how, as he was driving along Brixton Road, his front-seat passenger, PC Harris, had asked him to stop, and how, when he did so, PC Harris had got out of the vehicle. Sergeant Norris had then watched in his wing mirror as PC Harris had approached the defendants and the white youth, and had seen PC Harris place his hand on the white youth's arm, and the youth attempt to pull away from him. He had then witnessed PC Harris attempting to restrain the youth by placing him in an approved hold, and the defendants seizing hold of PC Harris, and pulling him violently back. He had seen the other officers going to help PC Harris, and then the defendants engaged in a violent struggle with all the officers. He had then witnessed other youths becoming involved, and serious public disorder developing. He had therefore radioed for assistance, but had himself remained in the vehicle.

Neeta's cross-examination was brief. "You've made no mention in your evidence of what it was that caused PC Harris to ask you to stop the vehicle. So, obviously you didn't see what that was, did you?"

"No, I was concentrating on my driving, but, as I've said, I had a clear view in my wing mirror of your clients assaulting PC Harris."

"Thank you. No further questions."

The magistrate glanced at the clock. "I think this is an appropriate time to adjourn for lunch," he said, and the court rose.

As Neeta left the courtroom, she was joined by Alison, who was keen to ask her about what had gone on that morning, but Neeta said, "Sorry, no time to talk," and hurried up to the canteen, where she ate a sandwich and an apple, while rapidly reading what she had written during the morning's proceedings, and making more notes.

The first witness to give evidence after lunch was PC Hills, the second of the officers whom Peter and Thomas were charged with assaulting. He gave evidence that he had been seated next to the rear window of the carrier, and that, immediately after the vehicle had come to a halt, he had seen PC Harris approach the defendants and a white youth on the pavement. He had not been able to hear what was said by or to PC Harris, but he had seen PC Harris place his arm on the white youth's arm, and the youth attempting to pull away from him. He had then witnessed PC Harris attempting to restrain the youth using an approved hold, and the defendants seizing hold of PC Harris, and pulling him violently backwards. At this, he had opened the rear doors of the carrier, and he and the other officers there had got out and gone to PC Harris's assistance. They had tried to restrain the defendants, but the defendants had struggled violently, and, as a result, PC Hills had received a number of cuts and bruises. A group of black youths had then become involved, abusing the officers, and throwing things at them. The situation had only come under control with the arrival of other units, at which PC Hills and his colleagues had been able to get the defendants into the back of the carrier, and remain with them as they were taken to Brixton Police Station.

Again, Neeta's cross-examination was brief. "You've made no mention in your evidence of what it was that caused Sergeant Norris to stop the vehicle, and PC Harris to get out and approach the defendants and the other young man. So, obviously you didn't see what that was, did you?"

"No, but as I've said, I saw your clients violently assaulting PC Harris, and it was only at that point that I got involved."

"Thank you. No further questions."

PC James, the third officer, whom Peter and Thomas were charged with assaulting, told the court, in answer to a question from David Lane, that he had made his notes in conjunction with PC Hills, and he agreed, in answer to a further question from Lane, that his evidence was very similar to that of PC Hills.

Lane then told the court that he was tendering this witness for cross-examination, meaning that it was to be taken as read that the evidence in chief of these two officers was the same.

Neeta knew from the copies of the two officers' statements that she had been given that their evidence was in fact word for word identical. She asked PC James the same question as she had asked PC Hills and got a very similar answer.

PC Allan, the fifth officer to be called, gave very similar evidence to that of the previous two, except that he said nothing about what had taken place outside the vehicle before PC Hills opened its rear doors. He also said nothing about having received any injuries in the struggle with Peter and Thomas.

Neeta asked him, "You've said nothing about what happened outside the vehicle before you got out of it. So, you didn't see that, did you?"

"No, I wasn't seated by the rear window, so I couldn't see out of the carrier."

The remaining three officers to give evidence all told the court that they had made their notes in conjunction with PC Allan, and agreed that their evidence was similar to his, and David Lane tendered each of them for cross-examination.

Neeta, with the four identical statements in front of her, asked each of them the same question as she had asked PC Allan, and received almost exactly the same answer from each of them.

By this time Peter and Thomas's supporters were getting restive. They could not understand why Neeta had not asked any of the officers about why they had allowed Peter and Thomas's white friend to escape or why the injuries which they had inflicted upon Peter and Thomas had been so severe. In short, why had she not accused them of the racism and brutality of which they were so obviously guilty? They started to murmur among themselves that Peter and Thomas should have got themselves a more experienced lawyer, a man perhaps, who would not have been afraid to take on the police.

Even Peter and Thomas's parents were beginning to look a bit anxious.

The last prosecution witness to give evidence was Dr Johnson, the forensic medical examiner or police doctor who had examined PC Harris, PC Hills and PC James for the injuries which they had received in their struggle with Peter and Thomas.

Normally, Neeta would have agreed that the doctor's evidence could be read to the court, and that the doctor herself need not attend, but this time she had a reason for requiring Dr Johnson to give evidence in person.

In her evidence in chief the doctor gave details of her examination of the three officers and of the relatively minor injuries which she had found them to have.

Neeta rose to cross-examine her.

"You also examined my clients, the defendants, Peter and Thomas Lloyd, isn't that correct?"

"Well, I only examined them briefly, before having them taken to hospital for a full examination."

"And that was because their injuries seemed significantly worse than those of the officers?"

"That's true."

"I'd like you to look now at some photographs taken of the defendants' injuries two days after they received them."

The magistrate intervened. "Are these to be proved, Ms Patel?"

"Yes, sir. They're exhibited to a statement by the photographer which the prosecution have agreed can be read under section 9."

"Is that correct, Mr Lane?"

Lane tried to hide his discomfort. "Yes, sir."

"Very well," said the magistrate. "Then I'd better have copies of the statement and the photographs."

"Yes, sir," said Neeta, and handed these to the clerk, who passed them up to the magistrate.

This was exactly what Neeta had wanted to happen. She knew that the injuries received by her clients, however serious, provided no defence to the charges which they faced, but she believed that the graphic and shocking evidence of these injuries provided by the photographs could not help but arouse sympathy for her clients and some distaste for the actions of the police. She had therefore wanted to get this evidence before the court at the earliest opportunity. As the magistrate began leafing through the photographs, she pretended to be looking for something among her papers in order to give him the maximum time to absorb what he was seeing.

Rickard was shocked by the photographs, but he realised exactly what Neeta was doing, and said gruffly, "Yes, well, Ms Patel, let's get on with it, shall we?"

Neeta knew that she had achieved what she wanted to and completed her cross-examination quickly, simply getting Dr Johnson to confirm that the injuries shown in the photographs were those that the doctor had seen the defendants to have.

David Lane told the magistrate that Dr Johnson's evidence concluded the prosecution case.

It was now just after four o'clock, and the court clerk and the usher expected the magistrate to adjourn the proceedings until the following morning, but Rickard sat for a moment in thought, and then, suddenly making a decision, he looked down at Neeta, and said, "Would you care to address me at this point, Ms Patel?"

Neeta felt a sudden thrill of excitement, for the magistrate's suggestion meant that he was asking her to make a submission of no case to answer, that he was considering dismissing the case against her clients without her having to call any evidence or, as lawyers would say, 'to kick it out at half-time'. This was what she had been working towards, but she wasn't sure she had done enough. She was still worrying about the last two questions that she had asked PC Harris, and her own plan had been to review the situation that evening and to decide once she had done that whether to make a submission of no case to answer in the morning. Then, if she decided to do so, she would also have time to draft her submission overnight. Even now, she was tempted to tell the magistrate that she would prefer to address him in the morning, but she feared that that would be a mistake, for the magistrate was indicating that he was minded to find no case to answer and, if he thought about the case overnight, he might change his mind.

Slightly unsteadily she got to her feet, her mind racing, as she tried to get her thoughts in order. She was halfway to securing an acquittal for her clients, but she must not mess it up now.

"Sir, yes, thank you. I'd like to make a submission of no case to answer," she said, trying to sound more confident than she felt.

"And the basis of your submission is…?" asked the magistrate.

"Sir, my clients are charged with assaulting three police officers in the execution of their duty, and it is my submission that, at the time my clients carried out the actions on which these charges are based, the officers were not acting in the execution of their duty, because they were seeking to effect an unlawful arrest."

A sudden stillness settled on the court, as noise and movement among the spectators subsided.

"Go on," said the magistrate.

"PC Harris gave evidence that he told my clients' friend that he was arresting him for disorderly behaviour contrary to section 5 of the Public Order Act. Now, under this section…" Neeta paused, and picked up a copy of the Act from the desk in front of her, before reading from it, "*A person is guilty of an offence if he uses threatening, abusive or insulting words or behaviour or disorderly behaviour.*"

The magistrate interrupted her. "You're not suggesting, are you, that this young man's behaviour did not fall within that definition?"

"No, sir, but I would submit that it fell towards the lower end of the conduct covered by the section."

The magistrate made a noise in his throat signalling his unwillingness to endorse this suggestion, and Neeta felt annoyed with herself for wasting time on what was, at best, a weak point. She pressed on, "But the section goes on to limit the offence to situations where this behaviour takes place within the hearing or sight of a person likely to be caused harassment, alarm or distress thereby."

"Go on."

"PC Harris gave evidence that the only people present at the scene of this young man's behaviour, besides my clients and the officers, were the group of young men on the opposite side of the road, and that the reaction of these young men to his behaviour, far from being one of harassment, alarm or distress, was that, and I quote, 'They seemed to be enjoying it'."

"Quite."

"As for the officers, you have heard that none of them, apart from PC Harris, either heard or saw what the young man did before PC Harris purported to arrest him."

"Yes."

"That leaves PC Harris, who told you categorically that he was neither alarmed nor harassed by the young man's behaviour. It is true that, late on in his evidence, he claimed to have been distressed by this behaviour, but I submit to you, sir, that this is not a credible claim. PC Harris gave evidence that he has not been distressed by people hurling abuse and other things, presumably missiles, at him and his colleagues during major incidents of public disorder. He told you that that is something he and his colleagues are trained to deal with. So, is it really credible that he was distressed by a small, unarmed young man making a single rude gesture and shouting a single rude word at him and his colleagues from the pavement, as eight of them in riot gear were travelling along the road in a police carrier? He claimed that he was distressed by the young man's behaviour because it was an insult to the uniform, but was it really any more of an insult to the uniform than the abuse hurled at him by large crowds of demonstrators? I ask you, too, to consider the officer's demeanour. He is a big man who gave his evidence to you with confidence. He did not appear to be a man who would be easily distressed. And, finally, if I may, sir, I would like to refer you to the decision of the Divisional Court in the case of the Director of Public Prosecutions v. Orum."

"I am familiar with the case."

"Thank you, sir. Lord Justice Glidewell in that case, of course, held that, as a matter of law, a police officer might be a person caused harassment, alarm or distress by behaviour falling within section 5 but he went on to say, if I may quote..."

The magistrate nodded, and Neeta picked up the copy of the report of the case on the desk in front of her, and read, "*Very frequently, words and behaviour with which police officers will be wearily familiar will have little emotional impact on them save boredom. It may well be that, in appropriate circumstances, magistrates will decide, as a question of fact, that the words and behaviour were not likely to cause harassment, alarm or distress to the police officers. That is a question of fact for the magistrates to decide having regard to all the circumstances: the time, the place, the nature of the words used, who the police officers are and so on.* And, sir, I submit that the evidence in this case supports a finding of fact that PC Harris was not harassed, alarmed or distressed by the behaviour of my clients' friend."

Neeta paused, and then concluded, "In short, then, sir, my submission is that the behaviour of my clients' friend for which PC Harris purported to arrest him did not take place within the hearing or sight of anyone likely to be caused harassment, alarm or distress by that behaviour, and that, as a consequence, he did not commit an offence under section 5. It follows that PC Harris's attempt to arrest him for such an offence was unlawful, and that, therefore, when my clients intervened to prevent this arrest, PC Harris and his colleagues were not acting in the execution of their duty, and my clients cannot be guilty of assaulting them in the execution of their duty."

"Thank you, Ms Patel. Very clearly put, if I may say so."

Neeta sat down, feeling herself shaking, hoping she had done enough.

The magistrate turned to the CPS lawyer. "Do you wish to address me in reply to that, Mr Lane?"

Lane got to his feet. "Only to say, sir, that, in the case to which my friend has referred, the court clearly held that, as a matter of law, a police officer might be a person caused harassment, alarm or distress by conduct falling within section 5, and PC Harris has given evidence that he was distressed by the young man's conduct in this case."

"Thank you. That, too, was very clearly put. It is all you could say. But I'm afraid it is not enough. I agree with the submission made to me by Ms Patel. I therefore find that the defendants have no case to answer on any of the charges against them, and I dismiss all these charges."

There was a moment's stunned silence. Then a babble of chatter broke out among the spectators, and a young man in the upper gallery shouted out, "Good on you, mate."

The magistrate gave a stern look in his direction. "That's enough of that," he said firmly. "This is a court of law. Please all now leave quickly and quietly. Any talking you need to do can be done outside. The court is adjourned."

An immediate hush descended on the spectators. This was not a man they were going to disrespect.

The usher called, "Court rise."

Everyone got up, and the magistrate left the courtroom.

As soon as he had gone, the eight police officers, who had got up from their seats next to the witness box, turned, almost in unison, towards the back of the courtroom and marched, stony-faced, out through the door.

Neeta gathered together her books and papers, and went over to Peter and Thomas, who were waiting for her by the dock, where their parents had come in to join them. Peter and Thomas looked stunned, as if they could not take in what had happened. Their mother was in tears. Their father shook Neeta by the hand. "Thank you so much, Ms Patel," he said. "Now my boys have a chance to make something of their lives, which they wouldn't have got if they'd been convicted."

"Just doing my job," said Neeta. "And they deserved to be acquitted."

They all filed out onto the concourse, where Neeta was surrounded by people wanting to congratulate her and to shake her by the hand or slap her on the back.

She waited on the concourse until they had all gone, when she was joined by Alison, who said, "Well done. That was very impressive."

"It could have gone either way," said Neeta, soberly. "At one point I thought I'd blown it."

"Was that when the officer said he'd been distressed by the insult to the uniform?"

"Yes, I thought I'd asked him two questions too many, but fortunately in the end it didn't seem to matter."

They walked out of the court building and saw painted on a wall in large white letters:

NOT JUST ICE NOT JUSTICE

They looked at each other, and Alison said, "Well, not always, but sometimes."